WARMAIDENS

Also by Kelly Coon

Gravemaidens

WARMAIDENS

KELLY COON

DELACORTE PRESS

All rights reserved. Published in the United States by Delacorte Press, an imprint of Random House Children's Books, a division of Penguin Random House LLC, New York.

Delacorte Press is a registered trademark and the colophon is a trademark of Penguin Random House LLC.

Visit us on the Web! GetUnderlined.com
Educators and librarians, for a variety of teaching tools, visit us at RHTeachersLibrarians.com

Library of Congress Cataloging-in-Publication Data is available upon request.
ISBN 978-0-525-64786-7 (hc) — ISBN 978-0-525-64789-8 (lib. bdg.) —
ISBN 978-0-525-64787-4 (ebook)

The text of this book is set in 12.75-point Adobe Jenson Pro Light.
Interior design by Andrea Lau

Printed in the United States of America
10 9 8 7 6 5 4 3 2 1
First Edition

For my beautiful boys, Brady, Kaden, and Brennan.

Listen to your heart—and your mom.

—◆—

WARMAIDENS

CHAPTER 1

THE DEAD COULD rise on this kind of night.

In some ways, they already had.

The cool air nipped at my shoulders as I knelt in the dirt, encircled by an elite group of warriors called the Koru who protected the queen. Torchlight reflected off their copper scorpion helmets. The scars they wore on their bodies like badges of honor. It flickered in their eyes when they looked at me, the healer who had saved them all.

After more than a moon of restless illness, they'd risen from their sickbeds one after another. When I'd witnessed the life in them, their muscles regaining strength as they fastened into their greaves and plated tunics to return to their duties, I'd cried like a baby.

If only my father had been alive to see it. He would have been so proud that I'd healed them, and that the queen was honoring me this night in recognition, though he would have

1

scolded me for running myself ragged to get here. But that's what you did when you were a healer doing everything in her power to be the best she could be.

And failing.

I played with the clasp of my healing satchel, flipping it up and down and up and down. Fought the urge to bite my thumbnail. I had one more person to save, and her illness was nearly impossible to overcome. Mirrum was the last Koru still struggling to recover.

But I'd heal her, too. I *had* to.

In front of the sycamore trees, a small band of musicians *rapummed* their drums and clacked beaded shakers. My heart banged as Sarratum Tabni appeared at the edge of the circle and the Koru parted, chanting my name in their soft, round Manzazu accent.

"Kammani! Kammani!"

"Rise."

The queen nodded at me, a spiked gold crown on her dark hair, earrings skimming her shoulders. Behind the queen, a towering statue of their goddess Linaza was bathed in firelight. Her mighty wings were spread to the east and west, her scorpion's tail hovering in warning.

As I stood, something white flickered in my peripheral vision near the grove.

I turned, and a cold, dank breeze brushed my cheek. The sound of water slapping against a wooden boat filled my ears. It almost felt as though my feet were in the prow, the river Garadun rocking beneath.

Stop it, Kammani. None of that Boatman nonsense. Not now.

I'd seen his skeletal face in the tomb back in Alu, and he'd been haunting me ever since we'd fled. Nine long moons of his face hovering over my pallet at night. Nine long moons of his bony fingers grazing my cheek.

Shoving away all thoughts of him, I stared at Dagan standing tall and proud beyond the circle of warriors, and tried to calm down. He hadn't wanted me to come alone to the ceremony so late at night, so Sarratum Tabni had granted him access as my escort, though no one else was allowed to attend. He smiled at me encouragingly and placed one hand over his heart.

"It's okay," he mouthed. "Just breathe."

Grateful for his encouragement, I offered him a wobbly smile of my own as the queen approached. She unclasped a necklace from around her neck, a scorpion amulet dangling from a thick leather strap. She held it up. Its sapphire eyes glittered in the firelight, and I took a deep breath to calm my fluttering heart. For what she was about to fasten around my neck wasn't just a gift.

It was a promise.

She was saying the Koru owed me a favor, and I could call upon them to answer it at *any* time, even with their lives if necessary.

"Kammani, Healer from Alu, this evening, we grant you our highest honor."

She held the necklace up in front of the Koru. They leaned in to see it, some reaching out to touch the dazzling pendant.

"We grant you the symbol of Linaza, our goddess of love and war." She glanced at one of the Koru standing nearby. "Commander Ummi? Your assistance."

Ummi, black hair cut bluntly at her jaw, stepped forward and held my ratty curls so the queen could fasten the strap around my throat. The scorpion was cold, heavy, as it settled between my collarbones. My fingers slid across the slick metal.

Sarratum Tabni stepped back and met my eyes. Hers were hooded. Calculating.

"Mighty A-zu, *healer*, we grant you our thankfulness on this evening for all you have done for our city. You, a stranger in our land, worked to bring my warriors back to health. May the Koru repay your kindness with their allegiance."

At once, the warriors brandished their battle-axes and swords and shouted my name, a great wave of exultation that resonated off the homes scattered nearby.

As they chanted, I locked my hands together to keep from playing with my healer's satchel. I had only been doing my job. What I had been trained to do by my abum. Though healing all of them had been a challenge, since Mudi, the healer with whom I'd been working, tended to favor the spirit world to her own rational thought. She told me that my visions from the Boatman were gifts. That I should listen to what he was trying to tell me.

But all he brought to me were nightmares about Alu, a city I'd never be able to visit again.

"Do you accept the gift that we have given you, Healer?" Sarratum Tabni asked.

"Yes, my lady." Not accepting this gift wasn't an option. Arwia, our exiled queen of Alu, had told me so earlier. Rejecting their kindness could only lead to ill will, even if it felt like too much. "I accept it."

She smiled briefly. "Good. We ask that you use it wisely, letting the goddess guide your heart."

The queen turned to the Koru and raised her arms up high. "My Koru, warrior maidens of Manzazu, children of Linaza, I invite you to feast in the A-zu's honor tonight. Drink from Linaza's cup. Dine from her abundance. Let us celebrate Kammani's bestowal of her gifts upon our great city. We can rest easy this night knowing we lie in her capable hands."

The Koru cheered once more, a great ferocious roar, and my heart seized as I looked at them all. These warriors were part of a larger Manzazu army that protected *me*. The citizens of this city, our place of refuge, were now *my* citizens. Their illnesses, mine to heal. And though the thought filled me with pride, with a certain amount of unspeakable joy, it also filled me with an overwhelming sense of responsibility.

I couldn't let them down now. Though I'd barely begun to make headway in this city that would rather pray and whisper incantations than take the tinctures I gave them, I would build a successful, thriving healing practice here with my own two hands. I *swore* it.

The musicians took up their drums and shakers once more to play a quick, staccato rhythm. Some of the Koru gathered to dance. Some dispersed to partake in the food brought in from Linaza's altars. Others hoisted me to their shoulders to sway in front of their goddess, voices raised in excitement.

"A-zu, this is your night." Commander Ummi's face was bright with religious fervor underneath me. "Enjoy it." She and other warriors jostled me around to the rhythm of the drums. Writhing in embarrassment, I met Dagan's eyes at the perimeter of the courtyard. He grinned and gave a little wave.

As the warriors whirled, singing a rousing hymn about honor and war and love, I looked up into Linaza's formidable face. Sightless, she stared down at me, as empty and inanimate as the gnarled trees behind her. But right when I pulled my gaze away from her sandstone eyes, the tips of her wings fluttered.

Just once.

And though it didn't make any sense, *any sense at all*, I swore my new scorpion pendant twitched against my throat in response.

CHAPTER 2

—⧚—

"ARE YOU NERVOUS, Simti?"

My friend and I knelt in front of a looking glass, making final touches to our faces.

"A bride *always* feels nervous on her wedding day." She flashed me a wobbly smile, but her eyes were shining.

A circlet of copper sat on her black hair. When she moved, the dangling leaves shimmered in the light from the tallow candles spread on low tables around the tent.

The wedding would begin at dusk. Simti's bride price had been paid—a plot of land and a chest of coins. The dowry had been settled, too. Now? We would feast, and once she and Ilu spent their first night together, lost in one another's arms, the marriage would be complete.

Happiness flooded through me, but so did a nagging sense of worry over Mirrum, the Koru warrior who had yet to recover.

"All will be perfectly fine, my friend." I squeezed her clammy hand, trying to pour some reassurance into her, but whether it was more for me or for her was unclear.

Scratching my nose around the colored pastes and powders Nanaea had painted on me, I wrestled with my own nerves. I felt absolutely itchy. I *hoped* that Mudi was doing what I'd asked. Three drops of the tincture every thirty minutes. That was it. Not too difficult. But as Mudi rarely did anything I wanted her to, only time would tell if she followed my directions. For Mirrum's sake, I hoped she did.

It had been four days since I'd received the scorpion necklace, and Mirrum had still not recovered to full health. She was sitting up and even taking in some broth, but I wasn't satisfied. I'd been over to the sickroom constantly to heal her, and had only left her this evening to witness my friend becoming the bride she'd always wanted to be.

Only this time, Simti's groom was very much alive. Since we'd all escaped the tomb in Alu, she was free to marry whomever she wanted instead of a dying lugal.

"Kammani, you're not messing up my handiwork, are you?" Nanaea squawked from the corner of the tent. She knelt, a threaded needle between her lips, wrestling with the hem of Iltani's tunic.

A difficult task, since Iltani was currently in it.

"I wouldn't dream of ruining your efforts, Sister."

"Good. It's been nearly impossible to find more face paint in the Libbu. The merchants are carrying hardly any." She plucked the needle from her mouth and wriggled it into the fabric.

My heart swelled watching her work, dampening the worry about Mirrum. We'd become a family of exiles here in Manzazu, establishing our own home. Each of us doing our own share. I'd carved out a little space in our house west of the queen's Palace for me, Nanaea, and our little brother, Kasha, though it was filled day and night with the noise of everyone else who'd left Alu with us. I'd miss Nanaea when she eventually left me for her own marriage.

My stomach fluttered as I stood and busied my hands straightening up. I grabbed a basket and tossed discarded tunics and beads into it.

"Watch it, Nanaea!" Iltani grumbled, sipping on her cask of sweetwine, the Manzazu brew she couldn't leave alone. "I'll be dotted like a leper when you're finished with me."

Sweating, Nanaea pushed her damp black hair back from her forehead. "Stop fidgeting and you won't get poked. This is a difficult stitch!"

Nanaea had apprenticed herself to a seamstress and was excelling in her craft, though dancing was more of her passion. But since Manzazu had dancers in droves, it made more sense for her to learn a trade that could support her. I missed the shine radiating from her eyes when she danced, though, which was happening less and less the more she worked on her craft.

Maybe one day she'd have time to return to what she loved.

Iltani bent to a table, selecting a juicy bit of fish out of some oil and popping it into her mouth.

Nanaea tugged on a seam and looked over her shoulder at Simti. "How did you get the embroidery in your tunic so perfect?"

"You forget that I've been sewing clothes for my family for *years*." Simti bent to the looking glass, pursed her lips, and pinched her cheeks. "But not applying face paint. It isn't blended right."

"Didn't Arwia say before she left this tent that nothing you do will make you any lovelier?" I stuck my basket on my hip. "You're the most beautiful woman in the entire city."

She blushed. "Thank you, my friend. Now come here. I need to fix something."

I knelt, and she twisted a bud on my flower crown. "And you look beautiful today, too. You've slept recently, which is an improvement." She smiled, and the gold powder that Nanaea had dusted on her brown cheeks shimmered in the candle-light.

"And you are a stellar liar."

"Me?" She placed a hand on her chest in mock indignation. "I lie about nothing."

"Are you sure about that?"

She grinned. "Well, perhaps only once and that was to get Ilu's mother to love me as much as she loves Dagan. Is he here yet?"

"Yes, he walked with me from the Koru's sickroom. Mirrum is still fighting the illness."

Simti's eyes softened. "You look worried. Will she heal?"

"I think so. But there's a tincture that will hurry things along if Mudi will use it instead of just pleading with the Boatman."

He didn't help *anybody*.

Unease filled my belly as I recalled the Boatman scooping Lugal Marus in his bony arms and disappearing into the Netherworld from the tomb. Mudi had told me—repeatedly to the point of nausea—that the Boatman was once a warrior, cursed to his post for murdering innocents in war. She said he spoke to healers because he was trying to gain his freedom by helping prevent the deaths of as many lives as he took. But despite her telling me to listen to what he had to say, I couldn't bring myself to do it. The breaths I heard in my ear when I was pounding out a new tincture in my mortar made me shudder. The glimpses of his face right before I fell asleep every night stole my breath.

Communing with the spirit world went against everything logic told me to do.

Kasha burst into the tent, his dark curls falling down past his shoulders. Since he'd escaped the Palace, he'd refused any trimming, saying he'd been shorn like a sheep once too often in his life. Now he would live his life as he wanted. This morning, I'd made him wash himself, but I'd let him win the haircut argument. At least it was clean.

"Sisters, girls, all of you. You're wanted by the priestess. It's dusk." He swiped a cup of sweetwine off a table, dancing out of reach when I tried to grab it back. "It's time!"

Simti grabbed me by both shoulders and looked me straight in the eye. "Now you're going to wipe that worry line away." She ran her finger between my eyebrows. "This wedding is a joyous occasion."

I softened my forehead. Relaxed my shoulders. "I'm happy for you, Simti. I just worry about Mirrum. And I'll miss you around our house."

Simti shared the bedchamber with Arwia and Iltani. Huna used to share it as well, but she'd sickened and died from an infection she wouldn't let me treat. She'd never forgiven me for pulling her away from the riches and glory she'd expected in the afterlife.

Her eyes glistened. "And I'll miss you, too. All of you."

Iltani hauled us both to our feet, her warm brown eyes glassy, a smirk on her dimpled face. "You know what I don't miss? Our old rotten city of Alu. That pisspot. Coming here was the best decision I've ever made and praise be to Selu—I mean, Linaza—for that. I was a rat in that city. Here, I'm happy and feast like the goddess I am."

"Iltani, you wouldn't drink yourself into a stupor every night if you were happy."

"Spoken like a woman who can't hold her brew." Iltani's eyes dimmed for a moment before she tossed back the rest of her drink. "I couldn't be happier to leave the stink of Alu behind."

"Liar," Nanaea said, shrugging out of her sweaty clothes.

She wiped herself down, and pulled on a tunic as blue as a summer sky, one that matched my ummum's shawl tucked around her elbows. Stooping to eyeball herself critically in the looking glass, she smeared a dab of red on her lips, and topped it all off with a copper circlet on her shiny black hair.

"Now, *that* is the fastest I have ever made myself look presentable, so I expect your gratitude, Simti."

Nanaea approached, enveloping all of us in the scent of her rose oil. She draped one arm around my shoulders, and another around Simti, pulling the four of us into a tight, humid huddle.

"My family, this is a day to be joyful. We've certainly earned it."

We all squeezed one another, tears sparking in our eyes, connecting as friends who've found sisters outside of blood can. As sisters who have escaped death a time or two can. All we were missing was Arwia, who was no doubt somewhere outside the tent, making sure everything was perfect for Simti.

Savoring our sisterhood, I smiled at each one in turn. Our climb from the tomb was wasted—*wasted*—if a young woman struggling to heal wouldn't leave my thoughts long enough to enjoy this night. After a moment, I kissed Nanaea's cheek.

"You're absolutely right, Nanaea. Let's go to a wedding and celebrate."

We all cheered and went in for another hug, squealing and dancing around in a circle. My heart beat with butterfly's wings, certain I might burst from nerves or happiness or both.

"Come *on*!" Kasha held open the flaps of the tent, so we

followed him into the dusk, toward a wedding that would be filled with love and promise and joy.

To be followed by a life of more of the same.

❈❈❈

The sun dipped low, hovering above the horizon, casting a pink glow over the olive grove. Tents dotted the courtyard, ringed by torches scented with frankincense. Wooden tables full of Manzazu food—syrupy fruits, fish poached in oil, fire-roasted vegetables—were nestled inside each.

People sipped chilled sweetwine, and swayed to the lyres on either side of the path that led to the dais where the ceremony would take place. Kasha horsed around with a group of boys poking each other and making googly eyes. Dagan stood in the center of the platform with Ilu, Simti's bridegroom. He and his parents had become a sort of family to us, and we were repaying the favor by standing up in support of their union.

My heart thrumming madly, I lined up with Nanaea, Iltani, Simti, while we all whispered encouragement and final instructions to one another as the musicians played.

Simti, the bride, was first. She beamed as she turned toward her husband-to-be and began to dance down the narrow path toward him. Her red tunic flowed over her curves as she clapped her hands and swayed. The crowd tossed flower petals into the air and knocked their cups together to toast her health.

Nanaea went next, gracefully twisting and whirling to the

rhythm, until she reached the platform and climbed the stairs to join Simti. Iltani downed the rest of her sweetwine and gyrated down the aisle after her, wobbly on her bare feet, doing her own version of Nanaea's dance with much less grace and a lot more leg.

The smoke from the lit torches choked me as I squared my shoulders and stared down the aisle. The thought of dancing even a little bit in front of a crowd made me feel as naked as a freshly plucked bird. I was *not* graceful. Not by anyone's definition of the word. But I took a deep breath and swayed down the aisle as best as I could, my cheeks flaming hot up to my ears. When I reached the dais, Dagan reached for me with a calloused hand, worn from the mattock and plow, and the warmth of his palm pressed to mine made me forget all about my embarrassment.

As I stepped up, he pulled me close and kissed my forehead.

"You are stunning, Oh Great Dancing A-zu." He grinned.

"Stop it. That was the clumsiest thing you've ever witnessed." I blushed. "You are stunning, too, of course."

I took in his handsome features. The divot above his lip that made it impossible not to kiss him. The rough smudge of beard on his jaw, now beginning to thicken. The black eyebrows that framed his dark lashes so well. *My love.* My heart swelled. We'd made each other happy here in Manzazu.

Dagan wrapped an arm around me. He bent down, his lips against my ear. "My sweet, you're not nervous, are you?"

"About Simti? No. Why would I be?"

I looked at him, and the earnestness in his amber eyes made me squirm. He ran a finger down my chin, but pressed his lips together. Tight. Took a deep breath.

"Because," he started, his words tumbling out of his mouth quickly, "these last moons have been the best of my life. Living underneath one roof with you and everyone else. Caring for all of us together has brought me the greatest joy I've ever had." He tapped his fingers on my arm.

"Dagan, they're about to start. What is it?" I whispered, my eyes on the priestess ascending the platform, a ceremonial bowl of sweetwine in her weathered hands.

He cleared his throat. "What I am saying to you is—"

"Will the bride and groom step forward, please?" The priestess nodded to Simti and Ilu.

"Later," I whispered to him.

"Okay." A nervous smile flitted across Dagan's face as he looked at Ilu across the platform. Ilu flashed him a wink as Simti stepped forward, a dazzling smile on her face to meet him in front of the priestess.

Dagan and I joined hands with Nanaea and Iltani and closed the circle around them both as Ilu draped a bride-price necklace around Simti's neck. Ilu's mother dabbed at her eyes, and mine filled, too. We'd be losing her from our home this night. We'd spent so many evenings together, cooking, laughing, building a new life free from the threat of Alu's terrifying customs. It was tough to let her go. But Simti and Ilu had fallen deeply, wildly in love within a moon of our arrival, so how could we not agree?

I raised my hand linked with Dagan's and we all sang a collective praise to Linaza for joining these two. The priestess poured the honied drink on Ilu's tongue, then Simti's, so their words to one another would be sweet for the rest of their days.

When Ilu bent to kiss Simti and she wound her fingers into the hair at the nape of his neck, the priestess declared them wed. As the crowd cheered for their union, Dagan looked at me with such heat in his eyes, what he'd been trying to say before the ceremony was suddenly as clear as the river on a hot summer day.

He'd been trying to ask me to marry him.

He wanted this moment on the dais for *us*.

CHAPTER 3

TWO HOURS LATER, the wedding had exploded in celebration. The musicians pounded their drums and strummed their lyres with flashing hands. Nanaea was dragged to dance by nearly half the men of the city, and Iltani played game after game of twenty squares, taking everyone's coins right out of their purses.

Sandals kicked off near the gambling tables, curly hair bouncing, Kasha danced with a group of boys. I spied a table with platters of fruits and eased myself down in front of it as I watched him play. Back in Alu, he'd been taken from us and had been forced to live in the Palace to replace the lugal's son. But now he could just be a boy.

And though he could be carefree, I could not.

Swiping a handful of grapes, I popped them into my mouth and surveyed the rest of the crowd, my thoughts straying to Mirrum.

I'd left her for far too long.

I looked at the full moon shining overhead as I forced myself to swallow. A half an hour more. That was as long as I could possibly stay. A tug in the center of my chest connected me to her as though she were an anchor and I was the boat.

"There you are, Favored Dancing A-zu of the North." Dagan ducked around the tent's flaps. "May I have the honor of your presence?" He bowed graciously, arms wide like Linaza's wings, and I smiled at his attempt at the Manzazu tradition.

"You may, Oh Great Farmer of the Fields."

He laughed, and I placed a hand over my heart, grinning at our game. He made me happy, and had, for a long time.

Dagan settled in and grabbed some grapes from the platter, and we talked about the wedding. I grew more relaxed, less worried, the more we talked. I studied his broad shoulders as he leaned back on his elbows. Watched his mouth move as he popped the grapes in one by one and chewed. He caught me studying him, and the air around us shifted. I could smell the faintest touch of Aleppo soap on his skin. See the reflection of the torchlight shining in his eyes. Suddenly, what he'd been trying to say before the ceremony became a candle flickering between us, bright and hot.

"What are you thinking about, Arammu?" He nudged me with his knee.

So he'd play *this* game. Get me to bring everything up before he would. It was his favorite way to talk about something he wasn't sure I was ready to discuss. I dodged the question with a distraction.

"Mirrum. Kasha and Nanaea. And . . . kissing you."

He shrugged casually, but his eyes tightened at the corners. "That doesn't have to be a thought, you know. I am, after all, sitting right here." He opened his arms, a challenge in his eyes. An attempt to call my bluff.

But it was no bluff. A flush moving up my neck, I slowly leaned over, keeping my eyes on his, and kissed him. It was soft, at first. But just like always, our kiss deepened, and within a few moments, it grew feverish.

All thoughts of Mirrum, Kasha, Nanaea, the rest of my responsibilities, melted away as he grabbed my hips and tugged me onto his lap. The air buzzed with nothing but him as he slid his hands up my sides, and I wrapped my arms around his neck. After several moments of his warm mouth on mine, my body pressing against him—*closer, closer*—I broke away, breathless.

"Arammu," he whispered. His breath was ragged on my cheek. "Let's not play these games. You know I love you with everything in me. And that I would not fail you. Not ever."

He cupped my face in his hands. Kissed my forehead, both cheeks. My lips.

He'd ask the question. My heart pounded as I held on to his wrists for dear life. What did I want? A life with him? Surely. But I already *had* one, no wedding required, though I'd yet to lie in his embrace.

The thought heated me from chest to cheek.

"And I love you, too," I answered, breathless, as he kissed me again. And again.

"Then—"

"A-zu?"

A throat clearing and a jangling of weaponry brought my eyes up to two fierce Koru warriors: Commander Ummi and a tall, lean woman with sinewy muscles named Humusi. They stood purposefully outside the tent, knowing eyes fixed on Dagan and me.

I scrambled off his lap, adjusting my tunic, a flush spreading hot up into my hairline.

"I'm sorry to interrupt." Ummi's sparkling eyes made her look younger than she was. But I'd witnessed her deft use of a battle-ax in the throwing fields. She was no child.

"It's not a worry." My voice squeaked at the end.

"Sarratum Tabni asked us to stop by to see if you were well."

I sighed. The honor of the scorpion necklace was one thing. This checking up on me constantly was something else. They'd been following me since that night, stationing themselves outside our little home, accompanying me into the Libbu. "You mean to protect me? I told you before that I don't need it. What harm could come to a healer in this city?"

Ummi straightened her boxy frame, her armored tunic chinking against her breastplate. "My orders come from my lady, so if she tells me to protect you and Arwia and anyone else, I will."

Arwia had been taken under Sarratum Tabni's wing when we arrived, her mother being a former childhood friend. In fact, the queen had invited her to stay at the Palace, but Arwia had said she'd prefer to live with us. Sarratum Tabni had disapproved. Said it was her duty to protect the rightful queen of Alu and her friends, but I often wondered why she was so intent on it.

"I am very well, I can assure you." I flushed, looking back at Dagan. "Thank you both."

Her eyes twinkled. "It appears to be so. Please let us know if that changes." Ummi turned and squinted at some noisy revelers. "Come, Humusi. We're not needed here. And it appears we've a situation to attend to." Ummi flashed a smile, exposing rows of gapped teeth, and they marched quickly away. People cleared a path as they wended through the crowd toward the commotion.

These women had given up every possibility of marriage and children to be Koru warriors, the most elite fighters in service to the sarratum. In fact, I'd witnessed one warrior removed from the Koru altogether for being caught in a man's bed. The commitment had to be absolute, nothing to muddle their minds.

Yet tradition said *I* was supposed to marry. I was a young, orphaned girl with no father to put food in my stomach and clothes on my back, even though I was managing well enough on my own with my friends. But tradition *also* said if I did marry, my husband would be my legal guardian. He could make decisions for me. If we ever stood before a judge, he would speak for me. It was hard for me to think of entering a marriage where we wouldn't be seen by the law as equals. He could, under the law, take everything I owned and cast me out. I couldn't do the same. The power would not be mine as a woman.

When I was young, a man had once exercised his power with his wife, Zuzu. He'd said she was stealing the family money to squander it away. She said she was simply purchasing goods their family would need. He took her in front of Lugal Marus and had washed his hands of her. She ended up down by the well, begging for food while he remarried and another woman raised her children.

But Dagan would never do something like that, even though he *could*.

He was always kind, and worked hard for us. He'd been transforming the ragged patch of weeds behind our home into a plot flush with barley, which was nearing harvest any day. He'd been wanting to introduce the crop to this city, and had even told me of plans to take it to more cities in the north. Expand on it. Build a big, booming, prosperous business.

What if Dagan made good on his desires to move away from Manzazu? I was excited for him and wanted him to succeed, but if he left, that would mean I'd have to abandon the healing practice I'd been trying to build. What of my ill patients? Mirrum? Could I possibly give up everything simply for a tradition?

But Dagan's finger running down the back of my arm filled me with a low, deep longing, my body a traitor to my thoughts. Lying with him was getting more and more difficult *not* to do, but I didn't want my body to make a promise my brain hadn't yet decided. Iltani lay with whomever she pleased, and that was fine for her, though I'd begged her repeatedly to be careful. But for me? I knew what it would mean to Dagan. I swallowed as he softly played with the curls hanging down my back.

"My sweet? Will you look at me? You were lost in your thoughts again."

Outside the tent, Nanaea danced in the center of the crowd, her hair falling down to her waist, bouncing and swaying. She tipped back a flagon of brew, drinking deeply, then spluttered with laughter as a young man spun her around. How happy she could be while my insides were perpetually knotted like a rope. Beyond her, Simti and Ilu danced on the dais, their arms wrapped around one another, lost to the romance of the night.

I turned to look at his earnest, handsome face. A face with lips I'd kissed a thousand times and wanted to kiss a thousand more. I ran my hands over his warm shoulders. "I'm right here."

He took my hands in his. Kissed each one, then brought his amber eyes to mine. There was longing there. Hope. And at the back end, a little bit of fear.

"There's something I wanted to ask you."

Pinpricks covered my body. *Nerves or excitement? Both?*

"Will you let me make you as happy as Simti is this night?" His breath came fast. He licked his lips, his eyes pleading. "Be my bride, Kammani, Healer of Manzazu. Be my wife. And let me spend the rest of my life showing you how much of my heart you really hold."

My stomach flipped as my heart pounded. "But . . . what of my healing practice?"

His eyes grew confused. "Your . . . healing practice?"

"What if you want to go to the north to expand your crop and all of my work is here? I couldn't leave my patients."

Understanding filled his eyes. "Ah. Well, we could make an arrangement, could we not?"

"I wouldn't sacrifice what I've built, Dagan." I ran a finger down his cheek. "My work is too precious to me."

"But couldn't you establish a new practice if it meant I could better provide for a family? There is great opportunity in the north."

"No! I wouldn't want to do that just for better trade. Not until I'd helped as many people as I could in *this* city. Or . . . or . . . trained an apprentice or *something*."

"Well, marriage means we'd have to compromise. At least a little."

"But what if I don't want to compromise? By law, you could force me to!"

His brow furrowed. "Do you think I'd ever force you to do anything? You *know* I would never do that. We could make it work somehow. I swear it."

"Dagan, listen—" But my response was swept out of my mouth, out of my head, as a long, strangled scream tore the night in two.

"Who was that?" I whispered, panic spreading through my body like fire.

We leapt to our feet, and Dagan pulled his dagger from its sheath as shouts erupted near the far end of the courtyard.

He looked at me, fear twisting his features.

"That sounded a lot like—"

"—*Arwia*," I finished.

Hands clasped tightly together, we fled the tent.

CHAPTER 4

—∿∿—

WITH TORCHES HELD high, alarmed wedding-goers clustered in the corner of the courtyard near a small thatch of olive trees draped with silk streamers.

Arwia stood near Nasu, her face a sickly shade of amber, one hand pressed to her ear. Blood seeped onto her tunic and dripped down her long strands of black hair.

"Nasu!" Dagan shouted.

"Over here!" Nasu raised one lanky arm.

We weaved through concerned bystanders to get to the former Alu guardsman. He greeted us with worried eyes. "She's hurt. Badly." He flexed his angular jaw.

"Let me see your ear, Arwia," I demanded. Blood was seeping through her fingers.

She moved her small hand away from the side of her head with a wince, and I held in a gasp. Her ear was nearly severed from her head.

"What do you need?" Dagan asked me.

"For now? A clean cloth."

"Got it." Dagan squeezed my elbow and sprinted away.

I reached up to examine the cartilage. Blood oozed from the wound. She'd need stitches and a pain tonic. Immediately. But I'd have to get to my healing chambers to get those. I hadn't worn my healing satchel, which had obviously been a mistake. Within moments, Dagan was back and I pressed the clean dining linens he'd found against her head until I could sew her back up.

"What happened?" Dagan crossed his arms over his chest, eyes sharp. Pointed.

Arwia quivered from head to toe. "Everything was fine! I was dancing. Iltani was drunk, and I was trying to get her to dance with me to get away from that lecherous man who always grabs women in the marketplace." She took a shaky breath. "And then a man who was wearing Manzazu clothes, but in the wrong way, a very wrong way, pulled me over here near the olive grove. And before I could even think about reaching for my dagger, he had his own out and tried to slit my throat!"

She gulped and tears filled her eyes. "But the Koru were there, and the next thing I knew, he was on the ground and my ear felt like it was on fire."

Commander Ummi and Humusi and another young warrior, part of the queen's main army, pushed through the crowds, revealing a man facedown on the ground. Black blood stained the sand around his body, likely from a gut wound.

Wiping his blood from her battle-ax onto her tunic, Ummi hung the weapon at her side. She nodded to the young warrior, who looked no older than Nanaea. "Tell the sarratum and your regiment leader about this, and go to the wall. Humusi and I will stay."

"Yes, Commander." She ran out of the courtyard, her sickleswords bouncing on her hips.

"What happened?" I asked Ummi.

"This man tried to assassinate your exiled sarratum, it seems. I caught him in the act, and as he fell, his blade slipped from her throat to her ear."

She kicked the man over onto his back. He had a patchy beard and lean, rangy face that looked oddly familiar. Sucking in his breath, Nasu dropped to a knee next to the man. After a moment, he looked up gravely.

"I know him. He's an Alu guardsman. I used to spar with him near the Pit." He swallowed, throat bobbing. "He was quiet as a fox and lethal with his knives. Lugal Marus used to send him on missions like this, and now it appears Uruku is, too." His lip curled in disgust. "To think he'd attempt to kill the rightful heir to the throne of Alu."

Arwia's hands shook. "This is why I *left* Alu. I don't want anything to do with the throne ever again! I simply want to live in peace, which is what I keep telling Sarratum Tabni. She insists I must make plans to reclaim my throne."

"Wait a moment. How did Uruku know you were still alive?" I asked her. "For all he knew, you'd died in the tomb. He thought we *all* did."

She furrowed her brow. "I don't know."

I looked at Dagan. "What about the men you paid to dig us out of the tomb? They could have told someone that we escaped our death sentence. Maybe someone heard about an exiled queen living here in Manzazu, and Uruku made the connection."

Dagan shook his head, his hands on his hips. "Those men are loyal to me. They would have never done something like this."

"For enough coins? There are those who would slit their own ummum's throat to be wealthy," Arwia said, wincing when I pressed the cloth more tightly to her wound.

Dagan's faced darkened in anger. "Then they will answer to me for it. But I can't imagine that they would be so cold. I've known those men all my life."

Nasu stood, brushing sand from his hands. "It's not because there is talk of an exiled queen, Kammani. There is talk about *you* outside the city."

"Me?" I pulled the cloth away from Arwia's ear to check the bleeding, and as soon as I removed it, blood seeped again from the wound. I pressed it back firmly.

"On my last trading mission with Ilu's father, we stopped at Laraak, a trading encampment outside Alu. The traders gossiped about Manzazu's healer from the south who'd saved the warrior maidens. It was a big deal. Some of the traders there knew Mudi, your healer friend, and apparently she'd talked."

Dagan's face flushed and he pointed angrily at Nasu's

chest. "Why were you trading in the south so close to Alu? *You* were supposed to have died in that tomb as well to protect the maidens in the Netherworld! What if someone saw you in the trading camp and *that* is what led Uruku's men here?"

Nasu's face paled. "I was protecting Ilu and his men as I was paid to do. But I stayed hidden. No one would have recognized me with my hair shorn like this, anyway." He rubbed his close-cropped head.

Arwia threw up her hands, which were covered in dried blood. "It doesn't matter how it happened. We need to figure out what to do! If he's tried to kill me once, he'll try again once he knows he wasn't successful. Alive, I'm a threat to the throne he stole from me, even though Selu knows I don't want it."

"All of us are in danger." I swallowed roughly. "All of us."

Dagan's face twisted in worry. "You're right. Nanaea, Simti, Arwia, Nasu, and you—all of you escaped the tomb even though he'd commanded your deaths."

"Yes!" I held the cloth tightly to Arwia's ear. "Think of his panic when he found out! If neighboring cities thought he had allowed this disobedience to happen, they would believe him to be weak."

Nasu nodded, rubbing his lip. "And they could cast their lots with Arwia and take the throne out from underneath him."

"And he knew where to find us because I healed the Koru—"

"—and because Nasu probably led them back here." Dagan's face darkened.

"If I've done *anything* to put Arwia in danger, you can be assured that I will end the problem myself." Nasu raised his steely voice.

"Enough bickering." Arwia's mouth puckered in annoyance. Pain. "Uruku quietly wanted to take out the threat before we became a problem, so we cannot become a problem ourselves. We must stick together. Communicate. Figure out what to do next."

Dagan's bright eyes sought mine. "He has to kill all of you, especially now that word will spread of this assassination attempt. And quickly. More assassins could still be out here. He wouldn't send one man for so many people." He looked cagily around the courtyard and stepped closer to me. "We must get back to our home. Secure the doors until we've formed a plan to keep you safe."

"Well, I must go to the sickroom first. I'm to stay with Mirrum this evening while Mudi gets some rest, and I need to fix this ear or she'll lose it." My head buzzed with urgency. "Arwia, come with me. I have plenty of clean linens and sterilized threads there."

"We will go, too." Ummi hitched her belt, which was full of weaponry. "To protect you."

"My thanks, Ummi. That would be a relief."

"Do you want me to come?" Dagan ran a hand down my arm. "If not, I'll get Nanaea and Kasha back home." His amber eyes picked up the light from torches held by the growing, murmuring crowd.

"No, my sweet. But grab Iltani. Only the gods know where she is."

He nodded to Nasu. "Help me find her; then we can fortify the house. And warn Ilu. They may come looking for Simti, too."

"I will." Nasu turned to the Koru. "Protect Arwia with your life, do you hear me? She may not want the throne, but she has a right to it."

Humusi looked down her long nose at him and grimaced. Ummi flicked him a baleful sneer, as if she hadn't recently battle-axed the life from a man and casually wiped his blood on her tunic.

"Be careful. Stick close to the Koru." Dagan put his big hands on my shoulders and kissed me softly on the forehead. "Come home safely to me."

"You be careful, too."

They left, and the Koru, Arwia, and I trekked toward the sickroom, kicking up dust in the moonlit night. Eyes wary. Hearts in our throats. As we traveled, I kept the linen pressed to Arwia's ear while Humusi, ever watchful, gathered stones and tossed them into the brush, checking for assassins who might lie in wait.

As the sickroom came into view and my immediate panic about being caught on the road dwindled, Dagan's question of marriage floated up into my brain like a specter. For the moment, it seemed we had more pressing concerns to attend to.

I doubted Dagan would like knowing that the delay filled me with a quiet sense of relief.

※※※

Unease feathered up my neck as I picked up a candle burning in the dim hallway that led to the Koru sick chamber.

"Through here, Arwia."

We pushed past rows of beads hanging over the doorway, and stepped inside the room with neat pallets lying in two rows. Ummi and Humusi followed close behind. The overwhelming sense of river rot—the rank, mildewed stench of the fishing docks—greeted me.

The Boatman.

No. I stifled the feeling. *Stay away!*

But as I stepped into the gloom, the hair stood up on my head.

Something wasn't right. There was no candle burning near Mirrum's bed. There was no *Mirrum* in her bed, either. And where was Mudi?

"Stay back," Ummi commanded, and Humusi pushed Arwia and me into a corner, covering both of us with her body. Silently, she unsheathed two swords.

Is there another assassin here? For us?

My heart thrummed, fear flowing through my body.

Ummi dropped into a low fighting stance, both battle-axes drawn, and crept through the sickroom, peering under pallets.

I strained to see through the dimness, a single shaft of moonlight from the lone window. I held my candle up higher.

"Mudi?" I called out, my voice choking me.

"Be quiet, Kammani. Let Ummi listen," Arwia whispered.

Nobody answered me anyway.

"They're gone! Where could they have gone? Mirrum was too sick to go far."

She shook her head, a finger to her mouth, and winced against the pain of her ear.

Ummi poked under coverlets with her battle-ax and glided slowly, slowly toward the end of the room, her weapons flashing in the moonlight. Behind Humusi, Arwia and I shivered nervously, her blood soaking through the cloth and running down my arm off my elbow. I had to get her stitched, and soon. She was losing too much blood.

When Ummi reached Mirrum's rumpled pallet, she bent and flung back the covers to look underneath. She straightened, confusion on her square face.

"They're not here."

A horrible sense of dread rose into my throat.

"Ummi, there's a storage room. Around the corner."

And as soon as I said it, a sound of rushing water filled my ears. If someone was lying in wait, or if Mudi had taken Mirrum, then that was where they'd be. I placed Arwia's trembling hand against the cloth over her ear, and scooted away from Humusi, candle held high.

"A-zu, no." Humusi gripped my elbow.

I shook her off.

"Stay with Arwia."

If Mudi or Mirrum was in that room and had been harmed in any way, then I needed to be there to help.

Creeping between the pallets, each footfall enveloped by the shadows, I met Ummi's eyes and jerked my head toward the corner where the storage room was.

Ummi nodded and pressed her lips grimly together in a line. Her dark eyes hardened as her grip tightened around her battle-axes. Like a cat, she slid around the corner, both weapons in her firm grip, and shoved past the beads hanging in front of the storage room.

I expected a shriek of terror. Or a cry of surprise.

But there was only Ummi's guttural "Oh," the word whispered in an expulsion of breath. It was followed by a name softly spoken in the dark.

"A-zu?"

Mudi. Mirrum.

Sick with dread, I dragged leaden legs to the beaded doorway, my stomach knotted.

"Kammani, wait for me." Arwia's strangled command rang through the chamber.

But I didn't listen.

I pushed past Ummi, whose wide brown eyes were filled with a hard compassion. She tucked her battle-axes away and laid thick hands on my shoulders as I faced what I already knew I'd see.

No assassin was lying in wait in the storage room.

But both Mudi and Mirrum were.

Their throats had been slashed, and deep maroon blood was draped down the fronts of their tunics like aprons.

I sat down hard right where I was, spilling the candle and snuffing the light as their bodies swam in front of me.

Mudi. Mirrum.

A healer and a warrior so ill she couldn't fight back as she was trained to do.

Murdered.

My hands found my head and I moaned in agony. I was going to save Mirrum! She was going to heal! And Mudi. A sob rose in my throat.

Behind me, Arwia's quick cry, followed by hiccupping sobs, filled the room. Ummi barked an order to Humusi and they chatted quickly, frantically. Then Humusi left the room, her sandals slapping against the cool sandstone floor.

But I drowned them out as I clung to my rational thought. It was the only thing keeping me from tearing the room apart in sorrow. In panic. Because why they'd been targeted was only a mystery if it wasn't coupled with Arwia's attack at the wedding.

An assassin had been sent to kill a healer, and a healer he'd killed.

The problem was, he'd murdered the wrong one.

CHAPTER 5

I WAVED A cautious goodbye to Ummi and Humusi, who'd walked Arwia and me home in the dead of night. After giving me their salute, elbows pressed into their hips, arms open like the goddess Linaza, they jogged away, and two other Koru warriors stationed themselves outside our home. Arwia and I pushed open the door, and I tapped the dust from my sandals before entering the house. Carpets covered the packed floor, and Arwia was constantly fussing about us dragging dirt in, so even in the midst of chaos, I wanted to please her.

At a time like this, kindness was more important than ever.

Nanaea and Dagan were standing, shoulders tense, in the center of the common room.

"Oh, thank Selu you're home." Nanaea flung herself into my arms, nearly knocking me off my feet. The heady scent of her rose oil enveloped me, and I was grateful for it. It smothered the sick stench of blood, of death and gore and violence, from my mind. It wouldn't last, but it was all I had at the moment. I hugged her, worry and sorrow chewing at my guts like worms, and she eased away.

"Arwia, how is your ear? I heard about what happened! Are you all right?" Nanaea took my healing satchel from me and hung it on a hook near a basket of her colorful fabrics, where I always kept it.

"Your wonder of a sister has managed to save it." Arwia bent to remove her sandals, easing down at our low wooden table, the dazzling moonlight shining over the top of bowls and flagons from an earlier meal, casting long shadows. She eyed me warily. We had to tell them what had happened. Neither of us wanted to do it, though.

"'Wonder' is a strong word. Especially since your hearing may be impacted for a while, and there's little I can do about that while it heals."

Nanaea crouched by the fireplace, stirring a pot of steaming wheat porridge. "I'm sure it will get better and everything will be fine after a while."

Her ear might heal, but nothing would be fine for a long time. Not until we were all safe. Dagan engulfed me in his arms, burying his face in my hair.

"You're back," he murmured. "I knew the Koru could protect you both, but I was still afraid. Kasha is upstairs asleep. Iltani is in a drunken stupor in her room, snoring loud enough to call the Boatman from the river." He pulled me back and kissed my forehead. "Are you all right? You're—" He stepped away from me. "You're covered in blood." He looked from me to Arwia. "Is that all hers?"

"No," I sighed, running a hand down my face. "It isn't."

Alarmed, Nanaea looked up at me swiftly from the fire. I took Dagan's hands in mine and kissed them. The *last* thing I wanted to do was introduce more violence into their lives. We'd *left* all that. Manzazu was supposed to be a safe haven for us.

Nevertheless.

"The assassins came for me."

"What do you mean?" Dagan breathed. "Are you all right? Is that *your* blood?"

Nanaea's ladle paused over the bowls. "Did they hurt you, Sister?"

"No. I—"

The back door creaked open, and Dagan shoved me behind him, his emerald dagger out of his belt and in his hand, poised to throw as Nasu emerged.

"Easy, Dagan." Nasu closed the door quietly behind him, his warm brown eyes wary, his hands up in surrender. "It's me."

"Well, announce yourself, then!" Dagan sheathed his dagger forcibly. "I could've killed you!"

He'd erected a set of targets in the back of our home for sport, and I'd seen him throw hundreds of times, so I knew Dagan's aim was true and straight, his dagger rarely missing the heart of the target.

Warily, Nasu started to remove his weaponry belt but

seemed to think better of it as he stared at me, and kept it on. "What's wrong? What happened?"

"The assassins came for me, Nasu. Mudi and Mirrum were . . . dead when we arrived in the sickroom." My throat closed, the edge of a sob trying to elbow its way out. I lowered my voice, glancing up the stairs where my little brother slept. "They were murdered. Their throats slit."

"Come. Sit down." Dagan led me to our low wooden table, made roughly by Nasu's hands, and Arwia scooted over so everyone could fit.

Nanaea plunked bowls of steaming porridge in front of us. "It isn't flavorful, since the Libbu has been out of nutmeg and cloves, but it's warm and filling."

We murmured our thanks, and she joined us.

Tearfully, I described the grisly scene. Finding Mudi and Mirrum. Deciding to stay put and fix Arwia's ear while Humusi ran to alert the queen. The families coming to collect the bodies. As I talked, we all made a show of eating, though we mostly shoved the food around in our bowls, the gore pickpocketing our appetites.

At last, Nasu gave up and pushed his food away. "Well, you can rest assured that Sarratum Tabni has fortified the city. Ilu's mother is friends with the queen, and she heard that the warriors in the larger regiment have been dispatched to the wall, with troops combing the city in twos and threes to find any threats."

He folded his hands in front of him. "She also said that

the bastard Uruku has been causing trouble in the entire river region down by the sea. Some of his men attacked a group of our traders headed down to the ports. Slit their throats. Left them for the birds. And that Uruku is sending out raids, terrorizing people in other cities in the south. There's even talk he's sent a band of mercenaries to places closer to us. Up north."

Arwia bit her lip, thinking. Then she turned to me. "I need to go to Sarratum Tabni and beg her to house us in the Palace, which is the safest place for now. Though I am not sitting on Alu's throne, you are all my subjects and I plan to keep you safe. Kammani, will you come with me? She respects you and maybe she'll listen if you're there. She still thinks of me as a child."

"We will never be safe." I shook my head and shoved my bowl of porridge away. "Not here in Manzazu or anywhere else we go. You know that, don't you? We cannot stay locked up in the Palace forever. Uruku will not stop sending assassins or putting a price on our heads until he's murdered each and every one of us. He values that throne far too much to be dissuaded so easily."

"You'd think if he valued it, he wouldn't have attacked on Manzazu soil." Nasu played with his spoon. "The queen is fortifying our city, but she will answer Alu's threat, and soon."

Arwia nodded. "You're right. She can't let this go unpunished, which is why it's even *more* important for us to go to her and beg her to house us until this is all over. War brings chaos."

Not only chaos, but death and disease, too.

"What she *should* do is take out Uruku with a band of her Koru warriors instead of launching a full-blown attack," Dagan said. "Slide into the city in the dead of night and assassinate him. It would save countless lives."

"Murder to prevent murder?" I asked him. "*That's* what you believe in?"

"Even your abum would agree with that, my love. There's no shame in saving your own life and in rescuing others."

"What you're suggesting is different. It means planning to kill a man, not simply defending yourself." My insides twisted at the thought.

"Is it so different?" Dagan asked.

"The queen would never agree to that. An attack is more powerful," Nasu said. "It would show Manzazu's might. Then she could reinstate you on the throne, Arwia."

"But I don't want the throne." Arwia's face twisted in angst.

"It doesn't matter, does it?" Nasu asked. "You're the rightful sarratum. And you've been telling me that you feel guilty for leaving everyone behind in Uruku's claws, have you not?"

Arwia flushed and looked at her hands. "Sarratum Tabni tells me that by abandoning them, I've disgraced my ummum and abum. That my parents would be staring at me from the Netherworld, urging me to rule the city in peace." Arwia looked up at me. "But who would even want me on the throne? No one. I *left* them."

"Whether or not killing Uruku is the means"—I cast a hard look at Dagan—"I doubt there are very many people in

Alu who wouldn't welcome your rule. They loved you before, Arwia."

"Some did." She shrugged.

"Many more than 'some.'"

"But I'd have no idea how to lead."

"If you were queen, you'd have twelve ensis to help you if you didn't know what to do." Nasu stood and took his bowl to the washbasin by the door. He squatted down to scrub it clean.

"Yes, and those same ensis would have to agree by majority to reinstate me as well. How would we accomplish that if Uruku has been keeping them happy enough by his side? It's too much." She stood. "Too soon. We just *got* here."

"It's been nine moons. And whether you want this to happen or not, here we stand." Nasu dried his dish and set it on the shelf with the others.

"And would you come with me if I did suddenly have to rule Alu?" she asked us. "All of you? What of our lives here?"

"Oh, Arwia, of course we would," I said.

"Really?" Dagan sat back and stared at me. "After the conversation we had about me going north?"

"This would mean supporting a new queen, Dagan. Not commerce."

He sighed and rubbed his eyes. "Yes, that's true. I am tired."

I reached over and squeezed his hand. "We are *all* tired. This has been a terrible night."

"Kammani?"

Kasha's voice was raspy with sleep. He stood on the stairs,

a foot dangling as if to step down, staring at me with worried brown eyes that looked so much like my abum's.

"Uruku is coming for us? We are not safe?"

Nanaea, Kasha, and I had finally been able to be a family again here. I'd watched Nanaea work hard at her sewing, trying to be responsible, and watched Kasha run around with the neighbor boys, chasing dogs and shooting birds out of the sky with their slingshots. We were living normal lives filled with nothing more tumultuous than arguments over who was taking too long at the washbasin.

So what answer could I give this boy, one whose own father had died by Uruku's hand?

Pushing myself away from the table, I went to him and ruffled his dark curls, and kissed the top of his head, which still smelled of smoke from the torches and cookfires at Simti's wedding.

"We are as safe as we can be right now, and we are going to make sure it stays that way."

He relaxed as I walked him back up the stairs to his chamber. But after I settled him in and rubbed his back, I wondered how in Selu's name I was going to keep that promise to him. Would Arwia agree to ask Sarratum Tabni for an assassination instead of a war? And if so, would the queen even agree if what Nasu said was true?

While Kasha drifted off, I eased his angst with a childhood song from our ummum, my eyes drooping as I stroked his hair. "Sleep, little bug." I yawned. "Sleep."

When I finally made my way down the stairs and tucked

myself into the pallet I shared with Nanaea, she was already asleep, her measured breath blowing a single strand of hair back and forth in front of her face. I lay down, drunk with fatigue, and tucked the pillow under my chin.

But just as I was drifting off, a man's whispery baritone sang from the moonlit corner of the room:

The river is wide

The river is deep

I take their souls to earn my keep

I startled and sat up, my heart pounding, and squinted at the shadows.

"Hello?" I whispered.

A shadowy figure appeared like a strike of lightning near my old wooden rocking chair, then vanished.

I clutched my quilt to my chest. "Nobody wants you here. Nobody! Do you hear me?"

But there was no response, save for a lone dog barking somewhere in the distance.

"Sister?" Nanaea murmured, stirring. "Dreams again?"

"Shhh. Go to sleep. It's okay."

I stroked her hair with a shaky hand and stared at the corner of the room until my eyes burned and the sound of his voice faded from my ears. Until the cold fear gripping my heart relaxed enough that I could lie down and drift off into blackness.

CHAPTER 6

—ɯ—

THE CROOKED STREETS that led to Tabni's Palace were crowded with merchants coming to the Libbu to trade. Despite people milling about like any other day, the caution in their eyes made it clear that word of the assassination attempt had spread and orders had been issued.

The sarratum's army was present in full force, sicklyswords in hand, spears tucked against their sides, faces resolute. War carts and chariots were lined up in the Libbu, workers tending their wheels and loading them up with provisions and weaponry.

"Kammani, look what is happening in this city right now."

Arwia's brow was furrowed, the small birthmark that hovered above her lip standing out starkly on her face, which had paled due to the stress of last night. Her attempted assassination. The injury. And now, the question she was going to ask Sarratum Tabni.

Gnats tumbled in my belly, and I took a long, shaky breath. "Yes, I know. War is on the horizon."

"Just as we thought." Manzazu, our safe haven, was definitely preparing to retaliate.

Iltani shifted Nanaea's basket of dinner linens on her hip as she, Arwia, and I approached the Libbu. Dagan and Kasha walked a few paces back, both of them with daggers in hand. Dagan had been teaching Kasha to throw, and though my brother's aim was improving, I prayed to Selu he didn't need to fling the blade. Someone would likely lose an eye.

Behind them, two Koru warriors marched, hands on weapons, eyes on the people around us. One was Humusi, who always seemed to radiate a nervous energy, bouncing on the balls of her feet. The other was a bulky warrior named Higal, who had a scar down her left cheek and a scorpion tattoo on her right. They'd been stationed by our home and had immediately followed us when we left, though Higal looked aggrieved that she'd been forced to watch us.

Next to me, Iltani was bleary-eyed, her continuous revels over the last several moons no doubt taking a toll. I placed the back of my hand against her forehead and pulled it away when she batted at me.

"Iltani, the last thing I need to worry about right now with all that is going on is your health, so I beg you to keep it together. You've been drinking too much brew. Staying out too late time and again. Last night Dagan said he searched for you for almost a full hour and had to pull you, half-dressed, out of the bushes."

"Yes, and you slam the door when you come into the house late at night and wake everyone up," Arwia groused. She shifted our basket of offerings for Linaza to the other arm. We couldn't enter the temple without a gift, so we'd brought a selection of our favorite things.

"At least I am good at *earning coins*, if not at being silent like the rest of you walking dead."

Though she'd slept through our conversation early this morning, she'd jumped at the chance to leave the house. I'd begged her to stay behind, but she refused. Her ruse was that she wanted to sell Nanaea's linens. The two of them had teamed together since Nanaea had proven to be ineffective in bartering, whereas Iltani could wring coins from a stone. But if I knew Iltani, she'd be flush with money in a half hour and two cups of sweetwine deep before noon.

"Just sell them quickly and get back home." I lowered my voice. "There are people literally trying to kill us."

"Kill *you*. They want nothing to do with me. I was a poor rat in Alu. They have no idea I'm here or who I am. Anonymity, as I've come to find out, is grand, especially if you've been after another woman's husband."

"For the sake of the gods, Iltani." I scowled at her, but she just laughed.

We jostled around another group of warriors into the Libbu that encircled the Palace. Its six domes of rose gold glittered in the warm morning light, and jade-green tents were scattered around it like seeds in a field. People haggled with the merchants in front of them over baskets of fish and multicolored shawls.

Many of the merchants' tents, however, were gone. The spice tent had disappeared. The silks. Even quite a few of the stalls selling trinkets for children and scorpion amulets for praying to Linaza. A few weeks ago, I'd had to trade healing services for just the smallest bottle of arnica, and I was rapidly running out. Trade from the sea had been cut off by the skirmishes near the ports, apparently led by Uruku and his mercenaries. It was going to be severely problematic if it wasn't resolved soon.

A family went by, a little girl clinging to the mother's hand, a skinny father leading two roped rams at her side. Iltani's eyes dimmed as she followed the man with her eyes.

"Is that one of the husbands you've been hounding?" Shading my eyes against the sun's glare, I looked up at the rounded crimson temple that sat in the middle of the Palace's domes. Arwia had said that the queen spent the morning in prayer and we could find her there.

"No." She cleared her throat, and the twisted smile was back on her face. "Reminded me of someone from Alu. Now go. Shoo. Be gone. I have money to make, and your presence reduces my chances significantly."

As we reached the sandstone stairs, I felt a surge of love for this poorly mannered friend of mine and tugged Iltani into a hug. "Make smart choices. And stay with Dagan and Kasha. Think of them, if not yourself, all right?"

"You worry too much." She laid a big, wet kiss on my forehead and shoved me away. With a keen eye toward the merchants' tents, she wandered off, likely wondering who would be the most malleable clay in her hands.

"Kasha and I are going to get him a new blade and will keep track of Iltani." Dagan pulled me close. Tucked my hair around my ears. "Then we'd better get back to our home and lock ourselves in." He looked past me to the carts and the weapons and lowered his voice. "Do you think she'll agree to send in the assassins, Arwia?"

"Perhaps." Arwia's long braid slipped down over her shoulder, and she winced when it brushed the stitches on her ear. "Though I'm not sure I'm the best person to sit on the throne if she does manage to oust him."

"You're stronger than you think, my friend." I wasn't sure I agreed with asking to *kill* a man outright, but as I'd lain there trying to sleep, tossing and turning, the logic of it was hard to deny.

That didn't make it morally right.

I stood on tiptoe and kissed Dagan's lips softly. "Stay with Iltani. Please."

"Of course." He rubbed his thumb over my chin. Kissed me once more. "You have my heart, Kammani."

"And you, mine."

Disgust filled Kasha's face at our conversation, but Dagan

clapped Kasha on the back with affection, issuing a final warning for me to be careful. Together, they trailed after Iltani. The warriors behind us split. Humusi and Higal debated, then with a scowl, Higal followed behind Dagan.

Although I felt a prickle of unease spidering into my scalp as we ascended the stairs, only part of it was because of the likelihood of a second assassination attempt. The other part was because there was a good chance we were all going to be facing an entirely new tomorrow, depending on what Sarratum Tabni said today.

※※※

The temple glowed in the morning sun. The goddess Linaza with her scorpion's tail, wings stretched full and weightless from her back, was painted in vivid blue over the arched doorway. Ummi stood rigidly next to it, battle-axes in her belt, cropped black hair hanging from her helmet.

She opened her arms in the Linaza salute as we approached. "Sarratum Tabni prays. Do you have business with her?"

Tamping down my nerves, I bowed my head as Humusi edged past us and slipped inside. "We do. Will you let her know?"

"Of course. Wait here."

She followed Humusi into the cool interior, where the queen sat on a narrow wooden bench, facing an altar piled high with gifts for the goddess: Talents falling out of baskets. Gold coins, beaded jewelry, fruits, and even sheaves of wheat.

"I suppose this is it, then." The diminutive Arwia stood as tall as she possibly could, but her lips were trembling.

"What are you going to say?" I bit my thumbnail, then quickly dropped my hand.

"I'm going to ask her to advise me on how to keep you all safe, and perhaps she will invite us to stay in the Palace while we sort everything out. My first piece of business is keeping everyone alive. Then . . ." She blew out a breath. "I'll ask her to remove the threat and spare the Alu citizens."

"Even if that means you'll take the throne?"

She shook her head, her eyes bleak. "What else is there to do?"

Murmuring echoed from inside the cavernous temple, where Ummi and the sarratum stood talking.

The stately woman angled herself toward us, her thin eyebrows raised on her wide forehead. "Do not stand there darkening the doorway," she called. "Enter and ask what you will."

We both took off our sandals and walked toward the sarratum, bowing to the shrine of Linaza. We added our offerings—a sampling of embroidery, a few coins, some fresh honeycake made by Simti yesterday morning before she'd left to be a bride—and turned to bow.

"You may rise." The regal woman's voice was rich like a bell. "Ummi tells me you have business with me, Sarratum Arwia." She stared at us, eyes wide and honest. Gold glittered on her lids, while her mouth was tinted a purplish brown like a date. She folded her hands neatly over her crimson tunic.

Arwia dipped her head in acknowledgment. "Well—my lady—yes." She cleared her throat. "You've heard of the assassination attempt on me, and I'm wondering what you would do in my position. I have friends here, who are like family, since, as you know, my family is all gone to the Netherworld, and I don't know how best to keep these friends safe. Should we flee to Enlidu? I think I can get us all there in a day's journey with provisions, but I don't know if that would expose us on the road. It might be better to hunker down here in place, especially because Kammani here has a great healing practice—"

"Arwia, you're rambling." Sarratum Tabni studied her, brow knitted. Behind her, Ummi's eyes lit up with mirth.

Arwia twisted her hands in her skirt as she flushed furiously. "My apologies. I'm trying to keep my friends safe."

A flicker of a smile landed on Sarratum Tabni's face. "An honorable desire. What does your god tell you to do?"

Arwia blinked rapidly. "He says to protect those I love."

"So you should do that."

"But how would you suggest I proceed? Our home is not that secure."

Sarratum Tabni lifted a thin shoulder. "Do you want my best recommendation for your ultimate security and that of your people?"

"Well, yes, of course. That's why I am here."

"I'm waging war on Alu. I will put down that impostor

who rules your city, and will need to replace him with someone honorable and loyal. That, dear child, should be you."

Although we knew it was true, hearing the confirmation of her decision to besiege our city, our old *home*, felt like a kick directly in the gut.

Arwia nervously twisted her hands in front of her. "But how does that protect those *here*? With *me*?"

The queen furrowed her brow. "Don't you have an entire city under your veil of protection? One currently being ruled by a man who was wily enough to take your throne from underneath you, and punish those citizens he is supposed to serve? He is harming your people, Arwia. Did you know that?"

"I suspected it, but . . . it was not confirmed."

Sarratum Tabni crossed her arms over her chest. "My spies tell me a skirmish broke out several moons ago in your city—maybe right after you left Alu—between the poor and the wealthy. Those with coin, no doubt bolstered by the lugal's favor to them, began tormenting the poor. Taking their silver after trading in the Libbu. Harassing their women. Worse. A group of the poor banded together and entered the Palace to stand in front of Uruku. They called for something to be done. For someone to be held responsible for the crimes. When he did nothing, they set fire to the counselor's home. Several other homes nearby caught fire, too. That started the skirmish, which led to every single poor person who'd been involved in the initial group being killed in the Pit by the guardsmen as traitors."

Arwia's face drained of color. She pressed a knuckle to her lip beneath the birthmark.

"That is your new lugal's way. My spies tell me he kills anyone, especially the poor, who oppose him. He's been ransacking the ships that come in from the ports. Disrupting trade in the entire river region. Harming city-states much weaker than we are. That's the man you allowed to take your throne."

Sarratum Tabni looked up at the shrine of Linaza glittering in the soft light from the torches that lined the room. "Do you know why our goddess is so important to me and earns my daily worship?"

We both shook our heads.

"Because she knows there is a time to love and there is a time to fight. And when a mangy dog of a ruler brings a fight to me, I believe it is time to exact retribution."

"But how will you do that?" Arwia asked.

"We attack the city-state with every weapon at our disposal. The full force of the Manzazu army."

"But what of the innocents?" I blurted.

Arwia delicately stepped on my foot as Sarratum Tabni turned to me. When I swallowed, I was certain my gulp could be heard all the way down into the marketplace.

"My apologies, Sarratum Tabni. I spoke out of turn—"

"No, no." She smirked. "I like your forthrightness, and I admire your sentiments, but innocents are always lost in war." Her voice softened in fervor. "Our cause is holy. I will have retribution for the slaughter inside my city. He will pay tenfold with the blood of his citizens."

Arwia bristled. "Those are *my* citizens."

Sarratum Tabni pursed her lips. "Are they? You left those people in his care to save your own skin with no plan of taking back the throne. I would think someone desperate to care for her people would also be willing to do whatever it took to ensure his tyranny ceased. Taking him and anyone who stands with him down means peace in the region, a restoration of trade here in Manzazu, and protection for my citizens down the line. We must put down this rabid dog before he attacks with an even stronger bite."

Arwia's mouth opened and closed like a fish.

Sarratum Tabni looked up at the shrine, admiration in her eyes. "And Linaza supports my methods. It feels right to me in my soul."

A fierce sense of urgency flooded through my veins.

"But what if, my lady, we could get Arwia on the throne *without* war? Couldn't you simply send in a small band of Koru warriors to silently . . . kill him?"

My guts twisted that I was even saying the words aloud, as if taking a person's life was a normal daily occurrence. Even wicked men were to be shown mercy, my abum used to say. Even Alani deserved a just trial.

Arwia raised her chin, the flicker of a flame burning inside. "Your Grace, I . . . I support you in restoring me to the throne." She glanced at me nervously, her cheeks flushing, but continued when I nodded at her encouragingly. "You'd have a wonderful, loyal ally in me, and if you were provoked, I would *always* come to your defense. But Kammani asks a good question."

The sarratum snorted. "You know nothing of the world yet, Arwia. A healer and one of my own Koru were slaughtered right under my nose. I do not want Uruku *silently killed*."

"You don't?"

"No. I want Uruku delivered into my hands *very much alive*."

Chills ran up my backbone at the gleam in her eye.

"I must mount his head on my wall to display my strength in the north. The sarratum in Kush does not take me seriously enough as it is. And the lugal in Enlidu is even worse." She held a fist in front of Linaza, her eyes burning with passion. "If I take his city and put an ally in charge, they will *know* what I can do."

"My . . . my apologies, my lady."

She inhaled through her nose, stepped back, and clasped her hands in front of her. "You're forgiven. You're young. Naïve."

Arwia nodded. "Perhaps." But indignation simmered in her eyes.

The sarratum sighed. "Arwia, please come live with me in the Palace for protection." She held her hands out to us. "All of you. And when we're through putting down the dog and disposing of his loyalists, you can take your rightful place on the throne and solidify an allyship that will last a lifetime."

"Is that . . . an order, Your Grace?" Arwia asked, raising her chin just the slightest bit.

The sarratum assessed her coolly. "It is my strongest

recommendation. For now, go. You can take a few days to pack. I've preparations to make since we go to war in half a moon."

She flicked her eyes up to Ummi. "Commander, see them out, and keep them safe on their journey back home."

"Yes, Sarratum."

Ummi escorted us to the landing outside the temple and held out her hand. "After you."

Arwia gnawed her lip as we walked lightly down the long flight of sandstone stairs to the Libbu below.

"Putting me on the throne has been her goal since we got here, Kammani," Arwia murmured in a voice lower than Ummi could hear.

"Yes, I can see that."

"*Of course* she wants our loyalty and allyship. Alu is closer to the ports! We could potentially restore order in the south and help rekindle trade up here in Manzazu. I'm so *stupid*. I thought she was just being kind, but she wants me on the throne for her own uses."

"You're right. It's why she's been giving you her advice as queen and protecting us here in the city. *Nothing* is free."

"I see that now." She glanced worriedly up at Ummi. "But this is a serious problem. She'll hurt my people to restore me as queen, and they will have no reason to welcome me back if I align myself with the city that has just attacked it."

"Yes. *Uruku* is the problem, not the rest of Alu. We need him—and only him—killed!"

So how do you *do* that? Get him alone and slit his throat? My abum had died that way on the road to the Palace. Or poison? Gudanna, Arwia's former handmaid, had used monkshood on Lugal Marus. The poison was quiet and had caused very little fuss before I'd asked Dagan's ummum about it. She'd trained as a healer with my father, and had recognized the signs of his poisoning because of her knowledge of medicinal plants.

Healers, like me, knew how to save lives, but we also knew *how to take them.*

My throat closed.

Though we had a serious problem, we also had a very clear—if terrifying—solution. It was as plain to me as the city of Manzazu stretched in front of us. The Libbu with people bustling around like beetles. The wide, squat houses with smoke trailing up to the sky. And beyond them, the river Garadun, a blue serpent basking in the sunshine, its curvy body wending toward other cities and eventually to Alu.

My legs jittery, I glanced at the woman who was supposed to be my queen. "Ah . . . this *isn't* a problem, my friend." I swallowed my nerves. "The sarratum said they'd go to war in half a moon, which is actually *good* news if you think about it."

"How is that good news?" she squeaked.

"Well?" I lowered my voice, glancing back at Ummi, who was staring resolutely ahead. "It means we have half a moon to follow that river back home and . . . uh . . . *kill him ourselves* before Manzazu attacks."

She looked at me, eyes bulging. "How could we possibly—"

"Like Dagan said! Sneak in! Get the ensis on board with you returning to power and then assassinate him. And"—I sucked in a deep breath—"I know who should do it."

"Who? You?"

I blinked guiltily at her.

"What?" she squawked. "You're not an *assassin*. None of us are." She met my eyes and slipped on a stair, and I grabbed her arm to catch her.

"Are you all right?" Ummi asked from several steps above us.

"Just fine!" I waved.

"Yes, Arwia. *Me*." Though Kasha and Nanaea were going to be hysterical when I told them I was leaving them behind to try to save their lives. Though my abum would probably join forces with the Boatman and haunt me forever for even letting this thought cross my mind.

"I'm not an assassin, but I *do* know a thing or two about—" I looked over my shoulder "—poison. I also know the city inside and out. I traveled each one of those roads as a healer. Many people there owe me a favor for healing them. For my *abum* healing them. I'd have allies who could protect me."

"I don't like it. You're not a good sneak."

"Then I'll bring Iltani, too. She can talk anyone into anything, and nobody even knows who she is."

"As if Dagan would agree. Or Nasu."

"Dagan could come with me if he were disguised. He's of

the noble class. He can . . . I don't know . . . sneak around and convince the ensis to accept you and get the people on our side. Nasu could come along to protect us."

She stared at me, her black eyebrows coming together in angst. "Then I am coming as well."

"No! You're too precious. If something were to happen to you, then who would rule?"

"Kammani, stop it. We'll have to figure out another way. This is ludicrous."

"We can do this, Arwia. We can sneak into the city and send him to the Netherworld before that insane sarratum up there bloodies everyone in Alu."

"This is terrible." Arwia crossed her arms over her chest as we took the last remaining steps and descended into the chaos of the Libbu. A pair of donkeys pulled a creaking cart stacked high with spears, their sharpened blades a stark reminder of what was at stake.

"We'll be ghosts in the night, my friend. He'll never see us coming." I couldn't believe I was convincing her I would make a good murderer. I couldn't believe I *had* to.

After several moments, Arwia straightened her shoulders, but her eyes were bleak as she assessed the frenetic movement in the Libbu.

"You're probably right, Kammani, though I hate it. I hate the whole idea." She stared at the weapons gleaming in front of us. "But if we don't, we'll live the rest of our lives looking over our shoulders, waiting for the blade. She touched her stitched ear absently. "I have *far* too many plans for my life to live like that. Well, I *did*. I suppose now my plans include a throne." She stared gloomily at the weaponry cart.

"And I have plans, too." In Alu, I could rebuild a healing practice with my own citizens. I could build a home with Nanaea and Kasha. Spend a long life with Dagan in whatever form that took.

Uruku had already taken my abum, my good kind mentor who'd taught me everything I knew about healing. He'd stolen Mirrum. Mudi.

He'd stolen this safe haven of Manzazu right from under our feet.

Though it sent shivers of dread up into my hairline and guilt into my heart that I was already thinking of the deadliest poisons to use, I wouldn't let him steal anything else from me ever again.

CHAPTER 7

NANAEA AND KASHA walked next to me on the road to Alu, their sandals crunching in the silted sand, eyes squinted against the blazing sunshine. Their presence grated on my nerves. They'd refused my demands to stay in Manzazu, safe and secure with Simti and Ilu. Kasha had wailed in fright, beating his chest and threatening to sneak away and follow us if I left him. Nanaea had promised she'd help get us into the city with clever disguises and had argued that her life was on the line, not just mine, and wasn't she a grown woman now, too, so she should be able to do what she liked.

By the time she'd finished speaking, my head had been pounding, and I'd agreed to let her come if only to shut her up. We'd tearfully hugged Simti goodbye, promising we'd return with news of our triumph.

Obviously, we couldn't all just march into Alu's gates, so we decided to stop in Wussuru, an abandoned city-state a few hours' ride from Alu. Nasu and the traders had slept there before and said it was safe and had a working well. Arwia said that she needed to be near enough to claim the throne quickly should we accomplish our task, so she'd camp there until she got word. Since she couldn't stay alone, Nasu agreed to stay in Wussuru as her guardsman. We all convinced Kasha he should also camp with them to be an extra set of eyes and ears.

The rest of us would head into the city of our birth.

Nanaea to disguise us.

Dagan to pave the way for the nin's coronation.

Iltani to be the sneak.

And me to mix the poison.

My throat went dry even thinking about it. I still needed to find something deadly enough to do the job. My tinctures had dwindled since trade had been reduced, and I didn't have time to test any new plants or berries before we left. With Mudi gone, there was no one to go to for help, either. I was counting on Dagan's mother to have something suitable at the farm. If anyone would have a tincture to take down Uruku, it would be her.

I am going to kill a man.

My abum had always trained me to do no harm. Ease someone into death only if they're suffering greatly. Keep my feelings out of my practice if I was angry with the person I was treating.

Churning with dread, I brushed the damp hair out of my eyes and laid a hand on the packed, squeaking cart to steady myself in the blazing sun. We were disguised as traders, loaded down with carpets and casks from Ilu's father. Dagan and Nasu marched up front, flush with weaponry to discourage theft as we traversed down the busy road that wound near the river.

"You all right?" Beet red, Arwia sat under a thin linen on the cart, rocking gently with every bump and turn. We'd advised her to stay hidden as much as possible, but in this heat, it was difficult to be strict.

"Just hot. *Very* hot. The sun is relentless." A trickle of sweat rolled down my throat where my scorpion necklace should be. I had taken it off and stowed it in my healing chest for safekeeping.

"It is. But Nasu says we should arrive by nightfall." She blinked up at the sun and frowned. "Whenever that will be."

"See anything behind us?" I asked her, glancing over my shoulder.

"Not a thing. Just traders and travelers. That's it."

"Good."

We'd told Sarratum Tabni that we were going to go hide in Enlidu until the war was over in case Uruku tried again. Arwia explained that we didn't feel safe in Manzazu since the assassination attempt, and there was a high likelihood the sarratum didn't believe a word of what she said. She'd offered to send some Koru with us to protect us on our journey, but we'd declined. They could report on our attempt to subvert the war that the queen had planned, and we'd be hauled back to the Palace, likely in chains.

We'd been traveling for two days and two nights now, and the threat of them catching wind of what we were planning urged my feet forward. We'd lost two days planning in Manzazu before we left, so we only had about a week and a half to complete our mission.

Not nearly long enough.

"I'm going to check on Iltani," I told Arwia.

"Okay. Tell her to stay out of the sweetwine jugs. She can drink *water* if she's thirsty, like the rest of us."

"I will. Assuming she will listen to me."

"You can only try."

With a sigh, I jogged lightly up to where she was making a show of leading the donkeys, but was actually clutching their bridles for dear life so she didn't fall in her drunkenness and get trampled. She flashed a brilliant, lopsided smile at me.

"Please refrain from looking excited about all this."

She winked as she tripped over her own two feet. "'Excited' isn't the word I'd use. Or maybe it is. I can't remember."

"Why are you dipping into the sweetwine so heavily? We need that to barter or bribe! You remind me of my abum."

"No reason." She hiccupped, eyes glassy. "Maybe I like the brew. Have you ever thought of that? And I'll beg you to keep your opinions to yourself."

She poked me in the right breast and I swatted her.

"You are so crass sometimes."

She cackled and I turned away, irritated. We were in a precarious position, and she was being flippant about it. It boggled my mind.

Dagan glanced back at us, and I caught his eye and walked quickly to catch up with him. The Boatman could take Iltani.

"Hello up here. How is protecting our life and limbs?"

"No nefarious thieves in sight." He smiled at me, but it wasn't the easy smile he typically wore.

Our discussion about going back to the city had been tense, starting with his outright refusal to let me go, which had been met with my own objections about not being married so I could do as I wished.

He'd argued that just he and Nasu should go into Alu, and both Arwia and I had immediately thrown that argument aside. He was big and easily recognizable in the Libbu, so he wouldn't be able to get as close to the Palace like one of us girls could.

"Are you still upset?" I interlaced my fingers with his.

He brought my hand to his lips. "No. I'm worried. You are my *everything*, Arammu. You know how I feel about you."

"Yes, and I feel the same about you." I swallowed. I'd yet to give him an answer to his question of marriage, and he hadn't asked again. I supposed we were both waiting on this hairline of a precipice to see what would happen in Alu before plunging back into those waters.

"If something were to happen to you, I don't know what I would do." He looked ahead at other travelers on the dusty, winding road along the river. Clenched his jaw. "I don't think I could bear it."

"We have to try to do this, though, don't we? What other

option is there? Could you live with yourself if something happened to your ummum or your brothers in war and we hadn't tried? This whole thing was your idea to begin with."

"I didn't mean for *us* to do the killing, Arammu." He stared at his sandals. "And I'd like to get to the other side of this with you intact so you'll be alive to answer my question of marriage."

"Dagan . . ." But I let my voice trail off. What else was there to say right now?

He shifted the pack on his shoulders. "I know, I know. This isn't the time and I will not pressure you. There are bigger things to worry about."

"Yes, my love, there are."

"But I *will* pressure you to think about you and Nanaea waiting in Wussuru while Iltani and I go into the city ourselves. Consider that, please. For *me*." He looked at me with those amber eyes framed by impossibly thick lashes.

My heart swelled with love.

"I will, Dagan. For you, I will."

But even as I said the words, we both knew I was lying.

❧❧❧

Night fell swiftly on the road.

"It's right up here." Dagan's tired voice lifted momentarily at the prospect of resting. Exhaustion sat heavily on our shoulders like children we were too tired of carrying. My muscles ached for a soft pallet and a star-filled sky in our little house in Manzazu, though that was a senseless, painful wish, considering where we were.

The abandoned city of Wussuru loomed ahead, its walls crumbling. Dagan was concerned that bands of thieves might hide there, but Nasu's trip up the road early this morning had assured us it was still vacant.

A ghost of its former self.

An hour later, we crossed under tiled archways bearing the figures of gods and goddesses nobody believed in anymore. Inside the walls, past disintegrating homes, remnants of firepits, and shells of taverns, there appeared to be an old Libbu surrounded by a wall pulled nearly apart by climbing weeds.

And there was a crackling fire burning brightly inside it. Shadowy figures broke apart and approached when we neared.

"Dagan! Someone's here!"

Dagan shoved me behind him and had his emerald dagger in his hand before I could blink. Nasu threw himself atop the cart in front of Arwia, brandishing his sickleswords.

"Get down!" he hissed to her, and she ducked beneath the linens.

"Who's there?" Dagan commanded.

"A-zu!"

A woman's voice echoed from the Libbu, and before we could even make another move or better prepare ourselves for impending bloodshed, we were surrounded.

By Koru. Eight of them.

Commander Ummi, scraping her teeth with a stick, and Humusi, wiping her mouth with the back of her hand, stepped from the shadows. Higal followed, burly hands on thick hips near her battle-axes.

"What are you doing here?" I breathed.

"You are not a quiet plotter. I heard you and Arwia on the steps," Ummi said around the stick in her mouth.

"But we never said anything about going to Wussuru then. Did we?" If we were *this* bad at sneaking around our allies, what chance did we stand in Alu?

She spat something out on the ground. "You said it in your home."

"You were *spying* on us?" Nasu snapped.

Higal laughed, a full-bellied sound that echoed through the courtyard. "We do as we are told."

Arwia poked her head up from the cart. "Are you going to take us back to Manzazu and tell Sarratum Tabni what we're doing?"

Dagan stepped forward with his dagger poised to throw.

"Put it away, farmer," Ummi ordered, both of her battle-axes suddenly in her hands. "We're not here to turn you in. We're here to *help* you."

Nasu flicked his gaze from Dagan to Ummi but did not drop his sickleswords. "And defy your sarratum?"

Dagan stepped forward. "Yes, please explain."

"I could kill you in three seconds, boy."

"And I could kill you in two," Dagan growled, his dagger twitching in his hand.

"Stop it. Both of you." Arwia climbed down from the cart, her long braid trailing after her like a rope. "Sheathe your weapons." She looked around at the rest of the Koru who'd encircled us. "*All* of you." Her hands trembled as she held them out, but she did not back down.

Slowly, his eyes watchful, Dagan slid his knife back into his belt, but stood at the ready, muscles tense. Ummi twirled her battle-axes and sheathed them in one smooth move, smiling broadly around the stick in her mouth.

"Please tell us why you're here." Arwia held her hand out to Ummi.

"I told Sarratum Tabni that we'd accompany you to your destination to guarantee your safety. And here I am." She bowed. "She wanted you watched on the path to Enlidu. She doesn't know you're here in Wussuru or what you plan to do, because I kept that from her."

"Why would you do that?" I asked.

"Because I believe in what you said on those stairs, A-zu. If you move into Alu swiftly, with stealth, you could rid your city of that maggot and be done with it."

"Why do you care what happens in Alu?" Nasu looked at her pointedly. "It is our city, not yours."

"Is it because you owe me the favor?" Otherwise, it didn't make sense. "The queen granted me the scorpion necklace, but I know you are required to fulfill it."

Ummi shook her head. "The favor was granted by Linaza herself. The queen only acted as the medium to guide it to you. Our goddess has granted you her power, and I can only fulfill that favor when you ask me to, A-zu."

"What if my request goes against the wishes of the sar-ratum?"

"Linaza would not give you a desire that defies the sar-ratum."

Really.

"Well, then why do you care?"

"Two reasons." She shifted her stick to the other side of her mouth. "Strength is not always loud. Sometimes we are strongest when we are quiet. We'd show ourselves to be a better army if we could remove him from power without harming the citizens of your city. Sarratum Tabni believes otherwise, but"—she cocked her head—"she has not been in a war."

Higal spoke. "The second reason is Assata."

"The tavern keeper?" I asked.

Higal grunted. "You know her?"

"We all do. She's a friend of ours," Dagan said, and we all murmured our agreement. "She sent us with provisions when we first left the city. Provided Kammani's abum with food when he couldn't pay. She's a good person."

Ummi nodded. "She is. I remember her from when I was a child. When she first left her birth city of Kemet as a young woman, she traveled to Manzazu and trained as a warrior."

"Yes! Many of us in Alu knew she trained with you. She used to give sicklesword lessons to girls behind her tavern while their parents were inside," I said.

Higal nodded. "Sounds right. She trained me as a girl."

Ummi continued. "But once she fell in love with the merchant, Irra, she left Manzazu to follow him to Alu. I know the destruction we can bring," Ummi said. "We do not wish to bring harm to her, or to anyone else. Besides, I think she would help you if she knew of your plans. You must go to her. Tell her what you want to do."

"Why can't you just kill him yourself?" Dagan asked. "If you believe in this cause? You're more skilled than we are."

Ummi glanced between Higal and Humusi, who stood, arms loose at their sides. "We cannot defy Sarratum Tabni outright. She wants him brought back to our city alive. Linaza has told me to offer you our *guidance* on this night. To give you some tools to protect yourself in Alu. And then we will go back to our sarratum to bring war if you do not succeed. But I hope this gives you some time."

My heart fluttered. It was gracious. And completely dangerous for them to be here if Sarratum Tabni knew their intent.

"Thank you, Ummi." I nodded to the others. "Thank you for this. But how did we not see you on the road?"

She crossed her arms over her breastplate. "We move with craftiness, unlike you." A ghost of a smile showed up on her face, displaying the gaps in her teeth. "We followed you and not at a safe distance. No one but Nasu felt our presence, and that was only after the first day." She shifted the stick to the other side of her mouth. "We left at separate times, disguised as merchants. Traders. Mothers heavy with child." She barked a laugh at that. "You never saw us, not even once, for our disguises were crafted with great care."

On the other side of me, Nanaea perked up when she said that. But the hair stood up on my head. If they'd followed in costume and we were unaware, we had a lot to learn from them.

Ummi jerked her head at the Libbu. "Let us take some rest and do some training. You can sneak into the city by dark in two days' time. I'll post sentinels around the walls to keep all of you safe. Two of the Koru are walking the perimeter now. No harm will come to you when you are in my care."

"Our thanks, Ummi. Let's unpack." Arwia nodded and we dispersed. Dagan and Nasu grabbed our tents and some rolls of bedding from the back of the cart.

"This is a gift from Selu," Nanaea breathed into my ear as she passed me by, hauling her basket of sewing and a small cask of what appeared to be face paints. "I'm going to talk to the Koru about what they used to disguise themselves. See if I can sew some of the pieces for us to get into the city."

"Good idea, Nanaea."

I joined the others unpacking a few necessities, shaking out quilts, and talking about Alu as we settled in. A nervous, excited energy seemed to zigzag through the warriors as they carried supplies. At last, we gathered around a crackling fire, several birds roasting on sticks, fish nestled on grates over the coals. At my side, Dagan filleted some hot fish into bowls for us both while Nanaea squatted on the other side of the fire, concentrating on a bit of cloth. One of the Koru warriors worked with her, ripping the seam out of a garment. Dagan was relaxed as he smiled at me kindly and handed me the dish, but though my murmured thanks seemed calm, I couldn't help but worry about what might await us on the other side of Alu's wall.

In the corners of the Libbu, weapons of every sort—daggers, battle-axes, sickleswords, spears, and shields—were stacked in neat rows. Nasu was sparring with a woman in the far end of the Libbu, and another Koru warrior was teaching Iltani how to attack with a knife, though chances were good she already knew. That girl had a way of surprising me, even though we'd been friends since we were young. Two more warriors were doing drills by torchlight, their weapons clanging, an occasional "Ha!" or "Oh!" slicing the chilled air in two.

As I took a sip of the sweetwine that Dagan had poured for me, Ummi eased down onto the blanket at my elbow, a fire-roasted fish filet in her hand.

"Are you nervous to go into Alu?" She picked at the meat.

"I'm not *as* nervous knowing you're going to show me how to better protect myself."

I knew some basics, of course. Dagan had shown me how to throw the dagger, though I usually failed to hit the target at all. My training as a healer meant I knew where to cut a man if he needed to die, though ever having to use that knowledge against someone seemed terrible.

"I can train you right now if you like." She waved the fish toward the weapons.

"At first light, if you don't mind." I held up my cup with a small smile. "I've already drunk too much of this to be alert."

And I needed to sleep. Sometimes my worries kept me up late at night. I'd stare out the window of my shared bedroom with Nanaea, gnawing my thumbnail, asking myself questions for which there were never any answers. Would I be the kind of healer my abum wanted me to be with a practice of my own, one I could staff with my own apprentices? Was Kasha eating enough? Was he learning enough? Nanaea would often startle awake and join me at the window, laying her head on my shoulder, and we'd sit, talking, until I felt sleepy enough to return to the pallet.

Were those days gone for good or would they be replaced by Dagan's bed if I accepted his hand in marriage? And why *wouldn't* I jump at the chance to do so? It wasn't as though I didn't love him. He was my favorite person, and I longed to enjoy the pleasures that marriage could bring. Heat rose to my face at the thought, and his strong shoulder brushing against mine made me hunger, low in my belly, for just that.

But the unfairness of the marriage laws between men and women needled me. Even though he'd never treat me unfairly, he *could* and would be supported by the laws if he did. It wasn't right, but if I married underneath them, it would be as if I supported them. But what other option was there? I loved him and wanted to be with him forever.

Can we work it out as he said?

"You look serious, A-zu," Ummi said, taking another bite of her fish.

I looked at her strong jawline as she chewed. She and the rest of the Koru had given up the entire idea of marriage for the honor of serving in the elite circle of warriors.

"I'm curious. Why must the Koru be unmarried while the regular Manzazu army can wed?" I shifted on the blanket, leaning back on my hand.

Ummi remained sitting tall. Vigilant, even as she took up her cup and drank. Every movement was precise. Ready. Waiting for signs of danger. "I've been a Koru since I was your age. As soon as I could be. So . . . a number of years. In all that time, I've only known the sarratum to make one mistake. And that was in not listening to your advice to go into Alu quietly." She flitted her eyes up from her fish and settled them on me.

"So it wasn't a mistake to ask you to give up a husband?"

She grinned, revealing the spaces between her teeth. "A-zu, I was never interested in a *man*."

Ah. There were women who were not, but by law, if their abums gave them in marriage to a man, that's where they went no matter how they felt about it. "But some women who want to join the Koru warriors *might be* interested in a man and marriage."

Her eyes wavered from me to the fire and back. "And those women can choose not to be members of the elite. Only the willing go into this sacred service, and she cannot be married if she does it. She must be focused on the sarratum's commands. That's it. Not worried about tending her small children or listening to her husband."

"But what if her husband tended to her children?"

Ummi snorted, nearly choking on a bite. "Her husband? Ha!"

Dagan leaned forward to slice some meat from one of the birds, and I studied his profile. *He* would be the kind of man to care for a child. He would take a little one by the hand into the fields and teach the child his ways. The image of him with Kasha in the Libbu sprang to mind. There *had* to be other men like him, too.

"Well, why are there no men in the Manzazu army?"

She raised an eyebrow. "Why are there no women in other armies?"

"That's a good question."

"The Koru was started years ago as a small group of women who were part of a larger army of women *and* men. The sarratum wanted them so they could tend to her safety at all hours. But as the years passed, the men dropped out as more and more women joined, and the Palace realized that an all-female army was an advantage. Other cities often misjudge our strength to their great detriment." She elbowed me. "It's something you can use, too."

"Their underestimation of me?"

She stuffed the remainder of the fish into her mouth and chewed. "You can lure someone right into the palm of your hand. And then?" She squeezed her oily hand into a fist. "You crush them."

We rose at dawn to train.

After some lessons in finding places to hide and disguising ourselves in plain sight, Dagan and I left Iltani near Humusi's dagger targets to meet Ummi for grappling training. But before I could even breathe a word, she flipped me over her shoulder onto my back, and told me that I needed to learn the skill, too.

An hour later, I was regretting my agreement. Wiping sweat from my brow, breathing heavily, I squinted into the sun baking my shoulders. Dagan brushed sand from his legs.

"Once more!" Ummi pointed at me to go.

"Last time—then I must move on to something else. I am exhausted."

She frowned at me. "He's not even wearing armor."

"He is heavy!"

She rolled her eyes in disgust as I laid my right cheek on Dagan's left shoulder, stabilizing his thick, sandy bicep with my right hand, while wedging his forearm into my left armpit.

"Drop, twist, and throw. Go!"

With a grunt, I did the move I'd been practicing, twisting as I fell to my knees and using the momentum to fling Dagan over my shoulder onto his back.

He landed with a *whump*, sending up a shower of sand.

"I did it! That's seven times." Breathless, I wiped sweat from my forehead with the back of my hand.

Ummi grunted, pulling me to my feet, but Dagan groaned as he stood, dusted with sand. "Seven times too many."

"Seven times is not nearly enough, but it will have to do. As I told you before, you need to practice this to be sure you can use it when you need it."

"I will remember it," I panted. "Thank you for the lesson."

"You are most welcome. I'll meet you to do knife skills after I eat." She jogged away toward the smells of food being cooked over the morning fire.

"What about thanking me? It was *my* body being abused!" Dagan feigned offense as he pulled me into a hug. I squeezed him back as tightly as I could, my arms around his waist.

"Well, you were a brilliant assistant. I offer you my humblest and deepest apologies," I teased, pulling away from him and brushing sand off his bare torso, letting my hand linger on his warm chest. His heart beat under there, steady and true, a strong *thump, thump, thump* against my palm.

He took my hands in his, a grin playing around his mouth. "Perhaps you'd like to kiss me and make me better."

I gave him a quick peck on the lips. He came back in for another, but I laughed, blushing. "I'm a sweaty, sandy mess and everyone is around."

He trailed a sandy finger down my cheek. "You've never been more beautiful."

That was a lie. It was *he* who was beautiful. Some of his hair had shaken loose from its knot, and it reminded me of the first time I'd woken up under the same roof as him. He'd stumbled out of his room at first light, rubbing sleep from his eyes, his hair loose around his shoulders. When he spotted me at the table, he'd shyly run his hand through his hair to try to smooth it, and I'd been filled with such fire, I'd had to stop myself from launching into his arms that very second.

And now? He was standing there, pressing me to him, love—and a bit of hunger—in his amber eyes.

For me.

So why don't I say yes to his offer of marriage this minute? Take him back to my tent and show him how much I really love him before our futures go up in smoke?

"You're thinking. That line is between your brows," he murmured as he brushed sand from my shoulders. Off my arms. "But I have been thinking, too, Arammu."

"Of what?" Heat rose to my cheeks. Marriage? Had my desire for him been so clear on my face?

His eyes twinkled. "No. Not *that*."

I raised my eyebrows.

"I mean yes, definitely that, but that's not all."

"Oh no?" I smiled.

"No. I've been thinking about that *favor* of yours. The necklace."

Ah. "What about it?"

"What if you . . ." He raised a shoulder. "What if you used the favor to beg Ummi to take the Koru into Alu? You'd be safe. Uruku could be gone, and we could move on with our lives. But this?" He waved to the weapons on our right. At Iltani throwing knives with Humusi on our left. "This will not be enough if you're facing a group of guardsmen. And I won't be able to be with you every second in Alu. It worries me."

"But Ummi said she would not defy the sarratum. I don't want to beg her to break that vow."

"Even if it means your life? Or the life of Nanaea, who is so intent on going in with us?"

"I don't think Ummi would do it, anyway. She is as loyal to the sarratum as Nasu is to Arwia. And she may have less desire to help me later on down the road if I push her to break her vow."

I trailed my hands down his chest. Let them fall to my sides. "Let us see what sort of conditions we face when we get to Alu. If it is impossible, I will ride back here and beg her to use her skills to help us. They said they were not leaving Wussuru for a few more nights, so we have a little time."

He nodded, but his eyes said he didn't agree. "Then while we're there, I'll do everything in my power to ensure your safety."

"Dagan, Nanaea has been working on our disguises and will be done before we leave. Her skills will help ensure our safety, too."

"You have a lot of faith in a little needle." He raised an eyebrow at me.

"We all need to have faith in something."

CHAPTER 8

MOONLIGHT GLIMMERED ON Dagan's bare shoulders as Iltani, Nanaea, and I crept out from our cover in the scrub near the south gate of Alu and darted to the copse of sycamores where we'd stashed our cart of supplies. The donkey we'd hitched to the front stared at us mournfully, and I fed him some of our foraged watercress and rubbed his bristly nose.

"Soon, my friend. We'll have you tucked into a nice, cozy barn soon enough."

Nasu had told us that sticking to the south gate would be our best bet for entry, but that we'd need to be careful getting in because guards were *everywhere*. We'd counted at least four at the gate and several of them up on the walls, stalking vigilantly, bows in their fists, quivers full of arrows on their backs.

Though they weren't looking for Iltani as far as we knew,

she couldn't saunter right in with Nanaea, Dagan, and me in tow in case Uruku had instructed the guardsmen to watch out for us. So we'd had to devise a plan. Iltani had suggested setting fire to the sycamores outside the gate to create a diversion because of course she had. But that would create a scene, and the *last* thing we wanted was to make too much of a fuss. We wanted to slip in easily, unnoticed, like ghosts.

"You'd think one of them would at least have to relieve themselves or *something* by now," Nanaea whispered as we crouched along the Libbu wall in the trees. "Make it at least a *little* easier for Iltani to talk our way in."

"Exactly. What are they, camels?" Iltani tugged her costume down over her hips. Nanaea had painted lines on her face and wrapped her hair in scarves, pulling scraggly strands out the front, darkening them with mud so she'd look unkempt. Iltani would be a traveling prophet, and I would be her veiled apprentice. Failing to offer assistance to one of Selu's prophets could bring about bad luck, so we'd use the Alu tradition to our advantage. Nanaea would lie hidden in the cart under folded blankets, while Dagan was to be wrapped like a corpse and would ride in the back. Dagan had killed a gazelle on the journey from Wussuru, and we'd saved the parts of the carcass we hadn't smoked to arrange across the top of him to add bulk.

And stink.

"It would be ideal if we could get two of them away from the gate with a small fire."

"Iltani, we already said no to the fire."

She winked at me lewdly. "Fine. Maybe I'll have to start a fire of my own with one or two of them."

"We're not going to be bartering with—" I gestured to the length of her body.

She cackled. "I'll be the one talking, now, won't I?"

Dagan scowled at her as he slipped the burlap sack up to his waist. "No one has to barter with . . . *anything.* I brought coins. You can pay them to look the other way if they don't buy your story. And I will be waiting with my daggers drawn if things go wrong."

Iltani opened her eyes in mock indignation. "As if I couldn't defend myself and my dear addled apprentice over here. How dare—"

"Be *quiet.*" I wrapped the scarves we'd borrowed from the Koru around my waist.

"None of you are any fun at all." Iltani elbowed me in the side, her eyes clear and bright. I'd asked her not to drink from her flask so she could be watchful and wary, and more than once, I'd seen her hand straying to her belt where she'd stored it. She'd sworn there was only water in there, but I had my doubts.

"I'll feel more fun when we're through the gate and on Dagan's farm."

We'd decided that it was the safest place to set up a makeshift camp from which we could come and go, and Dagan's ummum had plenty of tonics I could use to mix a poison strong enough to fulfill our plan. Plus, it was far enough away from the city center that we would be unnoticed.

"Kammani, here." Nanaea handed me a dark shawl and studied me as I pulled it over my head.

"Can you see who I am?"

"No. I can tell you're a woman and that's it. It should be perfect. And if they ask you to take it off, the paint I put on you should disguise you well enough. I flattened your nose and made your cheeks more angular than they are. You don't look like yourself."

"Brilliant." Iltani knotted a last scarf rakishly over one eye and draped mismatched and poorly strung beads around her neck. Even *I* was almost convinced she was someone who could commune with the gods. "Let's get to it. I'm starving, and Dagan's ummum is a spectacular cook."

Dagan and Nanaea climbed into the back, and I planted one soft kiss on his lips before Iltani and I laid the stinking gazelle carcass across his body and tied him up in the sack.

"Oh gods, it smells so bad." His muffled voice warbled from inside.

"Breathe shallowly," I whispered. "And probably through your mouth. I'd rub some mint under your nose, but we're out." We wedged Nanaea tightly against the seat, stacking blankets on top and trunks in front of her, and she virtually disappeared.

My brain was a frenzy of nerves as we emerged from the trees, creaking and rocking on the cart. After a few minutes of our traveling down the path, the guards on top of the wall nocked arrows to their bows and focused them on us.

"They see us," I hissed.

"I knowww," Iltani sang softly under her breath. "Now shut up, and let me do the talking."

"Stop where you are," one of the guardsmen at the gate gruffly commanded when we were fifty or so handsbreadths away. He and the other men standing nearby also nocked arrows in their bows, and pointed them at our chests.

"Hellooooooo, gentlemen," Iltani called, pitching her voice deep and crackly, adding a round Manzazu accent that was thoroughly believable. My nerves jangled, a sharp contrast to her bravado.

"What business do you have here so late at night?" The guardsman leveled his arrow at us. "Come closer."

Iltani cracked the reins on the donkey's back, and with a snort, it ambled slightly faster until we were close enough to see the men's faces. The one talking had gray in his beard, but the other three were younger.

"I'm here to tell the fortunes of Alu's citizens." She added a leer that could have curled a man's toes. "Do you want to hear yours?"

"Go back home." The older guardsman jerked his bow toward the road behind us. "We don't want your kind in the city."

She laughed, deep and throaty. "But I am a prophet of Selu! Do you wish to bring bad luck upon yourselves and your families?"

The man scowled. "Get out of here."

Iltani squinted and leaned toward him. "I *knew* you would say that. The evil Alani whispers all sorts of things in my ear, like what you think about laaaaaate at night when noooooobody else is around." She waggled a finger at him. "You naughty boy."

His eyes popped open in shock. "Get out of here, I said. Go!"

Iltani tapped the donkey with the reins, but he balked, recognizing an order when he heard one. She sighed dramatically and smacked the donkey's behind with her hand. The beast wheezed and hotfooted it forward toward the men. She yanked the reins when we were in spitting distance. All four trained their arrows on our chests, and two circled back behind the cart, eyeballing the contents.

"Fine gentlemen, won't you let us in and spare yourselves some bad luck? We're simply two prophets earning coin to eat. We won't stay longer than a day."

"Let me see who is under the veil."

My heart banged behind my rib cage, and I dug my fingers into Iltani's arm.

"Sadly, this one was kicked in the head by a horse as a wee babe, and now tells fortunes with eyes that are permanently crossed. We only veiled her to spare you from having to gaze upon her hideous face."

Oh great.

"Remove the veil anyway."

"Ah, someone who doesn't mind a little bit of a thrill. Well?

As you wish." She yanked the veil from my head in a flourish. I crossed my eyes and looked in the man's direction, and Iltani nearly choked. Quickly, she threw the veil back over my head with a cough. "See? A tragedy."

"Yaryk," one of the guardsmen called from behind the cart. "They've got a body. And it stinks."

The older guardsman stared hard at us and tightened his grip on his bow. "What reason do you have bringing a corpse into the city?"

At that, Iltani stood, violently shaking the cart. "I warn you, guardsmen. Do *not* go near the body of my deceased husband. He has been cursed! I have to bathe him thrice in waters from the Alu well, or the entire city will go up in flames."

The guardsmen backed slowly away from Dagan.

All but one.

He kept his arrow trained on the sack enshrouding his body.

Please don't move, my love. Please.

"Is that so?" The guardsman stepped closer. A mere twenty handsbreadths away.

"It is, sir, it is!"

But before either one of us could stop him, he fired his arrow into the burlap sack.

No!

"Oh well, now you have done it!" Iltani shrieked, panic on her face. I clutched her hand. "You have awakened the wrath of the gods for violating a dead man. Especially one who is cursed! Now his curse will spill out on you unless I reverse it in the sacred Alu waters!"

My heart pounded ruthlessly as I stared at the sack. A circle of blood bloomed on the burlap.

My love!

Under the veil, I bit my lip so I didn't scream, refusing to give in to panic. I could stitch a wound from an arrow if we moved quickly enough. I had everything I needed. We needed to turn around so I could heal him, *right now*.

"Iltani!"

She shook me off and spoke under her breath. "Wait."

The older guardsman rubbed a hand down his face. "Why'd you *do* that? Get away from the cart," he shouted to the man who'd fired the arrow.

The other guardsman shrugged, his eyes wide. "I was making sure they told it true! It *is* a dead body. It didn't flinch!"

"Dead men don't flinch, you imbecile!"

"Let us through so I may reverse the curse." Iltani pointed resolutely toward the gate, and the men backed away. "Your very *lives* are at stake if I do not. You've unleashed the Boatman's wrath!"

The older guardsman took two steps back, his jaw clenching and unclenching. "Get on with you, then. And be sure you do whatever you need to do to get rid of the curse. I have *a family*."

"I will pray for their souls." Iltani slapped the donkey's rump again, and we creaked through the gate, while the guardsmen all bellowed at the man who'd fired the arrow.

I tried to remain calm as we ambled away from their voices to head down a narrow path into the city. We came to a grove of fruit trees after several minutes of me hissing at Iltani to stop. She pulled inside the cover of the trees, hiding us, and I leapt out of the cart while Iltani freed Nanaea from her hiding space. Together, we frantically yanked at the ropes around Dagan's shroud.

"Dagan!" I whispered, my fingers working desperately at the knots.

"Get me out of here, Kammani." His voice was muffled and sounded off, and my heart wanted to burst.

When I finally yanked the sack away from his face, I was greeted by a grimace.

"Get this dead thing off me."

"Did the arrow hit you?"

"No. It hit the gazelle."

Iltani and I yanked off the shroud and I insisted on searching his neck, his chest, his legs for wounds as Iltani and Nanaea heaved the carcass off into the weeds.

"I'm fine, Arammu. Just don't . . . feel right." He clambered out of the cart and stood there, covered in gore, eyes watering. Then he lurched away into the brush. Several seconds later, the sounds of him retching reached our ears.

"Are you okay?" I called after him.

"Just need a second. And, ah . . . new clothes. These stink and I cannot bear it."

I dug around in our things and took him a new tunic.

He was bent over by a bush.

"Do you need anything?"

"Just hand over the tunic. Um . . . please. I will be fine in a moment."

I did, and walked back to the cart to give him some time to sort himself out.

"I hope he feels better. That had to be difficult," Nanaea said, sitting heavily on the edge of the cart while we waited for him.

"Much more so than lying under some blankets." Iltani poked her.

"I'm grateful you gave me the easy job. Thank Selu you can think on your feet!" Nanaea shivered as a gust of wind fluttered the leaves above our heads.

"Yes, though you're lucky I don't deck you for putting me on the spot." I nudged her. "Crossed eyes?"

Iltani cackled. "Let me say that for the rest of my life, if I ever need a good laugh, I'll be pulling up that image of you in my head."

Nanaea giggled. "Show me what you looked like, Sister."

"No," I protested, my face heating. "I refuse on principle."

"It was like this." Iltani crossed her eyes and bared her teeth like a donkey, and before long, we were laughing so hard, stifling our voices with our tunics, that I was certain I might explode. After a few moments, we eyed each other, sighing in relief. We were through the gate. And now we could get to his farm.

Nanaea pulled us both into a tight hug. "Iltani, we can always rely on you to think on your feet, you know that?"

"That's why I'm here." She planted a loud kiss on each of our foreheads. "To keep you fools out of harm's way."

And we laughed again because that was typically the furthest thing from the truth.

CHAPTER 9

HALF AN HOUR later, after finding a good spot to tie up the donkey and cart away from prying eyes until we could come back for them, I gave Dagan a precious pinch of dried ginger to rid the nausea from his guts. Then we were on our way. A thin veil of clouds clung to the night sky like spiderwebs. The square, tiered Palace loomed ahead, shimmering with torches in the dark. Houses stacked close together filtered into view once we got through the olive trees.

"Be quiet and stay low," I whispered to everyone as we passed within shouting distance of the poor part of the city to get to Dagan's farm. As we kept to the wall, avoiding the main roads and other people's watchful eyes, it was clear that Alu was not doing well at all. Dagan's eyes grew round as we took in the devastation in my old neighborhood. Many huts were burned to the ground, and those that stood held more occupants than could possibly fit. People had erected tents on sticks with old quilts and were sleeping underneath them while burning embers held cookpots that had been scraped clean.

"Why is everyone asleep?" Nanaea's worried eyes met mine.

"Must be a curfew," Iltani said.

"Malnourishment, too," I whispered. "It makes you very tired."

My hand on Nanaea's back, I directed her around a scraggly patch of weeds. Even in the middle of the night, you'd usually hear songs and laughter floating from nearby huts. It was comforting, in a way, that life went on even when you slept.

But this was not the Alu I remembered. A dark, somber silence had settled over the citizens like a funeral cloak. We passed thirty handsbreadths from where my family's hut should've been, but it was a blackened pile of ruin. There was nothing left but the top of my abum's broken healing table, which was partially buried in the ground. Nanaea stopped and put a hand to her mouth.

"Kammani." Her eyes welled.

"Come on." I tugged her away from the memories of the times we'd spent in that old hut together. "No use thinking too much about it. There's nothing we can do."

We trod past a spot near the wall where my abum had planted a row of yellow chamomile, and my heart fluttered. I ran my fingers over the sunshiny buds that still struggled for life as Nanaea sniffled behind me. This strain of chamomile used to be my father's favorite flower because of its uses. The feathery stems soothed. The color, bright and cheery, pulled moods into the light. When ground, the leaves relieved storms in the mind.

For me, they would be forever tied to my mother's cold, dead face as she lay prepared for burial, cradling baby Bellessa. My father had covered her body with the flowers after I'd tossed the first mound of dirt into the grave, and as the stems landed on her, I'd expected her to laugh and swat them away. Her stillness shocked me. It was as if she'd been carved from sandstone. Her features, certainly hers, looked like those of another woman. Never before had I realized how important the soul was to the face's shape until she lay there looking like herself, yet unrecognizable.

All at once, Iltani pushed me down into the grasses along the wall. I tugged Nanaea after me, and Dagan dropped to his belly.

"Iltani, what—"

She held a finger furiously to her lips and pointed. A torch bobbed along the pathway, illuminating a pair of guardsmen armed as if going to war. Maces and sickleswords swayed at their sides as they checked their surroundings. Daggers gleamed at their waists. They even wore helmets like the Manzazu army, something they'd *never* done in the city while in service to our former lugal.

My hair stood on end as they marched by, weapons clinking with their footfalls, mere handsbreadths from where we lay in the scrub. After they retreated into the gloom, we got up but stayed low, ducking and crouching toward what would be our base camp in Alu.

We scooted past Iltani's home before we ducked into the fields. She let her gaze linger hungrily on the little hut that looked as though it bulged at its sides, too many people stuffed inside to be comfortable. But after a moment, she looked away and hustled up to Dagan. Iltani had been flippant about leaving her mother and father in Alu. She never had any siblings, and never seemed to care that we'd left. In fact, not until this moment did I realize that she had any feelings about leaving them at all. Whenever I'd asked, she'd waved her hand and said that "of course" she missed them, but she'd always planned to leave Alu anyway, and felt fine about never seeing them again.

Maybe that wasn't even close to the truth.

Dagan's farm looked different than I remembered as we approached, looking over our shoulders for more guardsmen. His home was dark save for one lone torch in the front and a candle flickering from an interior window in the back. There was no noise, either, except the occasional bleat of a sheep and the chirring of the cicadas as we crossed through the golden-brown emmer fields.

Dagan stopped, one hand on his dagger, his eyes watchful. Nanaea and I trudged up behind him.

"It's so quiet," she murmured, still blinking back tears.

"Yes, and I don't like it. There are four boys in that home, and not one of them is making noise?"

"But a curfew out here at the farm?" Iltani plucked one of the stalks of emmer and placed an end in her mouth. "The only way to enforce that is with—"

"Gods! Get down!" Dagan pulled me to the ground, his arm around my waist. We lay together, Dagan's chest pressed against mine, one big arm flung across my waist. "Iltani, lie low."

She sat but refused to lie down, though Nanaea had curled into a ball, arms over her head.

"There are guardsmen around the house!"

"Selu save us," I whispered. If there were guardsmen on the farm, that meant we didn't have a safe place from which to work inside the walls of Alu. Anywhere else would be too close and exposed. Out here, nestled amid the crops with outbuildings scattered across the land, we would've been protected.

Not anymore.

Next to me, Dagan breathed heavily. He kissed my head absently, but his eyes roved around. "I'll have to sneak up there. Someone is in my home, and I need to see who it is."

"Now it's my turn to say no! Guardsmen are likely living in there!"

"Well, where are my brothers? My ummum?" His eyes were anguished. "If anything happened to them . . ."

"I'm sure they're okay, my love." I grabbed his chin. "We just have to figure out what to do now."

"I have to check on them. I only left Alu because I wanted to be with you. I should've forced all of them to come with us, too."

Iltani lifted one shoulder, freckled from the sunshine. "You'd never have forced your ummum to do anything she didn't want to do, Dagan. You know that. That woman is as stubborn as a mule looking at a new gate."

"That's true," Dagan answered hoarsely. "But I'm going to find out where they are. There's a path through the fields we plowed years back to make it easier to get from one to the other. I'll take that to go check on them and I'll stay down low. If I don't come back in half an hour, leave here and go back to Wussuru. This night. Do *not* come after me. If they see any of you—well, besides you, Iltani—they will know that we've come back, and they will torture us until we tell them where Arwia is."

"But I—"

Gently, Dagan rubbed his thumbs down my cheeks. "Promise me. Please, I beg you. Do this for me. If you've ever loved me, do not follow me. Swear it on Kasha's and Nanaea's lives."

His eyes were fierce, though his words and his touch were not. He'd never once asked me to swear. He was serious.

"I swear it." He was his own person and could make his own choices.

He kissed me on the mouth with enough heat to melt the skin from my bones, and took off into the fields in a low crouch. I watched him go, a piece of my heart going with him, wondering if that kiss would be the last one I'd ever get.

"Listen, if I'd known Dagan could kiss like *that*, perhaps I *would* have tried to win his heart myself years ago."

"You've seen us kiss plenty of times before, Iltani."

"Not like *that*." Iltani lay on her back, her knees in the air, not caring a whit that her backside was exposed for anyone to see. She picked the oblong berries off a stalk and crunched them raw between her teeth, likely to annoy me.

"And as I stated, you wouldn't have stood a chance. None of us did. That boy has loved my sister since we were children." Nanaea lay pressed down in the emmer, her black curly hair spread wide around her head. A cloud meandered over the waning moon, obscuring her face from my line of sight.

Chewing the skin around my thumb was doing nothing to quell my nerves. We hadn't heard any shouting or screams, or even any commotion, but Dagan hadn't yet returned.

It's nearing time to leave.

I pushed up to my knees.

"What are you doing?" Nanaea whispered. "Someone will see you!"

But I ignored her, peeking over the tops of the emmer to catch a glimpse of the house. It was still, the flickering light in the back room snuffed out, the house barely illuminated by the torch in the front. I looked up at the clouds over the moon and cursed them to Alani for not letting me see. My heart in my throat, I sank into a squat.

Then I heard rustling.

It was fast. Swishing through the grain behind us. A deep voice rumbled.

Nanaea sat up, her eyes wide, but Iltani refused to move.

"Get up!" I fumbled in my healing satchel for my herb knife.

"I'd rather take my death lying down."

Clutching the knife, I prepared to strike. To protect my sister at all costs.

The swishing grew louder, and at once, a man was upon us.

"Kammani!" Dagan's whisper cut through the night, and relief coursed through my veins.

"You *terrified* us!" I whispered, my heart pounding.

He eyed my knife, and I tucked it into my satchel and hugged him tightly.

"Is all well?" Nanaea stood, hands on hips, her eyes round in the moonlight. "How is Shep? Your ummum? The other brothers? Did the guardsmen see you?"

"I'm sorry to say all is *not* well. Uruku has commandeered most of the fields and forced my brothers and the field hands to work them from dawn until dusk. They've raided our supplies. All my mother's tinctures."

"Wait. *All* of them?" I asked.

"Yes. Shep says nothing is left." He looked at me grimly.

"Well, then I cannot mix a poison!"

"I know." He set his lips. "We'll have to get some elsewhere. And Rish—"

From the direction of the house, I heard a plaintive cry, and a chill ran down my arms. "What's wrong? Is he ill?"

"He's been wounded. And it doesn't look good."

"Your ummum couldn't heal him?"

He shook his head, his throat bobbing. "She can't because she has been taken by the guardsmen to the Palace for some untold reason. Shep told me they came a couple weeks ago. That's how Rish got hurt. Trying to protect her."

"Oh Dagan, no." I caught his big hands between mine. "Can I go to him? To look at his wound, at least? Are the guards there?"

"No. They've just left. They come back in the dawn, Shep says." He stared morosely over the fields he used to work daily.

"Well, let's go! I can heal him. And we can determine where we can get more tinctures and a safe place to camp until we take back our city." I tugged my healing satchel up on my shoulders. "Come on. Nanaea, stay with me."

❀❀❀

Rish, a round-cheeked boy of eight years, stood in the common room, clutching a forearm that was slashed from elbow to wrist. Shep, just a year younger than Dagan, stood next to Rish, rubbing his head. "We tried to sew it up, but . . ." He let his voice trail away.

Nanaea pulled both of them into tight hugs, Rish wincing when she brushed against his wound.

"Let's sit." Dagan's voice was hoarse, anxiety twisting his features as we crossed over the threshold and closed the door quietly behind us. "We don't have long."

We formed a tight circle, Shep's and Dagan's eyes roving the room, ears perked up like a dog's.

"Are Marduk and Qishti asleep? And the field hands?" I asked.

Dagan patted the ground next to him for Rish. "Yes, they're in their beds, thank Selu."

Shep spoke. "I sent the field hands home. The guardsmen are working all of us hard and taking most of the crop. We still have enough to trade and eat, but you'd barely believe Marduk is fourteen from his face." His voice took on an edge. "He looks as though he's aged five years. And Qishti. He was always skinny as a stalk, but now his tunics hang on his frame. He's starving himself out of worry for our ummum."

Rish patted his pudgy tummy. "I'm still eating good."

Dagan's worried eyes filled with warmth. "You *are*, little man. For that, I am grateful. You eat your fill. You don't need to worry, because big brother is here to take care of you." He pulled Rish, entirely too big for such doings, onto his lap, and Rish settled back into his thick chest.

I held my hand out to Rish. "Can I take a look at your arm, my sweet?"

Rish's eyes grew round when I scooted close, and he pulled his arm away from me. Even in the dim candlelight, I could see the infection starting down at the bottom of the slash near his wrist. Could smell the bad humors beginning to fester. I pulled out my bone needle and thread from my healing satchel, but tucked them into my tunic so he couldn't see them.

"What happened, bub?"

He buried his face in Dagan's chest, and Shep's nostrils

flared as he answered. "Guardsmen came to the farm and grabbed Ummum. A couple of them held me, Qishti, and Marduk back. They thought we were the only ones who could hurt them, but they didn't count on Rish." His eyes momentarily glowed with pride. "He flew out of the house with a dagger and slashed a guardsman's leg with it, and the man got mad and yanked the thing away. Sliced him right up the arm. He's lucky he didn't get him in the throat. It came close."

"Did they say why they took her?" Iltani took a swig from her flask.

Shep looked Dagan in the eye. "I suspect it was because of you. They're probably *torturing* our ummum to find out where you've gone. They have to suspect you left with Kammani and the nin, though no one has said anything about it."

"Uruku's likely afraid to admit it for fear of looking weak," I said.

Shep's amber eyes, so similar to Dagan's yet set in a lean, rangy face, glittered with malice. "When I get a chance to repay Uruku for doing this to Rish and taking Ummum away, he will regret it. I promise you that."

Dagan met his brother's eyes over the top of Rish's head. "And I will help you avenge them both. Are there others who would help? We need to get Arwia back on the throne, and we'll need a majority voice from the ensi's council to do that."

Shep nodded. "I *know* there are others who would help. Ensi Puzu only sits on Uruku's council to try to stop him. I've spoken with him in Assata's Tavern. He says that Uruku is the evil Alani's puppet and there are several of them who agree. Uruku maims or starves or kills those who don't listen to him, so people have been quiet."

"But no one else has tried to challenge his throne?"

"He kills anyone who's tried."

"Tell me what's been going on," Dagan insisted, and Shep launched into the details.

While they spoke, their deep voices resonating softly as the locusts chirred, I gently tickled Rish's tummy until I got a grin.

"Rish, please. May I see your arm? I'll make it so it doesn't hurt as much."

His fat lower lip quivered for a moment, and two round drops appeared in his eyes and fell down his cheeks. I smoothed my hand over his brunette curls. "My sweet, I can make you feel better. Will you trust me as your big brother does?"

After a moment, he scowled, but held out his arm. The wound was infected. The stitches were much too wide, and specks of dirt filled the spaces in between.

I looked up at the group when Shep and Dagan finished talking.

"Shep, will you get some Aleppo soap, some sikaru, and a cask of boiled water? Oh! And some clean linens?"

"I would, but we're out of almost all of our supplies. I do have a little bit of soap, but no sikaru. And none of the tonics that Ummum would use on him. I can't even help him with the pain."

I sighed. "Well, what about your neighbors? Would they at least have some sikaru that we could use?"

"In the dead of night?" Dagan looked at me as if I'd grown two additional heads.

"Yes. If it means properly tending to him, we could surely wake someone up." I rolled my eyes.

Shep shook his head. "Nobody has any. Trust me, I've looked. The Palace has confiscated most of the brew, and none of us have shekels to buy it at Assata's Tavern."

Frustrated, I sat back on my heels. "Dagan, I cannot heal him without sikaru to properly cleanse everything."

Shep stood. "I can at least get you the rest of the stuff. I put a pot on the cookfire outside already. Ummum told me boiled water was important for treating wounds."

Iltani held out her hand toward him. "And I'll help."

She grinned, and he assisted her up from the floor with a glint in his eyes.

Gods, this was not the time to flirt.

When they left, Dagan looked at me, confused. "Can't you simply wash his arm with the soap?"

"Yes, but he needs to be restitched. I can't sew him up without the sikaru, because the soap won't kill all of the bad humors inside."

"But *look* at it." Dagan held out Rish's wound. It *did* look garish and was obviously causing a lot of pain. "He's hurting. And we can't wait until we can get some more sikaru because the guardsmen will be returning at first light."

"Well?" I sighed, thinking through the meager tinctures I had in my healing satchel. I took them out and sorted them by the candlelight. "I *do* have a little bit of myrrh oil. It isn't a good enough alternative, though." But then I brightened. "Why don't we go to Laraak to get some brew? We have to go there to barter for more . . . you know . . . since your ummum's things were taken." I glanced at Dagan. "We could just take Rish with us tonight. Camp outside Laraak's tents in the cart, and approach them in the morning for what I need."

"You can't take him tonight," Shep said as he and Iltani toted in the water, linens, and a small cake of soap, both wearing secret grins on their faces. When this was over, I was going to have to talk to both of them about their complete inability to flirt at appropriate times.

"The guardsmen check on us in the mornings. We can come and go as we please throughout the day if we're not working, but they check to make sure we're here morning and night. They said they'd kill Ummum if we didn't show up for one of their checks. I think it's so Uruku can use us as leverage if Ummum doesn't work out. But I can take care of Rish tonight, Kammani, if you tell me what to do."

"We have to do *something*, Arammu. It smells bad," Dagan said, his brow furrowed anxiously.

Do no harm.

Rubbing my hands down my cheeks, I blew out a big breath. I was tired. Not only were my nerves keeping me up at night, but Iltani had snored like an old sow in our tent in Wussuru. How Arwia and Simti had gotten any sleep with her in their bedchamber in Manzazu was beyond my comprehension.

"Okay. I'll clean it as best as I can with what I have. Take out the stitches. But I can't sew it closed without clean tools and a way to make sure no dirt is left inside. I can wrap it, but even then, it could get *deeply* infected, because he's a little boy and bound to mess it all up. So I'll have to stitch it on the morrow as soon as we find some brew. Somehow." Either we'd have to get back into the city with a bribe or we'd have to get Shep to bring him to us. I rubbed my eyes wearily. Nothing was easy about this. Nothing at all.

I looked at Shep. "Can you help him keep it clean? Change the bandages if he gets them dirty or wet?"

"I can do my very best."

"Good. I'll do it." A sense of dread welled up inside me, but I moved forward anyway. There was nothing else to do. "May I have your dagger, Dagan?"

He took it from his scabbard and placed it in my palm. "Thank you, my sweet."

Nanaea looked worriedly from me to him. She leaned over and grabbed a candle and sconce. "I'll hold this near so you can see."

I dug in my satchel, holding the little jars up into the glow from Nanaea's candlelight to read their contents until I found what was left of an arnica hemp blend to ward off pain. I sprinkled some under Rish's tongue.

Dipping my hands into the hot water, I scrubbed myself and Dagan's dagger with the soap and plunged Rish's arm in to wash out all of the visible dirt. He flinched and tried to pull it back out, but I murmured reassurances as I washed him. Once that was finished, I drew his arm closer to me and slipped the knife underneath his stitches, pulling out the filthy threads one by one. He grimaced with each gentle tug. After I dosed him with the tiniest bit of poppy, he fell into a light slumber in Dagan's arms. When I was certain he was asleep, I dripped myrrh oil over the open wound and tied Shep's linens around his arm tightly. For now, it would have to do.

"I'm all set." I sat back and began to pack up my things. "We have to go."

"Why, though?" Iltani nudged Shep's foot with her own. "I vote we pick an outbuilding and stay put."

Shep nudged her back. "Sadly, they search those almost every day looking for more stores to steal. You wouldn't be safe."

Nanaea tapped a finger against her lip, thinking. "What if we bargained with the traders to stay right inside the trader encampment? They're close by, and probably would have poison. When we sneak into the city for Iltani to . . . um . . ." She glanced at Rish slumbering in Dagan's arms. ". . . deliver our surprise, Kammani can also see Rish to stitch him up."

"They're thieves and are known to hide criminals, according to Nasu." Dagan shook his head. "We can get supplies there, but we cannot stay. It'd be better to camp in the open air as Kammani said. In the grove where we hid before."

"Why *can't* you stay there?" Shep said. "They have a lot of goods and are loyal if they like you. They liked Ummum because she tried to help those who were sick, even when they couldn't pay her. Tell Yashub, the main trader there, that you're her son. I bet he'd hide you. He hates Uruku."

"Thieves and criminals. Sounds like a great place." Iltani raised her eyebrows. "At least they'd have brew."

I rolled my eyes at her. But Nanaea was right. They were close, but not *too* close. And trader goods meant that they likely had more tinctures than I could ever get elsewhere.

"We *should* stay in Laraak. Our whole point in being here is stopping the war that Manzazu is going to bring by getting Uruku off the throne. We can't do that without supplies."

"And safety." Dagan shifted Rish onto his shoulder, then stood.

"There's safety in numbers." I stuffed the rest of my things into my satchel and stood. "And less opportunity for someone to chance upon us out of the blue. We'll blend in."

After a minute, he agreed. "You're right, of course." His eyes softened, and he reached over and ran a knuckle down my cheek. "My Arammu. So beautiful and so smart."

"Oh, for the love of Selu." Iltani hopped to her feet and yanked Shep up as well. "Please, for the sake of all of our stomachs, may we go? I'd like another drink of brew in this lifetime before I meet the Boatman on the river."

Dagan smiled sheepishly, but Nanaea gazed at him with pride on her face, poking me in the arm. "He's a good man," she whispered as Dagan left the common room to lay Rish down in his chamber.

"He really is."

Maybe even good enough for marriage. But now is not close to the time to think about it.

"Wait a minute," Shep said. "How are you planning to get out of Alu? How did you all get *in*? They're being really picky about who they let in and out unless you have enough coins." He leaned against the doorjamb as we stepped out into the chilly night air.

"The south gate." Dagan pointed the way we'd come.

"You didn't use Gala's gate?"

Dagan brightened. "Gala? The Merchant's Son?"

"Yes," Shep said. "Remember him? Weak-chinned, always kind of embarrassed about it?"

"I do. He's a guardsman now?"

"Yep, and he's at the *west* gate. Closest to Laraak. I assumed that's how you entered."

"Uh, no. We used . . . different means." Dagan shook his head as we walked out into the starry night. "Much different."

"Do I want to know that story?" Shep grinned, baring his sharp incisors.

"Not in this lifetime." Dagan grabbed my hand and interlaced his fingers with mine, looking back at his brother with warmth in his eyes. "Stay safe, Brother. Take care of the others. I'm counting on you."

"You know I will. Safe journeys." Shep's soft farewell echoed down the path.

Iltani blew him a bawdy kiss over her shoulder.

"Is that an offer?" he called, his wolfish smile lighting up the night.

"A standing one." She held his eyes as we slinked away under the silent moon until the dark swallowed him up.

But as we ducked through the fields toward the west, her eyes dimmed and her hand strayed repeatedly to the flask at her waist, and despite draining it, she never lost the thirsty look hanging around her like a ghoul.

CHAPTER 10

SHEP WAS CORRECT. After retrieving our cart from the grove, we went to the west gate and watched it from a safe distance. Gala, Dagan's old childhood friend, stood there whittling a stick, his silver breastplate winking in the torchlight.

No other guardsmen were around.

His shocked expression and knife-slash of a smile when Dagan approached was all the confirmation we needed that he would let us pass through.

Nanaea, Iltani, and I scuttled out from our cover, our prophet's veils over our heads so Gala wouldn't know our identities. Dagan explained that we were his servants, and asked for Gala's silence that he was in Alu. To trust him that he wasn't there to do any harm, but to help the citizens. Gala looked warily at him for a second too long, but a handful of talents, enough coins to feed his parents and siblings for many hungry days and nights, was enough to secure his promise.

Then we went to Laraak.

Yashub, the head trader, turned out to be a man of my own height, nearly as wide as he was tall. His two front teeth were missing, so his words were softened by a significant lisp.

Despite our showing up in the middle of the night like thieves, he was still wide awake, sitting around a fire, laughing, drinking, and casting lots over six goats with a few of his associates.

Moonlight illuminated rainbow-colored tents that were flung across the encampment like toys scattered in the sand. The rest of the traders seemed to be asleep, their dreams likely punctuated by Yashub's wheezing laugh.

"Protection?" He squinted weathered eyes under a pair of gray, bushy eyebrows as he scratched his belly. His head. "We don't have guardsmen here. We deal in goods. Animals. Weapons. Nothing else."

"We don't need you to take up arms for us," Dagan explained. "We'd simply like to stay here, out of sight. As I stated before, you'd be rewarded with food and riches beyond compare. I'm the wealthiest farmer in Alu, and my brothers have been producing grain for the lugal. I can get you as much as you'd need."

Easy with the promises. I shot Dagan a worried look, but he stood with the confidence of ten men, powerful arms crossed over his chest as if he'd negotiated deals like this hundreds of times. In a way, I supposed he had. He was always the one to bring his family's produce to the Libbu for trade, and since we'd been in Manzazu, he'd been doing his own bartering there, too. This was simply another transaction to him. A deep, resonating pride filled me.

"I'd need something now to tide me over until these riches made themselves available."

Dagan patted a satchel at his waist. "Step closer and I'll show you what we have to offer."

A man at the fire stood, and Yashub shoved him down, stumbling a bit as he did so. "Ach, this young man isn't going to harm me. He needs me." Scratching his head again, he peered into Dagan's satchel and raised his eyebrows in appreciation. "That's a good start, my boy. But not nearly enough."

"My healing services are yours if I could have usage of a tent, and supplies. It looks to me like you've a rash or lice in your clothing and hair, and I could heal you." I held my hands out to the men. "I could help all of you."

Yashub caught himself scratching behind his ear and brightened. "You a healer? I do itch something awful and wouldn't mind a powder to fix it, but we are not well stocked in medicines. You'd need to head to the Libbu for those."

My heart sank and Dagan frowned. Half of the reason we were *here* was for medicinal tinctures. Now we'd not only have to sneak into the Palace to deliver the poison, but we'd have to sneak into the Libbu to *buy* the herbs to make one!

A man around the fire spoke. "And we got gobs of lepers who followed us up from Nur, and ol' Yashub couldn't turn them away even though one of them stinks halfway to the gates of the Netherworld. All that 'Unclean! Unclean!'

business don't keep 'em far enough away. The kids still run over there. They need healing or to get out, if you ask me."

"Nobody asked you," Yashub wheezed.

Behind me, Iltani cackled loudly, and I resisted the urge to whack her with something hard and squarish. "Indeed, sir. I am an A-zu and can help. I've been trained by the best healer in Alu, Shalim, Healer's Son. And in the north, I was trained by Mudi, who is—was—skilled in the ancient arts, too. A guardsman friend of ours said you might have heard of me— I'm the healer who saved the warrior maidens in Manzazu."

Yashub's eyes grew round. "That's *you*? But you're nothing but a young *girl*!"

I shrugged. "Ahh, yes. I am young—and a girl—but somehow, I managed. And I would have continued to heal in Manzazu, but we have something more pressing to attend to at the moment." I pointed at Alu. "And we need to stay here so we can . . . do that."

He looked sidelong at me, using his tongue to get a bit of food from a back tooth, finally resorting to using his finger.

"Any friend of Manzazu is a friend of Laraak. And that lugal in there"—he jerked his chin toward Alu—"doesn't deal squarely with my traders. If you're a good healer, I can give you a tent, but you'll have to get your own supplies. And if you fix me and mine here and our wives"—he gestured to the group around the fire and out to the tents—"you'd be welcome to stay as long as you'd need, although we have plans to pack up and move on soon. We've stayed here longer than we should've already, but my third wife is with child and doesn't want to move until it comes."

He squinted at me, and raised an appreciative eyebrow at Iltani and Nanaea. I'd told both of them to keep their lovely eyes on their feet, but Iltani had flat refused, and Nanaea's beauty was hard to mask.

"Those your servants or other wives?" he asked Dagan.

Dagan blushed from his chest up to his hairline. "Ahh, no. My sisters. Ones I would be remiss to have harmed." His eyes hardened as he looked around the fire at the men ogling both of them.

Yashub placed a meaty hand over his heart. "On my honor, the girls will remain as chaste as they are this night." He wheezed a laugh, which rapidly turned into a cough, but Iltani met his eyes over the burning fire and, because she didn't have one dram of sense in her head, winked.

❁❁❁

After we were shown to our tents and purchased food and drink for us and our donkey, we slept through the night to the sounds of snores from the traders around us.

Early in the morning, Dagan trekked back to his farm with the cart to gather some produce and grain to distribute to the camp, while I tended to Yashub's health. He was infested with lice, as were his wives and children. I saw to his immediate inner circle, too, but rapidly ran out of the melaleuca-and-vinegar mixture that could keep the vermin away. My tent in the center of the encampment was almost useless because it was empty save for what I'd carried with me in my healing satchel and a few extras in my healing chest.

If I were going to keep acting as a healer to keep our place in Laraak, I'd need fresh herbs for grinding into tinctures. Large swaths of linens for wrapping and bandaging the people in the leper colony on the edge of the encampment. Needles, sterilizing bowls, mortars and pestles, drying racks, knives, suctioning reeds, and more. The lack of supplies was worrying, though not as worrying as procuring a poison. We determined that this very day, we would sneak into the city in disguise to do just that.

While I worked to heal, Nanaea, an apt pupil of the Koru warriors, went around to give the men in the camp a close beard trimming with Dagan's dagger. She left them freshly shorn, if puzzled, but returned to me and Iltani with their hair trimmings in a sack and a look of firm determination on her face. We spent the next two hours stitching beards together with sticky bitumen and remnants of cloth, and shrugged into borrowed tradesman clothing to help us become the traders we were supposed to be.

Then we headed to Alu.

"It is impossible to breathe in this beard. Nanaea, you did *not* account for us having to stay alive while we sneak."

"Be quiet!" I glared at Iltani. "You're the one who insisted on going into the city as a man, too. You could've been safe as yourself, and you know it. So please, for Selu's sake, stop fidgeting."

My throat tight, I ducked under Gala's arm with Nanaea and Iltani as he let us through the west gate. Dagan had introduced us as diminutive tradesmen from Laraak, and we pressed coins into his hands silently as we moved past to make sure he at least pretended to believe us.

Nanaea had shaded circles under my eyes and darkened my eyebrows, but I couldn't seem to get my voice low enough to please anyone. So I was to feign muteness. Iltani, her voice pitched deeper than a drum, with a hint of a rasp, would do all of our bartering.

Dagan had been given a Laraak trader costume as well, sewn furiously by Nanaea to accommodate his height and breadth, and with the Koru's gray paint in his beard and tiny lines expertly painted into his forehead and around his eyes, he looked twenty years older than he was.

In the daylight, Alu was even more of a mess than I thought. The impoverished section of the city along the wall wasn't just half-burned; the residents here looked half-starved as well. My throat tightened as we walked by a little boy, his shoulder blades stuck out from his back, cheeks hollow, holding up a bowl. I dropped a handful of shekels into it as we passed, and Iltani roughly grabbed my arm.

"The street vermin will give you lice, Azizi."

"He is dying." My chest tightened in sympathy for the boy.

"And Laraak tradesmen are crude. Anything else will give us away." She looked around us at the busy streets, teeming with malnourished people going about their business.

She was right, of course. If anyone was skilled in the art of conniving and trickery, it was her.

"Are you set?" Dagan whispered out the side of his mouth, around his grizzled beard.

"Yes, are you?"

Shep had asked Ensi Puzu to meet him and Dagan at the house of Widow Girru, a sympathizer to our cause. Dagan would tell him of our plan to try to get his support for a majority vote. Then Shep would hand Rish over to Dagan, and they'd go to Assata's Tavern for sikaru. We'd meet them there so I could sew up Rish's arm and ask Assata to help us convince the other ensis to support Arwia for the throne.

He took a deep breath and nodded. "And if I don't make it to Assata's for some reason, go through Gala's gate and I'll meet you in Laraak."

"You'll be fine. I promise. Just hunch over a bit. You're too tall." My words were brave, but my heart was hammering. There was so much risk. So much to lose.

"Just remember to leave immediately if anything feels off." He jerked his chin at Iltani. "All of you."

"We will. Now go. Get on with it. We're wasting time." Iltani waved him away, fully embracing her character.

Dagan smiled at me softly, then shuffled away, hunching to make himself smaller.

I resisted the urge to call after him. Tell him I loved him with everything inside me. For if something went wrong, this might be the last time I ever saw him.

"Are you ready?" Nanaea raised her eyebrows. Her black lashes were thick and full, luminous eyes radiating her health.

A storm cloud of foreboding hanging over me, I swallowed the lump in my throat. Maybe our disguises weren't good enough. Maybe someone would recognize her as the Sacred Maiden who'd graced their Palace not so many moons ago. Maybe Dagan would never come back to me, and I would always wonder what it would have been like to be his wife.

Setting my sights on the Libbu pulsing with merchants in the distance, I blew out a shaky breath, unease working through my neck and shoulders.

"I don't know. But there is only one way to find out."

CHAPTER 11

THE STENCH OF rotting meat greeted us as we joined the throngs headed into the bustling trading center of the Libbu.

And as we were jostled in the crowd through the archway, I understood why. Atop the wall, where once grew climbing vines of lavender and gold, men's heads were impaled on spikes. At least fifteen of them. Their cheeks were bloated, flesh partially decayed. Eye sockets cleaned out by birds. Nearly unrecognizable as men.

Save for one, however, who wore a big black beard that was unmistakable.

Irra.

The three of us gasped.

"Sister." Nanaea rapidly blinked away her tears. "That's Assata's husband!"

"I know. I know. Don't stare. We have to blend in."

Why had *he* been killed? He was a good man! Had he defied Uruku in some way?

At once, the air around me grew cold, and my questions were replaced with the familiar sound of rushing water. Irra's head swiveled toward me, his jaw opening and snapping closed, the stench of rot rolling off his bloated tongue. All of the heads pivoted on their stakes, ghastly, empty eye sockets blinking in the sunlight. Their jaws opened wide, unhinging with sickening cracks, as they moaned in one decaying, synchronous chorus.

Vomit burbled in my belly, and I fought the urge to hurl my stomach's contents onto the feet of wealthy Alu citizens going to trade. Some cast horrified looks at the heads as they walked by, but most ignored them. Covering my mouth with the back of my hand, I stumbled toward the merchants' stalls. The tents were shades of melon and dandelion, and the cheery colors were a shocking contrast to the stench. Next to me, Nanaea coughed, eyes watering with nausea.

"Keep it together," Iltani warned, casting one worried look at us both. Her false beard was peeling slightly from her cheek, the dark bitumen goo melting in the sweltering sun. "Ears open. Eyes aware. We need tonics and information about how we might get into the Palace. Don't let it get to you."

"I won't. It's just the heat."

Tearing my gaze from the decaying flesh, I followed Iltani and Nanaea into the heart of the Libbu to find the booths with tinctures. Merchants stood stone-faced in front of their stalls, sicklesswords in hand, daggers plunged into their belts to discourage theft. Guardsmen in their heavy maces and clanking armor filled the once-happy marketplace with unspoken threats.

"Over there." I pointed to a couple of tents in a far corner with tiny bottles and casks arrayed haphazardly.

Sweating in our disguises, we walked past booths overflowing with grains likely taken from the farmers' fields. Thick shanks of roasted goat and baskets of ripe eggplant, fresh onions, plump tomatoes, and mounds of other vegetables.

"All this food, yet people starve," I murmured.

Her face hard, Iltani weaved around a man carrying two spears over one shoulder. "May the gods grant them ugly children and loose bowels." She shook her head. "The prices are sickening."

She was right. Sixty minas for a small basket of pomegranates! An entire talent for a measly cut of meat. Only the richest in the city could buy.

So we had two bits of information to note. First, the poor people were being starved, likely so they wouldn't be strong enough to rise up against Uruku. Second, guardsmen were *everywhere*. It seemed as though Uruku had doubled the number, though some of them were boys called into service, armor too big for their shoulders, greaves hanging from bird legs. But their hands held sicklesswords the same as the men. These boys—maybe a year or two older than Kasha—were called into the service of bloodshed.

This isn't right.

Hopefully, with Uruku's downfall, we could turn it into a city to be proud of.

Pressing my own beard to my cheeks with the back of my hand, I approached one of the booths arranged with potions and tinctures. My eyes roved hungrily over the pots, my needs almost on my tongue before I could silence them.

A robust woman with shrewd eyes, in enormous jade earrings, wrapped a length of thread around a small carafe, and set it aside.

"Here for trade, men? I have the best tonics in this Libbu. Do not venture past without securing the curatives you need to keep your young wives bearing you many children."

The sun beat down on the tops of our heads mercilessly as I rifled through the tonics at her station. I needed tinctures so I could continue to tend to everyone in Laraak—and something a little more lethal for Uruku. A bottle slipped from my sweaty palm and the tradeswoman flashed me a warning look.

Dear Selu, don't let the heat melt off my disguise before I've had a chance to buy what I need.

I glanced worriedly at Iltani's glistening face under her brownish-gray beard as the woman rattled off incorrect names of herbs and the wrong ingredients for ailments from headaches to incontinence. Sorting through her mixes, I put my senses to work, smelling and dabbing my fingers into them to check for grittiness or solvency, laying some of them on my tongue when I knew they were safe. Here was hemp.

There, a smear of aloe in the bottom of a jar. But I couldn't find a poison, or anything more dangerous than blue cohosh.

The merchant studied me as I poked and prodded.

"You're a real A-zu, aren't you."

She reached across the booth to grab my hand. Roughly, I tugged it away, panic winding through me.

Iltani laughed politely, smacking me on the back hard enough to jostle my front teeth loose. "This one has many ailments and needs a lot of help from your wide assortment here."

Nanaea picked up a small, red glass bottle sitting in the back corner of her booth and held it up to the light. "Can you tell me about this one?" she asked gruffly.

Iltani nudged me as I picked up some myrrh, poppy, fennel, chamomile, arnica, and cinnamon. The tradeswoman took the little bottle from Nanaea and launched into a description. My ears perked up when she said the word "nerium."

Nerium was often mixed with aloe to smooth the skin, but if ingested in large enough quantities, it could put someone to sleep for hours with their eyes wide open, giving them the appearance of being dead. My abum had once told me a horror story of a woman who'd been buried alive because of it.

My scalp prickled. What if we knocked Uruku out with it somehow and then just entombed him? Or killed him when he was being prepared for burial and wasn't being guarded? My throat constricted at the thought of what that might entail, but I held my hand out for it.

With a calculating gaze, the woman set it back on the table. "It's too expensive for the likes of you."

I met her stare. Nudged Iltani.

"How much?" Iltani crossed her arms over her chest like Dagan did when bartering.

"A hundred and sixty minas for half," the woman challenged, raising a bushy eyebrow.

I blanched inside my makeshift beard.

It's way too much! But we need it!

"You'll never convince anyone to pay that amount." Iltani spat on the ground. Her direct approach was the opposite of how she usually bartered with flattery and trickery.

I tugged Iltani's sleeve and nodded at the bottle.

The tradeswoman narrowed her eyes. "Why does your mute want it so desperately?"

Iltani lifted her chin. "We need to put down a dog that's got the mange."

She chuckled. "Perhaps you need something *else* that will suit your purposes and costs next to nothing."

I gritted my teeth. I wanted the nerium. It was a good option! But I didn't have nearly enough coins on my person.

From underneath her booth, she pulled out a small blue vial of serum.

"What is it?" Iltani squinted at it.

"Gochala." The woman's eyes glittered. "I've put down a dog or two with it. Works really well."

My heart raced. Yes! A drop or two would cause a person to suffer from insufferable headaches for moons, but that whole bottle would be deadly. My father had once mixed an antidote for one of his friends who had tried taking a little to "make him feel funny."

Sweat dripped down my forehead into my eyes, but I fought off the urge to wipe it away and ruin Nanaea's face paint. I nodded eagerly to Iltani as I reached into my linen bag, feeling for the coins. Counting.

"How much for that one?" Iltani rasped, her baritone resonating clearly across the booth.

The woman smiled dangerously. "That depends. How badly do you need to put down your dog?"

Iltani eyeballed me, a deep frown on her face. Her beard slipped again and she coughed, covering her mouth with her hand, and pressed it back on.

The woman's gaze went back and forth between me and Iltani, speculation heavy on her brow. She placed her fists on round hips. "One mina and twenty-five shekels. And then you'll need to be on your way."

I nodded. It was a decent price, and we needed to move. Now. The woman was suspicious of us. I held out the tinctures I wanted, along with some linens and a small spool of stitching thread, and set the payment on her booth. She wrapped everything up but the gochala, and gave me the parcel.

I jabbed Iltani with my elbow, nodding at the blue bottle.

"We paid for that one, too." Iltani nodded gruffly at the tincture.

The woman smiled, but it did not reach her eyes. "You

haven't paid nearly enough. The tonics cost more than the measly amount you paid, and I need you to get out of my sight. I smell something off."

Iltani looked at me, but my pockets were empty. I shook my head, alarmed, and she sighed, digging around in her bag, a coin purse hidden somewhere inside. As she moved, the folds of her linen cloak pressed against her, outlining her curves. The merchant studied her form, and looked down Nanaea's body, which wasn't nearly square enough to be a man's. Nanaea dropped her gaze to her sandals, her thick eyelashes resting on soft cheeks.

Sweat poured down my forehead, no doubt smearing the face paint, and Iltani couldn't locate the coins.

At long last, her hands shaking, she produced the coin purse, removed additional payment, and slapped it onto the table. But as she did, the woman slammed her hand down on Iltani's and sneered. "You three are *women*! And up to something. You stink of it!"

Iltani snatched her hand away, and I grabbed her arm.

"Let's go!" I hissed.

"May Selu reward you for your silence," Iltani whispered, grabbing the tonic of gochala. Her beard was falling off the side of her face, bits of black bitumen clinging to her cheek, but the woman didn't care a whit for Selu's rewards.

"Guardsmen! *Thieves!*" she bellowed, her booming voice causing heads to turn from all over the Libbu. Iltani upended the booth in the woman's face, sending tinctures and casks flying. Startled, people screamed, looking around in alarm.

But Iltani dropped to the ground and stuffed her satchel with as many tinctures and potions as she could.

"Come on!" I yanked Nanaea's arm, hauled Iltani from the ground, and ran toward the Libbu gate to flee as people pointed at us, at others, alarm on their faces, cries in their throats. But Iltani pulled all of us in the opposite direction.

"What are you doing!" I screeched as she tugged us around booths toward the Palace.

"They're going to be looking for three women dressed as men at the Libbu gate. We can't go out looking like this." She yanked me around a Libbu stall where two young women were shooing flies away from baskets of fish stinking in the midday sun.

"Hide us," Iltani barked at the women. One of them, drooping in an emerald-green tunic, belly filled with child, looked up with mild curiosity. She shrugged a plump shoulder and looked at her friend.

"We should hide 'em."

Her friend paused, a handful of grapes halfway to her mouth. "You always do this, Bikku. Such a bleeding heart. They're probably thieves."

She frowned at us, and Iltani growled. "I'll slit both of your throats if you don't. Your choice." She flicked the robe away from her thigh, where she'd strapped a long, gleaming blade.

The pregnant woman—Bikku—clutched her belly protectively and jerked her head behind her booth. Both went back to eating their fruit as we sneaked around behind the stall.

"Dear Selu, what is *wrong* with you?" Nanaea glowered at Iltani as she tugged us to the ground into a pile of fish guts, scaring a dog away that was eating its afternoon meal. All at once, I felt something prickly on my cheek, as if a finger was brushing against me. The image of the Boatman holding out his bony fist with something tucked inside wavered up into my vision, and I gasped, pressing the heels of my hands into my eyes.

"Stop it! Stop!" I whispered.

"Sister, what is wrong with *you?*" Nanaea crouched low, peeling the beard from her face.

"Nothing," I responded shakily. *Everything. Dead men's heads moaning on a wall and cold fingers of the Boatman on my cheek are not normal. Not normal!*

"Well, figure it out." Iltani slapped my thigh. "You're squawking like a chicken, and we need to plan our next steps."

"Yes. What are we going to do?" Nanaea looked around the Libbu, the place where she'd stood not long ago, receiving the so-called honor of being a dead man's bride.

"I'm not sure." I bit my lip, swallowed the panic that had settled in my throat, and tried to think about it logically. Rationally. We needed to get to Assata's to meet Dagan and figure out a way to give Uruku the gochala.

"Well, *I* am. We're going to the kitchens," Iltani said.

"What? No, we're *not.* We need to get out of here! People are looking for us!"

"No, stupid. Listen to me." She grabbed my hands and I ignored the insult. "It's the easiest way into the Palace. It's how we left when we were running away after you found the monkshood, remember? There's that narrow passageway down the back. Since we have that gochala stuff, there is no way we're leaving here without poisoning that worm Uruku with it. We'll put the whole bottle in his food and watch him die."

"What? Stop it! We can't go do it right now! We don't have a plan!"

Besides, we were being watched. Bikku and her friend were chewing their grapes, openly staring at us. They turned back around when Iltani bugged her eyes half out of her head at them.

"This is the plan! Right here, right now. We're doing this." Iltani pulled Nanaea and me so close, her brew-drenched breath assaulting us. "We have poison. We sneak in through the kitchens. I run up there and pour it down his throat."

"Yes, and then you *die.* Iltani, we need to think things through. Take our time and deliberate—"

She grabbed my shoulders and gave me a little shake. "NO, we will miss this opportunity if we don't act now. Sometimes you need to go with your gut and make a move!"

"We told Dagan we'd meet him at Assata's so we could plan, and that's what we need to do. Anything else is too risky. Besides—" I lowered my voice, for who knows if these women were loyal Uruku followers. "What's the point in doing you-know-what this very second if the ensis aren't in agreement to let Arwia take over the throne?"

"Well, we could figure it out." She cocked her hands on

her hips, which looked ridiculous considering she was wearing a man's beard.

I stared at the walls of the Palace, which were merely fifty handsbreadths to our right. At Nanaea's face, which was too beautiful even if she put the beard back on. At my own shabby disguise that was rapidly disintegrating in the midday sun. How many times could we get back in here to do this? How many more times would we be this close?

"Kammani, surely with the level of poverty in the city, a majority of ensis would welcome her in," Nanaea said. "People are starving. Wouldn't they want to get out from under his rule?"

It *would* only take a few hours to ride back and get Arwia. If we delivered the poison, and he died, the Palace would be in shambles trying to figure out what to do. In that time frame, we could ride in with her and she could announce that she'd never died in the tomb and take her throne. In fact, if Uruku was already dead, Sarratum Tabni would likely send in her army to make sure it went smoothly. Without Uruku pulling the strings, surely the guardsmen of Alu wouldn't fight.

Would they?

I chewed on my lip and took the blue vial from Iltani's bag. As I did so, I felt unease flowing through me. "Iltani, getting into the Palace will be difficult and dangerous. It will mean risking all of our lives. Besides, Dagan will be looking for us at Assata's soon."

"We can get in and out of the Palace in an hour. Easy," she said.

"We don't even have *food* to deliver it in."

"What about those *grapes* the fishmongers are eating?" Nanaea eyeballed the women, who were glancing at us out of the corners of their eyes.

Gods of the skies.

But . . . they *did* have a point.

I rubbed my forehead and sighed.

We *had* to do it. For the sake of the rest of our lives. For the sake of *all* of their lives here in this city.

I held the bottle up to the sunlight and shook the serum. "Fine. But we'll need different disguises."

"Haha!" Iltani rubbed her hands together. "I knew you'd come to your senses."

"I can take care of that. Hand me your beard, Kammani." Nanaea stowed her own beard in her pocket. "You'll be dressed as a noblewoman. You'll wipe all of that off your face, but walk with a straight back and keep your chin up. As if you're truly wealthy."

"Without any disguise at all? They'll know who I am!"

Iltani snorted. "Oh please. You are not as remarkable-looking as you believe, as much as Dagan thinks otherwise."

I bristled. "Iltani, I've had about enough—"

"Shh!" Nanaea whispered, looking at the fishmongers. Bikku was openly staring at us. "You will blend in, and that is an extreme virtue. Now hand over your beard if you want to live. We must walk out of here different than we came in."

Begrudgingly, my pride stinging from Iltani's bluntness, I

135

peeled the beard off, and Nanaea picked the bitumen off my cheeks as I winced.

Nanaea attached my beard to her face, and stuck a bit of the black goo onto her front tooth to make it look as if it were gone. She let her long black curls go free, tied a scrap of linen over her forehead, and flipped her vest inside out. Suddenly, she was a different person.

"And I'll deliver our gift as plain old me." Iltani pulled the beard off, stepped out of her long cloak, took off the trader scarf, and wiped off the heavy lines that Nanaea had painted on her forehead and around her eyes. "I've a better shot at going unnoticed as a poor girl than a trader in the Palace."

Nanaea looked her up and down. "You're right. It'll work."

Iltani eyeballed me speculatively as I tried to make myself appear to be a wealthy noblewoman, smoothing down my hair and shrugging out of the trader cloak to reveal my plain linen tunic.

"It isn't enough." She shook her head. "Nanaea, look at her."

Nanaea fussed with my hair and belted up my tunic to expose more of my knobby knees, but neither appeared satisfied with the results. Annoyed, I yanked my tunic back down. "There's nothing else to do."

"Oh yes there is." Iltani jerked her head at the fishmonger sitting next to Bikku. She wore a deep purple tunic, which was clean, expertly woven . . . and about my size.

"What?" the woman asked around her bite, eyeing us suspiciously.

Out of her pocket, Iltani produced a mina. "Give us your tunic. We'll give you the tradesman cloak in return."

The woman stuck up her pert nose. "Go to Alani. This is my favorite." She swiveled on her stool, and before I could stop her, Iltani was out of a crouch and had the woman on her knees, one hand in her hair, the other pressing the dagger from her thigh into the woman's throat.

"Well, you lost the opportunity for payment. Now you're wagering with your life. Remove your tunic."

"Take it! Take it!" the young woman screeched.

"Iltani! Let her go!" I glared at her.

Ungracefully, she dropped the woman to the ground. Just as the woman was opening her mouth to scream, I grabbed the mina from Iltani and thrust it into her hand. "For your silence. And"—I looked at Bikku—"we're going to need your grapes."

"For Lugal Uruku?" The woman's round face was swollen in the heat. She had to be miserable in her condition.

Iltani's eyes hardened into copper coins. "I don't care if you're with child," she growled. "I will beat you senseless if you open that mouth of yours."

"Iltani, stop it!"

She pointed the knife at me. "You may be an A-zu, but that doesn't mean we *always* have to heal people, my friend." She slowly slid the dagger under the woman's nose. "I've killed before, and I'm not afraid to do it again."

"You've never killed anyone, Iltani. Be quiet. Put the dagger down."

Bikku blinked at me, unfazed by Iltani's threats. "You're an A-zu? I always wanted to be one of them." She wiped a trickle of sweat from her temple. "No, what I meant was that if you were talking about that man pretending to rule, I can help you. You can have the grapes. Her tunic." She pointed to her friend, who was sobbing on the ground. "That Uruku killed my husband, and he's called a bridal gifting to happen in two days' time. One of my friends is being gifted in the ceremony so her father doesn't have to pay the dowry."

Bridal giftings often happened west of us, in other cities, but not down here in the south. Young women were rounded up like cattle in the public square, usually the poor and those from noble families who had gotten to a certain age and were not receiving offers of marriage. The men of the city were given their choice of brides, wealthiest men choosing first. Neither a bride price nor a dowry had to be paid. I gritted my teeth for those poor young women sitting in a holding pen somewhere, some likely younger than Nanaea.

"And the scum Uruku is allowing this to happen." The thought made my skin prickle with disgust.

She pursed her lips. "Lugal Uruku says it is his gift to the poor. Providing a life of means for their daughters."

Likely his way to try to get them to calm down, though it seemed that any unrest was being squashed immediately by the lack of food.

I studied the woman closely. Her eyes lacked any kind of affect in them as she talked, and I realized what I was seeing. It was the same face I'd seen many times on those who had experienced the stark tragedy of a family member gone too soon: shock. But burning inside there was a small fire, too. She was serious. And though it went against my better judgment, something else burned inside, urging me to *go, go, go.*

"How can you help?"

"I'll get you into the Palace in the fish cart. Through the kitchens, like your wild friend over here says."

Nanaea stood and straightened her beard. She looked more manly than I could have thought with the added bulk of the vest. And Iltani was a poor girl, likely sweating over bubbling pots of stew.

Will this work? Or will we die?

"Don't even think about changing your mind—I see your brain working in there." Iltani poked me in the temple. "I'm already geared up. If we get to land our heels on that bug and squash him, we should all take every risk we can."

CHAPTER 12

MY HEART POUNDING, hands shaking, I crept with Iltani and Nanaea around the ovens in the courtyard kitchens as the Palace workers bustled about, faces flushed. The fishmongers had dropped us off in the cover of some olive trees, the grapes tucked into my sash. Once inside, we'd find a bowl from one of the lower storage rooms, add the grapes, and lace them with the gochala. Then Iltani would deliver them to Uruku as a serving woman, and we'd pray he ate them swiftly.

Bikku had sworn not to tell anyone we were sneaking inside, but her friend looked cagey. We'd threatened her entire family with a swift, painful death if she alerted anyone to our scheme, and terrified, she'd agreed to keep her trap shut.

But just in case, we bound and gagged them in their wagon

in a grove of fruit trees behind the Palace. If only I'd had the nerium to knock them out.

My plan had been to act like we all belonged and saunter right in, but with the number of guardsmen around, it didn't seem like the smartest move.

They glowered from their posts, hands on the hilts of their sickleswords, likely to prevent theft by the kitchen workers as they sweated in the afternoon heat. The workers kneaded rounds of bread, pulling and twisting the dough. They chopped dates for desserts, and stirred great vats of stews over open flames for Uruku and Gudanna's tables.

Dogs wandered in and around the savory smells, noses lifted high, saliva hanging from mangy jaws. But no scraps were thrown to them. Any bits of fruit or fish or vegetables left over from these meals likely went into the mouths of the kitchen workers, though it wasn't much, apparently. Their arms trembled with fatigue; their faces hung with the gray appearance of malnourishment. How awful it must be to work with food you couldn't eat.

But we could not help them right now.

Soon.

"On three." I clasped Nanaea's hand. Her deep brown eyes determined, pretty cheeks flushed, she set her chin.

Iltani squatted in the dirt in front of us like a jackrabbit. She whipped her head around, dimples flashing with excitement. "One . . . two . . . *three!*"

We darted from one oven to the next, hiding between it

and the scraggly bushes lining the perimeter. The heat was suffocating, especially in the heavy silks of the noblewoman's tunic. According to my memory, we'd need to run into the back corridor, find a staircase, and head up a long, narrow set of stairs in order to maneuver through the vast corridors to get to Uruku's chamber.

"Once more, and we're in," Nanaea whispered.

"Again, on three. One . . . two . . . and . . . *three!*"

We bolted for the Palace, but as we rounded the corner, out of eyesight of the kitchen workers, someone reached out and grabbed me and Nanaea around our waists. The grapes tucked into my tunic spilled all over the ground as we wriggled and squirmed.

"Let them go!" Iltani demanded.

The arms around us slackened, and with a firm yank, we tugged away from a young guardsman wearing gear too big for him. He unsheathed his sicklesword and leveled it at our throats. Iltani's hand stilled on her thigh, close to her hidden dagger.

"Why are you creeping so close to the kitchens?" The boy's voice cracked with youth.

Flustered, I said the only thing that came to my mind: "Because they're unclean! Stay away from them!"

He took a step back, his face distorted with fear. "What do you mean?"

"They've contracted leprosy!" I hissed. "Stay away or you will be infected yourself!"

He took two more faltering steps backward, his brow furrowed. "Why are they not bound with cloths, then? Where are their sores?"

Another guardsman stepped around the corner, sickle-sword drawn. Iltani, Nanaea, and I stood closer together. This one was still young but had cunning eyebrows and a scowl. He pointed his weapon directly at my heart, which was beating so hard, I was certain they could see it through my tunic.

"What are you doing with this tradesman and a poor gutter rat, noblewoman?"

"I'm . . . I'm taking them to the temple to pray. They'll die soon of their illness. Leave us to our business."

"No, get out of here. The Palace doesn't need to be filled with disease." He shooed us away from the corridor with a frown, but that would *never* do! We needed to be *inside* the corridor and on our way upstairs!

"They'll die!" I growled. "Let us pass."

Scowling, he advanced, holding his sicklesword in his barley stalk of an arm. And though it was thin, his arm did not shake as he pointed the weapon at my sternum.

"Stay away," I told the guards, holding my hands out as if to protect them. "The flesh-eating disease will infect you if you breathe the air that they expel." I eyeballed Iltani and understanding filled her eyes immediately.

She coughed openmouthed in their direction, and their faces twisted in fear. They backed away, ducking their chins into their chests, but the guardsman with the sword continued to train it on me.

"We should kill them. Put them down."

"But they're sick!" the younger one argued.

"So? Fewer mouths for the city to feed."

"My ummum says it is of Alani to kill the weak! We'll be cursed!"

The older boy frowned. "She said that?"

"Yes!"

"Well," he sighed, looking between us and the younger boy, as if debating himself. "Stay here with them. I'm going to find Lamusa. He'll know what to do."

The younger guardsman nodded, and the older one disappeared around the corner.

"Now stay put." The boy trained his own wobbly sickle-sword on us. Iltani looked at me with a glint in her eye, and I knew she had a plan. She sidled up to him, hips swaying, the grin of Alani on her face.

"You're much too handsome to be wearing that awful frown." She smirked. "Smile. Show me those teeth."

The boy flushed crimson. "Stay where you are."

She pressed her fingertip against the edge of the sickle-sword. "Ooh!" She winced. "That's sharper than I thought!" She sucked her finger. "I think I've cut it bad." She looked up at him, eyes wide.

Nanaea and I tensed, looking for an opportunity. A moment of weakness.

And in one second, we had it.

"Let me see." The boy dropped his sword a handsbreadth, and that was all the space we needed.

Iltani kicked him between his legs, and he doubled over with an "Ooof!"

I knocked the sword from his hands. "QUICK! Get his arms!"

Iltani and I wrestled his wiry arms behind his back while he gurgled in pain, and Nanaea whipped the linen from her head and knotted it around his wrists.

"His mouth!" I hissed as I held him still. "We have to shut him up like we did with the women!"

"I've got it." Iltani took the blunt edge of his sicklesword and whacked the boy in the temple with one swift crack. His eyes rolled back into his head, and he was still.

"Get his legs. We have to hide him." I spotted some scrub and hoisted him under his arms. "Over here!"

Yanking and tugging, we managed to pull him over into the bushes and threw some branches on top of him. I checked his pulse to make sure Iltani hadn't *killed* the poor boy, but he was fine. I wasn't sure he would be when his friend came back.

"Let's go! We won't have much time. We have to find more food since that stupid boy knocked all the grapes into the sand!" I whispered, and we darted into the cool, dank corridor, my heart beating hard and fast. There were empty doorways up and down.

"Look into each one. They *must* keep the stores in one of these. Go. Go!" Iltani commanded.

We raced from one room to another. But though I found

dough rising in the warmth of the sun, hanks of meat hanging from hooks, and a room stocked with linens, there was no fresh food.

"Kammani! Here!" Nanaea popped her head out of one chamber and motioned me across the hallway. The three of us ducked into a narrow pantry with shelves bearing casks of oils, nuts, and grains. The tang from baskets of overripe fruits filled the room, and assorted copper platters, bowls, and trays for serving gleamed with a high shine.

"This is perfect! Let's get some food and get it up there, *now*."

From the corridor, sandals slapped against sandstone bricks, and we ducked behind a barrel of wheat as the older boy thundered past the room with a burly guardsman. After several beats, they left, but another pair of guardsmen marched past as an entourage of servers scuttled by, carrying platters of food. One tray dipped and wavered on a servant's arm, and a dish of almonds mixed with dried, honeyed dates fell to the floor and scattered.

"Watch what you're doing, Sippar!" a boy servant screeched as the girl righted her tray and glanced fearfully at the mess on the floor. "Clean that up! And get back out to the cook and have her prepare another! These are for Lugal Uruku. He will *not* be happy with a delay."

Squatting farther down, I gnawed on my thumbnail. Getting up to Uruku's corridor was going to be a real problem. "There are too many people around."

A clatter of guardsmen passing by the pantry doorway raised the hair on my neck, and I ducked.

"No one will notice me. I'll blend in." Iltani got a wicked gleam in her eye, flicked her tunic back from her thigh, and exposed the dagger. "One way or another, he will be dead on this day."

My hair stood up on my head. "You're *just* delivering the poison and then getting out of there. That's it."

"I'll do what it takes."

My heart sank. Because she absolutely would. And if he didn't eat the food we laced, she'd plunge that dagger from her thigh into Uruku's throat and be killed by the guardsmen herself.

There was only one thing to do.

"You're not going up there. *I* am." Voices sounded in the corridor, and we shrank from the noise.

"Kammani, why?" Nanaea asked, eyes round.

"Because I will follow the plan, and she will not." I jabbed my shaking finger at Iltani's chest.

"Dagan would murder me if I let you go." Iltani frowned.

"Better to die at his hands than Uruku's."

She pinched me. "You listen to me. *I am going—*"

"In your own words, Iltani, *shut up.* I am doing this." I stared at her hard until the smile melted off her face. But within seconds, she recovered.

"Fine, but if you die, I wash my hands of guilt and refuse to mourn you. I'm swearing it now."

"That's not even close to true."

"But you can't go up there dressed like that." Nanaea ran her hand down my silken tunic. "Only servants and guardsmen are going up there."

"Then make me a servant. I am, as Iltani said, plain. No one will remember me!"

Hastily, Iltani and I exchanged tunics, and I loosened my braids down around my shoulders, pulling some tendrils around my face as the other servants' hair had been a bit ragged. Nanaea reached into a flagon of oil and spattered some on my tunic as if I'd been cooking all day, then smeared some on my cheeks. She rubbed dirt from the floor under my eyes and cheekbones to make me look haggard and hungry.

"You look the part, but what will the two of *us* be doing while you're up there?" Nanaea inspected me, tugging the hem of my tunic this way and that.

"You'll be leaving and going to Assata's to meet Dagan."

"Yes, the person who would pull out our toenails for abandoning you in the Palace." Iltani shook her head. "No. Not happening."

Nanaea bit her lip. "We don't have time to argue! Soon enough, the cook is going to come in here looking for replacements to make that dish, and we can't be in here when they do."

I brightened. "That dish! The dates and almonds! *That's* what I can take up there. The servants aren't that far ahead of me."

We stood and Nanaea selected a small bowl similar to the

one that had gone flying off the serving girl's tray. Iltani and I ripped the tops off barrels and dug through sacks of grains looking for a replacement for Uruku's meal. There were small pots of coriander, cumin, saffron, and fenugreek. Dried leeks and long stiff branches of rosemary. Dried, salted mutton and duck. In the back, there were casks of honey near the bags of lentils, and finally, the dried fruits.

"Iltani, here!"

We opened bags of figs, apples, apricots, and quinces until Iltani found the dates right by two casks filled to the brim with dried almonds.

Perfect!

We filled the little bowl with a mixture of the dates and almonds. With trembling fingers, I pulled out the blue bottle of gochala from Iltani's bag. Carefully, I dripped four drops onto the nuts and fruit, trying to hide the poison as best as I could. Iltani yanked the gochala from my hand and spattered it all over the dish.

"It needs to be disguised!" I hissed, and jerked the bowl away. When I did, I knocked the bottle out of her hands, sending it skittering into the corner of the room, end over end.

"Well, I hope you're happy. That was all of the poison we had! It had better work." I scowled at Iltani, but she grinned wickedly.

"I think we added enough." Nanaea pried open the cask of honey and dipped into it with a finger, drizzling the sweet nectar over the top of the fruit until it looked appetizing.

Wiping her hands on the front of my tunic, adding another note of authenticity, she smiled, wobbly and worried, with her dazzling white teeth.

"Kammani, I bid you blessings for safety from Selu himself. I will do as you've said and will make sure Iltani and I get to Assata's. She'll hide us until Dagan comes." She hugged me tightly.

"It will be fine, Nanaea. I promise you." Steadying my heart, I sank down onto my haunches, waiting until the corridor was clear to exit.

"You're gonna need more than blessings, Kammani." Iltani pulled the dagger from her thigh and wrapped it tightly around my own. "If you have to use it, plunge upward, under the ribs until it pierces the heart."

"How in Selu's name do you know that?" I frowned at her.

She grinned, dimples slashed on her cheeks. She looked more dangerous than she ever had.

"The Koru. You missed the lesson on stabbing a man to death, but I didn't."

⦻⦻⦻

No one was around. I took the back staircase and arrived at a long hallway that was once strung with beautiful handwoven tapestries under Lugal Marus's watch. It was now painted in garish colors with murals of the gods feasting and dancing.

The strap holding the dagger against my thigh chafed. My hands shook holding the bowl of poisoned treats. Would this work? What if I hadn't used enough? What if Iltani had poured too much and he could taste it from the first bite and every single kitchen worker was killed for it?

Do no harm.

A final turn brought me to Uruku's chamber, the door with the lion's head and three blooms bringing back a floodgate of emotions. My grief as I'd learned that my abum had been murdered on the road to the Palace, by Uruku's men, who *knew* my father would've figured out that Gudanna was poisoning Lugal Marus long before I did.

The ache of desperation I'd felt when I knew I was losing Lugal Marus.

The shock at seeing the streak of blue on my tunic when I'd discovered the monkshood flower crushed underneath a stool. The fear from the flash of Nasu's sicklesword against Dagan's throat when he'd sneaked into the Palace the night after we'd first kissed.

All of it had happened right here at this door.

And now it was flanked by a guardsman and a swarm of servers bearing their trays of delicacies.

"Where are they?"

The soft, lullaby-sounding question was followed by a crash, a meaty slap, and a high-pitched scream. A serving girl was flung from the door with a cry.

"He wants the dish!" the girl barked to a serving boy. The boy just stared at her.

"Go find out what's taking so long!" she yelled, wiping blood from her nose, and the boy immediately took off.

I looked down at the bowl in my hands. I had to get it to Uruku before he or Sippar returned with a replacement!

Taking two steps forward, keeping my head down, I willed my hands not to shake. My heart to still. The dates and almonds glistened in the honey, but underneath, poison that could end his life lay in wait.

If it works. If a taster doesn't eat it first.

The thought stilled me. He could have a taster! I melted into the shadows, my nerves crackling under my skin.

A child! A boy or girl stolen to be in the Palace and used expressly to ward off those with ill intent. *Like me.*

Could I sacrifice a lamb to kill the wolf?

No! I can't!

But, almost as if I was a puppet and someone else was pulling the strings, I found myself walking toward the doorway anyway, playing the odds like Iltani did when she gambled. Odds were good he *didn't* have a taster. If he did, odds were good that the taster wouldn't get one of the pieces with the poison. If the taster *did* eat one, odds were good that if they only ate one, they would be fine. They might suffer a severe headache from ingesting a little bit. Experience some vomiting. But they would be all right.

It would be fine.

It would.

Kneeling down by the girl, angled away from the scent of rosemary and goat stew emanating from the doorway, I held out the bowl, my hands shaking so much I could barely hold the dish. "A replacement." My voice was low, eyes averted.

She looked up into my face in confusion, casting a side-long glance at the other servants, and went to stick her finger into the dish as if to taste it, but I moved it out of her reach. "Do not touch," I whispered. "These are for the lugal only."

Her eyes widened, but she must have seen something on my face that convinced her or was simply angry after being slapped, because she set her bloodied lips. "Give it to me. My many thanks."

"Hold here at the bottom," I whispered, and pressed the dish into her small hands. She swallowed a look of terror that came over her. A shadow fell over my shoulder, casting the silhouette of a man against the wall, and at once I knew it was him. Uruku. The feeling of his slimy mouth on mine in the dungeon came reeling back like a shock of cold water. Ignoring the urge to wipe my lips clean from the memory of it, I held myself still in my squat, fear rattling my bones as he stood there, tapping his foot. Sighing impatiently.

"My almonds, girl. Hand them to me." When the girl didn't immediately move, terror rooting her to her spot, he snapped. "Quickly!"

I stilled my quaking, my head bowed, praying to Selu and Linaza and any other gods who could hear me that he would not recognize me. Would not even notice me cowering on the floor like a mouse afraid of being squashed.

The girl struggled to stand upright, blood smeared on her cheek. She tried to wipe it away, but Uruku interrupted her.

"No," he said softly. "Leave it."

The girl cast her eyes to her feet. "My lord." She held out the dish.

"Ahhh, yes. There it is." He eased the bowl away from her with long, clean fingers, and she dropped her hands to her sides. "Go now. Be gone. All of you." The door squeaked on its hinges, but before it shut, a muffled voice echoed from within.

"Wait."

It was a woman. All the hair on my head stood up. *Gudanna*.

"I want to see the girl who brought the platter without it being complete."

Pulling my tendrils more closely around my face, I tried to shrink away into myself. Uruku might not remember my form, but Gudanna was different. As Nin Arwia's former handmaiden, she'd seen me many times from a variety of angles throughout the Palace.

The serving girl stood stiffly at my side, and several of the other servants fled down the back stairway. The others held themselves still in various states of movement, as Nanaea and I had playing statues as children. One touch and we'd freeze, giggling, trying not to move. The game was over when someone lost her footing.

But this was not a game.

The door squeaked open again and Gudanna's voice echoed, her shadow fusing with Uruku's on the wall in front of me.

"Senseless girl," she spat. The sound of a slap, and another, echoed through the corridor. Next to me, the girl was nearly knocked off her feet. "Remember your tasks next time or you shall be thrown in the Pit with the last one. Have I been understood?"

"Yes, my lady."

Another slap echoed off the halls, and my fists bunched in my lap. I fought the urge to stand and defend her.

Uruku's voice murmured, "Remember to stay calm, darling. You shouldn't fuss. Not now."

The shadows jerked apart.

"I am *fine*, I have told you." Gudanna's voice carried a touch of annoyance. "Now get off the floor or you'll be cleaning it with your tongue."

My body began to tremble when I realized she was talking to *me*.

I rose slowly, keeping my head down, Gudanna's heavy breathing the only noise in the hallway. She sounded . . . ponderous, the way her voice hitched. Uruku shifted and light from their chamber threw her shadow on the wall again, showing off a large, round belly.

She was *with child. Uruku wanted her to be calm because she was with child!* My heart fluttered. If she ate the almonds, she would die, and so would the baby.

An innocent sacrificed for crimes it hadn't committed!

Shame bubbled up inside me as bile climbed into my throat. There was nothing to do now. Nothing at all. I couldn't take it back.

Do no harm.

"Now be gone! All of you rats go back to the kitchens!"

Gudanna's voice was like a whip cracked over the top of a horse, and I fled, jogging toward the staircase, anxiously trailing behind those who would not hurry enough.

Move! Move!

But had I not been last, had I not been willing the servants to move faster down the stairs, my body pleading by its proximity, I may not have heard the sound that brought hope, then thunderous guilt, into my chest: the distinct crunch of someone biting down on a handful of almonds.

But I couldn't look back to find out who it was.

CHAPTER 13

WHEN I FLED the Palace, sticking to the side streets and keeping my head down, I was exceedingly thankful for my plain face.

No one paid any attention to me as I ducked past rows of houses until I saw Assata's Tavern. Creeping past empty barrels stacked behind, I creaked open the door into the dim storage room to find Dagan pacing, his face constricted in worry.

"Selu be praised!" he exploded, pulling me into a tight hug as soon as I stepped inside. I shook in his arms as he pushed the door closed behind us and locked it.

Sitting in the corner on stools were Nanaea, her beard in her hands, and little Rish, whose face was twisted in pain. Next to them were my healing satchel and Iltani's bag from the marketplace.

"Are you okay? Tell me you're okay," Dagan murmured into my hair. "I can't believe you did this."

"I'm fine." My body quivered with relief that I'd made it out of there alive.

"Did you succeed?" he asked. "I was terrified for you when Nanaea told me what you were doing. You were in the Libbu to get information so we could all sit and plan something carefully together, not act on a whim!"

Whether he agreed with what we'd done or not, I could not squash the surge of pride in my chest that I'd accomplished it. "Yes," I said, my throat tightened around my words. "He ate the poisoned almonds. Whether he eats enough, we will have to see."

And whether it was actually him *remains to be seen as well.*

He kissed my forehead. After a moment, he released me. "That's all we can do at this point, then. We will wait. And we will pray to Selu that it works."

I looked behind him to Nanaea and Rish.

Prickles ran up into my hairline.

"Wait a minute. Where's *Iltani?*"

Nanaea lowered her eyes.

The prickles turned into fear.

"Nanaea? Where *is* she?"

"It isn't my fault." She pulled her curls over one shoulder and twisted them nervously. "Iltani ran off the second we left the Palace, and I couldn't keep up. I looked for her, but a guard walked by and I was afraid he'd recognize me. So I came back here, figuring she'd meet up with us like she was supposed to."

"What?" I whispered.

She winced. "You didn't see her?"

"No! I was busy trying to *assassinate* the *lugal!*" I hissed.

"You know how Iltani can be," Dagan said.

"I know. I know. I just wanted someone to keep an eye on her. She hasn't been right lately." I chewed my thumbnail. "You have no idea where she went?"

"I don't. I'm sorry," Nanaea whispered. "I tried to follow, but she is so fast. She lost me on purpose."

That absolutely frustrating, lovely idiot. Where had she gone? Anything could have happened to her!

I closed my eyes, trying to block her possible fate out of my mind. "It's all right. We'll find her." It *wasn't* all right, of course, but when Iltani wanted something, there was no stopping her. "She must have tried to do something herself. I hope to the gods she wasn't stupid."

"She's too wild for her own good." Dagan rubbed my shoulders. The sounds of tavern-goers on the other side of the wall told of a subdued group. More eating and drinking in silence or soft chatter than laughing or playing dice as they might have in the past.

"Did you have any success with Ensi Puzu?" I asked Dagan as he sat heavily next to Rish.

"Some. He was astounded that Arwia wasn't dead. Said the entire city believes she passed with her abum into the Netherworld because she went into the tomb with all of you."

"So we were right on that account. Did he say he'd support her?"

"Yes. With delight, since by law, she has claim to the throne. He will not provide aid in helping to assassinate

Uruku, though. He says he has no interest in getting his hands dirty in that way."

"I understand that. I don't want any part of that, either, but—"

"Here we stand."

"Here we stand indeed."

Dagan smiled at me sympathetically. "One problem he foresees is that the other ensis will claim it isn't her. They watched Arwia go into the tomb, so they could use that as an excuse to disavow her and then take the throne themselves."

"We'll need to convince them it's in their best interest to support her, then." I blew out a breath. "Seems easy."

He laughed grimly. "Perhaps Assata can help."

"Is she out there with her customers?"

"Yes. She said to wait in here and she'd come talk to us the second she could be free from her duties. But while you wait, will you take a look at Rish's arm?"

"Of course!" In my worry about everything, I'd ignored the boy. Guilt twisted my insides as I put on my healing satchel and knelt in front of him to inspect his wound.

"You took off the wrap?" I asked Rish.

Dagan ruffled his hair. "He fell in the mud this morning, so Shep took it off. I washed it at the widow's house, but it doesn't look good."

"You're right. It doesn't."

His skin was red all along the gash, and there was oozing pus down by his wrist once more. I should have never left a child with a severe wound overnight without stitches. I was a healer, but it seemed I was hurting people more than I was helping them.

"It's okay, sweet boy." I tickled his knees until I got a grin. "We'll get you all fixed up."

After thoroughly examining his wound, which still had bits of grime inside it, I spent the next thirty minutes working on him. I drained the infection, which had only worsened, and applied some of Assata's sikaru to try to kill the bad humors. Then I stitched it with boiled threads I'd tucked into my satchel. All the while, I kept craning my neck to look out the small window to see if Iltani would come.

The interior door to the tavern squeaked open, and Assata slipped in, a ghost of her former self.

"I only have a few minutes or so." Her clipped Kemet accent, usually so robust, was as thin as one of Nanaea's threads. Her once-square shoulders were curved. Her deep brown eyes, which used to sparkle, were dim with gloom.

"Assata!" Nanaea pulled her into an embrace, her eyes tearing up.

"Healer's Daughter," the older woman murmured.

"We saw Irra." Nanaea's eyes glistened. "On the wall."

Assata swallowed roughly. "Alu is not the same city you left, I'm afraid. And Uruku's punishment affects you and me most of all, young farmer."

"Yes, I know. They took my ummum! Why? Is it because I left?"

Assata sighed. "Yes. And everyone noticed, Dagan. Shortly after you fled Alu, the young women of the wealthy class starting talking."

Dagan's face grew puzzled. "Why would they care about *me?*"

"Look at you!" She rubbed her forehead with a shaky hand. "You're the most eligible husband for these women and you've suddenly disappeared? With no word? When you have great wealth and even better prospects? It didn't make sense. And the Palace watcher heard about you being missing, and told Gudanna that his charge, a little boy named Kasha who'd once belonged to Shalim the healer, was missing, too."

My heart jumped and as if sensing it, Nanaea linked her arm through mine.

"And Gudanna, who is not a stupid woman and knew that Dagan was close to your family, Kammani, told Uruku that something was wrong." Assata took a deep shuddering breath, her voice beginning to hitch. "So they cracked the seal upon Lugal Marus's tomb in secret."

"Just as we figured." I pressed my lips together so tightly they hurt.

Assata's face went grim. "When they discovered that it was empty, save for Lugal Marus, they sealed the tomb again and quietly went to the two places they could go to find out what happened."

"My farm," Dagan said hoarsely.

"And to your tavern," I supplied. It only made sense. Everyone knew to go to Assata's Tavern if you wanted to hear the real story behind anything going on. She had connections and information. It was why *we* were there right now.

She closed her eyes, putting a trembling hand to her lips. "Yes." Her voice cracked. "In the middle of the night."

"What have they done, Assata?" Dagan's chest began to heave. "What have they done to my ummum?"

For a moment, Assata didn't speak, swallowing around the anguish clearly choking her.

"Uruku took your ummum, Dagan. And he took . . . my Warad. My son." Her voice went high before it collapsed. She gasped out the rest around her tears.

"They killed Irra. Slaughtered him in our chamber. The place Warad was born. They killed him there on the floor when he couldn't answer their questions about Arwia's location, because he, of course, knew nothing. He never has known anything! I'm the one who sent you with provisions, not him! So they killed him with their sickleswords right in front of us even though I begged them to stop and told them we didn't know where you were. And before I could get my own weapons, they took Warad away to the dungeon and I was called in to see Uruku. My son and your ummum are gone, and they will likely be dead before the new moon if we don't do something."

My heart wrenched. Nanaea had gone unusually pale and held hands to her cheeks, her black eyes filled with worry. Dagan's hand hovered on the hilt of his dagger.

"And what of Nasu's family? Or Huna's? They were here, too. He didn't take them?"

"No." She hugged herself. "They left shortly after you did. In the night before all of this happened. We *all* should have left. We were stupid to stay."

"Well, what did he want?" Dagan's lips tightened. "If he's using Warad and my ummum, what did he want you to do?"

"What else?" Assata spat, roughly wiping away her tears with the backs of her hands. "I must deliver Arwia to him or he will kill my boy. My only son." Her voice broke apart again. "And he's likely torturing your mother to find out where you went."

Dagan spoke. "But, Assata, their pain is almost over. We cannot bring Irra back, but we are about to save Warad and my ummum."

She blinked up at him. "What do you mean?"

I swallowed around the lump in my throat. "Well, to-day—" I lowered my voice to a whisper. "I may have killed . . . Uruku."

Her eyes grew round. "What did you do?"

"I delivered almonds laced with a poison that should, ah . . . do the job very quickly. If he eats enough—" I bit my lip.

"How long will it take?"

I shrugged. "To be honest, I'm not sure. I haven't done this before." Red crept up into my face. "I know it can put down a dog. So says the merchant in the Libbu."

"You bought it from a merchant? Here in the city?" She looked at me incredulously. "She likely reported you right away. Uruku probably already knows you're here!"

"No! We were disguised! There is no way she knew—"

She stuck her hands on her hips. "If the merchant didn't warn the Palace, and *if* a taster didn't get the poison first, and *if* he eats enough to actually die, it will *still* take many days—maybe even a full week—for the ensi to pull together and announce his death. They'll want to quell panic and have a plan in place before doing so. This isn't fast enough. My son will be dead before then. I *must* do his bidding on the very real chance that your plan did not work."

"How long ago did he give you the command?" Dagan asked. "How long have they been gone?"

"Two weeks and three days. Two weeks and three days of torture for Warad and your ummum."

"Well, why haven't you set out to find her yet?" I asked her. "If you're so dead set on turning her in?"

She lifted a thin, brown shoulder. "Don't speak to me like that, girl. I'm *not* a child. You *know* why I haven't." She hung her head, her chin resting on her chest, and looked back up and met each of us in the eye.

"When Arwia is handed over, he will put her to death. That isn't something to take lightly. But I've sat here and wrestled with my conscience, all while he keeps Warad locked in chains. But now?" She shook her head. "There is nothing else for me to do. I am a mother, and Warad comes first to me. And, Dagan, he was *your* friend when you were children. And Nasu's!"

Dagan reddened. "I *know* that. But—"

"No! I am going to find her. If you're here, she can't be too far away."

She wasn't. She was back in Wussuru under the Koru's and Nasu's watchful eyes until we returned. But Assata couldn't know that!

"Please, just wait and let us see if the poison will work. If not, we will try again! Listen to us!"

At once, her face went hard and she gripped me violently by my arms, her fingers digging into the nerves above my elbows. I winced and tried to pull away. "No, *you listen to me!*" She shook me. "I cannot sit by any longer and debate this. I will rescue my son and if she has to die, then that is what Selu wants. She was supposed to have died in that tomb, anyway."

"Assata—"

"No, Healer's Daughter. Don't argue with me. I can make this difficult or I can make it easy. Tell me where she is and I will free Dagan's ummum and my son from whatever is"— her voice broke—"happening to them." She shook me again, desperately.

In a blink, Dagan's dagger was out of his sheath and aimed at Assata's heart. He grabbed her upper arm, pinching the skin. "Release her."

Assata's eyes hardened as she stared Dagan down. "I can disarm you and have your throat slit before you blink. You forget who I am."

"Please, Assata." My chin trembled in pain, and after a moment, her face fell. She dropped her hands, and Dagan sheathed his dagger. I rubbed my arms where she'd hurt me, and she stepped back, numbly shaking her head. She was hanging on by a thread at the most.

"The whole reason we are here is to rid Alu of his terrible reign." I tried to touch her shoulder, but she flinched away. "If we put Arwia back on the throne, she will release Warad and Shiptu. Will you delay going to find her until we can do it? Help us, even?"

Assata raised her chin, her eyes wet, but filled with a bit of command she must have had on a battlefield in another lifetime. "You may choose to do anything you'd like, but I have already wrestled with my conscience for weeks, each one a reminder of my child rotting in a dungeon, likely tortured. Starved. I won't wait another second."

"But I've given him the poison! Can you simply—"

"No!" she shouted, then glanced toward the door leading into her tavern. She leaned close to me, every word a lash. "I'm getting her and turning her in, and whatever will be, will be."

Her spine went rigid. "Now go. I'll give you an hour to get out of the city. After that, I'll track you down and find out where the nin is by any means necessary."

"Assata, please listen—"

But she shook her head, gave us one last, hard look, and shoved the door open into the subdued noise of the tavern.

The slap of it closing behind her sounded like war.

CHAPTER 14

"WHERE IS THE pain?" I probed along the woman's swollen belly and she winced.

"Low, deep in my womb."

"Lie down here for me, please." Gesturing to a small pallet I'd put together that morning, a multicolored quilt fresh from the drying lines atop, I looked worriedly out the tent flap toward the trader encampment.

No Assata and still no Iltani. After Assata's threat, I'd put the beard back on my face and we'd fled to Laraak. We'd bribed our way onto a cart laden with goods leaving Alu for the ports out the north gate, where no one had seen us enter or exit before.

And though I'd waited up half the night for Iltani, she'd never arrived.

Dagan had sneaked back into Alu late last night and dispatched Shep to look for her. He'd also met with Ensi Puzu to update him about what I'd done and to see if he had heard whether or not Uruku had sickened. He hadn't heard and neither had Gala. Gala *did* mention that Assata had been through the gate and had asked him about us, but he'd remained loyal and had stayed silent.

Smart man.

Practicing in my healing tent while waiting for Assata to make good on her threat, Iltani to return, or to discover whether Uruku would die was the only thing keeping me from running into the streets and screaming in terror.

Was Iltani hiding out somewhere safe, biding her time to return to us? Or had she been captured by the guardsmen while she tried to run away? Did Assata find her? And if so, was she currently torturing her to learn Arwia's whereabouts?

But I had to stay focused on this woman before me. It was all I could do right now until Dagan was ready to go back into the city. Ensi Puzu was going to meet us later with more council members so we could plead for their support.

I'd been leaving my tent to go find Dagan, when a line of ill patients demanded my attention. Yashub had ordered me to tend to those in need if I wanted to keep our safe haven in Laraak, so I'd done so, one after another. One had been a man from the leper colony, and I'd ushered him back to his tents and laid out fresh linens and a tincture of nut oil that my abum had once used to treat the disease.

This woman had been behind him, and she was the last.

She moaned.

"When did you last receive the blood of the moon?" I

pressed a warm cloth I'd heated in a cooking pot and steeped with chamomile to her abdomen. Her face immediately calmed when the warmth hit her belly.

"Yesterday evening."

"Ahh, so now I see maybe the issue. Is it always painful like this?" Squatting down, I scrubbed my hands with Aleppo soap in a basin, rinsed them in myrrh water, and felt along her cheeks and her forehead for fever and her throat, armpits, and groin for swollen glands that would tell me she was fighting off an infection.

"Yes. Always. It's always been terrible." Her face was pale, her straggly hair damp along her temples.

"Although we've been cursed with the moon blood, we don't have to suffer each time it arrives." Taking a mortar and pestle from my healer's table, I ground dried fennel, dill, and chamomile into a fine powder. I added ginger for discomfort of the bowels that often came with moon blood, and cinnamon for the nausea.

Quickly, I steeped a tea from the mixture I'd ground and asked her to sit up and drink while I heated the cloth and placed it on her abdomen once more. The tension between her brows calmed even more, and I felt satisfaction rising into my chest. This, I could do. Healing. It was what I was *meant* to do.

Rinsing out the pot, I looked out worriedly into the encampment and spotted Dagan jogging toward Yashub's tents with Rish trailing behind, wavering on his legs. I'd told Dagan he *had* to stay with us last night, and Shep could tell the guardsmen he had died if they asked after him. I'd cleansed his wound with more myrrh and given him garlic and vinegar to ward off infection, but I was worried it wasn't enough. The poor boy had tossed and turned all night at my side, his fever never breaking.

A shout echoing across the encampment in a few of the traders' deep voices caused my hair to stand on end.

Maybe Iltani? Or news of Uruku's death?

Throwing my healing satchel over my shoulder, I told the woman to rest and to venture home only when she felt better. Racing along the path behind Dagan, I scanned past the tattered roofs and tunics flapping on lines, and saw a group arguing near Yashub's tent.

The copper helmets and the scorpion face tattoo were unmistakable. It was Commander Ummi and Higal! A woman shifted into view from behind them, and my blood froze.

Assata was with them.

Picking up my pace, I caught up with Dagan and Rish and tugged them both behind a tent.

"What are you doing?" Dagan asked. Rish stood next to him, a sort of glazed expression on his face.

"Assata is with the Koru," I told him as I placed my hands on Rish's cheeks. He was burning with fever again.

"Ahhhh, no—that's not good."

"No, it isn't. She found us. Easily. We have to get out of here! And Rish needs tending to again."

He set his mouth grimly. Ruffled Rish's hair. "Of course she found us. We're right here near Alu! The problem is, no matter where we go, she'll track us down." He bit his lip and ventured a look around the corner of the tent. "But why are Ummi and Higal here with her? They wouldn't let her hurt us."

"Who knows if they would? She trained them when they were young. They're going to be more loyal to her than to us."

"Not more than they are to you. You have their favor!"

"Yes, but would that negate a lifetime of loyalty? Right now, we need to just go back to your tent and think. Gather our stuff in case we need to run away. Find Nanaea." I glanced back toward the women, then at Rish. He held his injured arm to his chest. Swiftly, I examined his stitches. Pus bulged from the holes. *Selu save us.* The infection had worsened! Maybe it was deeper than I even knew. Down into the tissues where I couldn't see. My heart sank. "But we can't do any of that until I work on Rish. His infection is worse." I swallowed.

In one motion, Dagan picked up his little brother with a grunt, and Rish lay on his shoulder like a boy smaller than he was, his eyes tight with pain.

"It's worse?" He shifted the bulk of Rish's weight on his shoulder, casting a furtive look around the tent at Assata and Ummi. "Is it because he got the dirt inside when he fell?"

"It's not his fault. I should *never* have left him without stitching the wound. I *knew* better than that, but I did it anyway."

"Oh, Kammani." He frowned as he hiked Rish up farther onto his chest. "It's not your fault. I asked you to do something for him, so if it's anyone's fault, it's mine."

"No, it isn't. I knew what should've been done. I probably harmed him *more* than if I'd just left him alone until I had supplies."

"There was *no* perfect solution."

A boy's voice, one I'd heard a hundred times in my own home in Manzazu, shouted across the encampment. "Kammani! Where are you? These men won't let us through!"

Kasha.

My heart lurching, I turned back toward Ummi and Assata. Sure enough, there he was.

Dagan eyed me worriedly. "They've got him. They better not be using him as a bargaining chip, or I swear to the gods—"

I laid my hand on his arm, fear rising in my chest. "Let's go see."

As we approached, Assata was jabbing a finger into Yashub's face while other tradesmen encircled them, backs stiff.

"Let us see them," she growled. "These warriors will annihilate your men if you do not."

At that, traders' hands went into the folds of their cloaks to draw out daggers and small axes.

Yashub held up his meaty hands. "We don't need that now."

"We're here!" Dagan called. "Everyone calm yourselves."

Assata looked past Yashub's shoulder, squinting against the glare. Her face softened into recognition when she met my eyes. Kasha wriggled away from Ummi's hold and ran to me, almost tackling me in a hug.

"My brother! Are you okay? Has Assata gotten Arwia?" I murmured into his ragged curls as he held me tight.

"No—why would she want Arwia? They want to talk to you."

"I'm sure they do." I glared at Assata and the Koru as they strode roughly past the traders. They'd obviously brought Kasha to me to show me what power they held. How easily they could control me.

Yashub scowled at us and wiped his mouth. "These warriors better not be bringing trouble to me and mine."

"They're not." I cast a long look at Assata over Kasha's head. "We will talk. Civilly." I buried my fingers in Kasha's hair and kissed his forehead.

"We can talk over here," Dagan said to them. He shifted a moaning Rish on his shoulder and headed away.

Unease clawing at me, I followed him back to his tent, and we stood near the little seating area that he'd arranged in the dirt beneath a fledgling thicket of tamarisk trees. Dagan laid Rish on a blanket, and I sat next to him, trying to quell my dismay as I looked at the angry infection around my neat stitches. Took in the unusual paleness of his tan cheeks. I sprinkled some arnica into his mouth for the pain.

"I found Arwia." Assata crossed her arms over her chest.

"I heard." I looked up from Rish's swollen arm.

"Wussuru is an obvious place to hide, and the traders talk. Wussuru is a few hours if you're riding fast. It's where I'd be if I were her."

"Did you turn her in to the Palace?" An ache welled in

my chest at the thought of what she might be going through if Assata had. Maybe she was seated by Iltani in a dungeon right now.

"No." She paused, glancing at Ummi and Higal. "My old friends here told me the sarratum of Manzazu is planning to go to war to unseat him, so there is no need. There were hundreds of warriors from the queen's army in Wussuru, waiting on her command to attack. Warad will be released as soon as it's accomplished."

Fear bloomed in my chest. "More warriors have arrived, Ummi?"

She nodded. "The sarratum finished preparations earlier than expected. We are assembling and forming a plan now, but more will arrive any moment so we can strike."

"*Why?*" The question exploded from the very heart of me. "We are *here* trying to get him off the throne before you can lay waste to the city! We've only just begun. I've poisoned Uruku, and we're meeting with some ensis to make sure she'll have a majority vote. Can we not see if this works before you kill a bunch of innocent people?"

"No. Manzazu needs to strike *hard*. And swiftly." Assata spat on the ground. "My son lies wasting in a dungeon. Shiptu is likely being flogged. Or *worse*. You *know* what they will do to a woman in captivity!"

"Assata, peace." Dagan wearily rubbed his brow. "Please. I know what they can do. But you can't go murdering people in the city to get to them! Have you *seen* the poor?"

"I've seen them, but they are not my priority. My *son* is."

175

She looked hard at Dagan. "And your mother should be, too. You're simply afraid to do what you must!"

My throat felt raw as I spoke. "We are *not* afraid, Assata. I took him the poison myself! But everyone forgets the poor. Everyone forgets that lives are taken when war is waged. The Manzazu army will go into Alu, and anyone in their way will be slaughtered, bloodied, and maimed. The guardsmen have doubled since we were last there, and even boys barely older than Rish and Kasha are called into service. They stand no chance against this army!"

"Nor *should* they, if they serve Uruku." Her eyes were hard, sweat beading across her forehead.

Her rage and sadness were blinding her. This was not the Assata who so lovingly helped people out at her tavern whether they had coin enough to pay or not. Had given food to my abum and had lent an ear when he was drunk and mourning my mother. This wasn't her. This was a woman bent on revenge.

"Why are you even here? To remind me of your strength? To throw it in our faces that you can do as you please?"

Ummi lifted her chin. "Arwia asked me to bring Kasha to you. He is not safe in Wussuru if we go to war."

"And I came to tell you that you need not fear me, unless you get in my way to support Manzazu in their strike against Alu. I'm joining them," Assata said.

Suddenly, Dagan stood, his hand in the air. "Shep! Here!"

Shep, his long hair a mess, rode up in a flurry of dust on horseback. He dismounted swiftly and led the horse to us. His eyes, always so playful, were bleak. His cheeks were smeared with dirt.

"Brother. I have news."

Dagan met him and clapped him on the back. "What is it? Have you found Iltani? Or is it word of Uruku?"

Shep rested a heavy hand on Dagan's shoulder. "Uruku is alive, I'm afraid. A friend saw him vomiting on his way to the bathhouse behind the Palace. He must have eaten some of your almonds, but they didn't work."

"No," I whispered. "The merchant must have sold me a watered-down version of gochala. That *stupid* woman!"

He swallowed. "I also have news about Iltani, and it isn't good, either."

My hand stilled on Rish's head. "What is it?"

Shep swallowed roughly. "She's in a holding pen with the other girls."

"A holding pen? What do you mean?" Dagan asked.

But my stomach sank because I already knew what he was going to say. Bikku, the fishmonger with child, had mentioned it yesterday.

I hung my head after Shep met my eyes, pity in them. He cracked his knuckles as he explained. "My friend said Iltani was caught by a group of guardsmen outside the Palace gates, claiming to be a member of the nobility. They asked around about her, but nobody knew who she was. She's to be given as a bridal gift on the morrow to the first man who wishes to wed her."

Heat seared through me as I stared at my hands.

My frustrating, beautiful friend had been stolen.

Uruku still lived because the gochala hadn't worked.

Manzazu was poised to attack.

As tears sparked in my eyes, my guts churned and bubbled. Because we were facing nearly insurmountable problems, and it appeared that everything I did, every single move I made, only made things worse.

※※※

The inside of Dagan's tent was stifling, but it was better than crying in front of Assata and Ummi. Better than the sharp tang of terror on my tongue. Better than thinking of the complete catastrophe we were all in.

I dug through my satchel, tears streaming down my cheeks, while they talked loudly of battle plans outside.

My hands quivered as I tended to Rish's swollen arm, sniffling. I soaped it and bathed it in sikaru, and stuffed him full of as many tinctures as I had, giving him poppy to sleep before pouring vinegar and melaleuca over his oozing sutures. Eyes wide, Kasha squatted next to me, intent on helping in some way, fumbling around, picking up bottles and laying them back down until I barked at him to go back outside while I worked. Then I cried all over again for being so gruff. I removed Rish's stitches, drained as much of the infection as I could, and scrubbed the new threads with so much myrrh oil, nothing would ever cause an infection again.

With each stitch, I berated myself. This child could lose his arm. Because I'd done more harm than good. *Needle into the skin and pull through*. Iltani would lose her freedom. Because I'd allowed us to take a foolish risk by going into the Palace. *Needle into the skin and pull through*. Warad and Shiptu could lose their lives because I didn't want to wage war. *Needle into the skin and pull through*. I knotted the end and poured more melaleuca over his arm for good measure.

I needed to fix all of this, but I didn't know *how*. A coldness descended upon my shoulders as I looked at little Rish, his black lashes fluttering on his plump cheeks, whimpering as he slept. Something brushed against my cheek. Startled, I jerked around, but nothing—no one—was there.

And yet—something *was*. A damp sensation washed over me, bringing with it the scent of rotted rivergrass. A creak of a boat moored at a dock. I blinked and the tent's walls seemed to pulse like a heartbeat.

No. Not now. I need a level head, not this.

Blinking, gasping for a breath that wasn't filled with the stench of rot, I stood, but when I did, something dark, something dank, wavered in front of my vision. A man. No! Not a man. A—figure. As I stifled a scream, my feet twisted on Rish's blanket, and I fell to my knees as my vision went dark.

All at once, I was kneeling in the prow of a rickety wooden boat, looking at the shoreline as I bobbed and weaved in a current of blue water lapping at the sides. The stench of decay filled my nostrils, but my limbs felt light as a cool breeze wafted over me. On the shore, his cloak blowing in a stiff wind, the skeletal Boatman stood, shifting in and out of my vision in a spectral haze. On his hip, he wore a small bag, similar to my healing satchel. He flipped up the flap and pulled something from its depths.

A small cask or bottle.

He raised it into the sky and opened his mouth in a war shriek, as the hood of his cloak slipped off his head. For the briefest moment, the image of a black-haired warrior with sharp cheekbones and a tortured gaze flickered in the Boatman's stead. He wore a leather chestplate and greaves on his legs. Behind him, hundreds of warriors stood shoulder to shoulder, holding the same little cask over their heads, ferocity ripping from their throats. The Boatman's eyes bored into mine as he held the bottle toward me, but after a moment, the warriors behind him disappeared, and he was replaced with the shadowy, skeletal figure once more.

My mouth flew open in silent terror, and when my eyes cleared and little Rish appeared once more in front of me, I was shaking so badly I could barely stand.

But I did, pushing myself out of the tent into the bright sunlight, panicked gasps tearing from my throat.

"Sister? What's wrong?" Kasha asked.

I shivered. Nanaea was now standing with everyone, her face screwed up in concern while Assata and Ummi argued with Dagan. Dagan tore his gaze away from them as I stumbled to the washbasin.

"Are you all right? Is it Rish?" He laid a hand on my back as I knelt down in front of the cool water. "What happened?"

"I—" I closed my mouth to stop my teeth from chattering. "It was hot in there and I felt a little nauseous. Rish is okay. Resting."

"I'll stay with him." Shep ducked into the tent behind me.

But Dagan didn't know what had happened in there. I'd seen him again. I'd seen the Boatman in full as I'd felt his touch on my cheek behind the fishmonger's stall. Just as I'd seen him in the tomb with Lugal Marus. Was Mudi right? Was he trying to contact me to help me? Trying to show me something? Or was he trying to get to Rish? Was the boy so far gone?

Of course not!

Rish wasn't that sick from his arm. Not yet. I knew it and I could trust the facts. My father always said to trust the evidence because it always told the truth. But my mother said there were forces outside of us at work, and we never knew what could happen if we let ourselves trust in *them*. The Koru trusted in them. They trusted in Linaza more than their own minds.

I dipped into the barrel of water and washed the sweat from my face as Dagan rubbed my back. As I dabbed my skin dry, a thought occurred to me that raised the hair on my head.

The Koru trusted in *Linaza*.

So much so, in fact, that they'd given me a scorpion necklace and a favor supposedly on her behalf.

If I needed one more chance to poison Uruku and rescue Iltani, then perhaps, I could do both things if I used the favor—now!

Dagan rubbed my shoulders, his handsome face screwed up in concern as Nanaea and Assata bickered. "Are you ill?"

"No." I shook my hands off to dry them and stood, wiping them on my tunic. My knees were wobbly, but I was more than fine. I walked over to my sister, and whispered in her ear to go fetch my scorpion amulet from my healer's chest. When she ran off, I approached Assata, who stood next to Ummi and Higal. I laid a hand on Assata's forearm. On the bracer covering Ummi's. Higal crossed her arms over her barrel chest.

"I've heard from Linaza in the tent, Ummi. An imminent attack is *not* what she wants."

Over Assata's shoulder, Dagan raised his eyebrows in disbelief.

"Just a few seconds ago, she told me to go rescue my friend Iltani so she isn't given in marriage by Uruku. And she also said to give Uruku a poison made by my own hands."

Hadn't the Boatman shown me a bottle? There was *bound* to be some monkshood or belladonna growing along the riverbanks, and I could just start over. I didn't need the merchant's tables. I could find something myself!

"And I can *do* that. I swear it." That wasn't *entirely* the truth, but . . . close enough.

Assata frowned in disbelief. "Linaza, the goddess of love and war in Manzazu—spoke to you?"

Breathless, Nanaea walked up to us, holding my gold scorpion amulet. It glinted in the sun as I took it from her.

"Yes. She did." I wrapped the amulet around Ummi's throat. "She granted me a favor from these Koru warriors. And now"—I clasped the necklace and stood back—"I'm calling it in."

Ummi assessed me coolly. "I cannot stop the attack, and I will not defy the sarratum, Kammani. Linaza would never give you a desire or a message that goes against Sarratum Tabni's desires." She trailed her fingers over the slick gold of the scorpion. "So what would you have me do?"

"I'm not asking you to *defy* her. I know Linaza guides the sarratum's voice. I'm simply asking you to *wait* to bring war so I have enough time to save my friend and get Uruku out. That's it! Couldn't you halt the army's battle preparations a little bit? Some last-minute things that need tidying up? That will not change anything too much from where you stand, but it could mean *everything* to me. To Iltani. To everyone in Alu. Could you not speak to the army leaders to delay? As the commander of the Koru, you outrank them, don't you?"

"Each Koru outranks the regular Manzazu army." She frowned and shifted her stance. Reached up and felt the scorpion necklace while she studied me, apparently searching my soul for signs of sincerity. "How long of a delay to poison him and rescue your friend?"

"A few days. That's it. Enough time for us to try once more."

Higal spoke. "Commander? A word?"

Ummi and Higal stepped away from us and talked to one

another heatedly, much too low to be heard. While they discussed, Assata alternated between rolling her eyes and glaring at me. Eventually, Ummi held up one hand to Higal, and walked away from her toward us.

Ummi opened her arms in Linaza's salute to me. "I will give you this favor, but"—she reached behind her, and unclasped the necklace, and handed it back to me—"keep this as a reminder of what I have done. When you look at it, remember the sacrifice I am making for you, for going against the sarratum is not an easy thing, even if Linaza commands it. Sarratum Tabni will not be pleased to wait."

"This is not of the gods," Assata spat, livid. "A delay means more torment for my son!"

"A delay means saving the city from slaughter." My eyes filled. "You *know* I'm right, Assata."

Higal crossed thick arms across her chest. "Ummi does not speak for me."

Ummi looked sideways at Higal. "I'm the highest-ranking Koru, and have made my decision. We will grant her the delay."

Higal spat on the ground. "Sarratum Tabni has given the command."

"And *she* answers to Linaza, who has granted this favor," Ummi fired back.

"No." Higal shook her head. "I will gather the army together under *my* command. We will fulfill the sarratum's wishes."

"And I will stand by your side as your second, Higal." Assata's eyes glittered with danger. "So we can rescue my son."

The woman who used to add cloves to my sikaru and feed me honeycake until I felt like I would burst leaned in close to me, so close I could see the broken blood vessels in her eyes and the bags underneath. Likely from crying herself to sleep every night since her son had been taken and her husband murdered.

"Assata, please—"

"No, Kammani. This is how it is. So if you're going to rescue your friend and finish the job with Uruku, you'd better do it quickly.

"For we are coming. And you'd better believe we will bring all of our might."

CHAPTER 15

THE YOUNG WOMEN were linked together like cattle headed to slaughter. Hands tied in front of them. Dried reed ropes around their waists leading from one to another to another. Some of them looked like little girls who were barely of age.

We were inside the Libbu, next to the old well. Dagan sat by my side, a cracked pot with a few shekels in the bottom at his filthy feet. He'd rubbed sheep dung into his garments to complete his disguise, and the stench coming from him was close to unbearable. Guardsmen swarmed around us like plated beetles, their faces watchful. *Looking for us?* From time to time, they pulled big men around and stared them hard in the eyes, then shoved them away.

We must be careful.

I gritted my teeth. All of my choices had consequences. My abum had once taught me that. When you acted as a healer, administering a dosage with good intent, there were always risks. Side effects, he'd called them. And one of the side effects of Iltani's recklessness was my having to come and rescue her from her fate.

But it was impossible to be angry at her. She'd been stolen, and *that* wasn't her fault.

Angst welled up in my throat as the young brides walked past me, a make-believe beggar in filthy scarves. Nanaea had bound some of my fingers back with rags as if the digits were missing, and she'd painted my face to look haggard, old, and— completely unassuming.

But underneath my robes, stowed in my healing satchel, was a poison of monkshood and belladonna that would deliver someone to the Boatman in seconds. Earlier in the day, Dagan had met a guardsmen who was less than loyal to Uruku to arrange safe passage into the Palace to deliver the tincture. For enough coins, he told Dagan he was willing to look the other way. Dagan had also met with Ensi Puzu, who claimed that he and four other ensis would support Arwia's rule, which meant we only needed to convince two more men to make it a majority. Ensi Puzu said he'd bring the ensis most likely to listen to us to Laraak later this evening so we could convince them.

Everything seemed to be falling into place. And as soon as I watched the bridal gifting to make sure Yashub made good on his bargain with us, I would take Uruku out if it was the last thing I did.

Their hair swept up and away from their slender necks,

the girls in the gifting kept their eyes down at their dirty feet. Hordes of wealthy men, with thick, beaded necklaces around their throats, threw elbows and shoved one another for a better view of the girls paraded past their greedy eyes.

My insides felt as if they'd been boiled in oil as they trailed past me. When Iltani walked by, red rouge caked over her freckles, lips smeared with gold, I reached out and grabbed her foot to try to tell her it would be all right, but she was not in her head. She kicked my hand and yanked away from me, her face screwed up in rage as she was tugged along. She looked garish. Dangerous. And itching to fight. Dagan murmured something soothing, but his words were lost to me.

My friend.

Iltani spat insults to those who crowed at her as she was half marched, half dragged to the center platform. There were at least thirty girls in white gifting tunics—maybe more—shoved into a cluster like little sacrificial doves. Iltani looked too beautiful for her own good. The wealthiest men, who got to choose first, would select her, and Yashub was not the richest by far, though Dagan had tried to give him ample proof otherwise. Yashub's purse bulged with coins, and a silver headdress glittered on his grizzled head.

Dagan sighed bleakly as the girls were arranged on the dais. He picked a callus on his hand. Opened his mouth to speak. Clamped it shut. On our trek into the city, we'd barely spoken a word. Every time he'd opened his mouth, he'd closed it, as if thinking better.

After a few minutes, I could take it no more. "What's wrong? Do you not agree with our plan?"

He rubbed his eyes. "It's not about the plan," he whispered. "I'm upset about Rish. I'm *really* upset, actually. I couldn't sleep last night while he suffered."

I twisted my hands in my lap. "That's my fault. I should have known better than to leave his wound open."

He flushed. "I'm not upset at *you*. I just wish he weren't in such pain."

A noose of guilt tightened around my throat.

Shame pulled it tighter.

"I do, too. I should have listened to myself, and he would probably be healing instead of suffering right now."

He glanced furtively at the crowds milling about, while vendors sold food too pricey for the starving people at the edges of the crowd to buy.

"Are you listening to yourself now, though?" He laced his fingers together over his knees. "That's what I was trying to say. Maybe Mudi was right that the Boatman is trying to commune with you? You told me last night that he'd taken a bottle from a satchel he was wearing. But yet, you mixed a poison from flowers you found by the river. Are you sure there wasn't something in your healing satchel you could have used? Did you look?"

"Of course I looked. There's nothing else in there, or I would have saved myself the trouble."

Besides, I wasn't even completely sure what the Boatman

had been trying to tell me. I didn't *really* believe in Mudi's theories, and couldn't even swear it was a bottle in his hands. I closed my eyes in frustration, and when I opened them, Gala, Dagan's friend, had joined the guardsmen and ordered a young bride next to Iltani to move over.

"What is Gala doing here?"

"When we crossed into the gate, I heard him say he was going to the gifting."

"Why would they need Gala? I've counted at least fifty guardsmen in the Libbu alone."

Beneath his filthy grime, Dagan's face bloomed red. "He's not here to work. He . . . ah . . . well?" He scratched his neck. "He . . . wants a wife. From what I overheard him saying to the other guardsman as we slipped through the gate, no one he's asked will give them their daughters without a considerable bride price. He doesn't have the coins to pay much." The last words came out in a mumbled rush, and his face reddened even brighter beneath his filth.

My eyes bulged. "So he'll simply choose a bride this day, one who is placed against her will? Will he choose Iltani? Did you tell him you knew her and not to take her? He's never seen her face! She's been covered every time we've gone through the gate."

Dagan looked down at his hands. "I couldn't say anything without risking us. I didn't know the other guardsman. Gala was joking and laughing like a big man about getting a bride with none of the price, to draw attention away from us as we went by." He played with the frayed edge of his tunic.

"Perhaps another beauty will capture his attention more, and at least that girl would be getting a fine man for a husband instead of someone else who would treat her poorly. Gala is a good person at heart."

"Do you hear the words that are coming from your mouth?" Blinking, indignation rising in my chest, I fought to keep my composure. He didn't understand.

"That came out wrong. I *know* this is terrible. But whoever Gala chooses will get a kind husband. He'll try to love her. I know he will."

I gritted my teeth at his lack of comprehension. Why couldn't the women choose whom they wanted to marry? How would the men feel if the roles were reversed? If boys were up there on the dais while women vied for their hands? Guilt crept along my spine because I was currently in the position to choose and most of my fellow women were *not*. Dagan was at my side, begging to marry me, and I loved him.

So why was I so unwilling to give him an answer?

Look around.

The women were going to be owned by the men who selected them. And even though Dagan wasn't any kind of man like that to me, the thought that he would lawfully be my keeper would not shake free from my head. That *must* be it. Because the other parts of marriage—save the children that could inevitably come—I welcomed. But I didn't want to be owned by anyone. Not even by the man I loved with everything inside me.

On the dais, Iltani was refusing to cooperate, despite a

guardsman with arms as thick as trees and a tangled brown bush of a beard ordering her around. The man backhanded her across the jaw, and I clenched my fists so tightly, my nails bit into my palms. He went through the rest of the group, arranging girls this way or that. He tugged a beautiful girl, no older than fifteen, to the front near Iltani. Her round eyes were luminous with unshed tears, but the streaks of kohl underneath were evidence of the many she'd already shed. Her cheeks were flushed, and her hair was knotted into two long braids down her shoulders over a white filmy shawl.

From the corner of the Libbu, in a group of underfed people with ragged tunics, a small man with eyes the exact replicas of hers cupped his hands around his mouth. Told her to bow her head meekly. Her shoulders drooped as she surveyed the men clamoring for her attention at the base of the dais. One reached up to take hold of her foot, and though she shrank away, the man laughed, displaying a mouth full of rotten teeth.

The stocky guardsman gestured to the men around him. "Gather round," he scratched out, coughing into his fist, and the men in the crowd drew close, already pulling bags of talents, minas, and shekels from their waists. "Show me your wealth and we'll see who gets to pick first."

Yashub got in line behind a group of men, one hand on his dagger, the other on his coins. The line moved slowly as one by one the men went by, opening their purses, boasting of their sheep and homes, some slipping the guardsman shekels as they clasped hands. Yashub was one of those men, though he passed an entire talent to the guardsman. The man grunted appreciatively and slapped Yashub on his back. Gala walked several paces behind, and when he went up to the guardsman, he showed him a rather small bag of coins. But he leaned in, cracking a joke, and the older man laughed uproariously. My heart sank. Could Yashub's bribe influence the man to give him first choice more than the connection he had with Gala?

Relationships were often worth *more* than gold.

The guardsman finally arranged the men in line from wealthiest to poorest.

"Dagan, look!"

"I see! Yashub is third right behind Uruku's head merchant and that young priest."

"We must pray to Selu above that no one else selects Iltani before he gets to choose."

The merchant, a slight man with gray streaked through his beard, sturdy sandals on his feet, pointed to the young beauty who'd been crying near the front. The head guardsman grunted, and she broke into fresh sobs as she was dragged down from the dais and into the hands of the merchant. But she was the only one displeased in the matter. Her poor abum jogged lightly up to the nobleman and bowed his thanks over and over again as she was led away.

A guardsman pulled Iltani closer to the center of the dais. She snarled at him, kicking his shins, and the men standing in line whistled and catcalled. Anyone who selected Iltani had better not close his eyes in sleep with her lying by his side. My heart ached for my friend, and I wanted to signal to her that all was well. We were going to save her. I tried to catch her eye, but she looked past me as my disguise intended her to do. I cursed it for preventing me from giving her some small measure of comfort.

But her eyes widened when she spotted Yashub. Frantically, she searched the crowds, squinting. Maybe she'd recognize Dagan's big frame and see me. Maybe.

The guardsman laughed and held up his hands. "This one is beautiful, my good men, but she is a thrasher and needs to be tamed! Who is man enough to bring this wildcat to heel?"

No! Be quiet! Do not point her out!

The men let out a collective roar and raised their fists, their eyes lit with the challenge, save for the young priest in front of Yashub who waved his hands in disgust and selected a small, quiet girl near the back of the group instead. Stark resignation in her wide eyes, a look I'd seen often in the dying, she followed the priest away with a bowed head.

Wheezing, Yashub smiled triumphantly, and put his hand in the air. "And now I must select a bride!"

Iltani stepped forward, her face twisted in a false smile. "Choose me!" Desperation strained her voice. Hope bubbled up in my chest that we might save her from her awful fate.

Yashub reached forward for her bound hands, but as he did, Gala stepped in, a hand raised between them.

"Wait a moment," he said to his fellow guardsman. "You've placed me behind this old trader, but are you sure you meant to do that?"

The men around him laughed and chided him.

Yashub shoved Gala. "Wait your turn, boy!"

"But what if I want this pretty woman?" Gala slapped Yashub's shoulder good-naturedly, but his eyes were hard.

My heart lurched and I snaked a hand out to grab Dagan's forearm. "How much did you put in Yashub's purse to prove his wealth?"

"Thirty talents."

"But what if that isn't enough? Gala may have more."

"He couldn't. He can't even afford a bride price, so there is no way. He isn't a wealthy man." Dagan cracked his big knuckles.

"Step back, boy! This one is mine!" Yashub growled, shoving Gala's shoulder.

A different guardsman stepped up, his hand on his sickle-sword and a frown on his face.

"Please!" A skinny man broke away from the group of fathers, his hands clasped as if in prayer, and I recognized him immediately. The certain tilt of his scruffy head. The way his scrawny shoulders sloped down on the right. It was the exact replica of Iltani from the back.

Once, he was a coppersmith by trade, dealing in metals he could never afford to own. Yet, he managed to keep his family afloat. On this day, his tunic was in tatters, his skin hanging on his bones. He was drowning.

"She's my daughter," he begged. "I should be allowed to give her in marriage."

His protests were quickly silenced by guardsmen, who

hauled him away from the proceedings and out of the Libbu with threats of death if he interfered. He stood by the archway, hopelessness on his face, rubbing his grizzled beard. Iltani briefly looked at him, her lip quivering as if she'd recognized what he had tried to do.

But the squabble over her hand rose. Yashub barked an order to the head guardsman to hand Iltani over. He grabbed her arm, but Gala pulled her out of his grasp.

"She doesn't want an old sweaty man like you in her bed. Leave her to me."

"Let me go with him!" Iltani wrestled free from Gala. "He has wealth and you have none!"

But instead of getting angry, Gala was transfixed.

The men around him laughed, calling over the guardsmen. "He has coin enough! Let him have this feisty one!"

"I will take care of her. I swear it." Gala placed both hands over his heart in supplication. Beside him, hordes of wealthy men stood, eyes alight with the contest, looking back and forth between Yashub and Gala to see who would win the prize.

"She's mine! I am farther up the line than you. Stand back!" Yashub wheezed, his face dripping with sweat.

"No! She will be *my* wife!"

Gala grabbed Iltani's arm once more, and the men around him shouted and cheered and banged on the dais with their fists. They clapped the guardsman on the back as Iltani squirmed. One man, a wealthy merchant by the look of him—silver rings squeezed over fingers, a tunic of the finest silks draped over his shoulder—pressed gold coins into Gala's hands, his face awash with sikaru.

The merchant yelled above the fray. "A young man needs this girl, not an old goat like that one over there!"

He pointed at Yashub, and Gala smiled, his weak-chinned face radiating with the prospect of winning.

I clutched my hands together. "Gala has a fist full of gold! He'll prove himself wealthier than Yashub."

"That's it! This is the end of it!" Yashub rasped, wiping a meaty hand down his face. "I'm taking her. I need a young woman to carry my seed, as the old hags are all dried up."

He looked up at the head guardsman, waving his bag of coins.

"I'm the man with more wealth and was put in line in front of this one. So hand her over! There are options on down the line for this young man. He doesn't want this girl, who'd likely slit his throat in bed." Winded and red-faced, he held a hand to his gut.

The guardsman looked from Gala to Yashub, indecision in his eyes.

Yashub laid a heavy hand on Gala's shoulder, sweat dripping from his temples. "I'll give you three goats and a ration of my last trade to let this one go."

But Gala looked down the line at the other prospects, his eyes going down to the shekels in his purse and the new coins in his hand. He showed his new wealth to the head guardsman and leaned in close to have a fervent, quiet discussion. After a minute, it was decided.

"This girl goes to Gala, guardsman of Alu!"

The scruffy guardsman swept his arm out to Iltani, who looked ready to gnaw the ropes off her own wrists with her teeth. "Sir, come collect your prize and take her to wife before you sleep tonight. Got a funny feeling you might never wake up!"

The men all laughed, but Gala just stood at the foot of the dais, dazzled, looking up earnestly into Iltani's beautiful sneer.

"Touch me and lose your manhood!" she yelled at him over the shouts of the men at her feet.

His eyes went wide, but he flushed and smiled as the men around him guffawed and congratulated him with full cups of brew. Yashub stalked to the head guardsman, gesturing wildly toward Iltani, but the man waved him away. Yashub glanced sideways at us as if we held the answers.

"Dagan, he's *your* friend. Go tell him she is our friend!"

Dagan's eyes were bleak. "All I can do is tell Gala the truth and pay him to release her."

Bile filled up my throat and I fought the urge to vomit. "It'll have to be *today*. This very day before he takes her as his wife. It *must*."

Beside me, Dagan stood. "I will speak to him right now."

"Be careful!" I whispered as he stumbled toward Gala, the stench of him receding as he walked hunched over, clutching a cask of sikaru to his chest as if his life depended on it.

He could *not* let the guardsmen know who he was!

"I will make you love me," Gala told Iltani loudly, his hand over his heart. "I swear it."

And he likely means it. But a woman given against her will into marriage is not a woman who would willingly offer her love, no matter the intentions of the man who'd selected her.

Iltani's eyes glittered dangerously as they led her down the dais to Gala, who stood there, hands on his hips, contemplating his new bride.

"Shall we?" He swept an arm out in front of him and nearly knocked Dagan backward.

Dagan tugged on his tunic, but Gala ignored him, his eyes fastened on Iltani.

Again, Dagan tugged on Gala's tunic, but Gala swatted him away and pulled Iltani's ropes on her hands toward what I could only assume was his home. She ground her heels in the sand. "You'll have to carry me. I'll never go willingly."

Gala's shoulders fell, his eyebrows knotted in confusion. "I've been told by all the women in Alu that I am handsome. Do you not find me so?"

Dagan turned back to me, a question in his eyes, but other guardsmen surrounded Gala, clapping him on his back, congratulating him on his choice, and one kicked Dagan in his backside, sending him sprawling into the dirt.

"You stink, beggar!" He yanked him up by the back of his tunic and looked in his face. *Really* looked. "You look familiar to me. Who are you?" He furrowed his brow in concentration.

Dear Selu.

Dagan pretended to retch, acting stupidly drunk, fear in his amber eyes, and disgusted, the guardsman shoved him away. Sweating, Dagan stumbled back to me and plopped down, breathing heavily.

"That was too close. He nearly caught you."

"I know. I'll have to try again. At his house. Privately. But she can't leave him, Kammani. Not without a justifiable reason. And being taken to bed by force will *not* be considered one."

"I know, Dagan. I know it well."

Guardsmen encircled Iltani like a pack of mangy dogs, but she stood bearing their congratulations, the briefest flicker of grief flitting across her face before it was replaced again by rage. No one else would've noticed it but me. She always kept such a brave veneer, laughing away any hurt or insult, mocking anyone's sensitivity, but that one glimpse gave me a hint at how she really felt inside.

And it was up to me to save *her* now, too.

Save the city. Save my friend. Save little Rish's arm. All of it was a pressure, building up inside me, a burden I was forced to bear. But bear it I would.

There was no other option when people's lives were at stake.

Clutching my healing satchel under my cloak in defiance, I watched as Gala pulled away from the group to whistles and indecent suggestions. When Iltani stood her ground and refused to follow, he simply picked her up and carried her, then stalked away from the gifting with his prize.

And though Iltani lay quietly in his arms as they receded from my sight, her face was anything but docile.

Her eyes were full of murder.

CHAPTER 16

BEFORE WE WENT to Gala's home, dodging guards-men, hiding in shadows and beneath overhangs, scuttling into scrub and behind barrels, we sneaked to the northeast doorway where the disloyal guardsman was supposed to be waiting to let us through.

But no one was there.

"Where *is* he?" I asked Dagan as we ducked around a cor-ner to avoid a pair of young guardsmen walking past. "He was supposed to be here!"

Dagan wiped a trickle of sweat from his brow. His stench, heightened by the heat of the day, almost knocked me over.

"I'm not sure. We'll just try again after we rescue her, Kammani," Dagan said. "Don't worry." He rubbed my arm and smiled, but both of us knew something was wrong.

By the time we got to Gala's home in the outskirts of the wealthy neighborhoods bordering the huts and hovels near the wall, they'd beaten us there. They stood inside his little one-story house with a few scraggly bushes in front by the cookfire and a roof that badly needed repair.

Hidden in the fruit grove behind, we listened to his muffled attempts to talk to her. He flattered her. Asked her about her parents. She responded with cutting wit and scathing insults, and in time, he gave up and came outside to the back porch and plopped down on a barrel, whittling with a dagger.

"Gala," Dagan whispered, emerging from the scrub.

"Who's there?" Gala dropped his stick and unsheathed his sicklesword in one motion.

I stayed back, hidden. Our plan was twofold. He'd tell Gala that Iltani was our friend, and try to negotiate with him to release her. I'd give Iltani the means of defending herself if Gala failed to give her up. I'd sat in the scrub and mixed a concoction with what I had in my satchel. It would have to do.

Dagan walked toward him, hands up, and Gala's eyes widened in recognition. He clapped his hand with Gala's, and the gesture nearly made me choke.

"Remember those three servants who first came with me through the gate? Well—" I heard Dagan say as I tiptoed around the side of the house to the common room in the front, where Iltani was. She was squatting in a corner, her arms around her knees, a look of stark grief and unbridled war on her face.

My heart leapt. "Iltani!" I whispered through the window.

She stumbled to her feet, lifted momentarily by the sound of my voice. Casting a long look over her shoulder toward the back of the house, she crept over to me and grasped my hands over the sill, laying her forehead on our interlaced fingers.

"About time." Her voice was too loud. Too much. As was Iltani's way.

Tears sparked in my eyes. "Iltani, be quieter. Gala is going to hear. I want to get you out of here right now, but you could face the council if you leave and *no one* would decide in your favor."

She shook her head vehemently, eyes red-rimmed. "We can't risk it. I mean, I'd risk it for me. But they'd kill my abum and ummum if I left him. Gala already warned me on the road here when I ordered him to let me go. He says *he* would never hurt my family, but his other guardsman friends would if I ever left him. He says some of them are cruel, and with Uruku in power, they're bolstered even more. The stinking hogs."

"Do you really think they would?" I whispered, one ear straining to hear Gala and Dagan's low, rumbling conversation.

"Yes!" she whispered harshly. "And now they know who they are, too. My abum came to the bridal gifting and announced who he was like an addled donkey." She waved her hand around and nearly knocked a vase of wilted flowers off the windowsill. "If I left, the first thing they'd do is find him and demand to know my whereabouts, and he wouldn't know because he never knows anything." She lowered her voice. "And then they'd kill him. They might anyway for what he did, standing up and trying to reclaim me. That *ignorant* man." Her words were harsh, but I knew that they were driven by a wild, protective love.

"But you cannot stay here and . . . and . . ."

"What?" Her eyes suddenly brimmed with tears. "Become his wife in word *and* deed?" As she spoke, her voice rose, and I shushed her, but she didn't listen. As if I really expected her to. "Well, isn't that a quandary, because that is what will happen, Kammani. He's going to try. He can't be the man he's so desperately trying to be without giving it a whirl."

"Iltani, Dagan is trying to pay Gala off for you this instant. Lower your voice."

But she kept speaking, her voice rising with every word. "And there is nothing I will be able to do about it but try not to murder him." Her voice caught as her chin quivered. "If I did that, they would find me and kill my parents. So I'll have to take it or fend him off as best as I can." She closed her eyes, pressing her lips together until they were white, misery making her writhe.

I clutched her hands in mine, staring hard down the side of the house, praying to Selu that Dagan was making headway in his conversation. She squeezed me with all the ferocity she had in her, hanging on to this brief connection with me like a drowning woman about to sink under the river.

My voice broke. "My friend . . . ," I whispered.

She laid her forehead on my hands, but she did not cry. She breathed in the scent of my fingers interlaced with hers and, after a moment, laid a loud kiss on top.

"It's okay. Get Arwia on the throne. Once she's restored, she'll have Gala put to death, and I can choose who gets the supreme privilege of sharing my bed."

"I may be able to help you before then, if Dagan does not succeed."

I reached down into my healing satchel, buried under thick robes padded to disguise my shape, and pulled out a clay bottle.

"Add a fingernail of this to his food, but be careful not to eat it yourself. Wash your hands after you touch the powder."

Her eyes glittered as she took the little bottle, squinting at the contents. "What is it? Will it kill him? As long as it looks like an accident, I am *more* than willing—"

I swallowed nervously. "No! No, but it might make him *wish* to die, at least for a little while. It's a mixture of aloe vera juice, senna, and turmeric. It should cause severe stomach cramping and loose bowels." I shrugged. "A man in pain will have a difficult time performing his husbandly duties."

"A fingernail, huh? What about the whole vial?"

My smile wavered. "Well, he'd likely die, as his blood would thicken and slow in his veins because he'd lose so much water."

She took the cask and put it in the waistband of her tunic, her face thoughtful. "Hmmm."

"Iltani, please don't murder him."

"We shall see. If he contracts a deadly illness, who am I to question the gods?"

"You could *seriously* be compromising your own safety if not your *soul*—"

"My soul is probably already going to perish. Look what we've concocted for Uruku. Is that not murder?"

Guilt flooded through my veins. My cheeks reddened. "It will save so many lives if he's dead. It's . . . different."

"Is it?" She met my eyes. "I wonder."

"You object?"

"Ha!" Her laugh was mirthless. "I wish I could watch the light fade from his eyes myself. I just wonder about how *you* will fare if we succeed."

My throat tightened as I met her steady gaze. "I'm doing what I must. My soul will be all right." But was that the truth? I'd been trained to heal, *not* to harm. Killing Uruku went against everything I'd learned from my father. Show mercy, he'd told me time and again. We are all just people trying our best.

But Uruku's death would save the lives of many, so in a way, I was doing everyone a favor, wasn't I? We *had* to do what we'd come to do, or we'd live the rest of our lives in fear!

Do no harm.

Iltani nodded. "Good. And my soul will rest easy enough if that man out there sits on the chamber pot for days. My thanks for this." She patted the bottle with nonchalance, but the mask she usually tied so carefully about her face had already slipped. I'd seen past it.

"Do not thank me," I whispered. "It's my fault you are here.

I should never have left you and Nanaea alone. I know how reckless you are." I gave her a mildly reproving look.

Grief filled up her eyes for a moment, and she shut them against her flood of emotion. "Don't be daft, Kammani. You're better than that. It's my own fault." She looked down at her hands. "I wanted to see my parents. That was all." She bit her lip when it trembled. Hard.

"That's understandable."

"It was *stupid*," she spat.

"Well, so was *my* idea with the almonds. Now we have to figure out another way to give him the poison. I've made some that will actually work."

Behind the house, Gala's and Dagan's voices rose in anger. *Oh no.*

Her face fell. "Ahh, well. At least he tried." Then her eyes grew alarmed. "He better not make Gala too angry. He could tell Uruku!"

"Good point. Let me go see."

"Wait, before you go, give me a task to do. I'm going to be here for a while. Something. Anything. For Gala is stupid." She looked over her shoulder at the back door, where Gala and Dagan's voices were punctuated with fire.

"I think he believes that he will actually win my heart." She laughed, a dry brittle sound like a twig snapping in two. "So I can use that. Give me something to ask him, and I'll help you take down Uruku. I'll work Gala like a puppet and make him dance to whatever song I sing."

I gripped her hands fervently. "*There* you are. That's my

Iltani with the fire inside her." But what could give her purpose until we could get her out? *Give her a reason not to kill him?*

"Keep your ears open when the guardsmen come to visit. Find out where Uruku goes outside the Palace and is exposed. With the support of the ensis behind us, we could seize him when he is at his most vulnerable and force the poison down his throat."

A shout and a curse were followed by Dagan's rigid form stomping around the house toward me, his face a thunderstorm.

Iltani's right. He failed.

He nodded sympathetically at Iltani, then jerked his head toward the road. "We have to go, Kammani. And hurry. Gala said he'd win her to him with his love, but if I didn't leave his home right now, our deal at the gate was off."

"What?"

He looked at Iltani. "I made him swear as a favor to me that he won't touch you unless you agree."

Iltani barked a laugh. "Let us pray that he values your friendship as much as his reputation as a man. Now go. But you must promise me one thing."

"Anything," I whispered.

"When Uruku is unseated and Arwia restored to the throne, I will have my day with justice." She gritted her teeth, her big brown eyes shining with tears she wouldn't dare shed, not even in front of me. "Promise me!"

I kissed her hands and reached out to touch her freckled cheek. "You will have it and more, my friend. I promise."

As we left Iltani, I swore on my life that I would take down Uruku, Gala, *all of them*. Dagan and I sneaked to the Palace, dark intention heavy on my heart. But when we arrived once more to check the doorway where the guardsman was to have met us, it was flanked by two guardsmen armed to the teeth, and the Libbu was bustling with people muttering something about Warad, Assata's son.

Why is his name on their lips?

"You! Both of you!" One of the guardsmen, with long, matted hair and a mace in his fist, shooed us away from the Palace. "Get out of here! No begging near the doorways! You lot have been told before!"

"Go! Go!" Dagan murmured to me urgently.

"But we need to find another way in there!"

"Kammani, no. It isn't safe. There's something in the air."

And I felt it, too. A strange tickling at the back of my throat, a whisper of dread across my brow. We melted into the crowds, sliding away from the guardsmen, but as we followed along to try to exit the Libbu, the crowds led us to a dais erected in the center of the Libbu, where once Nanaea had been chosen to die as a Sacred Maiden.

"It's Warad!" I clutched Dagan's arm.

Dagan sucked in a breath. "And he looks terrible."

Warad stood in the center of the dais on tree-trunk legs, filthy and sallow-cheeked. His hands were shackled in front of him and his shoulders drooped. At his knees was a sandstone block, covered in dried blood. Someone in the crowd screamed his name, and he blinked at her wearily in the blinding light. The surly young guardsman who had pointed his sicklesword at me in the Palace kitchens days ago stood behind him with several others holding maces and spears, sicklesswords and daggers.

People surged around the platform, Warad's name rolling off their tongues. As we neared, pushing to the edge of the crowd to stand in the shade of a tamarisk tree, a throaty trumpet announced the arrival of Uruku's caravan.

He rode in from the dusty roads leading from the Palace in the back of a wooden chariot, garish red paint slashed along the sides. The black mares tugging him toward the dais were healthy and thick, their coats shiny. How well cared for the animals of Alu were compared to the people.

"I can hardly stand to look at his face. He was supposed to be dead!"

"You tried, Arammu," Dagan said, but his words sounded hollow.

The caravan came to a stop, and Uruku dismounted from the chariot in ragged jerks, his face a sickly shade of amber.

Hope fluttered into my chest with tiny wings, beating desperately against my breastbone. *But he is ill.* At least somewhat from the gochala's side effects. With him in a weakened state, any poison I gave him—even a few drops—would send him to the Netherworld. Delivering it, though, was proving to be a problem since we couldn't get into the Palace. We needed *another* way.

Uruku took the stairs in two stumbling strides, and a few of the guardsmen on the platform took a half step backward. Some stared with open disgust. Not *everyone* wanted him on the throne. I looked around at the murmuring crowd. Did *any* of these people besides the wealthiest few approve of his rule?

Uruku opened his mouth to speak and winced, grasping his head with a trembling hand. I cursed myself for purchasing an ineffective poison.

And in fact—my guts twisted as a sinking realization raced up into my hairline—I should be cursing myself because of my *idiocy*. Not only had I bought a useless poison, delivering it had worked *against* us. My little stunt had actually *alerted* him that someone wanted him dead.

I was going to be sick.

"Gods of the skies, Dagan, we have to leave. Right now." I tugged on his arm. "Uruku knows! He realizes he was poisoned, and that someone is out to get him. That's why Warad is here! He's—"

But Uruku interrupted me. "We have a traitor in our midst." His voice was controlled, though agony twisted his features in a knot. "Someone seeks to gain the throne by killing me. Trying to kill my wife and heir. But we will not be torn down!" He pointed a shaking finger out at the crowd, and some shrank from him, although many of the wealthier citizens cheered. "I put some of the traitors' heads on stakes, but there is another in our great city, *still*."

He paused with a grimace, holding the heel of his left hand to his eye socket.

I fell back against the tree trunk, my heart in my throat. I'd acted stupidly. I gave him the poison and it made our situation worse! He would take revenge. He thought it was *Assata* who had given it to him. Everyone in Alu knew she was a warrior. He believed it was her acting against him because he had her son! Frantically, I pulled on Dagan's arm, but he was ignoring me, staring at the dais with a clenched jaw, his right hand hovering over his emerald dagger.

"We have to go, my love!"

Uruku grabbed Warad by his hair and pushed him down on his knees in front of the sandstone block. "People of Alu! I will not tolerate disloyalty and threats!"

Warad's big, round face was resigned, his eyes dry, chin firm, under his scraggly beard. If Assata were here, she would slash her way through this crowd, annihilating everyone in her path to rescue her son, and we were sitting on our heels. But there was nothing we could do. Not right now.

"We need to get out of here to plan another way to poison Uruku," I hissed to Dagan. "Come on!"

Dagan shook his head. "We can't just leave!"

Uruku was bellowing on about loyalty and traitors in a ragged voice, wincing as he spoke, a hint of madness played at the edges of his words.

"What else are we going to do? He thinks Assata delivered the poison, and he's going to punish her by murdering Warad!"

"But if he kills him, Assata could become unwilling to co-operate."

"Uruku is not a rational man. And I pushed him over the edge with the gochala." My plans weren't working. I was harming more than I was healing! *He will kill Warad because of me.*

"So this—*this*—is what we do to traitors in Alu, citizens." Uruku's commanding voice echoed from the dais. "*This* is how we deal with them!"

He turned to one of the guardsmen behind him and snapped his fingers. "Your sword."

The man unsheathed it with a soft snick and handed him the hilt.

Dagan pulled out his dagger.

Panic tightened my throat. "Dagan, *do not* even think about it."

"I'm an excellent marksman, Kammani."

"And they'll see who threw it and kill you, too!" I pleaded, my eyes welling.

"Would they? We don't know that!"

"Warad, Tavern Owner's Son," Uruku continued. "Your abum, Irra, was a traitor. Your ummum, Assata, lives as a traitor. And now you shall accept punishment for their crimes."

Uruku nodded to the guardsmen on either side of Warad. "Secure him."

The guards grabbed Warad and shoved his head down to the block. Warad writhed and jerked, trying to squirm from their hold. The crowd surged forward, some screaming encouragement, others yelling in protest.

"My love!" Tears spilling from my eyes, I grabbed Dagan's arm again. "Please. We have to leave!"

Shaking with rage, with sorrow, Dagan stared at the dais, the emerald dagger in his fist. He grabbed my shoulders fiercely. Kissed me on the mouth and shoved me lightly away. "Go!" he whispered. "Run back to Laraak and let me end this. No one would suspect a beggar!" He licked his lips and looked at the dais. "I can do this."

"No!" I whispered at him while the people around us shrieked. "I cannot risk losing you! What are you saying?"

Uruku drew the sicklesword high up over his head.

"Come *with* me!" I yanked at his elbow. Reached for his dagger. I couldn't stand by and let this happen!

"Stop it," Dagan growled as he drew his arm back. His eyes were closed to slits, his shoulders tense.

"Dagan! If you do not leave with me now, *right now*, I will run up on the dais and take Warad's place. It's *my* fault he's there. It should be me dying on this day."

He looked at me hard. Still resolved.

Guardsmen converged on the crowd, keeping those protesting in line with backhands and shoves. Women screamed as Warad squirmed on the block, but two more guardsmen held his legs while one yanked his tunic away from his broad shoulders to give Uruku a clean target.

"Is that what you want, Dagan?" I shook him. "You want me to run up there and take his place? Because I will do it. I swear to Selu I will. Watch me." Desperation clawed at my throat. Because I meant it. I would.

"You will not threaten me!" Uruku's voice boomed like thunder over the shrieks of the crowd. "I will not abdicate! The throne is mine!"

"Dagan please!"

Finally, Dagan's shoulders fell and his eyes softened as he looked at me. At the sobs about to choke me. His lips quivering, he gently sheathed his dagger.

I rubbed his shoulder as I cried. "That's it. That's the way. Come on. Let's go!"

But before we could move, we watched, struck with horror, as Uruku brought the sword down on Warad's back with a sickening crunch and a spurt of crimson. The crowd roared as Warad shrieked and thrashed. Blood rolled down his sides, soaking into his tunic and pooling on the platform.

"He missed!" Dagan breathed. "Dear Selu, he missed!" His face twisted in disgust, he turned away and began nudging me through the crowd out of the Libbu while Warad screamed in pain. "Go, Kammani. Go."

With a mighty yell, Uruku raised the sword again and buried it once more in Warad's back. Warad bellowed like an ox on the slaughterhouse floor.

"He's missing *on purpose*, Kammani. He's punishing Assata," Dagan said, eyes wild.

"We have to keep moving and get back to Laraak." My voice was nigh on hysteria. "Regroup!"

As we fled toward the gate, I sobbed, turning back toward the platform repeatedly as the platform grew smaller and smaller. As Warad's thick legs thrashed on the dais and muffled screams tore from his mouth.

But soon, his cries were replaced by gurgling moans, and not long after, they were replaced by the soft, still silence that can only come from the dead.

CHAPTER 17

MY SCORPION AMULET in my hands, I sat in my medical tent, gulping in air, tears coursing down my cheeks. Nanaea crooned into my shoulder.

Ensi Puzu and the two councilmen we were supposed to convince—Ensi Adda and Ensi Mudutu—had just left and were on their way back to Alu. I'd tried to give Ensi Puzu my poison to use on Uruku at the first opportunity, but he repeated that he would have nothing to do with assassination. He'd only promised to support us should Arwia take the throne. We'd done our best to convince the other two ensis that Arwia would be the best leader for the city, but whether they'd support her remained to be seen. Neither had sworn allegiance to her.

"*Nothing* is going according to plan. Nothing."

"Shhh, Kammani. Shh. It will be okay."

Warad was dead. Iltani was stuck in a marriage without

her consent. Dagan was on his way to bring Rish to me. I'd looked at his poor arm the second we'd gotten back into Laraak, and it was violently red and festering.

All at my hands.

My stupid, useless, ineffective hands.

I'd left Rish's wound open. I'd caused this agony to happen to him, just as I'd given Uruku the poison, causing Iltani to get captured and him to blame Assata and kill Warad.

And Manzazu was poised to attack. In fact, they could be on their way this very minute!

"I'm doing more harm than good, Nanaea. I'm hurting everyone."

"Selu will make sure things work in our favor. He's listening to us, even if we don't feel him." Nanaea pressed her forehead to mine. Kissed my cheek. She took my ummum's threadbare blue shawl and wrapped it around me.

"No, he isn't. Selu doesn't listen to anybody."

Wiping my tears on the shawl, I stared at the pointed tail of the golden beast on the necklace and thought of Mudi's advice. She'd told me that the Boatman was trying to earn his way out of his post, trying to replace the lives he'd taken as a warrior long ago by helping healers. That I should *pay attention* to him. That I could trust my instincts.

If that was the case, the Boatman really wasn't helping me at all.

Or is he trying to and I am not listening?

The image of the Boatman standing on the banks of the river with his band of warriors behind him flickered into my sights again, and I held it there, watching him. He took a bottle from his satchel, and from the way the light was hitting it in my memory, I'd swear it had been red. A deep crimson like the nerium bottle on the merchant woman's booth. But I didn't have the nerium or a different red bottle of tincture! I rummaged around in my healing satchel again to check, but nothing was there that looked even close to the bottle he held.

And how can I get to Uruku without hurting more people, even if I did have the right tincture? It will be impossible to sneak around as we've been doing, and I've already done so much harm!

My spirits fell even further as my tent opened and Dagan appeared at the opening, Rish in his arms. The boy was writhing in agony, his arm oozing, swollen to twice its normal size. The tinctures I'd given him weren't working. Cleaning the wound wasn't working. His arm was primed to kill him if I didn't do something about it.

Do no harm.

But in Rish's case, the harm was the healing.

"I'm going to go. I'll be back later, all right?" Nanaea's eyes filled and she fled the tent, and honestly, it was all I could do not to follow her. Because what I was about to do would probably be the most difficult thing I'd ever done.

Tears ran down my cheeks as I eyeballed the bone saw glittering in the basket near the doorway as if it were a sea monster with rows of sharp teeth. Though it would be horrible, and would require more courage than I probably even had, I'd have to take the arm so I could spare his life.

I met Dagan's tortured eyes as he kissed Rish's head softly.

"I'm not ready for this, Kammani," Dagan said, his voice breaking.

I just nodded because there was nothing else to say.

Dagan paced in front of Rish, who wailed and thrashed on the pallet like an animal caught in a trap. Clenching and unclenching his hands, Dagan stopped and looked at me warily.

It had been half an hour, and the arnica and hemp weren't even dulling the pain anymore.

"Dagan, I *have* to do it now. It's inhumane to wait any longer."

"I *know* this is the only way to heal him." He ran a hand through his hair. "I don't want to believe it, but I know it's true."

My throat closed around my pain. "I need to fix him, and I need to do it before the infection travels farther than it has. He's suffering, my love!"

I bent over my healing table and mixed a poppy mixture heavy enough to send him into his dreams through the agony of the surgery and into the night.

At last, Dagan nodded, tears in his eyes. "All right. You can give it to him. I don't want to let you do this, but . . . we must. And I can help you."

My hands shaking, I handed him the vial. "My many thanks," I whispered. "He needs to drink this."

His eyes in torment, he walked to his little brother and got on his knees beside the pallet, crooning softly into his ear while Rish wailed. He sat him up and poured the tonic into his mouth, encouraging each swallow until Rish's eyes grew heavy and eventually his lashes rested on his cheeks. Dagan was the picture of love and support to him, a man worthy of being called an abum one day.

The thought striking me as bizarre at this terrible occasion, I wiped my trembling hands down my tunic and walked to the water I'd had Kasha tote in from one of the Garadun's tributaries and boil. As I grabbed the soap, Dagan stepped behind me. My eyes welled at his nearness. No matter *what* sort of harm I caused, he was still there for me. No matter what. The warmth and heady smell of his tunic stilled my hands, and I craned my neck around to face him.

He touched my cheek, his eyes filled with tears.

"My love . . ." My eyes welled as my lip trembled. "I'm sorry. . . ."

"Shhh, shhh, shhh, Arammu."

"I did more harm than good." My voice broke.

His chin bunched. "This isn't all your fault, Arammu. I *asked* you to treat him, and we were trying our best. Isn't that a healer's job? To do their very best? Try to ease people's pain? You tried. And that's all we can do."

"I should have listened to myself, though. I knew not to leave the wound open!"

"Well, then you must learn to pay attention to what your instincts tell you. You will only be a better healer for it. And I should have just listened to what you recommended and shut my mouth!"

I nodded, not trusting myself to speak.

Easing away from his touch, I plunged my hands down into the warmth of the washbasin, scouring with the bristle brush and the soap. He went around to the other side of the tub. Dipped his own hands into the water, too, and began to scrub right along with me.

"I should have stepped up with Rish and helped you find a different solution instead of pressuring you to heal him. *Something.* You are not in this alone, my sweet. You are not in *this life* alone."

The words rubbed me raw, because though he took some of the fault on himself, it really wasn't. I had known what needed to be done and I didn't do it. Period. I scrubbed the bristles under my fingernails, removing the grime and the dirt. Scrubbing and scrubbing and scrubbing some more.

Under the water, Dagan took the brush. Rubbed his thumbs over the tops of my hands. I met his eyes. "Forgive me for my part in this, Kammani. Forgive yourself," he breathed across the washtub. "Remember how much I care. I will help you with Rish, and I will help you moving forward. Whatever you need."

Stifling the tears in my throat, I nodded. After several moments, I wiped the tears from my eyes with my arm while my hands dripped over the basin. "I'll need it. This is a—trying task."

"It is, and likely one of many we will need to endure.

Together." He swallowed, and I looked up at his handsome face. Tears ran down his cheeks. "My family needs us both to be strong." His throat bobbed. "I don't think I'm doing a very good job."

"Yes, you are," I whispered.

He finished washing his hands. "I hope my ummum still lives. I feel guilty being happy that it wasn't her being killed on the platform." He wiped his eyes on his arm, keeping his hands clean as he'd seen me do. "And angry. I feel so—angry for what Uruku has done." He shook off the water and grabbed a cloth stitched with little red rosettes. Nanaea's handiwork. He handed me one, too. "I am not a violent man, as you well know. But there's nothing, outside of risking your life, I wouldn't do to stop him, Kammani. *Nothing*."

"I know. We just need to find a solution to *do* that." Rubbing my fingers over the red rosettes that Nanaea had stitched at the bottom in beautifully neat little rows, I was suddenly struck by a thought.

Nanaea and her sewing could be the key.

She'd been so clever with her disguises that perhaps she could devise something else now to help us get into Uruku's chamber or throne room. We'd need a diversion and a sneak attack. Perhaps Higal would help with some of the Koru since they were itching to fight anyway. And no one knew who they were and would underestimate the women, as Ummi had once told me they would do.

So if we played into that and disguised them as something helpless—

I racked my brain, thinking of what women's position would be the least assuming in this city-state, as the warriors would never pass as servants. Iltani's mournful face as she stood with the other women on the dais dressed like maidens to be wed floated into my memory.

"Brides!" I said to Dagan. "We can make them brides to be given to Uruku!"

"Make who brides?" Dagan looked around the tent. "What are you talking about?"

"He'd never suspect them if they were given from a group of traders. Once they got to his chamber, they could kill him, and we could restore Arwia to her rightful place. It can work, Dagan, it can."

"Are you . . . talking to me? Or to yourself?" Dagan finished drying his hands, his face puzzled.

My heart beating madly, I set aside the cloth and picked up the bone saw to clean it in the basin.

"I'm sorry. I'm sorry! I'm just thinking out loud. Dagan, what if we prevented war by turning the Palace's own sick deeds against them?" I asked as I scrubbed. "We can pretend that a handful of the Koru are brides and *give them to Uruku*! Nanaea could dress them in finery!"

His eyes lit up with the prospect as the realization of what I was saying sank in. "Yes. Yes, that's a very good idea. He wouldn't turn a group of women away. He'll underestimate them!"

My heart lifting momentarily, I pulled the saw from the water once it was clean and laid it on a linen next to my other supplies. "Yes! And we need to talk it all through with you and Nanaea and everyone else after our work here is done."

"Then we'll do that. But—" He took a deep breath. "First things first, though, right?" His eyes softened as he looked at me, then at his brother.

I nodded as I slowly breathed in through my nose and out through my mouth. "Yes, of course. First, little Rish."

My abum once told me that you must excise the cause of infection for the good of the body or it would fester and spread. In Rish's case, it certainly had.

Just like Uruku was infecting the city of Alu.

Filled with purpose, I stared down at the bone saw. The needle and thread. The sterilized dagger for the easier work. The myrrh, sikaru, and the clean cloths. I mentally worked through the steps I'd need to take to sever Rish's lower arm from his body.

And when I was finished, I'd cut Uruku out of the body of Alu with the sharpest blade in the entire fertile valley: the Koru.

CHAPTER 18

—⌇⌇⌇—

IN THE ABANDONED city of Wussuru, the Manzazu warriors lined up in neat rows like markings on a tablet, their copper helmets shining in the sun. In their fists were maces. Spears. Sickleswords. Battle-axes. Bows. Their armored cloaks glimmered like snake's scales when they moved, shifting a battle-ax to a better hand. Repositioning a spear.

I would not want to be the recipient of this army's punishment. In front of them, several of the army's commanders stalked, their faces stony. And next to them walked Higal and Commander Ummi, gesturing angrily at one another.

Dagan stood in front of Assata, who'd changed into the Manzazu uniform. She looked lethal with the sickleswords in sheaths at her waist, an armored tunic on her back. Dagan's face fell in grief as he finished telling her of Warad. When he stopped, hands on hips, head hanging, she screamed and shoved him hard in the chest, tears springing to her eyes and rolling down her cheeks in fury.

We'd debated telling Assata at all about Warad. But after talking with Arwia, we decided the only compassionate thing to do was to relay the news and pray it redirected her to join forces with us in our bridal scheme.

Unfortunately, that wasn't the case. Assata pushed Dagan once more, slapped his cheek, and stormed away, howling and beating her chest.

Dagan stood there a second, kicking the sand, before walking back toward us. He rubbed his jaw where he'd been slapped and Nasu clapped a hand on his shoulder. Tears flooded my vision. That poor woman.

"Well, that was a terrible idea. She'll never forgive us," Dagan told me as he shielded his eyes from the sun. He and I had made the trip to Wussuru, leaving Nanaea to care for Rish and Kasha for the day we would be gone. While she did, she and the weaver friend would make the Koru's bridal tunics. Rish's skin had pinked up immediately when the infected arm had been removed, and I'd stuffed him full of enough poppy to sleep for a full day. There was once a time I wouldn't trust her to the task of watching him. But now? She was proving herself competent and efficient. Startlingly so.

"Never is a long time." Arwia inclined her head regally, tucking her long hair over her stitched ear. It was healing nicely, though she'd have a wicked scar for the rest of her life. "Assata has to realize it is not your fault."

"She knows no such thing." Dagan put his hands on his hips near his daggers.

"And she won't care anyway." Nasu glanced back at her wailing on her knees. "She wants blood." .

"And she'll get it," I told Nasu. "Tomorrow morning. We'll send in a small band of the Koru dressed as brides for Uruku, and they can kill him. Once he is gone, Arwia can take back her city."

Nasu shrugged. "You're too late, Kammani. Look at them all." I took in his warm brown eyes, flashing back to the moment he'd tried to slit my throat in the tomb while we'd kissed, and my hand instinctively went to the scar left behind.

"Higal and Ummi have been fighting about the delay that Ummi gave you. Half of the troops and their commanders support Higal, and want to march *now*."

Nasu jerked his close-cropped head at the thick warrior who looked as ferocious as a lion.

"And to be honest, she's probably right. It seems needlessly risky to continue trying to poison Uruku when Higal has a good plan. She'll send in warriors to attack the gate and get through the city to the Libbu. Once she's there, she'll lure out many of the guardsmen with war, and a small faction will get inside and capture Uruku. They'll kill his ensis, then parade their corpses, and him in chains, all the way back to Sarratum Tabni, where she'll put his head on the Manzazu wall."

"Well, that is not what *I* want at all." Arwia crossed her arms over her chest. "I *only* want Uruku dead. We can get the rest of the city's allegiance another way. With gifts! Or even *food*. Kammani says they're starving!"

"My lady." He bowed slightly, pressing his lips together. "The nobility stand to lose if Uruku is taken, so they will not go willingly into your service. They must be killed, or they may rise up against you one day. Same for the guardsmen who serve him. I want to listen to you, but I believe you're wrong."

"You supported us before, Nasu. What changed?" Dagan asked him.

Nasu blew out a breath. "I suppose I owed you the chance. But you couldn't accomplish it. Why keep risking your lives? Let's move on. Sarratum Tabni will march whether you succeed or not at this point."

We continued to debate as Assata wept herself dry near the warriors. But after a while, she came to her feet with great care, the weight of her grief trying to press her into the ground. At once, as if deciding something to herself, she dried her eyes with the backs of her hands, squared her shoulders, and marched up to Higal, speaking desperately into her ear.

After a few moments, Higal nodded, her mouth hardened into sandstone. She broke away from the greater regiment and stood next to Ummi. Assata took Higal's spot in line, her face twisted with ache.

Higal raised her hands to the warriors in the Linaza salute, and nearly half of them snapped to attention. The other half looked confused.

"Warriors! This is your call to arms!"

Next to Higal, Ummi gritted her teeth. "Stand *down*, Higal!"

Higal ignored her. "Our sarratum has commanded us to war against Alu! We march tonight!"

The warriors raised their weapons in the sky, roaring in response to Higal, and my spine tingled with the memory of the vision of the Boatman. The hallucination. Whatever it was I'd experienced. The warriors in my vision held tinctures, though. Not weapons. Fighting the innocent was *not* the way forward.

"Higal!" I yelled. My heart was screaming that harming the innocent to get what you wanted was foul. Indecent. Unforgivable. I may go into Alani's claws for attempting to kill Uruku, but I'd accept that fate. Killing the innocent was *not* the same. My hands up, pleading, I strode over to her.

"No, Higal, no war. Send in some of your Koru to go in dressed as brides, as we've explained. They can sneak in and remove the threat."

Coiled like a snake, Assata broke rank and ran up to me, unsheathing her sicklesword. She grabbed my shoulder and flung me down to the ground while the warriors behind her yelled. Dagan rushed up behind Assata, his daggers already out of his belt, but Ummi launched herself between Assata and me, her eyes hard.

"Step back," Ummi told Assata.

Assata's eyes grew cold. "I'm helping you remember your sarratum's bidding, Commander."

Ummi leveled her battle-ax at Assata's throat. "We owe

the A-zu the delay, and I will not back down on that promise. We do not act until I give the command." She stared hard at Higal. "In case you have forgotten your *rank*."

"No, Manzazu will have WAR!" Assata cried, the warrior she once was still present in her mother's hands and belly, sloped shoulders and threads of gray at her temples. Maybe more present because of those things. "This army with their warrior hearts will follow Higal because she is following their sarratum's orders!"

"Not if they want to please *Linaza*." Ummi stepped up to Assata and drew the other battle-ax from her belt. The blade flashed in the sun as she rotated her wrist. "We do not have to come to blows, but we will. The A-zu saved our lives. We owe her our debt."

Assata's lip curled. "Your allegiance *should* be to your *queen*. And my allegiance is to my son! My husband! The warrior who lives inside me! She has consecrated us for bloodshed, and I will have it on the morrow. This girl does not control me!" She pointed her sicklesword at my chest. "Everyone who stood there and watched my son die deserves to meet the Boatman." Her eyes were hard with rage. "*Everyone*."

I shrank back into the sand, holding up a hand to ward off an attack, and the brick wall of Dagan stepped next to Ummi between me and Assata. He held both his daggers in his massive hands, his eyes hard.

"Assata, I do not want to fight you, but if you make any more threats against Kammani, I will. Warad and my ummum were dead the moment Uruku took them. We will likely not get my ummum back alive, either. It's a fact that kills me. But the *only* thing that is important now is removing Uruku from that throne and putting her back on it." He pointed to Arwia. "People will be loyal to her. They know Uruku is a monster who lusts for blood and power. It would be different if he'd made the city prosperous, but he has failed the citizens of Alu."

Dagan held his arms out to all of us. The warriors, too. "You think we haven't been doing our duty, but all of us have been working hard. Kammani poisoned Uruku. Iltani gains inside information from Gala. I've been counting the weak and the strong and ensuring the ensis will let Arwia rule. There are more poor than rich in Alu now by a lot. Maybe eighty percent! All but a handful of the nobility are starving. Many of them are angry, Assata, and they would likely take Manzazu's side if they came in as saviors. There is no reason to go in slaughtering."

Assata laughed long and loud. "You stood by while Warad was killed, and now you want Higal to have mercy on his murderers?" she roared. "His head likely joins his abum's on the wall, and you want her to stop this?"

"Yes." I held my hand up in defense. "Higal can take a troop of bridal warriors in to capture Uruku and kill him. Then you can parade his body all the way to Manzazu and Enlidu and Kush and anywhere else you see fit."

At that, Arwia pointed to Assata. Then Higal. "All of us

need to work together or we will not succeed. How can we be fighting among ourselves and hope to win? We must be a force united! Please listen!"

Assata studied Arwia, smiling at her mirthlessly. Then she nodded to Higal. The Koru warrior thrust one meaty fist into the air. "Those warriors who are with me and your *sarratum*, meet me in the courtyard. *We. Will. Wage. War.*"

She jogged out of the Libbu walls, and nearly half of the women followed her. Assata spat on the ground near my feet and jogged behind them all. Nasu stood next to Arwia, his hands on his hips, a look of indecision on his lean face. Arwia tugged his elbow and he lowered his head, their conversation too quiet for me to hear.

Ummi stood there, watching them go, her features turned to stone.

Dagan reached down and helped me stand. "They won't be stopped, Kammani."

"Commander, will you help us? We could leave here with a small band of the Koru. Right now. Go to Laraak for disguises, then enact our scheme before she brings war. If we already have Uruku dead by the time she arrives, she won't need to march!"

"I promised a *delay*, A-zu." She gritted her teeth, her eyes flashing. "Now this is causing me trouble with my own warriors."

"Trust yourself, Ummi. You *know* in your heart that this is right. You *know* it. It will prove your Koru wise and strong when you quietly show your strength as you said before. You and Nasu can command the team. With his knowledge of the Palace and your skill in battle, you can lead these Koru in, overtake him, and stand victorious. I know it!"

Dagan looked over my shoulder. "What does he think he's doing?"

I looked over to Nasu and Arwia, but Nasu was striding purposefully away. Toward Higal and Assata. Higal's barks of commands could be heard echoing off the city walls.

Arwia cast worried eyes over at us, her long hair falling over her shoulders. "Nasu stands with Higal. He believes she is right and that I will be challenged for the throne if I do not attack brutally. He is loyal to me, but . . . he says he's tried it this way long enough. He believes we must use force."

Nasu exited out the Libbu archway into the courtyard, and an exultant cry rose from the warriors standing out there. But there were still half of the warriors in here and all of the Koru except Higal. Many souls willing to listen to *our* way of thinking.

"What do *you* want, Arwia?"

She blew out a breath. Looked hesitantly at me, then over her shoulder to where Nasu had gone. "If Ummi agrees, then I choose to protect our citizens. I'll go with you, and we will take down Uruku quietly. I'd rather try once more this way."

"Ummi, please say you'll do this. Please help us end this war before it begins."

She dropped her head and looked at me with fierce determination in her eyes. "If Linaza is directing your vision, I will."

I wasn't so sure it was she who had put this spark in my

belly and fanned it into a flame, but if saying that it was Linaza meant saving the lives of innocents, I would. I'd say it a hundred times.

"It is so, Ummi. Linaza is the goddess of war, but also of love. And I love my city. Help me protect those who live there."

She put a heavy hand on my shoulder. "Then we will do it."

"Good." Arwia looked from me to Ummi, flint in her eyes. "Now let us go pry that wriggling maggot from my throne."

CHAPTER 19

—ᴍ—

THE HALF-DAY RIDE back to Laraak was made faster by the speed of the stallions beneath us, the hands of the Boatman on my shoulders urging me onward with cold dread. He was *there*. He was ready to take souls to the Netherworld. And I couldn't let him.

Arwia raced her white steed through the night next to Dagan and me. The horse's muscles strained and stretched beneath its ivory hide, and her hair followed after her in silken waves as we galloped hard. The warriors who were with us sneaked stealthily in twos and threes, seamlessly disappearing in the crowds on the great road that passed between city-states. Only Ummi and the Koru brides stayed with us on their horses, their faces resolutely forward wherever we might lead.

"Faster," I breathed into Dagan's ear, and he tightened his hand over my arms that were encircling his waist as we sped, together, toward the safety of the encampment.

Toward Nanaea and Kasha and little Rish.

Toward a plan that would hopefully secure Alu for Arwia and restore the city that had raised me, had chewed me up and spat me out, but still resonated in my heart. Still beat within my breast. Still held the bones of my family.

I was a healer, and I had an entire city counting on me to get rid of the infection that had festered for far too long.

I couldn't let them—any of us—down.

❂❂❂

They were the most powerful brides I'd ever seen, and my heart practically leapt with hope, something I desperately needed. Rish had been awake when we'd arrived early this morning, and his stitches had not only looked good, but he was in bright spirits for someone who'd been told they could never use an appendage again. He'd shrugged his shoulder and said he was glad it was gone because it had hurt him something awful. After stuffing him with honeyed dates and all the sweet figs I could find, I left him with the young woman who suffered from moon-blood pain. She was telling him a story about their night goddess at Laraak, and Rish, his eyes wide, was enraptured.

His stump, however, nearly broke me. For the rest of my life, whenever I saw it, it would remind me of how I'd hurt him. But I left my worry behind for the moment. I couldn't let it deter our plans.

The brides standing before me made me believe they might actually work out.

Ummi looked fit for her wedding day, as did the other Koru. Ummi's hair was brushed into a short tail at the base of her neck, and her lips were painted gold. Thick strokes of kohl outlined her big eyes, which peered out from her filmy veil with more ferocity than was safe. She'd refused to remove the bracers about her forearms, so Nanaea tied silks over them down to her wrists. All of the Koru looked mildly uncomfortable, poking one another and laughing shyly. Humusi, the lean Koru warrior who'd discovered the assassin in Manzazu with us, bobbed around like a cat until Nanaea practically had to tie her down to dress her. Ummi's face flushed red as a trader walking through the camp whistled, but Arwia scolded him.

"What an unusual situation to be in," Ummi grumbled. "I'm not used to being at anyone's mercy. I am in charge."

"I *know*." I laid a hand on her arm. "But this is temporary."

"And necessary for the entire region." Arwia surveyed Nanaea's work. "For *your* citizens, Commander. When I'm back in the Palace, I will restore trade to the north." She blinked, her nerves bubbling through. "Somehow."

"We will all support and help you, Arwia." I twisted to get at my healing satchel, which was situated strangely under my robes.

"Hold still, Lady Trader." Nanaea knelt in front of me, lacing one of my sandals. She finished and stood.

"Lady Trader. What a sickening thought. Any woman who could give her own sisters away to be used however a man would like is a shame to all humanity."

"But why?" Kasha asked. "If they are going to be wives? Why wouldn't they want to be married to their husbands?" He stood next to Nanaea, his eyes wide, holding a stack of linens from which Nanaea would occasionally pull and tuck into different places on the Koru's bodies, accentuating a hip here or adding color to bring out their eyes there.

Nanaea combed her fingers through the front of his hair. "There are things you don't know about marriage, Brother."

He frowned. "No?" He looked at Nanaea. "You get married and you love each other. Like Ummum and Abum."

Nanaea met my eyes over his shoulder. "That's not always how it works, especially if a woman is forced to take a husband she doesn't want. Like Iltani has been."

"Who wouldn't want a husband?" Kasha blinked at me, and I felt my cheeks coloring as I thought of Dagan and his own question posed not that long ago.

"Some women do." I glanced at Dagan, but though he was listening, he was studiously avoiding looking as though he was.

"But some do not."

I looked around the trading post, a sheep's pen in the distance catching my eye. "Think of it this way," I explained to him, straightening the vest over my robe. "Go roll around in that pile of dung shoveled from the sheep's pen."

He furrowed his brow. "What? No. Gross!"

"What if your loved ones told you that the pile of dung smelled great? That you were stupid for not wanting to lie in it? And what if you didn't have a choice? What if I made you go sleep in that pile of dung for the rest of your life?"

"That would be terrible. I would hate it."

Nanaea met my eyes over his head as she tied a belt a little more snugly around Ummi's waist. "That's exactly right. And brides who are given in marriage without their consent hate it, too."

He curled his lip in disgust. "I'm never going to marry."

"Not all marriage is like sheep dung, Kasha. Some are like feather beds." I ruffled his hair as Nanaea laughed, her bubbly voice diminishing some of the tension that had settled on my shoulders. From over the tops of the Koru's heads, Dagan was watching me, holding back a hint of a smile.

I tugged Kasha and Nanaea into a hug, burying my face in their hair, and met Dagan's eyes over their shoulders. My family.

"Stop! You're crushing me!" Kasha wriggled away and dumped Nanaea's linens into her arms, then bolted to my medical tent to see Rish.

"I still believe I should go with all of you. I could make my case before the ensis to reinstate myself on the throne as soon as it is abdicated." Arwia reached out and tentatively adjusted a warrior's necklace.

Nanaea stuck her hands on her full hips. "Remember, I have plans for a costume that will make the ensis worship the ground you walk on. It's necessary! We must make them believe you were strong enough to escape from the tomb. You must look like a warrior maiden who can lead the city in no uncertain terms." She eyed Arwia's simple, drab tunic in a dirty beige. "And you cannot do it in *that*."

Dagan walked back to me with another trader from Laraak we'd hired to add to the authenticity, securing daggers on their belts.

"Ready to go?"

"We are." I pulled Nanaea into another hug and murmured into her rose-scented hair. "Look after Rish. Give him the tincture I've been telling you and—"

"I know," Nanaea interrupted, holding me at arm's length. "Take good care of him. I will. Don't worry about us. You go and do *not* be afraid, you hear me?" She kissed my cheek, her eyes suddenly bright with tears. "And come back to me safe and sound, or I'll be mad at you forever."

"I promise." I laid my hand on the top of her head, which was warm from the sun, letting it fall to cup her cheek before pulling away.

As the Koru, Dagan, the trader, and I headed past the edge of the Laraak tents, Nanaea and Arwia linked arms, meandering toward my medical tent. Dagan joined me at my side as we set our sights on the walls of Alu, glimmering pink and gold in the late-morning heat.

"Sheep dung, huh?" he asked.

When I went to swat him, he'd already darted away.

242

Gala, his face gray, holding an arm to his midsection, was at the gate when we arrived with the eight Koru, and I resisted the urge to grab Dagan's dagger and press it to his neck and make him release Iltani or face death. But I would mess everything up for Iltani's family if I did, and I couldn't break my promise to stay silent and let her work her magic. *Soon*, I promised myself as he waved us through, tying the sack of coins that Dagan handed him to the belt at his waist.

Soon.

At least for now, it appeared that the tincture I'd given Iltani was doing its worst. I only prayed to Selu that it had prevented him from taking her to wife.

"Ummi," I whispered.

"What, A-zu?" Ummi craned her neck around to look at me.

"Trader, you mean?" I laughed, my nervousness making it come out high and strange. "I have faith in you and your fellow Koru. But if something should happen, I want you to know—"

"Hush." She smiled underneath her heavy, sunset-colored makeup. "You've yet to see us in action. Nothing will happen."

As we traveled to the Palace, the beige, tiered structure shimmered proudly in the center of the city as if calling me to it. The blue temple on the top was a beehive of people swarming in and out of the arched doorways.

What is going on? That many people were not usually up in the temple this time of day.

As a prickle of unease swept through me, I said a quick

prayer to Selu for our safety. For what I knew we'd face when we arrived. For what I *didn't* know.

The spectacle of our brides created a commotion as we walked. Whistles and lewd comments followed us as we trudged down the dusty lanes toward the Palace. Dagan, dressed as a trader, with thick kohl around his eyes, his beard streaked with gray, rings on his fingers, and a pouch around his waist to make him appear well fed, strode with confidence at the front of the line.

The Koru wore dejected expressions and hung their heads, giving some of the people of Alu the bravery to come up and grab hold of them, planting sloppy kisses on their ears or pressing their bodies against them.

"Stop it!" I yelled ferociously when one man grabbed Ummi's breast under her cloak, but Ummi nailed him so hard with her forehead, she snapped his nose. Blood gushed over his lips and down his chin while his friends laughed.

I reached forward to comfort Ummi, reminded of Uruku's rough paws on my own body, but her chin was firm. She glanced over her shoulder at the man who'd grabbed her.

"He's received his due."

"Not too much longer," I whispered as we passed by a man and his sons, who were running away from the Palace so fast, they didn't spare us a second glance.

And they weren't alone in their haste.

As we neared the city center and the huge sandstone Libbu wall, more and more people crowded the roads headed away, tugging their children's hands, expressions twisted in fear.

Screams resonated from inside the Libbu, and the unmistak-able clang of metal against metal rang out in the morning air.

Ahead of us, Dagan and the other trader stopped, and Dagan held up his big hand, turning toward the sounds.

Abandoning my post near the rear of the line, I trotted up to him. "What is it?" A clash followed by a scream made us all flinch. "What is *that?*"

"It's war, Kammani. Listen." His mouth went grim, and his left hand strayed to the daggers on his belt.

"Dear Selu." My hand flew to my throat. Because from where I stood, a few streets away from the Palace Libbu, peo-ple streaming past us, abandoning their belongings, their bas-kets for trade and begging, it suddenly dawned on me what I was hearing, too. Clangs of sicklesword against sicklesword. Shouts. Ragged shrieks. Ummi jogged up next to me, bringing Humusi and the other Koru with her, round eyes watchful.

"Ahh, A-zu," Ummi whispered, a glitter in her eye. "The war you were trying to avoid is upon us already. Higal must have beaten us here."

CHAPTER 20

—ɯ—

BEDLAM WAS WAITING for us in the dusty Libbu. Carts were overturned. Booths ripped to shreds, people screaming and sprinting in all directions. Assata climbed to the top of the Libbu wall, flanked by the heads of her dead husband, dead son, and all the other traitors to Uruku, and raised her fist up high with a cry that pierced the din.

The tradesman we'd hired dropped the Koru's ropes and fled back toward Laraak.

The warrior women who were on Higal's side, arrayed in their copper tunics and scorpion helmets, battled like lionesses on the hunt, swinging battle-axes and maces into the skulls of the guardsmen who were brave enough to challenge them. One warrior screamed, streaks of dirt on her face as she sliced through the abdomen of a guardsman. His mouth fell open in surprise as he caught his own guts in his hands.

Near the left, Nasu, his face spattered with blood, his

muscles straining as he swung his sicklesword, fought the guardsmen with whom he'd once been brothers.

I screamed, my hands over my ears, tears pricking my eyes. Dagan unsheathed his daggers.

"We must proceed, A-zu!" Ummi cried. "The battle has already begun. There is nothing left to do but help my sisters in war."

She cut herself out of her bridal tunic, and her armor glimmered as she plunged into the fray. Humusi and the other Koru shed their own disguises like snakeskin and followed closely behind, weapons drawn.

Dagan pushed me toward the entrance to the Libbu. "Get back to Laraak! Now!" he commanded, his whole body radiating with focused intensity.

Dagan's brothers Shep and Marduk, who must've gotten word of the battle, yelled as they parried through the clangs and curses, darting toward the rear of the Palace near the kitchens. Shep, baring his incisors like a dog, carried a sicklesword stolen from some guardsman, but Marduk carried only a mattock from the field on his bullish back.

"Dagan! What are they doing here! Where—"

"Go!" Dagan yelled, terrified, into my face. "I need to get them!"

I flung myself once around his neck, kissed him, and sprinted away, dodging screaming, starving people running for their own lives.

The Boatman was chasing us, his cavernous mouth open and ready to swallow us whole.

But I didn't run for Laraak. I ran for the corner of the Libbu near the well in a thicket of trees. I wouldn't abandon Dagan. Even if I had to watch him die. Even if I was forced to my knees and killed myself, I would not leave him behind.

Scrambling into the prickly weeds beneath the sycamores, I dropped onto my belly. My heart thrummed in my chest. My hands, underarms, forehead, and back were slick with sweat. I touched the healing satchel at my waist underneath the thick trader's cloak and covered my ears against the screams of war. Cursing. Shrieks of agony and rage from the Manzazu warriors and guardsmen who were viciously fighting right in front of me in the Libbu.

Humusi climbed to the top of the Libbu wall with a bow and arrow and fired at the guardsmen in range, knocking them down one by one. Time stood still as the horror rained down upon us. There was nothing more than clanging metal. Billowing smoke from a fire started near the Palace entrance. Crashing bodies and broken bones as both the nobility and poor were caught in the fury.

And where were Dagan and his brothers? They'd run toward the kitchens, our way *in* when we'd poisoned Uruku before. But though they might be able to get into the Palace, they'd never get Uruku. Not this way. He was likely already in hiding, scared off by the sounds of bloodshed.

Pulling myself up to follow them and warn them away, I gasped and slid back down to hide as a young man in rags thrust a dagger into the chest of a nobleman mere handsbreadths away. He collapsed, writhing amid the mayhem, a hand pressed against the blood. A rich man, covered in gore, snuck up behind the poor killer and swung at his neck with a gleaming sicklesword. The young man dodged the first swing, but the rich man was stronger and faster and ran him down, hacking off the poor man's head with several furious, bloody strokes.

Dropping my head into my arms, I sobbed among the screams of the dying. People were fighting a war they didn't even understand. There was no reason to kill that poor man and no reason to fight the nobility, either. They were *both* caught up in Uruku's madness. They should be working together to get Uruku off the throne! I wept and watched as a reserve of guardsmen, looking bigger and stronger than those who'd been in the Libbu before, poured from the Palace with a great war cry. They flooded the marketplace and the Manzazu army spread out, some scaling the walls to hurl spears, others fighting hand to hand. But the women were outnumbered by a lot. By *quite* a lot. Assata joined Humusi and fired arrows at the growing number of guardsmen.

Tightness gripped my chest as they fought relentlessly through their terror with bravery.

Yet, I lay in the scrub, cowering.

No. The word surged through me. I didn't have to lie here. Though I couldn't help those who had died, I could do *something* about those who still lived.

I pushed myself up from my belly with shaking arms to wobbly legs. Men, women, guardsmen, and a few Manzazu warriors lay strewn about like broken dolls beyond the safety of the weeds. Their legs were twisted beneath them. Their bodies seeped blood. With my hand, I stifled another sob rising in my throat. Others writhed in agony, hands pressed to gaping wounds.

The soft groans from some people lying farther down toward a more secluded area of the Libbu—away from the battle zone—compelled me from behind the tree with shaking, faltering steps. I ducked underneath the cracked branches, grasped the rough trunk of the tree to steady myself, and took a few tentative steps out into the open.

No one attacked.

My heart thudding, I ran as fast as I could around the side of the Palace to a man who lay near an overturned cart. He was a young guardsman. His helmet lay nearby, dented. A bright blue tunic woven with gold threads covered him from waist to knees. Beautiful leather sandals wound around his feet, which were splayed to the sides of his body. Somebody cared for him. Cared enough to make him these lovely clothes. His mother? A young wife, perhaps? Crouching down to assess his wounds, I studied his face. He was handsome. No more than sixteen or seventeen—my own years. My belly tightened involuntarily as he reached for me, agony twisting his face, pale with the loss of blood, which was seeping from a long laceration in his left arm.

"Please," he whispered.

"I'm here, I'm here," I crooned.

Just then, a woman's voice called to me, and I saw a pair of Manzazu sandals sticking out from behind an overturned cart. "Help me," she moaned.

But this boy needed me, too!

"Please, it hurts so bad," the young guardsman whispered.

"I'm here!" Using the blade I kept in my satchel, I cut off the long strap from his fine sandal and knotted it around his arm to stem the blood flow. He turned, groaning in pain, and I saw the deep gash on his back and the pool of black blood darkening the sand beneath him.

"*A-zu,*" the Manzazu warrior cried.

"I'm coming!"

My heart ached with pity for her. But this guardsman needed my help. Probably a cauterization, which I could not do at the moment. Carefully, I removed his breastplate and wedged it under his back while he writhed, pressing the metal against his skin to help stem the flow until I could assess the Manzazu warrior. I rifled through my healing satchel and found the poppy and tapped some into his mouth to help him drift off.

That will have to do for now.

My heart lurching, I left him and raced to help the warrior. I needed to at least see how bad she was. If she was fine, I could go back to the guardsman. At least pull him out of the dirt and the grime, build a fire, clean the wound, and cauterize to hold it until I could tend to him properly.

The woman lay sprawled, hair matted to her forehead, her

helmet near her feet. I dropped to my knees. Grasped her hand. Her grip was weak. I traced my finger along her arm for the beat of her bloodline. It was also weak. Slowing.

"Where does it hurt?" I whispered.

"Here." She swatted at her left side.

I laid her hand gently on her belly and shuffled to the wound. Dark, black blood covered the ground, and the laceration continued to gush.

She groaned and tried to push herself to her elbows.

"Stay still!" I cried. I needed a bandage. A cloth. Anything to stop the bleeding.

To my left, a corpse of a man lay, a war-stained tunic around his waist. *No.* Something else. I looked quickly to my left and right, hoping for a stray horse blanket or a bit of torn clothing. Anything I could grab that wouldn't put me in harm's way. The battle continued to rage from the other side of the Libbu. I looked back to the dead man. To the boy beyond him who desperately needed my help, too. Bile filled my throat when I knew what I must do.

"Hold on!" I smoothed her hair, then scurried over to the corpse, glancing around wildly, my nerves jangling. *Hurry! Hurry!* I ripped a portion of the tunic from his body, and screamed when his leg flopped against mine.

I raced back to the warrior, who was trying to speak.

"Shhh," I whispered. "Lie still."

With shaking hands, I tried to tear the tunic into a strip I could use.

"Please," she groaned.

"I'm sorry!" My chest tightened as I tugged the material. It was too tough! I put it to my teeth and tried to tear it again to form a bandage to stem the blood flow.

She pointed with trembling fingers beyond my shoulder. "Over there," she moaned.

I glanced up from my work. The battle drew closer. A band of figures clashed their weapons together with grunts and roars. The Manzazu warriors were fighting bravely, but there were so many guardsmen! There were women fighting two and three men at a time. A guttural cry of *Retreat!* in Higal's round Manzazu accent echoed off the walls.

"I must hurry," I told her frantically. "Why were you fighting under Higal, anyway? I had a plan to prevent this!"

Frustrated with myself for not being strong enough to tear the fabric, I balled the tunic up and pressed it against the gaping wound in her side.

She whimpered, tears brimming in deep-set eyes framed with thick lashes. "I needed to keep Manzazu safe. Higal said we must listen to our queen's command."

"It's okay." I smoothed the hair from her forehead. I licked my dry lips and looked back to the war, my heart hammering. "I need to stitch you up, all right?"

Rish's bloody stump swam in my mind. If I sewed her right there without cleansing the wound properly, she would die anyway, just later rather than sooner.

"I need to get some help to move you." I could grab Dagan and Shep and Marduk. We could get a cart and pull this warrior to safety.

She grabbed my arm, suddenly stronger. "Don't leave me." Her bright eyes begged.

"I must! Help is close by. I can't carry you alone." I pressed the tunic into her side, and her clammy hand against the tunic. "Keep this cloth here. It's important."

"A-zu, don't leave me!" she cried, looking after me in horror.

"I'll be right back with help. I *promise.*"

Tearing myself away from her, I crouched behind the cart. When I went to stand, coldness bathed me from head to toe, and the Boatman brushed against me, the young guardsman in the bright blue tunic cradled like a babe in his arms.

The boy met my eyes as he went past, raising a bloody hand as if to say goodbye.

❈❈❈

Get it together! Together, Kammani!

Near the kitchens where I'd seen Dagan and his brothers race, a low groan and a voice that sounded achingly familiar echoed from behind one of the massive ovens. Nobody else was about. The kitchens were abandoned as if they'd been left during preparations for the morning meal. Ducks lay partially plucked on tables, dull brown feathers spread all over the ground. Black smoke trailed from the ovens, rounds of bread burned to a crisp inside. Great casks of sikaru were spilled, flies buzzing above. I prayed to Selu that Dagan was safe. But that voice behind the ovens made my hair stand on end.

"Who's there?" a harsh voice, cracked with grief, echoed from behind one of the sandstone structures.

"You first!" I shouted, clutching the bodice of my trader robe. It could be *anyone*. A guardsman waiting to kill me!

"Arammu?" the man asked hoarsely.

Dagan. I ran with wild abandon toward his voice. He was sitting in the grass near the Palace entrance, Shep's bloody body in his arms. Marduk was nowhere to be found.

"Selu save us," I cried, running to them and throwing myself down. My hands fumbled in my healing satchel under my cloak for tinctures. Threads. Anything. "What happened?"

"A guardsman surprised us at the corner. He was lying in wait, prepared when we walked in. Shep was first inside, and the guardsman caught him in the neck with his sword."

His voice broke and great sobs racked his body, his shoulders shaking. "I couldn't stop him!"

"Let me see him, Dagan. Let me see him. I can do *something* to help. Where is he hurt?"

Dagan pulled Shep away from my fumbling hands. "No! He's gone, Kammani. Don't you see that? You're the A-zu!" His words lashed out like a horse whip against hide.

"Look at him!" he moaned.

He held his body up for me to see, and sobs immediately flooded over me, too. Because his life's artery in his neck had been severed. His face pale. Slack. Amber eyes, so much like Dagan's, wide open to the Netherworld. I gently prodded along his neck for his pulse, pressing and pressing to see if there was any chance of life inside, but Dagan was right. He was gone, gone, gone. Gone like my abum and ummum. Gone like my baby sister. Gone like Irra and Warad. Probably like half the Manzazu warriors right now.

"And Marduk?"

He wiped a hand down his face. "He saw Shep die, Kammani. He saw him die. And he ran to the farm to be with Qishti, who they said was hiding in my chamber under some of my ummum's quilts. I didn't stop him. I wanted him safe. The guardsman ran off, but for how long?"

"Let's go. Higal has called for retreat, but that doesn't mean she's going to give up. We need to leave so we can intercept whatever her plans are next and figure out what to do. This cannot happen again. We *must* stop this!"

"I'm not leaving him for the dogs. I'm not."

"We'll bring him! And bury him in Laraak."

His face shattered with grief, Dagan picked up his younger brother's broken body, grunting, and we crept around the side of the Libbu toward the west gate, where we could flee to Laraak.

As we passed the overturned cart where I'd tended the warrior, I gasped because I'd forgotten her when I'd found Dagan. But she was not there. There were smudges in the dirt—drag marks—as if she'd been pulled to safety by someone else.

But not sixty handsbreadths away, at the end of the trail, she lay in a pool of black blood with eyes that stared into the

Netherworld, the tunic I'd given her to stem the flow of blood abandoned nearby.

How tenuous was the thread that bound us to life. How easily it could be severed.

As we ran toward an abandoned cart outside the Libbu and hoisted Shep's body into the back, I wondered if she, Shep, and the young guardsman on the other side of the war were on the same boat to the Netherworld together.

CHAPTER 21

—⁓—

DUSK BURNED WITH the heat of a thousand fires, and most of it radiated from Dagan's skin. We stood at the outskirts of Laraak's encampment, Dagan and Nasu shouting at one another. The eight Koru brides, including Ummi and Humusi, sat with various degrees of injury on pallets inside my healing tent. Though they'd lived, many of those who'd chosen to follow Higal had not. After stitching and slinging as many of her warriors as I could, I healed these eight in my tent, with Nanaea, Arwia, and Kasha acting as my aids.

The rest of the Manzazu warriors who'd come to Laraak with us, who still stood with us, had made their camp closer to the river. They hadn't even known of the bloodshed until Ummi, a vicious laceration across her back, had ridden out to tell them. A small faction of warriors still believed in Higal and had made camp with her down the river. Ummi had tried to unite them, but for now, they were broken into two.

The fight outside intensified, Dagan yelling and Nasu replying sharply, "It was the better way."

"You're *obviously* wrong or we wouldn't be standing here right now!" Dagan connected his huge fist solidly with Nasu's jaw, sending Nasu's lanky body sprawling into the sand. He sprang up to his feet, his face twisted in rage, bumping up against Dagan's chest.

"I will *not* fight you, Farmer." Nasu jabbed his finger into Dagan's face, a trickle of blood from a split lip trailing down his chin. "In honor of your brother who had *no business in battle*, but if you hit me again, I will be forced. Do not test me."

Dagan shoved him backward. "He fought for *me*! And for his mother!"

"He should've never been in there! It isn't our fault!" Nasu threw up his hands.

"It is!" Dagan growled, throwing Nasu back down into the sand.

"Stop it!" I screamed. I yanked on Dagan's arm, but he was a man filled with Alani's fire. His eyes were wide with mournful anger, dark and menacing, and he shook me off him as if I were a fly.

This isn't him. This isn't my Dagan!

"Leave me, Kammani. I will deal with this guardsman who has *killed my brother!*"

Assata stepped in between Nasu and Dagan, one finger in Dagan's face. "If there is anyone who should be angry, it is *me*. My son is dead because you sat on your hands and waited to act."

"No," Dagan told her, his hands in fists. "Shep is dead because you and Higal and Nasu wrecked our plan. We *could have gotten* Uruku. We were at the Libbu. All we had to do is get inside." He pointed at her chest. "And because you were too impatient—"

"Too *foolish*," Arwia filled in from near the fire, her hands folded neatly in front of her, head held regally as if it already wore a crown.

"You didn't act as a head guardsman, Nasu. And you didn't act as a skilled warrior, Assata. Both of you plunged in thoughtlessly. And now we have dead Manzazu and dead family members. Neither of you considered the consequences of your actions. Your decisions were muddled by emotion— your loyalty to me, Nasu, and your grief, Assata. They distracted you from working together with Kammani and Dagan to come to the best solution. And now we all suffer."

Dagan clenched his fists at his sides. "Stand, Nasu! Your choice cost me my brother." His voice cracked on the last word. "And your actions could have cost me *everything* in this life, do you hear me?" He looked at Assata. "Kammani was in the Libbu in harm's way, and I couldn't protect her."

His shoulders heaved and he fought back tears. My big, steady Dagan was falling apart.

Assata pounded her fist into the palm of her hand. "I tried to save your ummum, Dagan. Do you not see that? I wasn't acting simply out of grief!"

Dagan's rage softened, fading to a quiet bleakness. His

voice was a whisper as his fists unclenched. "She is as good as dead anyway. She's likely *already* dead. There isn't a point to *any* of this. Rish is broken and Shep is gone, and I need to accept that my ummum is, too."

At that, he stalked toward his tent, shoulders bowed, and my heart went with him.

I peeked into my tent, where Ummi had lit several candles to brighten the twilight. Nanaea was crouched near the pallet, stitching a bloody slash across one of Humusi's knees.

"This laceration split back open, Kammani, so I'm fixing it." Nanaea poked the needle steadily into her skin and pulled the thread through, while Humusi sucked in a breath.

"Please tell me you took care to—"

"—sterilize the threads and the needle? I burned the needle and rubbed the threads in myrrh as you showed me. But I didn't believe it was clean, so I did it all again and scrubbed my hands with soap and doused them with sikaru to be sure." She pointed at her neat stitches, running perfectly in line. Better than my own.

My heart squeezed. So calm, so efficient. Who was this young woman she had suddenly become? She'd been busy costuming Arwia while we were gone. She said her idea would *ensure* the nin would be taken seriously when she made her claim to the ensis, but neither of them would tell me how they were going to make her appear to be a warrior when she was so small. According to Nanaea, I had to see it to believe it.

I glanced past Humusi and Nanaea to Rish where he lay

on one of my pallets, sleeping soundly, his silky curls spilled across his forehead. He clutched his stump to his chest in his sleep, but the bandage was clean. No blood. No seepage. He was *healing*.

And now to tend to Dagan.

Kasha squatted, grinding pokeroot into aloe with the mortar and pestle near the tent flap for someone who'd been burned with pitch. "Will you hand me my healing satchel? I want to give Dagan something to calm him."

"Sure." He reached behind him and pulled it up by the strap, then handed it to me. "I accidentally knocked into it and some of the bottles fell out, but I put them all back in and the rest of the ones in that bag over there, too." He pointed to a small sack that lay near my healing table, hidden underneath a pile of blankets. It was the sack that had held the gochala and the rest of the tinctures that Iltani had stolen from the merchant. I'd forgotten all about it!

"My thanks, Brother. Now focus on your task. I'll be back soon."

He bobbed his head and I left the tent, striding purposefully around Nasu and Arwia, who were both staring stonily at the fire. But I slowed my pace as I walked past Assata, gently squeezing her shoulder. She flinched, her eyes haunted by ghosts.

Dagan sat on a quilt in the corner of the tent in darkness, his head in his hands. His big shoulders shook with grief. Tears filled my eyes and love blazed through my chest as he sobbed. Quickly, I lit several candles, and knelt by him.

"Arammu, look at me. Look at me, at your Kammani. Please, my love."

I took his face in between my hands, but he was inconsolable, his grief cracking his spirit in half. "First Rish was hurt and now Shep is dead. He *can't* be."

Sitting next to him, I wrapped an arm around his shoulders as he wept, and tried to pour comfort from my heart to his, but nothing would give him solace. Eventually, though, he lay down on his side, and I stroked his hair, murmuring in his ear, found the chamomile oil in my healing satchel, and dabbed several drops on his tongue. Before long, his thick black lashes fluttered closed, and his even breathing told me he'd fallen into a fitful sleep.

Wearily, I eased away from him and returned the chamomile oil to my bag. As I tucked it into one of the pockets near the poppy, a strange red glass bottle nestled next to the laurel caught my eye. I pulled it out, and nearly burst from excitement.

The red bottle the Boatman had taken from his satchel.

It was *nerium!* My hands shook as I looked at it. Iltani must have picked it up when she'd knocked the merchant's table over, and Kasha had put it inside when he'd cleaned up.

I could use it! *But how?* I racked my brain, but Mudi's voice rang in my head. *Listen to your instincts. Trust.* I sat, thinking for a moment, trying to stay calm and let my gut take over, and an idea flickered to life.

Maybe we could make the *guardsmen* fall asleep with it, then get to Uruku with a few members of the Koru. I chewed my lip. We likely would never be even able to get into the Libbu again. They certainly knew someone was fighting for the throne, though whether they knew *we* were here was anyone's guess.

But what about *an ambush* when he was outside the Palace walls?

As I thought about it, running through the possibilities, my head swam, my eyes blurred, the sound of Dagan's soft breaths melted into the background, and I was once again on a rocking boat in the center of the river Garadun. Terror filled me to the brim, but I forced myself to look at the shore. I would not back away from this gift. I would *not* shrink in fear.

My hair whipping around my head, I searched the shoreline until I found him. The Boatman. He stood, dressed as a warrior that perhaps he once was, but in an explosion of light, he morphed. His sharp features broadened. His frame expanded into someone larger until the curve of his shoulder took on a shape I'd felt underneath my own hands. His face grew a short, scratchy beard I'd felt against my own neck. His eyes went from a black-brown to the amber color that reflected the love they held for me inside.

He morphed into . . . *Dagan.*

And beside him, at his elbow, someone who looked *exactly like me* stood, too. My healing satchel was at her waist. Her brown, curly hair blew in the breeze as she reached into her bag and pulled out a red glass bottle. The *nerium*! Her face grew delighted as if she'd made the most amazing discovery. But as she lifted her gaze to study me on the river, a line of worry grew in between her brows. Her hand went to her mouth, and she chewed her thumbnail like I did! She reached up and took Dagan's arm in hers, but he frowned and walked twenty paces away, ferocity on his brow. The girl's face twisted with terror as Dagan pulled his emerald dagger from its scabbard and aimed it at her. As fear squirmed inside my chest, I watched, horrified, as Dagan threw the blade with all of his might.

At her.

At *me*.

The dagger plunged into my neck with shocking force, and blood spurted into my hands. I crumpled immediately on the shore, but felt my own knees giving way on the boat, too. Suddenly, my vision was blurred and something warm was pulsing down my neck onto my tunic, and when I looked down, Dagan's dagger was sunk to the hilt in my throat.

Dagan stood on the riverbank, anguish and horror scrawled across his face, but as the world went dark, he shifted back into the Boatman, and a single sentence exited the Boatman's mouth in a cry that seemed to come from the depths of the watery graves over which I was floating:

"*Beware.*"

※※※

"Kammani—wake. Arammu? Wake. Please."

Dagan's tear-streaked face hovered over me as I spluttered out of my vision. As I pushed away, the horror that he'd thrown his dagger at me knocked the wind from my lungs, and the small red bottle fell from my hands.

"Get away from me! Don't hurt me!" I cried. Cowering, I crawled, knees, hands, knees—*faster!*—to the corner of the tent, my heart hammering as I got my bearings.

"I never would! What do you mean?" He stretched one hand out to me. The other went over his heart. "I would never *hurt* you. I love you!"

Clawing at my throat, I searched for the dagger that had been embedded, but it was nowhere near me. It was safe, in Dagan's scabbard where it always was. My stomach churned, bile rising to my throat.

"You fell," Dagan said simply, letting his hands drop to his lap. "You fell over and woke me, but you were screaming and clutching your throat." His anguished amber eyes searched my face. "Do you think I would ever hurt you? Because I would rather die than cause you pain." He flexed his hands open and closed into fists.

I felt my throat. *I am safe. Nothing is wrong. It was a dream. A vivid one, yes. But a dream nevertheless.*

But what if it wasn't?

What if it was . . . a *message?*

Breathing in through my nose and out through my mouth, I calmed myself, considering the possibility. The *distinct* possibility.

I hadn't listened to my instincts before, and Warad had died and Iltani had been stolen. Rish's arm severed. Maybe it was time to bear heed to my gut, no matter what my brain told me to do. My *gut* felt as if the message was clear. It felt true. Real. As real as the nose on my face. The digging of the blanket into my knees.

My voice shaking, I held out my hand. "Give me your dagger."

"Why, Arammu?" His eyebrows came together in confusion.

"Because I need it," I squeaked. I held my hand out again. "Please."

He pursed his lips and thought about it, but gently pulled it from his waist and looked at it in his hands. It was encrusted with emeralds. Sharp. Gleaming with danger. "Why do you want it?"

"Because the Boatman warned me that one day you would kill me with it, Dagan." I forced my chin up, though my hands shook. "And I haven't been listening to my gut, and maybe this is what I should've been doing all along. Listening to the Boatman. I don't know why he sent me a message or what is going on, but he did! Again! He tried to reach me in the tent with Rish. Broke through, but I pushed him away. He held a bottle in his hands, and I think we must use it somehow. Mudi told me he's trying to earn his way out of his post by helping me save lives and that I should listen to him! And just now, he showed me that dagger embedded in my throat. Maybe he's trying to save my life, too, so I can help others." I laid my hand flat, fighting the nausea rising in my belly at asking it of him. At not believing in Dagan. "So please, hand it over."

"You'd leave me defenseless."

"You have another dagger in your belt."

He blinked, his other hand straying to his backup blade, and tossed the emerald dagger to my side. Raw hurt and a flicker of grief crossed his face, and his shoulders slumped. "You must think little of me if you believe I could ever hurt you." He swallowed roughly. "You must not trust me. I know you have been through a lot in your life, Kammani, but I never thought you could ever think me so callous as to *harm* you."

At that, my heart tugged inside me. Picking the dagger up, I ran my fingers over the hilt, still warm from its proximity to Dagan's body. It was heavier than it looked. He'd have only one dagger to protect him, but nothing at which he was so skilled a marksman with. I'd never seen him without this one in any kind of situation. He threw this one at targets on the outbuildings. Had killed wild lions and wolves who'd tried to get his sheep in Alu. If Nasu should retaliate for his threats, or if Higal should call the Manzazu warriors still loyal to her to attack, he'd be left without his primary way of keeping himself alive.

My gut told me to keep the dagger far, far away.

But my heart said to give it back.

"Dagan?" Trembling, I offered the dagger to him.

He glanced at the weapon in my hand as if it were a snake.

"I trust you. I swear."

After a moment, he squatted in front of me and took it.

"Arammu." His voice was husky, his amber eyes anguished. "What have I possibly done to make you feel so threatened?"

"It wasn't you. It was the dream about the Boatman and—it scared me."

I didn't know what to believe. The strange visions from the Boatman that were difficult to interpret, or the tug of my heart. Could both be right? Could Dagan actually harm me without intending to? I couldn't be sure, but I did know, and could feel, the earnestness radiating from Dagan as strongly as I could feel my attention being pulled toward the little red bottle of nerium that had rolled out of my grasp.

It lay in the corner of the tent, winking in the candlelight, calling to me. Maybe there really was someone out there in the darkness, saying my name, trying to help me save lives so he could escape his fate. Maybe my heart *and* my gut were right.

Crawling forward, I picked up the bottle, and felt inside my bones, that it was important, especially to *me*.

"What is that?" Dagan tucked his dagger back into his belt.

"I think it's a tincture that is supposed to save us."

"How?"

"I honestly do not know." I sat with it in my hand, weighing the contents.

At once, the tent flaps were thrown back and my dearest friend in all the world stepped inside the tent, her face a little less glib than it usually was, a little less carefree. But her eyes were as fiery as ever. Maybe more so.

"Your war killed many guardsmen, my friend, but not the one who mattered most. My dearest husband, Gala, still lives." Iltani tossed her hair over her shoulder. "You should be spanked by a long, splintered broomstick for that mistake."

"Iltani!" I stood and hugged her until she squirmed. "Has he touched you?" I murmured into her hair.

"No. He tried. But in his sickened state"—she pulled away, grinning wickedly—"he was unable."

Dagan spoke. "But Gala could make you stand trial if you flee from him."

She waved her hand at Dagan, some of her carefree attitude hanging on to the surface of her, but I knew better. Her eyes were haunted as they'd never been before.

"Do you think me so foolish as to endure the threat of his bed, and the violent sounds of his retching now that he's been incapacitated, and escape with no good plan? Come now, Dagan. You should know me better than that. I'm here because I've been given leave of my dear husband for the evening while he helps with the wounded guardsmen and tries to keep his own bowels inside his body. He knows I'm your friend and says we should have you all over to dine one day."

She snorted. "He's the only guardsman as far as I can tell who knows that Arwia escaped the tomb, however. Most of them believe that a band of female warriors are trying to overtake the throne so *Assata* can rule. They still think Arwia is dead. That's the rumor that Uruku has spread."

"Good. Better they're confused." I hugged her again, relieved that she'd been spared his proximity this night at least. "While you're here, do you have any thoughts as to how we could use this?" I held the red bottle of nerium out to her.

"What is it?" She pulled the bottle from my hand and studied it.

"The nerium you stole from that merchant woman. It slows the heart, making people unconscious so as to appear dead. But it has to be ingested or be put directly into the blood."

She thought for a moment, shaking the nerium powder. Then her eyes lit up. "I have an idea."

Dagan's amber eyes, still swollen from grief, looked at her from under his heavy brow. "By all means let us hear it, Iltani, for life isn't making much sense anymore."

"I can't promise it'll make any sense, but it involves a little nakedness and maybe some idiocy provided by the man who lives in my house."

"That sounds . . . ridiculous. But I trust your instincts." I squeezed her hand.

Iltani looked down at me quizzically. "You trust my *instincts*? I'm sorry, is your name Kammani? Where is my friend who only trusts in cold, hard, unrelenting *facts*, which, by the way, are inaccurate half of the time? Can you find her for me? There's a usurper here, trying to bed this delicious man of hers."

I rolled my eyes. She wasn't trying to be mean. She was blunter than she needed to be, but honest nevertheless.

"Not anymore, my friend. My heart will guide me for the rest of my days."

She raised an eyebrow. "Should we put a wager on that?"

I smiled benignly. "Wait and see."

CHAPTER 22

THE SIKARU IN the jug sloshed as I, along with Dagan, Iltani, Humusi, and another Koru warrior named Taram, stopped next to a low, crumbling wall in the bushes. Commander Ummi had told me she would come to protect us, but I'd asked her if she'd try to unite Higal's troops with hers instead, so Arwia could be escorted in victoriously. She said she'd do everything in her power, but that she could make no promises.

We were well fed, well watered, and disguised in dark cloaks to blend in with the dense olive grove flanking the path that led from the Palace to the royal bathhouse. A tributary wending throughout the grove and underneath the squat sandstone structure gurgled as we stooped below the brush line.

My robe was bulky as I knelt in the dirt, my healing satchel twisted underneath. Nanaea had thrown long cloaks over

Higal and Taram to disguise their weaponry, but the clanking under their getup was loud enough to wake Alani and pull her from the depths of the Netherworld.

The aftermath of Higal's failed coup had left the Libbu and portions of the city near the Palace in shambles. Carts overturned. Market tents ripped apart. Flies buzzing over the bodies of the dead that had been stockpiled like sunbaked bricks near the east Libbu wall. Someone had half-heartedly draped a swath of linen over a few of them, but many of their bloodied faces were exposed to the night air.

The crows that pecked at their eyes.

The Manzazu warriors who had fallen had been piled into the back of a funereal cart, which would be taken outside the city and burned. Humusi and Taram had both vowed retribution for the slight.

The people whom we'd passed to get to our current destination in the wee hours of the night—some stumbling home in various states of drunkenness, others walking with weapons drawn and wary eyes—hadn't seemed to mind our presence, as it was likely they were up to no good as well. A poor, starved family had scuttled behind us, their meager belongings stuffed into packs on their backs, big-eyed children in tow. They were headed toward Gala's gate, apparently hoping to escape Uruku's rule and brave the unknown to make a new home elsewhere.

"It's heavy, Iltani. Are you sure?" Dagan set the jug down, his voice lowered to a whisper.

"How heavy can it be?" She hefted the jug up with a grunt

and positioned it on her hip. "It'll be fine. I've carried far heavier burdens than this."

She's carrying a heavier burden than this right now.

I'd told her of Shep's death after our conversation in the tent, and she'd walked away from me and Dagan to sit underneath a tree. Her weeping could be heard over the soft sounds of the merchants settling in for the night, but when I'd tried to approach her, she'd ordered me away. When she'd pulled herself together, she'd been more determined than ever to enact our scheme.

I glanced past her to Gala standing with other guardsmen off in the distance, the torches on the outside of the bathhouse illuminating his green face. A grimace twisted his features. Apparently, his "ailment" hadn't improved.

Iltani tugged her tunic down, exposing more of her cleavage, pasted on a smile, and looked over her shoulder at me with a wink. "I'll have them eating the nerium directly out of my hand if the brew doesn't work."

The jug of sikaru on her hip, she tossed her head and sashayed slowly toward the group of guardsmen who were standing at attention near the entrance.

"Husband!" she cried when she was well away from us.

Gala weakly answered, then gasped and clutched his belly. The men around him laughed.

"I feel bad giving him the nerium. He would have helped us if he'd known what we were up to." Dagan's lips were pinched as if in pain.

Taram, Humusi, and I all stared at him with baleful eyes.

"Funny. I don't feel bad about it at all."

Not about Gala. But I did about Dagan. His shoulders, always so strong and straight, sagged forward, Shep's death weighing heavy on them. Even my doubt in him had wounded him deeply. When he smiled, it didn't reach his eyes. I ached for the ease that he usually carried around. Would he ever get it back? Or would what we'd been through and were still going through haunt him for the rest of his life?

Iltani sauntered up to the guardsmen, hips swaying, shoulders thrown back, a move that had to be costing her. But it was probably a bittersweet moment, since revenge was to be hers if they took the bait. I'd added enough nerium to the jug of sikaru to knock out six men, and since there were only four on guard outside the hidden bathhouse, I figured we'd be safe. Gala attempted to take the jug from her, but he couldn't lift it, so another guardsman stepped in. She hugged him in thanks, the sign that she was fine and we were to move.

"Let's go. She's there," I whispered, and we crept agonizingly slowly closer to the bathhouse, hidden among the trees. From somewhere above, an owl hooted plaintively as we slunk like dogs, our steps watchful of stepping on a branch. Every soft clank of the Koru's armor caused us to freeze, panting, nervously awaiting our discovery.

When we arrived a mere hundred or so handsbreadths from the back of the building, we sat on our haunches and waited. I longed to see what Iltani was doing, but she was out of my line of sight. The chirps and chirrs of insects calling to their mates and Iltani's far-off high-pitched laughter were the only sounds eviscerating the full belly of the night. Stars were scattered over the bits of the jasper sky we could see between the jagged branches of the sycamores.

Iltani's conversation grew in frivolity, the men hooting and laughing, and we stared at one another in silence, all of us contemplating our own worries.

"He'd better be in there," Dagan whispered.

Gala had told Iltani that Uruku bathed in the bathhouse we now crouched behind to attempt to heal his piercing headaches with the steam, and that Gala himself escorted him there almost nightly.

"There is a reason there are four guardsmen outside this bathhouse." I willed calmness into my bones, resisting the urge to chew the rest of my thumbnail off my hand. It was worn down to a nub at this point. "I'm remaining hopeful." I ran my fingers over Dagan's arm. "Do you think the ensis will come through?"

He shifted back on his heels. Stared at his hands. "Ensi Puzu told me he'd convince them, but I suppose we'll see. I'm having trouble believing in anyone right now."

Moonlight fell over Dagan's noble features, illuminating the grief in his eyes. I rubbed his knee. "It will be all right."

He offered me a half smile. "I'm just wondering about Gudanna."

"We'll have to find her later. She has no power once Uruku is off the throne anyway, since she wasn't born to reign."

Humusi spoke softly, her round eyes watchful. She was even jumpier than usual, fidgeting with her bracers. Touching her battle-axes over and over again. "So the guardsmen fall asleep, and we go inside the bathhouse and secure Uruku. We question him about Shiptu's whereabouts, and then kill him. Then we ride to Laraak to gather the rest of our army. When the day breaks, Ummi leads the warriors in with Arwia at the forefront to claim the throne."

My knee bobbed. "Yes, that is the plan."

When she put it that way, it seemed too easy. Much too easy. But there were so many people involved. So many things that could go wrong. We didn't have time to wait any longer, though. If Ummi failed to unite the Manzazu army, Higal's troops would try again, bloodshed on their minds. Either that, or Sarratum Tabni would hear of their failed coup and would send reinforcements. We had to act, *now*.

After what seemed to be a full hour, the laughter of the men died away and Iltani peeked through the brush like a wraith, a wicked gleam in her eye. "They're all asleep like fat babies after they've drunk their mother's milk. Let's go!"

"They all drank the brew?" We stood and slunk toward the bathhouse. "Each one of them? Even Gala?"

"I made it a game and they were all too enamored with Gala's 'fiery little wife' to turn me down. The idiots. Come on. They'll be awake soon enough."

We crept around the wall, darting as quickly as we could to the entryway of the bathhouse where the guardsmen once stood. All four were in a deep slumber at the doorway, a look of death heavy on their features, two of them with their eyes wide open, staring into the Netherworld.

Maybe I mixed too much?

I stooped, feeling along their throats for that unmistakable surge of blood in their veins. They were alive, though Gala's pulse pounded wildly. We dragged two of them behind some potted tamarisk trees, but propped Gala up at the doorway as if he'd simply fallen asleep at his job, in case anyone came by. Iltani kicked him over, hard, and Dagan pulled him back up, a look of consternation on his face. As we crept into the shadowy interior of the sandstone building, the air was noticeably more humid inside. The feel of the Boatman's riverboat beneath my feet came back into mind as a draft of salty, wet air washed over me.

We ducked into a side room stacked high with bolts of cloths for drying, baskets of Aleppo soaps, eucalyptus fronds, and rose-scented oils. Moonlight glowed through the square window to the right. Taram and Humusi carefully took off their tunics to reveal their breastplates and scaled capes. Their eyes were watchful. Wary. Taram drew a dagger and a battle-ax from her arsenal, and rotated the ax with quick, calculated flicks of her wrist. She looked skilled. Dangerous. Like death personified. Humusi drew a short dagger and a mace from her belt, and the effect of her muscles pulling taut beneath her shoulders as she tightened her grip on each and grinned, her bright smile shining through the gloom, was enough to make all the hair stand to attention on my head.

Tucking the herb knife from my satchel into my waistband, I warily eyeballed Dagan as he unsheathed both daggers from his waist and moved into the corridor, and down a dark, curved hallway that seemed to lead to the main bath-house chamber. Iltani pulled her blade from the band around her thigh as Dagan held a dagger to his full lips, shushing us, and we crept slowly toward what we could only hope was Uruku. Iltani and I stayed close behind him with Taram and Humusi following, weapons chinking softly.

As we rounded the corridor into the main breezeway, two guardsmen stood, flanking a thick, heavy door upon which the lion and blooms crest of Lugal Marus was carved. Torches crested the wall.

One pockmarked, the other as wide as Dagan, the guards-men flinched in surprise as we filed into the breezeway. But Taram and Humusi were on them before they could even draw their weapons.

With stealth and efficiency, they slit the men's throats with their daggers and had their bodies dragged away to the side of the room before I could even open my mouth to protest.

"Dear Selu!" I hissed.

I walked to the men and knelt, as they spasmed, gasping through their severed windpipes.

"Did you have to kill them? They were just doing their *jobs*! We could have tied them up until we got Uruku!"

"Yeah, well." Iltani grinned malevolently. "Now they can do it for Alani in the Netherworld."

"You could have just put them to sleep." I stared hard at the warriors.

"Too much of a risk, A-zu," Humusi said.

Sickened, I dug into my satchel and found the nerium,

then dabbed a little on each of their tongues so they wouldn't suffer as they met the Boatman. I knelt there as they stilled, then tore my eyes away as I stood, bile rising in my throat. It wasn't right. But I was on this path and could not get off it. I'd chosen to align myself with bloodshed.

The warriors nodded to Dagan. His face grim, he took a torch from the wall as Humusi held up three fingers. Then she dropped to two. Then one. And when the final finger dropped into a fist, Dagan flung open the door and Taram and Humusi charged in, weapons drawn, bellowing like beasts. A woman screamed, and Dagan slipped inside with the torch and one of his daggers.

"*Get up get up get up get up!*" Humusi commanded.

"Leave me alone!" the woman cried. "Guardsmen!"

It was *Gudanna*! But where was Uruku?

There was scuffling, water splashing, shocked grunts, and a massive sploosh as something fell into the bath. But eventually, Gudanna was dragged, sopping wet, out of the bathing room, her belly bulging in the bolt of linen haphazardly draped around her. Scars wrapped up from her abdomen, around her throat and chin, from the fire that had killed her family so long ago. Her ankles were swollen and face puffy from being with child.

"Where is Uruku?" Dagan asked Gudanna as he exited the room dripping wet, discarding the snuffed torch to the side as he walked around to face her. His voice was low. Menacing. Darker than I'd ever heard it.

Humusi and Taram pulled Gudanna tight on either

side and wrestled her up closer to Dagan. I fought the urge to shrink away from the air of violence heavy in the humid chamber.

"He's not here." Gudanna's lip curled up, twisting at one corner from the scars. Her hair was plastered to the sides of her face, framing bright, intelligent eyes flashing with indignation. "He did not want to come today. Said he felt the presence of Alani, and now we know why."

Dagan stepped forward and pressed his emerald dagger to her throat. She tried to tug away, but the warriors held her firmly.

"It is no matter," Dagan said. "Tell us where he is! NOW!"

She sneered. "I *knew* you'd come back to save your mother, Farmer. You're too senseless and weak to do otherwise."

Dagan stood taller, his lip curling with unmitigated rage. "Tell us where he is, woman, or I'll cut out your heart."

At that, Gudanna's face twisted with interest up at him. "Liar," she challenged.

Dagan gritted his teeth and sliced down her bare arm in a jagged cut. She gasped as blood began seeping from the wound and rolling down her arm.

"For the sake of Selu, Dagan!" I yelled, but he was not listening to me.

"Where. Is. Your. Evil. Husband!" He held the dagger directly in front of her right eye, shaking with rage, and for a moment, Gudanna looked afraid. Truly afraid.

"He's in the Palace. In our chambers."

"Then take us to him." Dagan clenched his jaw.

"Yes! Good idea," I told him, my heart nearly bursting with nerves. "*She* can escort us into the Palace and tell the guardsmen to stand down or—"

"Or what? You'll kill me? Ha!" She sneered. "You need me alive to get to my husband."

"But we don't need that brat in your womb," Iltani said, her eyes lit with malice. "Kammani is a healer and she can cut that kid right out of you if you don't do what we say."

Gudanna's face went white. She looked at me. "You wouldn't let that happen. I *know* it. That isn't in you."

Iltani continued. "You have no idea the level of death and destruction in this girl's heart. Yes, she would! So you will lead us safely into the Palace and tell the guardsmen to stand down. *Now choose!* Your husband or your child!"

"What a terrible choice to have to make," a voice echoed from the narrow hallway.

We turned around to see Uruku emerge, weakened with poison even more, it seemed, his face yellowish, wan, eyes sunk in his head. He was flanked by two burly guardsmen holding spears. But before anyone could react, those spears shot through the breezeway and landed squarely in the bellies of both Taram and Humusi, below their breastplates. The warriors fell to their knees, blood oozing from around their wounds, and Gudanna fled to her husband.

Dagan and Iltani both charged Uruku, daggers drawn.

"Secure them!" Uruku bellowed, and one of his guardsmen—a big, hulking man—was on Dagan in a flash, tying his hands with rope. Dagan thrashed, knocked the guardsman in the mouth, then received a headbutt in exchange. He growled and tried to rip his hands free. The other guardsman punched Iltani in the jaw and she screamed in rage, her blade clattering down the dark corridor. He snatched my dagger from my hand before I could conceal it.

"Run away!" Dagan yelled to me, eyes wild as he thrashed against his restraints, but I immediately fumbled over to Humusi, tripping on my own feet, slipping in her blood. I pressed my right hand against her abdomen, trying to staunch the flow. She twisted and lurched, moaning in pain, and fell backward at an awkward angle with a groan, eyes in torment, gory hands weakly tugging at the weapon.

"A-zu!" she gurgled as blood bubbled up into her mouth.

"No!" I screamed, but a guardsman hoisted me up and away from her. Iltani attacked again, clawing at his face, but he knocked her to the floor once more with an elbow to the side of her head.

The guardsmen pulled me and Dagan to stand in front of Uruku while the Koru warriors groaned in the background.

A sob in my throat, I stared hard at Gudanna.

She looked up at her husband. "Ahh, love, but you know I'd never choose anyone over you, even this child."

With something like softness in his eyes, Uruku looked down at Gudanna and planted a kiss on her forehead, his face pale with pain. "Well, you don't have to make that decision now."

"Please." I desperately tried to claw out of the guardsmen's hold. "We only want Shiptu and we'll be gone forever. Please."

Gudanna smiled. "I understand wanting something you can't have. My children, burning alive in the hut while I was on the other side of the city, still cry for me in my dreams. Your abum failed them, and they still scream my name when I close my eyes. But I can't have them back any more than you can have what you want."

She stepped forward, her eyes glittering. She smiled at me once, ran a finger down the smoothness of my cheek, authority in the tilt of her chin, her belly protruding out and hanging low in such a way that I knew, as any good healer did, her time to deliver was drawing nigh.

"They must be questioned about Arwia, my lord. And if they give her to us, maybe we will free them." She looked over her shoulder at him, and he tilted his head, studying us as if we were bugs.

"Or perhaps"—he winced with the pain his words were costing him—"if they do not give her to us, we will cut off their heads."

They dragged us out of the bathhouse and around the splayed feet of the guardsmen still lying like corpses. But as we wended around their prone bodies, a muffled note of surprise broke from Iltani's mouth. Because there were only three men lying there.

Gala was no longer propped against the doorjamb.

He was *missing*, and apparently not as lovesick as Iltani believed.

CHAPTER 23

LESS THAN ONE year ago, I stood on this same carpeting in the extravagant throne room, marveling at the softness beneath my toes. The gurgling water in the fountains. The beautiful tapestries and murals adorning the walls.

The torches hanging on either side of the thrones looked different this evening than they used to. They were off-kilter in their sconces, splashing ragged, twisted shadows across the sandstone walls. Illuminating the bloodstains on the rugs from past punishments.

People had gone with the Boatman in this room.

Evil lived in this place.

Gudanna sat on Arwia's old throne in a soft blue tunic, her swollen ankles encircled with copper bells. A heavy lapis lazuli headdress with gold rosettes sat atop her hair, and her dark eyes had been outlined with kohl. Her belly sat on her lap, and faint rings of sweat darkened her tunic under her armpits. I watched her for any signs of distress that her baby was trying to descend from its wicked mother's womb, but outside of a faint grimace that could mean everything or nothing at all, she was still.

Uruku sat on the central throne—the one reserved for the lugal—his hair slicked away from his sickly face, the bronze headdress hammered with the lion and blooms of Lugal Marus. He hadn't even bothered to change the emblem, perhaps recognizing on some lower level of his baser self that he was usurping a city-state that did not rightfully belong to him.

Dagan stood on my right, his nose bloodied, eyes bruised, back lashed in stripes. He'd been beaten in the dungeons, where we'd been hung against the wall for many hours to try to get me to talk. They'd end the torture if I told them where Arwia was. They'd end his suffering. Dagan's eyes had found mine again and again, and through each strangled cry that came out of his mouth, he'd told me to hold firm. Not to speak. He could bear it. I'd cried in agony for him, but it was less pain than knowing that Dagan, whom I loved with all that I had in me, who wanted my hand more than anything in this world, was hurting.

Iltani was about to be whipped for trying to poison Gala, but he had begged his senior guardsmen not to lay a hand on her, citing "an illness of the mind." But since he'd taken the afront personally, he'd agreed to let them shave her head.

Through the door of our dungeon, he'd told us he would have been willing to help if we'd let him in on our plans. He'd suspected something was off with Iltani since she was so nice to him, and he'd faked drinking the brew and run away in case she was planning to kill him. He *knew* she was unhappy. And then, when Iltani had said she'd wanted a hug, he'd come into the cell and embraced her, and she'd practically torn off his ear with her teeth.

Now she stood next to me, her shoulders thrown back in defiance, head shaved, looking like a cat that had been bested in a street fight.

"Where is she?" Gudanna's voice echoed from the throne.

"Who?" Iltani said belligerently, and was immediately knocked to the floor by a swift backhand from one of the guards. Where were the pitiful child guards? It seemed as though Uruku kept the strongest around him, and left the smaller, younger guardsmen to battle outside threats, his own people be damned.

"I'll ask one more time. Where *is* she?"

"We do not know," Dagan wheezed, holding his likely cracked ribs. "The last we heard, as we . . . repeatedly said . . . ," he panted, "she'd been taken to wife and died in childbirth."

In one swift motion, Uruku stood to his feet. "LIES!" he yelled, wincing in pain. Angrily, he gestured toward the corridor, holding a knuckle to his temple. "Bring them out!"

Bring *who* out?

A rattling of chains and a scuffling noise, followed by a low moan, echoed from the corridor. Three bedraggled figures were tugged from the depths, their torsos and heads stuffed in linen sacks. A man and two women, judging from their bodies. Guardsmen standing nearby yanked the sacks from their heads, uncovering Shiptu, whose bones jutted from the tunic as if she'd been starved, and two people I was *not* expecting to see:

Nasu and Assata.

"Ummum!" Dagan strained against the ropes they'd tied around his body.

Shiptu gave Dagan a brave stare despite her thinness. Despite the fact that two of her teeth had been knocked out. "I am here, my child. Where are your brothers?" Her chin bunched with unshed tears, but she recovered. "Are they well? Have they been harmed?"

Dagan's voice went hoarse. "They are all well, Ummum. Well and whole."

Could she hear the falseness as I could?

Rish was not whole, and poor Shep was gone to the Netherworld.

My stomach dropped when she closed her eyes and said a prayer of thanks to Selu, clasping her tied hands in front of her mouth. She was wearing a filthy tunic and her feet were bare. Her hair was matted, but aside from the missing teeth, she didn't look as though she'd been beaten.

But it was not the same for Nasu and Assata. *And why are they even here?*

Nasu didn't look good. He had been whipped bloody,

matching Dagan stripe for stripe. His lashes wrapped around his shoulders in jagged red welts, even extending up across his jaw. But he wore defiance like a crown, jaw set, eyes hard, feet resolute.

Assata, on the other hand, looked strange. Almost as if she were severely injured, but . . . off. She limped and moaned, holding her hip, but if she were really injured on that side, she'd be limping the *other* way.

As I studied her, she caught my eye. And when she did, one eye closed in a wink so brief, I wouldn't have caught it if I weren't paying attention.

She is faking her injury.

But why?

Gudanna gestured to Nasu. "This one and the tavern wench were attempting a coup with several young women dressed as warriors, similar to the ones we found with you. The women killed some of our best guardsmen, but though a few of them escaped, the rest were dispatched to the Netherworld."

My eyes welled as Gudanna prattled on, oblivious to the pain she was continuously bestowing upon us. "The tale this traitor guardsman spins about Nin Arwia is different than yours. He claims no knowledge of her current whereabouts, indicating she is alive. You've stated she died in childbirth. Who tells the truth?"

"The nin is likely dead!" Nasu's voice was strained. "I didn't know!"

Uruku frowned. He pivoted on one heel, taking in Dagan's sagging, bloodied body with his shrewd eyes.

"I believe you to be more sensible than this blubbering twit behind me, Farmer. And if not you, your healer." He waved in Iltani's general direction. "Or whoever she is."

Gudanna hoisted herself from her throne, her center of gravity off due to the growing baby. Holding her belly with one hand, she descended the stairs and walked toward us. Uruku weakly walked over to assist her. They stopped a few handsbreadths away.

"We know she is alive and wants to take over the city." Gudanna pointed her finger at my chest. "Healer's Daughter, if you have any good sense about you, tell us where she is or we will add Shiptu's head to our collection on the wall."

"I don't know." I met her eyes with the lie, hoping she'd buy what I was selling. "I swear it."

Uruku waved her away with a thin arm. "No, no, no, we won't add her head to the wall. It doesn't do any good. We need the *nin*, which requires more *finesse*. Nobody cares about death by decapitation. It needs to be more personal." Uruku's eyes, too close together, focused narrowly on me. "Besides, what would be the sport in a quick dispatch? We will have a Trial of Ordeal and let the gods decide which one of them is telling the truth."

He tipped his head after he said it, as if he were simply suggesting the obvious. We're tired, so we should sleep. We're dirty, so we should bathe. As if he weren't about to punch the wind from my lungs. Knock the legs out from underneath us all.

"A Trial of Ordeal?" Dagan strained against his ropes, his

face twisting in pain. "That's for criminals who've said"—he gasped—"they didn't commit the crime of which they're accused. We haven't been accused of a crime!"

Gudanna held her belly and grimaced. "Yes, you have. You're accused of lying to a ruler about the whereabouts of that brat Arwia. But if you tell the truth, that the nin really is dead, you won't die in the trial. Selu will save you." She looked up into Uruku's sickly face. "So which should we choose? The drowning?"

I closed my eyes. The drowning trial meant that we would be tossed into the river Garadun with our arms and legs bound. If we were able to keep ourselves afloat for a day, we'd prove our innocence and be rescued. But if we drowned, it proved our guilt. Nobody was ever proven innocent in that trial.

"No." Gudanna's hand absently rubbed her abdomen as she argued with herself, and a line appeared between her brows. *The beginning of labor?* "I think not. I should think two strong young men like the farmer and the guardsman over there should have a better trial than that. One that utilizes their strength."

Uruku's sunken face brightened. "Indeed, wife. You're correct, as always. We should have them battle in the Pit."

"Battle what? Lions? Tigers?" Gudanna rubbed her belly, looking around the cavernous throne room as if drawing inspiration from the nature scenes painted on the ceiling and walls.

From the corner, Nasu barked a note of surprise as Assata

stumbled against him. He made a move as if to try to catch her with his tied hands, but she crumpled in a heap. She raised her head, appearing to be woozy, and scrabbled against the wall as if trying to get up.

Shiptu stared down at her in despair.

Uruku and Gudanna contemplated the situation; then Uruku pointed to one of the guardsmen near Assata. "Take her out back and finish her. She's been as useful as she can be."

My heart sank as they dragged her away, kicking and biting, and I gritted my teeth at my inability to save her or us or anyone else. I was completely useless.

Uruku stuck his hands on his lean hips, going back to the question at hand as if sending someone to their ancestors wasn't anything more than a nuisance.

"No, not tigers or lions, my sarratum. I think it best that they battle each other, don't you? The guardsman and the farmer, fighting to demonstrate who is honest and who is not? These two here"—he pointed to Iltani and me—"can watch with us. Perhaps when they see that one of their own has been slaughtered by another friend's hands, they'll cooperate."

"We won't do it." Nasu, like Dagan, strained against his chains. "I'll never fight him."

"Yes, you will." Uruku smiled almost gleefully, turning away from the three of us. "For every minute you do not fight, I'll cut off a finger from one of these two young women."

Iltani raged, the veins in her neck standing out against her skin. "You absolute piece of sheep manure. *You call yourself a lugal?*" She was backhanded to the carpet, yet again, by the guardsman's heavy paw. She got up on her knees, her eyes glittering, and rammed her head into his groin as hard as she could. The man bellowed, and she was knocked sideways by the hilt of another guardsman's sicklesword, but this time, her eyes rolled back into her head and she lay still.

"But Dagan wouldn't stand a chance against me." Nasu pulled with all his might against his chains. "He's not a fighter."

Next to me, Dagan bristled. "I certainly knocked you to the ground before."

"Ha!" Uruku's sharp laugh of delight echoed throughout the throne room. "A quarrel already!"

Dagan strode forward, pulling the guardsmen with him, his passion making him forget his pain. "Uruku, listen to me. Set us up in a Trial of Ordeal. I will fight Nasu to prove I tell it true. But you must let them and my ummum go free." He jerked his head to me and Iltani.

Gudanna smiled at Dagan, self-satisfied like a cat. I could imagine her with a gray tuft of squirming prey in her mouth.

"You are in no position to bargain, boy. But I will promise you this: If you best Nasu, and deliver the nin, you can have the girl of your choice. If it's one of them"—she pointed her eyes like daggers at me—"so be it." She looked at Shiptu, who stood quivering near Nasu, her shoulders stooped. "And your ummum will be released."

As they tugged us out the entrance Nasu, Assata, and Shiptu had been led in, a scuffle sounded around the side of the Palace wall. The clash of metal against sandstone brick. Soft grunts and a throaty cry from Assata. A man's angry curse. The wet squish of a weapon hitting flesh.

Then, moments later, it was still, and the only sounds were our own uneven breaths and the chains chinking together as we were dragged toward the Pit and whatever the gods had decided our fates should be.

CHAPTER 24

—⁓—

SHIFTING TO RELIEVE the pressure of the ropes around my hands, the press of my healing satchel against my belly, I tried to drift back into the few moments of restless slumber I'd managed since being tossed into this outbuilding near the Pit. Before posting themselves around the perimeter, the guardsmen had left Nasu's and Dagan's weapons with them for the trial, warning us that if we used them to end our own lives, they'd kill Shiptu, Dagan's brothers, and Iltani's parents.

Shiptu had been taken back to the dungeons to await the ending of the trial. My heart hurt at the thought of her down in the damp, not knowing whether her son would live or die. Either Assata lay dead in a gutter somewhere, her eyes picked from her head by the birds because the guardsmen had gotten the best of her, or she'd simply used her apparent weakness to her advantage and led them into a trap. I pictured her free from the city, racing toward Laraak to gather the warriors who would come in and free us all, Arwia—no, *Sarratum* Arwia—at their head. My throat ached with all the ways it could go wrong, but I was clinging with all my might to hope. Assata had winked at me. It had to mean something.

They'd chained the four of us up in the corners. Gala had requested that both Iltani and I be tied by our waists so I could treat her, but both Dagan's and Nasu's arms were linked to rusted bronze hooks set into the wall. Brown bloodstains dripped down from previous prisoners waiting for their turn in the Pit, and I shuddered, imagining the atrocities that had been committed in this building.

Nasu slept fitfully, his beard grown in sparsely, his hair longer since we'd been away from Manzazu. Dagan sat nearby, blinking into the moonlight that streamed in from the cracks in the rushes of the ceiling.

"Dagan?"

His brow lifted, but he did not answer. I'd given both Nasu and him arnica and hemp for pain, and though they needed salve for the lacerations on their backs, both had told me not to bother as they'd likely have wounds again on the morrow.

"Arammu?" I tried again.

He shook his head, nodding at Iltani sleeping in the corner, curled in a little ball, a piece of jagged pottery she'd found buried in the dirt clutched in her fist. Once in a while she murmured the word "no" in her sleep and jerked as if flinching from a blow.

"I want to talk to you," I whispered, pushing myself up

awkwardly to sit, using my wrists as leverage. "Please. You're upset and you're willing to fight Nasu, but what if you lose tomorrow—" My voice cracked as I spoke, but Dagan turned toward me, blinking his bruised eyes, a small smile on his cracked lips.

"Then you will be free from answering my question of marriage, won't you."

His reply brought tears to my eyes. "Do you think I wish you to die so we will not be married? You *cannot* believe that."

He smiled, but there was no joy in it. Just a deep well of ache, one in which he might drown.

"No." He shook his head. "Forgive me, Arammu. Of course I do not believe that. It is my weakness talking. Self-pity."

"No, Dagan. Don't say that."

He looked at Nasu bleakly. "The real question is what if I win, Kammani? Could you look at me the same way if I kill our friend? Could you love me as you do now if I send him to the Netherworld?"

He blinked his swollen eyes at me and shifted toward the wall.

My heart throbbed with pain for him. His spirit had been crushed. He'd lost his brother Shep, lost his ummum to Uru-ku's lair, was being forced to kill his friend, and doubted the love I felt for him. Part of that was *my* fault. I hadn't gone out of my way to show him that I loved him with all that was in me, as he'd done for me, time and again.

Dagan had only ever told me the truth. I was a skilled A-zu, as the loyalty of the Koru could attest, but though my skills were good, I had much to learn about trusting my gut, and Dagan had helped me be the best healer I could be by encouraging me to do that. He knew the dreams I carried with me and helped me shoulder them when they got too heavy.

It dawned on me then how important he was to my craft. He helped me. He supported me. He championed me, trying to push me further.

With him by my side, I was *better* at what I did, not worse. Tears pricked my eyes.

He didn't hold me back, he held me *up*.

The tears in my eyes rolled down my cheeks. "Dagan."

He turned his head.

"I love you."

He nodded, a small, sad smile on his face. "Don't cry, my sweet. I love you, too."

My voice broke. "And I'll love you no matter what happens with Nasu, all right? We're together in this, like you said before when you helped me with Rish. And together we'll find a way out. I swear it. I *swear it*."

I held his eyes as I cried. After a moment, his eyes filled, too, and he stretched across the outbuilding as far as he could, extending his long leg to try to reach me. I stretched as far as I could, too, and could just barely manage to brush my sandal against his.

We were a partnership, and for both of us, that meant giving. I wasn't sure I was ready for marriage, and didn't think I owed him that. But now, sitting here, looking at that amber-eyed boy, I knew what I wanted: a life with him. I was a healer, but I was a healer in love with my broad-shouldered, bighearted Dagan, and for the first time really ever, I realized that didn't make me weak.

It made me powerful.

⊠⊠⊠

She is fair, she is fair, she is lovely and fair.

Singing my abum's song, the Boatman sits in the corner of my old hut, mist enshrouding his shoulders, candlelight flickering softly from the sconce near his head.

Nasu kneels at his feet, sharpening a dagger against a leather strap, and Dagan sits next to Nasu, a big grin on his face as he casts his final lots and beats Uruku in twenty squares.

"Aha!" he shouts. "You bet against me, and you will *lose* every time!"

He collects his golden coins and shoves them into his purse at his waist, but they all fall out the second he drops them in. Morose, Uruku picks up my brother, Kasha, by the scruff of his neck and marches toward the door.

I try to speak—to stop him—but my mouth has been sewn closed with tight, neat stitches. Nanaea appears at my elbow, the needle and thread in her hands.

Near my ummum's pallet, Iltani is braiding a rope, end over end over end over end, her tongue stuck in the corner of her mouth, a black cloak over her shoulders. Smears of kohl outline her eyes and run down her cheeks from where she's been crying.

She is fair, she is fair, she is lovely and fair.

Dagan looks up. "Did you hear that?" he asks me. "Who is singing?"

I raise my finger to point at the Boatman, but the bottle of nerium has been stuck to my hand with some of the sticky bitumen, and I cannot shake it off.

A cold wave of river water seeps under the curtain hanging in front of the doorway and begins to flood the room.

Get out! Get out! We're going to drown!

I want to scream as the water rushes in faster and faster. My hands find the end of the thread at my mouth and try to pull, but Nanaea's stitches are sure and strong. I stand and reach for Iltani, but she sinks underneath the water and is gone before I can catch her, her black-streaked eyes blinking at me beneath the surface.

The frigid water rises to my calves. Then above my knees.

Panicked, Dagan stands and pulls Nasu out of the water. But Nasu lunges at him with his dagger, and they square off, sloshing through the steadily rising tide.

We must get out! Now!

Nasu jabs at Dagan and he weaves to avoid the hit. Dagan counters with a thrust, and Nasu jerks backward. They fight, swinging their blades, splashing with each jab. Each near miss. The water rises to their waists. Their chests.

The water rises to my chin.

I'm going to drown!

I claw for something to keep me afloat, but the nerium bottle won't leave my hand. I bump into Iltani's cold, clammy body, and she shrieks at me, bubbles and black eels pouring from her mouth, while she tries to pull me under.

The water climbs past my lips. I choke as it goes up my nose and burns down the back of my throat, and a scream tears through my sewn mouth.

Dagan turns his head as if just noticing I am there, and as he does, Nasu pulls his dagger out from under the water and slits Dagan's throat.

Dagan!

He sinks beneath the waves, blood pulsing from his neck with every one of his heartbeats.

And before long, I'm not choking on water anymore.

I'm choking on Dagan's blood.

CHAPTER 25

DAWN BROKE WITH the crowing of a rooster from somewhere in the distance.

Though my dream had filled my mouth with bile upon waking, it had given me a glimmer of an idea. I just needed Nasu to listen to me.

He clenched and unclenched his fists in their restraints.

"Wait. A dream? You had a dream and now you want to do *what* with our blades? You aren't an expert at war tactics."

My face flushed. I'd done a lot of harm when I'd been trying to heal. And I hadn't trusted him or even myself, but now we needed to work together or we would all die.

"Well—"

Nasu twisted his wrists. "Don't even speak. Neither you nor Dagan have had any regard for the expertise sitting right in front of you this whole time."

Dagan's eyes were hard when he stared at Nasu. "Arwia

believed that we could sneak the brides in and take out Uruku, but you and Assata destroyed those plans before we could execute them." His voice was hoarse. "You've made plenty of mistakes yourself. Your coup alerted Uruku to our presence."

Nasu sneered in disgust. "Kammani's plan to give Uruku the poison is likely what alerted Uruku to our presence."

"Your failure to communicate one another's plans is the problem." Iltani spat. "Had you simply joined forces, as Arwia has told you time and again, Uruku's body would be feeding the worms as we speak. Yet here we sit."

"Wait, friends. Please." I held up my hands, misery wrapped around my throat. "Many of these problems came about because I was not listening to anyone, not even myself. But I want to now. The Boatman has given me an idea about how to save both of your lives until Assata does whatever it is she is planning to do." I'd told them about Assata's wink, but though they all thought it could mean anything, I was holding on to the hope that it was a message that she had some sort of plan to rescue us.

"But I need help putting it all together. Isn't it worth at least listening to me so you don't have to try to kill Dagan?"

Nasu sighed and looked down at his bare knees.

"Explain again what you want to coat the blades with?" Dagan asked me.

"The nerium. The blades will dry, and will make whoever is cut with the tip appear to be dead."

Nasu met my eyes. "According to the Trial of Ordeal, that

would prove the man standing to be honest, and would prove the man who'd 'died' a liar. But what then?"

It appeared he would work with us. At least for now.

"How long does the nerium last?" Dagan asked.

"Half a day. Not long enough for someone to bury you."

"But long enough for the person to be dragged away for burial rites without chains and without being watched." His eyes lit up.

"Yes. *Exactly.*"

Dagan craned his neck to see Nasu. "So in the Pit, you could cut me to make it look fatal."

Iltani piped up. "And when Dagan is dragged away, he can go to Laraak if Assata hasn't already done so, and bring the Manzazu army in to take out Uruku."

"And what will you say when Uruku questions you about Arwia?" I asked Nasu.

"Tell him," Dagan started, rubbing his chin against his shoulder, "that she's in hiding somewhere."

Nasu twisted in his restraints with a grimace. "Wussuru. It's a half day's ride away. He'll be forced to send some of the guardsmen to go looking for her and will move the numbers more in our favor with us. They'll have fewer to fight."

"Yes!" I sat up taller. "You could give Uruku a false message! He will be forced to give credence to anything you say once the gods have proven you to be true. Our ensis would kill him for sacrilege themselves if he did not listen."

"But once they got what they want out of you, they'll—" Iltani drew a line over her throat.

304

"Maybe," Nasu told her. "But hopefully I could draw out my usefulness until Dagan arrived with the Manzazu army."

The barest flicker of hope lit up Dagan's face. "Yes. It could *work*." But then his smile faded. "But what of *you* and Iltani? You'll be seated in chains watching the trial. If they go to Wussuru and find it empty, they'll kill you both."

Iltani snorted. "Do you think us incapable? Come, now. I can convince that ignorant husband of mine to help us." She smiled, but there was no mirth in her eyes. "The foolish, foolish child."

"That didn't work before, and now that you've tried to give him that poison and eat his ear, he'll never trust you again," Nasu told her.

Iltani shrugged her freckled shoulder. "I didn't try to *eat* it. I tried to *remove* it. But . . . he loves me in his own twisted way. I'll use that to my advantage."

Nasu raised his eyebrows in disbelief, but Iltani lifted her chin with the fierce determination I knew simmered under her flippant mannerisms. The sadness and anger that boiled together. "Kammani and I will survive, like we always do. And so will both of you if we trust one another."

"Are we in agreement?" I asked.

Dagan and Iltani both agreed, and after a moment, Nasu's quiet "yes" united us in our mission.

"Perfect. Give me your blades, then," I told the boys.

After much sweating and cursing, Nasu and Dagan were able to wriggle their daggers out of their scabbards and fling them in my direction. Each clattered to a stop across the sandstone floor, and Nasu's rested barely out of reach. I froze, waiting for the door to squeak open and a guardsman to enter, but nobody came. Stretching my foot forward, I swatted at the copper hilt, missed, and strained against the rope at my waist until I felt it would tear me in two, but finally, I managed to grab it between my toes and pull it to me.

Fumbling under my heavy cloak, I reached my healing satchel. Sweat dripped into my eyes, but I shifted so that a ray of light filtering in from the rushes overhead shone inside. There was the laurel and sage. The arnica. The small vial of poppy. The blue cohosh. Gently, I shook the bag so that I could see even more clearly, and saw the small sack of bitumen and the little red bottle of nerium.

After working them out of my satchel and up my cloak, I rolled each blade in the bitumen, then tapped more of the fine powder onto the sticky blades.

"Done."

Sweating, I stuffed the nerium and bitumen back into my satchel and looked up to find all three of them watching me. Dagan, eyes swollen and bruised, smiled at me softly with blood-crusted lips. Nasu nodded, a show of faith. Iltani grinned wickedly and made an obscene gesture.

"They're beautiful," she said.

Swallowing hard, I considered the two blades lying next to one another: Dagan's dagger with the emerald-encrusted hilt, and Nasu's dagger with lapis lazuli threaded on his.

She was right.

They *were* beautiful.

Twin blades of beauty.

Twin blades of death.

And now, they'd be twin blades that would cut Uruku's reign much shorter than he probably thought possible.

CHAPTER 26

—⟋m⟍—

AROUND THE PIT'S perimeter, row after row of clay-brick benches were crammed with citizens curious about the spectacle they were about to witness. Typically, a Trial of Ordeal wasn't held in the Pit. This bloodstained oval was usually reserved for known murderers and thieves. In fact, the freshness of the spatter spoke of many punishments that had been given under Uruku's rule.

But today wasn't a typical day. We were going to overthrow a ruler and use his punishments against him.

The Palace horns blared to announce the arrival of Uruku and Gudanna. The cushioned benches to our left, where they would sit in this sumptuous viewing box, were positioned just above the row of twelve ensis that made up Uruku's council.

"There's Ensi Puzu." I nodded at the man with the gray

beard oiled into a triangle. "I wonder if he managed to convince the two holdouts to consider Arwia's rule."

"Which ones are those?"

I pointed at the row of council members. "Ensi Adda is the bald one with the red tunic, and Ensi Mudutu is the younger one on the end with the long hair."

As if sensing that we were talking about him, Ensi Puzu turned back and looked at me. His face was swollen and bruised.

Dear Selu.

Someone had beaten him, probably to keep his mouth shut! Ensi Puzu shook his head at me and turned back around.

My heart sank to my filthy feet.

"If the ensis don't want Arwia in, we're in a lot of trouble."

Iltani bumped me with her shoulder. "No." She shrugged. "If Dagan goes and gets the Manzazu army in Laraak, then they'll just kill the entire council if they don't comply. Now it doesn't matter if they agree or not."

"It will to Arwia. She'll want them to approve her. And I think Alu needs to see that she isn't just a sarratum who kills people to get her way. She doesn't want to be like Uruku or even like Sarratum Tabni."

I met her eyes, then looked past her at Gala, who was much less ill since Iltani hadn't been around to administer the dosage of the stomach tonic, though his ear looked like a dog had gotten to it. As we'd walked by him, he'd acted the part of an abused husband, scowling and kicking at the sand, but Iltani, in a burst of inspired brilliance, had begged for his forgiveness for injuring him and for her trickery. The poor fool had actually forgiven her, and rubbed her freshly shaved head. Said he was looking forward to a new start.

I'd yanked her away before she could get another shot at his ear.

"I still cannot believe he removed our restraints." The ropes were coiled under the benches beneath us.

"He's as senseless as those stupid sticks he whittles day and night." Iltani winked at Gala and he grinned, blushing madly. She laid an arm across my shoulders, the smile falling from her face. "It's too bad that he found the shard of pottery and took it, because I was going to plunge it into Uruku's heart and be done with the whole thing."

"I understand the feeling." I lowered my voice and looked cagily over my shoulder. "But there's no sense sacrificing your own life now. We have a plan." I looked into her wide brown eyes over her bruised cheek from the many backhands she'd received as of late. "Nasu will pretend to kill him, Dagan will ride back to Laraak, and the Manzazu army will ensure Arwia can ascend the throne by coming into the city and capturing Uruku. Whether they kill him outright or just take him back to Sarratum Tabni is no longer our concern."

If it works.

She sighed. "Yes, well. This will be much less personally satisfying."

The smattering of applause from the noble crowd as the

caravan of Uruku's guardsmen and horses paraded down a path toward us was overshadowed by cries of anger from the poor. Uruku's crimson sedan chair with gold tassels came to a stop right below where we sat, and he stepped down, wincing with the effort, every move seemingly filled with pain. He ordered a guardsman to assist Gudanna, who was wearing a deep blue tunic that hugged her big belly. Her eyes were puffy, with dark circles beneath. She moved with obvious fatigue as she descended from the chair with a soft "oof," and stopped and clenched the guardsman's arm for a moment before continuing on slowly.

Uruku waved to the crowd and ascended the stairs toward our viewing box, shaking us slightly with each step. Gudanna, heavy with child, and pausing now and again, grunted up the stairs behind him. They crossed in front of us to get to their tufted seats, Gudanna holding her abdomen with care. Her eyes flitted once to me, some anxiety hidden behind them, but she looked away, sweat beading on her brow.

"She's going to have that baby soon," I whispered in Iltani's ear. Automatically, my hand strayed to my healing satchel, which was on my hip under the heavy trader's robe.

"With Alani's evil offspring, no doubt."

"Alani is a goddess, so your insult doesn't even make sense."

"The gods can impregnate whomever they want."

Several moments later, a great, shrieking groan at the left of the arena drew the crowd's gaze to the heavy gate swinging wide open on rusted hinges.

Dagan and Nasu walked out of the shadowy corridor,

blinking into the day's brightness. They both wore sickle-swords, daggers, and even maces about their waists, but no breastplates, likely so it'd be easier for them to deliver death blows. The sunlight shone on their bare chests, and even from this distance, it was easy to see the angry red welts and lacerations from their whippings

Without a word, Iltani pulled me into a side hug that was a little too tight. "Keep a brave face."

My stomach turned over. "I'll try." But the thought of them accidentally hurting one another as they feigned a fight was unnerving.

Both Dagan and Nasu wore masks of complete concentration. Dagan's eyes roamed the platform and the viewing boxes, and when I caught his eye, he sent me a tight-lipped smile, which only made me more nervous.

On the far corner of the benches surrounding the Pit stood a podium high above the crowd. The town crier laboriously climbed, his knees hitting his great belly, sweat pouring off his brow. With a mighty grunt, he hoisted himself up the last steps to speak. He paused, his face flushed with exertion.

I shuddered as he raised his hands, and the drummers rolled out a warning for the crowd to silence themselves, each strike on the hide matching the thump in my own chest. He lifted the trumpet to his mouth to project his great voice across the empty cavern of the Pit.

"Ladies and gentlemen of Alu!" His voice echoed off the sandstone walls. "I must speak of the unprecedented spectacle you are about to witness, made especially difficult to test these two young men since the lugal deems honesty such a worthy venture!"

From his cushion down the viewing box, someone was watching me. Turning, I caught the disgusting grimace of a smile from Uruku.

My knees bobbed beneath the heavy cloak, my healing satchel shaking, rattling the tinctures inside. I didn't like that look. Not one bit.

Below, the town crier reminded the crowds about the sacredness of the Trial of Ordeal, instructing us that today, both men would fight to prove they were honest. "He who dies will have been proven a liar by the gods, and he who lives must be believed, for he speaks the truth." He paused, glanced down at the clay tablet in his hand, and shifted his body to address Dagan and Nasu directly. The crowd leaned in to hear his words.

"Today, Guardsman and Farmer, you will need to truly earn your honesty. You'll be facing . . . an almost insurmountable task." He swallowed, his voice faltering. "You will *not* be fighting each other to prove your innocence, as you've been told. You will be facing a challenge even greater than that."

They weren't going to fight each other? Panic bubbled up into my throat. "Iltani, our plans aren't going to work if Nasu doesn't cut him with the blade!"

Dagan and Nasu glanced at each other, fear plain on their faces. I looked at Uruku, who was grinning widely.

The town crier continued. "But we know that you are strong. Able. And determined to share your innocence with all of us in Alu. The last man standing will prove his word is true! Young men, I pray that Selu keep you!" At that, the crowd roared. The town crier climbed back down the stairs, his hair dampened with sweat, and cast one worried look back at Dagan and Nasu as he left.

I gritted my teeth in panic. What were they going to do? Who did they have to fight?

The trumpeters blew once more, signaling that the trial was to begin, and Nasu spoke urgently to Dagan, his lips near Dagan's ear. After a second, they briefly bumped their forearms together, and Dagan drew his dagger and sicklesword from his belt. Nasu drew his sicklesword and a mace, and they crouched into a fighting stance, their backs together. Whatever they would encounter, they would face it together, as friends.

With a harsh grating sound, the massive gate swung open once more and a group of guardsmen marched out in battle formation to the sounds of the drums. Dagan and Nasu tensed, clutching their weapons in white-knuckled fists.

Then more guardsmen spilled from the corridor, pulling a large, covered cart, which creaked and groaned beneath the weight of its contents. The men tugged, their muscles straining, until they'd pulled it to the center of the ring. As they locked the wheels, Uruku stood, a dark smile pulling his lips toward his ears.

The soldiers marched back toward the gate, leaving the

cart standing where it was, the cover tied down with thick hemp ropes.

But something was under that cover.

Something *alive*.

Dagan and Nasu stood before it, crouched in anticipation. The crowd murmured below me.

"Iltani, what's in the cart?" My voice came out warbly. Wrong. Off-kilter, fear changing the tone and tenor. Below us, the crowd quieted.

"Only the gods know what that maggot has done."

As the guardsmen marched toward the exit, the last one pivoted and sliced through the rope, then ran to join the others behind the closing gate. The clang of the metal slamming shut reverberated around the Pit.

At once, the cover of the cart fell away as the rope split, and the contents of the cart were finally exposed.

Lions.

Two of them.

The male lifted its head and roared, and I screamed Dagan's name loud enough to fill the Pit, the city, and hopefully, the ears of the warriors all the way in Laraak.

Come help us. We need you.

❈❈❈

In horror, the people sitting closest to the Pit scrambled to find seats on higher ground, but the walls were much too high for the lions to escape. Dagan and Nasu, too.

My chest heaving, I wrenched myself out of my seat. "Dagan!"

Nasu unsheathed his nerium-encrusted blade, spoke quickly into Dagan's ear again. Dagan nodded and sheathed his sicklesword, then took up both his and Nasu's daggers.

"Stop this!" I screamed furiously at Uruku, who was tense, his hands braced against the edges of the box in front of him, a gleeful smile on his lips. He wanted to watch them die! He must not have even cared about Arwia or he already knew where she was. This wasn't a trial. It was a *slaughter*.

Uruku glanced at me and laughed, the violence about to commence bringing his bloodthirst out in full bore. He pointed to the fracas that was unveiling itself below.

"You can end this, Healer! Just tell me where the nin is."

"As I stated, I don't know!" I bellowed. He'd kill us all anyway if I told. They just had to survive and prove themselves to be true in front of the council. *Both* of them.

The lions, ribs protruding, had leapt from their cart and now prowled the perimeter of the Pit in full crouch, hungry rumbles coming from their chests, lips pulled back to expose the sharpest teeth I'd ever seen.

Dagan and Nasu stood back to back in the middle of the Pit. Both of their faces were pale, and I could see Dagan's hands shaking, even at this distance. At the side of the Pit there was a commotion, as Dagan's little brothers Marduk and Qishti shoved through the guards to yell to Dagan.

"Brother!" Marduk's thick torso strained to push past the

guardsmen stationed around the Pit. "Kill Nasu so you can be declared the winner!"

The guards roughly pushed the younger brothers against the stands, but they weaseled back through, shouting at Dagan.

"They're going to fall in." I grabbed Iltani's arm. "His brothers are going to fall in, Iltani!"

"Gala, do something!" Iltani commanded him.

"The guardsmen down there have it under control."

"*Gala!*" Iltani cried. "If you want to prove yourself a man, and were ever a friend of Dagan's, get those boys away from the Pit!"

He looked at Marduk and skinny Qishti, who were both shouting to Dagan in a frenzy, dangerously close to the edge of the Pit.

Gala rubbed his lip. "I'd like to stay here with you."

"Aren't you a guardsman, supposed to protect Alu's citizens? Those boys need your protection, Gala, not me. You don't have to watch me. I'll stay put. I'll never betray you again."

After a moment, his eyes lit up with what looked like hope. He nodded once, and raced down the stairs and around the Pit to do her bidding.

With a horrible growl, the female lion lunged forward and swiped at Nasu with a massive claw. Nasu swung the sickle-sword to counter, but missed. The lion lunged again. Nasu swung the mace with his left hand, and caught the lion on the side of the head in a sickening crunch. She growled, blood dripping down onto her face, baring her teeth, and prepared to pounce.

"Fight, Dagan!" I screamed until I felt my throat would bleed as Iltani wrapped her arms around me, tight.

Oh Selu save them!

Dagan drew back and hurled the first of his daggers in one clean move. The lion raised up, about to leap, and Nasu's blade plunged deeply into her throat to the hilt. The lion writhed and squirmed, rubbing her paws against her neck, trying to dislodge the dagger, but as she struggled, the nerium was taking effect, sending her to sleep. Her movements became thick. Unsteady.

Nasu lunged, reared back his spiked mace, and finished off the beast with a splattering crack. She sank down in the dirt with a massive rumble, blood darkening the dirt around her throat.

The crowd roared in approval as the lion fell silent. They chanted, "Turn them loose! Turn them loose!" but Uruku only stood straighter, arms folded tightly, puckering his mouth. He waved them off as if swatting away flies.

"Dagan! Over here!"

Marduk and Qishti were trying to push past the guards to throw a rope down into the Pit in some reckless attempt to rescue their brother, but Gala was in the mix this time, trying to keep them away.

Qishti managed to squeeze between two of the guards while they were busy with his older brother. Gala tried to wrench him back, but was knocked by a guardsman's elbow, end over end into the Pit.

Directly in front of the male lion.

Gala screamed as the lion roared. He tried to scramble away through the sand, half crawling, half running, but the lion leapt on him at once. Yellow teeth flashing, it tore into his leg and shook him violently from side to side. Gala wailed and unsheathed his sword, swinging with all his might as the lion mauled him, but swung wide.

Dear Selu, he missed!

I covered my ears. Shrank away as the shriek of the Boatman filled my head. But Gala's screams echoing off the walls pierced through anyway.

Iltani stood stock-still, staring at the carnage below. Her face was white.

"It's eating his leg."

"Stop it, Iltani. Turn away. Please!"

"Dagan and Nasu rushed over and are trying to kill the lion. Nasu is beating it with his mace!"

"Stop looking!" I screamed, shaking her violently, but she stared on, eyes unblinking. Mouth open in horror.

But after a moment, the crowd stilled and I chanced a look at the Pit. Dagan and Nasu took a step back, chests heaving as the lion slowly sank to its bloodied side. They stood next to it, wiping their faces of gore. Finally, the beast stilled, its tongue lolling out of its mouth. I dropped my hands to my sides.

The crowd grew silent as Gala writhed on the ground. He moaned, ashen-faced, holding his right leg, which was mangled to the thigh, blood pouring from the main bloodline.

No one spoke. No one moved. We stared, horrified at the scene below us. The wreckage of Gala's leg. The entrails of a lion. Two blood-spattered brothers-in-arms who'd fought to bring down a wild beast. Guardsmen tensed and ready inside the gate, waiting for instructions on their next move.

It was probably too late for Gala with an injury like that. But I could try to do something.

"Bind his wound!" I yelled, my voice echoing in the stillness. I *had* to try to save him. I was a healer.

But a hand on my arm brought my eyes to Iltani's face. Her eyes were shining with malice.

"Let him die."

"Iltani—"

"No. Do not give them any more instructions. Gala tried to lie with me without my permission, no matter what he promised Dagan. He laughed at me, Kammani when I told him to stop, and told him I'd kill him if he succeeded. He said he'd make me love him."

She met my eyes and I recoiled from the hatred burning inside.

"So he will die, and I am *glad* for it. I am *glad*."

I nodded, silencing myself. It wouldn't matter if I told the guardsmen who were coming to collect him what to do, anyway. It was too late. He'd lost too much blood. They opened the gate, slipped into the arena, and scooped the groaning

Gala into their arms. They carried him out as quickly as they could, black blood dotting the sand behind him.

I prayed he would die quickly. Iltani was likely praying he wouldn't.

Uruku raised his hands. Next to him, Gudanna fanned herself, panting heavily, holding her belly. It visibly contracted under her filmy tunic, and she grunted.

"Farmer and Guardsman," Uruku commanded, his face twisted in pain, the gochala still at work in his blood. "You *have not* proven your innocence to me or to this city." His face went white. "*One of you must die!*"

The crowds began to chant for them to be released. One lone voice in the back, then everyone joining in.

"*Turn them loose! Turn them loose! Turn them loose! Turn them loose!*"

Uruku's face contorted in rage. "*Guardsmen! Start the trial again!*"

Rage welled up inside me like fire the louder the crowd yelled. The council members stood, conferring with one another, some confused, some angry. As the people below us chanted louder and louder, stronger and stronger, Uruku shook with fury.

"Listen to the crowd, Uruku. Let them go!" I cried.

"Yeah, you lice-infested donkey!" Iltani screeched.

He turned to look at us, his eyes glittering.

"They have proven themselves true, so let them go," I demanded. Though it might cost me, I had to listen to my heart. And it was telling me to fight.

"Tell me where the nin is, and I will," Uruku said through gritted teeth, gripping the edge of the viewing box until his knuckles were white.

And as soon as I did, we would all be dead.

"No." My voice wavered with anger.

He slammed his hands down on the side of the box. *Tell me where she is, or you will join them in the Pit.*

Iltani spoke up. "You'd never accept her word, anyway, so why don't you just suckle Alani's teat in the Netherworld."

A grin spread across Uruku's sickly face as he stared at Iltani. "Then I'll take your little healer friend to the party!"

Iltani launched herself at him in a growl, but he punched her in the jaw to the floor.

Roughly, he grabbed my arm and dragged me down the staircase. Iltani heaved herself up and tried to follow, but two burly guardsmen held her back. She screamed my name and kicked and clawed, but they held her fast. We tore through the crowds, them parting as he shoved me through. He pushed me down a side ladder into the Pit, where I crashed into the dirt. He followed and yanked me up by my hair, locking his arm around my throat.

"Kammani!" Dagan yelled, panic flickering in his eyes as I came into view. Nasu raised a bloodied sicklesword.

I gurgled, kicking at Uruku's shins. I thrust my elbow into his breastplate and tried to wrench myself away, but he pressed a dagger to my rib cage.

Dagan called to us. "Free her, Uruku, and I will kill Nasu right now to prove myself innocent! I swear!"

Nasu squared off to him, anger rising on his face. "You'd never best me, and you know it."

"Why don't we see how this plays out." Uruku dragged me to the center of the ring, ten paces away from Dagan. Dagan's hand twitched, his dagger poised to throw, but Uruku kept me in front of his body. Dagan had no clear shot!

"Guardsmen! Finish the trial! Spare one of them. The other two must die!" Uruku screamed almost gleefully, his forearm firmly around my windpipe.

Gasping for air, I felt the horror of what was to come rain down on our shoulders like fire as the gate creaked open, and more guardsmen than I could count poured out and encircled us, armed to their teeth, shields flashing in the sun.

"Serve justice! We must have the truth!" Uruku cried in my ear, his voice heightened with malicious triumph.

The guardsmen stood shoulder to shoulder, helmets pulled down over their brows. They carried battle-axes and maces. Sicklesswords and spears. One accurate throw and we'd be done. Humusi's writhing body as she'd been impaled spun through my mind in nauseating waves.

So this is how we will die.

Dagan and Nasu tensed together, chests heaving, blood spattered across their faces. Dagan's emerald dagger glittered in his right hand, a sicklesword in his left. Nasu clutched one gory mace and his own sicklesword. No match for any of these men.

"Dagan!" I screamed, my throat raw, as I wriggled under Uruku's hold. My blood grew cold, and the Boatman flickered

to life in front of me and ghosted away. I grabbed for his image with my mind, but Uruku's forearm pressing, *pressing*, into my throat was making me see stars instead.

As the guardsmen slowly advanced on Dagan and Nasu, who stood back to back, ready to meet their fates, Uruku hurled me forward onto my knees into the sand, and retreated with a guardsman out of the Pit. Dagan's face was a mask of terror.

"*Run to the ladder!*" he yelled to me as a guardsman swiped at Dagan's head with his sicklesword while another stepped forward and lunged for Nasu. Another, his beard bigger than I was, advanced on me, a spear gripped in his mighty fist. My heart trembled in fear.

I held up my empty hands. "Please sir." I stayed on my knees, ready to dive should he throw it.

"Kammani!" Dagan screamed. His sicklesword clanged against a guardsman's shield on his right, and two more guardsmen advanced on his left. He was surrounded. "*Go!*"

A cry tore from my throat as the big guardsman took another step toward me. Then another. But my scream was not as loud as the shriek that rose from the gate of the Pit. Nor was it as loud as the resulting cries of terror—of fascination, of *triumph*—that rose from the crowd around me.

Startled, I whipped my head around to look, and sobs racked my shoulders as my eyes told my brain what I was seeing.

Chariots. At least thirty of them.

Thundering through the gates toward me. Toward the melee.

All being driven by a band of female warriors too fierce, too powerful, to even believe. And they were led by Commander Ummi and Higal, who both wore vicious determination about their shoulders like they were born for exactly this kind of revenge.

CHAPTER 27

THE WARRIORS, COPPER helmets gleaming in the sun, mouths wide open in battle cry, would not stop coming through the gates with chariots and whips. Riding panting horses. Swinging battle-axes and firing arrows and throwing spears. Assata thundered by me astride a gleaming chestnut mare, a broken arm holding the reins. She swung a sickle-sword into the guardsman advancing on me as she raced into the fray. He fell to his knees, blood spurting from his throat. I scrambled away, to the side of the Pit, fear, *relief*, choking me. The heavy trader's tunic was sweltering, and I ripped it over my head and kicked it off, freeing my healing satchel. Terrified, I pressed myself against the Pit's wall.

The warriors clanged battle-axes, bloodying the sands with shrieking men. An arrow thunked into the shoulder of the man fighting Dagan, and Dagan swung his sicklesword and finished him with one jagged slice. His face was grim. Resolute. He spun around to help Nasu with another attack.

And at once, my hair prickled on my neck. A whisper at first.

Then a roar.

A mighty rush of frigid wind descended on me as if I were caught up in a great storm, and from the center of the battle, over the horses kicking up sand, the warriors' twisted, ruthless faces, a figure rose.

The Boatman, casting stark light from his eyes, his mouth, his hands, ascended from the sand in his ragged cloak. He opened his cavernous mouth wide in dreadful terror and threw his hood from his head. As he raised his bony arms to the skies and shrieked, one word echoed through my head again, and again, and again.

Beware!

The same one I'd heard when I'd envisioned Dagan throwing his dagger at me!

The sensation of spiders crawling down my arms made me shudder as he continued to scream above the warriors, his bony jaw opened wide. No one else stopped to stare. He must only be showing himself to me.

The healer.

Dread wrapped its long fingers around my throat, and I began to choke.

But after a second, I realized that the fingers were *real*.

Someone is choking me!

Peeling brittle fingers away, I wrenched around to see the damp, sickly face of Uruku. He must have come down the ladder during the fracas! At once, he was on me again, choking me, thumbs pressing into my windpipe as his eyes bulged.

"You have done all this! You! You stupid girl!" Spittle flew into my face as he raged.

I wedged my thumbs into his eyes. When he thrashed but didn't let go, I remembered Iltani's well-placed kick with the young guardsman from the kitchens, and reared back and kicked Uruku as hard as I could between the legs. He dropped to his knees with a grunt and I bolted. But he reached forward and grabbed my foot, sending me sprawling on my face.

He was on me in a flash. He straddled me from behind and once again put his hands around my windpipe, squeezing. Squeezing.

Gurgling, trying to peel his fingers from my throat, my eyes stinging and watering, I pinched both of his hands in the tender part between thumb and forefinger, the place my abum had always told me would take a man to his knees.

Howling, Uruku let go. I scrambled to my feet and ran, but he caught up to me and grabbed me again, pinning his forearm against my throat. I couldn't breathe! The memory of being shoved from the window in the Palace all those moons ago, of falling and breaking my leg, of everything that came after, swam into my head. All of a sudden, coldness descended on me as the rotten stench of rivergrass flooded my nose. Straining toward Dagan, my eyes stinging, throat closed, I felt swept away, underwater, and heard, as if it were whispered in my ear, "Arammu" in Dagan's voice.

In the center of the Pit, Dagan stilled, staring at us as the war was waged around him. His emerald dagger was in his hand, his face filled with rage. Behind him, the Boatman, his cloak billowing, the stench radiating from him in waves, whispered in Dagan's ear. In one practiced move, as I'd witnessed him do a thousand times behind our house in Manzazu, Dagan reared his arm back and hurled his dagger toward Uruku with more force than I'd ever seen him wield.

But as it flew through the air with the grace of a fired arrow, Dagan's eyes widened in horror. For the path it was on was *not* in line with Uruku, its intended recipient.

The dagger was sailing directly toward *me*.

❂❂❂

Drop. Twist. Throw!

The memory of Ummi's training in Wussuru sprang to life in my body, and I jerked my left arm up, knocking Uruku's hand off my throat. At once, I dropped, twisted, and launched him over my shoulder. When I did, a wet thunk, followed by a strangled, burbling shriek, came from Uruku as he flew overhead and landed on his back with a whump.

He writhed on his back, kicking.

Panic buzzed through me, and I scrambled away from him—*Run! Run!*—but when I took stock of myself, I realized there was no need. Not anymore. Dagan's dagger was sunk to the hilt in Uruku's throat, and blood streamed from the wound.

He was down and wouldn't be getting up again.

I was *safe*. I was safe!

Uruku jerked in the sand, thrashing, hands wild and frantic around the blade. My body quivering, I crawled closer to the man who had caused me so much pain. He and Gudanna had murdered my father. Lugal Marus. Had killed so many others in their quest for power, but now he lay lurching in the filthy Pit, dying miserably.

Do no harm.

I reached for my satchel, my brain barely even registering what I was doing, as he opened and closed his mouth like a fish, searching for air that would not come. Rattling through my tinctures quickly, I found what I wanted: the nerium.

It would ease him into death so he did not suffer. The powder I'd put on Dagan's blade had likely all wiped off at this point, so Uruku would need the dose that I had left. My hands shook as I held the little red bottle in my palm.

Does a murderer like him deserve mercy?

My abum would say yes. He'd give the tonic and say vengeance was for Alani, not for us humans. We forgive and we move forward. We offer mercy to the evil *and* the good.

But what did *I* want? His slimy lips on my mouth. Hands on my body. The thought that he'd bashed the teeth from that woman so many moons ago, and murdered innocent people, filled me up with sorrow. With rage.

Tears sprang to my eyes, and I pressed a hand to my mouth, processing it all. He deserved no kindness, especially from anyone he'd hurt—but that had very little to do with *me*. I was a healer. I kept my feelings out of it. The Boatman had pressed this tincture into my hand time and time again, and I would show mercy because it was right and it was whole and it was the only thing separating me from this evil man.

My hand trembling, I reached toward his mouth, which was desperately sucking in his last breaths, and sprinkled some of the tincture on his tongue to ease him into his death. As his eyelids began to droop, he slid Dagan's dagger free from his throat, sealing his fate with the move. The blade had at least been blocking some of the flow, but now he'd bleed out within seconds. The Boatman would come. And quickly.

Kneeling at his head, my knees covered in the gore of this dying man, I looked into his brown eyes, hoping for something.

An apology. Remorse.

But there was nothing but a sort of bewilderment as if, in all his years, he'd never imagined anything like this could happen to someone like him.

He held a bloodied hand out to me, grasping the front of my tunic. I put my hand over his.

"My abum was a good, kind man," I whispered. "And I miss him every day. But you know what?" I leaned close so he could hear the last words anyone would ever say to him: "No one will mourn you once you're dead. Not your wife. Not your child. Not this city. *No one.*"

In a few seconds, his hand fell away, and his drooping eyes strayed from me to the battle. Finally, while he twitched and kicked, his eyes dimmed, and his dark soul slithered away to its doom in the Netherworld.

A sob rose from my gut and lurched from my chest in agony—in joy.

He was gone.

It was over. I covered my face with my hands and cried. For though I might have plotted to end his life, a fact that did not make me proud, I had shown him mercy in the end, and that was something.

That was *something.*

✖✖✖

The battle was ending, when I was calm enough to stand.

Light-headed and woozy, I stumbled away from Uruku's body, Dagan's dagger wiped clean and stowed in my satchel. A few warriors finished off the last of the fighting guardsmen who hadn't dropped their weapons and surrendered. I took in the carnage on every side as the women pulled their whinnying horses to a stop and the chariots stilled. A mess of twisted limbs here. A dying man there. Discarded sickleswords and helmets everywhere.

I'd need to help tend the wounded—and soon—but for now, I wanted only him. Dagan.

Where is he?

As I tromped through remnants of the battle to find him, one final white horse galloped into the arena, kicking up sand. I turned, lifting my eyes to see the rider.

It was *Linaza*, the goddess of love and war.

And she looked a lot like *Arwia*.

Streaming from her long black hair were red ribbons that shimmered as if they'd captured the sun. Atop her head was a crown of hammered gold, with what appeared to be fire inside.

She carried a flashing copper shield and wore a silver breastplate over a blood-red tunic that flowed from her shoulders long past her hands. Feathers had been sewn from shoulder to tip. On her back were gold wings that spread to the sky. Her horse was similarly arrayed, its mane woven with red roses and ribbons, its back draped in a long white sheet on which was painted a scorpion with its tail poised to strike.

The crowd stilled and horses reared in the arena as the women got down from their chariots and swept off their helmets one by one.

"Citizens of Alu!" Arwia yelled, her face painted to make her features look formidable. Slashes of eyebrows. Carved cheekbones. A red, dangerous mouth. "I am the daughter of Lugal Marus, Arwia, the Sarratum of Alu!" She raised her shield in the air and the crowds shifted uneasily, their cries of awe echoing across the large expanse of the bloody Pit.

"The goddess of war, Linaza, has freed me from the tomb! She gave me the power of her shield. *The power of the Koru and the great Manzazu army!* She commanded that I rid you of the torment from Lugal Uruku, who took this kingdom falsely."

The ensis on the council sat on their bench, mouths agape. Ensi Puzu stood and cheered, one fist in the air, and four other members joined him to support Arwia. But Ensi Adda and Ensi Mudutu remained quiet and seated with the other councilmen, observing. Perhaps they wanted someone else on the throne?

The crowd was hushed, but a man shouted in joy from the back. Shielding my eyes from the sun, I picked through the crowds to see who it was. The man jumped up and down, the set of his shoulders similar to a particular smart-mouthed friend of mine. Iltani's father. He raised his fist and Arwia answered with one of her own.

"He has starved you! Punished you! Torn your families apart! I have come to tell you today that we are *finished with torment*! You will work an honest day and receive a living wage. We will help those who cannot afford food. We will protect our city with our band of warriors who are loyal to the citizens of Alu, not their own coffers.

"I promise you that I will restore your faith in this crown!" she cried, holding her hands up high overhead. *"No one will suffer under my rule!"*

"All hail Sarratum Arwia!" Iltani's abum yelled hoarsely. *"All hail Sarratum Arwia!"*

And the crowd joined in. One after another after another. Standing in exultation. Arms overhead. Hands clasped together in prayer. Raised to the sky. The guardsmen standing in the Pit who had not been killed sank to one knee, their heads bowed.

Ensi Puzu knelt to her, too, and joined the chants of the crowd. *"All hail Sarratum Arwia!"* The four other ensis who supported her joined in. *"All hail Sarratum Arwia!"*

That made five.

As the crowds shouted and sang and called her name, Arwia held out a hand to the council members who remained silent.

"Good men! Please join me in reclaiming our city. Join me in making our citizens happy and whole! You will be rewarded for your support and will have a hand in shaping Alu into greatness."

After a moment of consideration, Ensi Mudutu nodded, then knelt and began to chant along with Ensi Puzu, his long hair falling over his shoulders. *"All hail Sarratum Arwia! All hail Sarratum Arwia!"*

Six. Their support was split.

Arwia held out her hand again to the rest of the men. "Ensis! Join me, for the sake of our broken city. Help me restore it so we are not vulnerable to others who do not care about our citizens as I do!"

Please. Please. We need this. It will mean so much for her reign to take the throne with support.

The men on the council deliberated, and two of them, contempt on their faces, left the viewing box and walked away.

But finally, with a look of resignation, Ensi Adda knelt slowly, his red tunic bunching around his knees. "All hail Sarratum Arwia," he said softly, nodding to her. Ensi Puzu elbowed him in the gut, and the man raised his fist and his voice. "All hail Sarratum Arwia!"

Seven. A majority.

It didn't matter that the remaining ensis refused to show her allegiance. It didn't matter. Because she had gotten approval from the majority of the council, and she was now Alu's queen.

The city was won.

The citizens of Alu stood on their benches and shouted for her as she rode around the Pit on her horse, her face fiery. Determined.

From across the arena, my eyes found Dagan. With Nasu, he grabbed Commander Ummi off her horse and paraded her around the other side of the Pit on their shoulders. On her mare, Assata cradled her broken arm, gritting her teeth in pain, but delirious in the victory nonetheless. Next to her, Higal shouted, mouth open wide, one victorious fist to the sky.

Crying with abandon, I placed my hand over my heart, the gesture of my city, as Dagan cheered in exultation. I took in the wreckage of the bodies all around me. The blood. The price of human life spent to further each side's aims. I cried, for we were safe, and those guardsmen were not. Everyone who paid the price of war certainly was not.

But for now, the weakest in Alu would be served by some-one who held their needs in her hands with more regard than her own power, and I prayed as I lifted my head to the sky, that she would serve them well.

We owed it to those who had died to ensure that she did.

CHAPTER 28

—⁓—

ARWIA CALLED FOR a couple of the Koru to go find Shiptu and release her from the dungeons, but I had one person on my mind and one only: Dagan.

People streamed into the Pit, claiming their dead and carrying their wounded to safety. I helped those I could as I wended around the chariots. He was in this Pit somewhere. It didn't matter that he'd be covered in gore. I would find him. I would fling myself into his arms and tell him I loved him until I lost my voice. I would.

My heart in my throat, I pushed past a pair of men carrying a dead guardsman between them, as a band of Koru headed out toward the dark passageway that led into the city. Arwia trailed behind them on her white mare, regal. Glowing. The sarratum she was born to be.

I turned to the Koru, clasping each of them on their shoulders as they trailed past. "My many thanks for the miracle you performed for us. My many thanks. Thank you for your help. We couldn't have done it without you. You saved us. Thank you."

One of them paused. "We were protecting our city as well as yours. We will stay to instate Nin Arwia on the throne, but after that we must return to our queen."

I placed a hand over my heart. "Of course."

She returned a Linaza salute and went on her way as Arwia called to me.

"My friend!" I grabbed her leg as she reined her horse to a stop. "You and the army came at exactly the right time. But how did you get through the gates?"

She declined her head regally, and up close, I could see all the work that had gone into her war attire. Nanaea must have spent hours perfecting it.

"Higal wanted to bring war, but I brought coin. Yashub let me borrow riches from Laraak to secure the victory. He had a whole chest of gold and jewels in his keep. I told him once I was sarratum, I'd pay him back double, and he took me at my word, especially when there were warriors at my back."

Yashub was wealthy?

He'd been holding out on us. He could've been the first in line to secure Iltani at the bridal gifting. We were going to have to have a word with him.

"So when we came into the city, I distributed the coins and jewels to the guardsmen's families to make sure we'd be allowed safely in. Most were willing to change allegiance. They only complied with Uruku's command because of his threats.

When I told them I'd be fair and would make sure they were paid decently, they were happy to comply."

Goose bumps covered my arms. "You're brilliant! You'll be a wonderful, strategic sarratum."

She smiled. "My thanks, friend. But Nanaea helped me feel like one, and both Ummi and Higal ensured it was so. They came together with the help of Assata. As Assata tells it, she disarmed the men who'd dragged her from the throne room, though they broke her arm, and sneaked out of Alu in a trader's cart. She hid until nightfall. When she came into Laraak, she ate, and asked the warriors—all of them—to follow Ummi and Higal into battle. And they did."

She looked back at Assata, who stood, talking weakly with Nasu, Higal, and Ummi at the entrance of the corridor, her broken arm already cradled in a makeshift sling. I'd need to set it soon.

Arwia reached down and stroked the neck of her horse. "But I have to go, Kammani, while everyone believes in me and the Manzazu army is still here. They're giving me a chance, and I don't want to mess this up. I want to show them that I'll keep my promises to rule with grace. And"— she glanced worriedly toward the horizon—"I'll need to repair the relationship with Sarratum Tabni. She wanted Uruku alive, so I have to send some messengers to her immediately with news."

"Well, I'll be here every step of the way to support you. Now I have to go, too."

To find Dagan.

She blew me a kiss, nudged the horse ahead, and trotted toward the gate.

My throat tight, I wedged myself through a line of warriors who were leading away the guardsmen who'd surrendered. Nasu, Ummi, Higal, and Assata stood at the entrance of the corridor, talking softly, and my heart squeezed. I couldn't just walk past.

My voice broke when I reached them. "Ummi, my friend! I used your grappling trick and it saved my life."

She nodded, her face weary, armor spattered with the blood of broken guardsmen. "I'm glad it could help you, A-zu."

I turned to Assata and buried my face in her good shoulder, reminded of long days spent playing outside her tavern. "And you! I prayed that wink meant something good for us. Hoped. But I thought you might be dead."

After a moment, she broke away, wincing. "I'm too old to be taken down that easily. At least you weren't praying for my death."

"Oh, Assata. Of course not. We didn't believe the same things about how to proceed, but we were always on the same side. Always. And"—tears pricked my eyes—"I am so sorry about Warad. I am. I was reckless. I caused Uruku to retaliate . . ."

She shook her head. "You were foolish, but it was brave to try. You're a healer. It's honorable to want to save lives. But had we simply coordinated our efforts . . ." She let her voice trail off, a haunted look in her eyes. One tinged with bitterness that would likely take years to diminish, if it ever did.

Nasu crossed his arms over his blood-spattered chest, weariness on his brow. "I'm just grateful Dagan and I were able to work together." He pointed toward the far wall. "He's over there, by the way."

"I'm grateful, too." I went up on tiptoe and kissed his rough cheek. "Thank you for taking our side in the end. I'll care for your wounds after, all right? And yours, Ummi and Assata?"

They all nodded at me, but Nasu spoke. "Of course."

With one final smile, I left them to go find Dagan.

The boy I had loved since I was old enough to walk stood behind a chariot in the Pit, staring down at a guardsman whose legs were twisted beneath him, unblinking eyes gazing into the cloudless sky above.

"Dagan?" Relief flooded through my body as I said his name.

He was alive, and there were too many guardsmen lying near us who would never hear their names spoken again. My chest ached as I took in his battered, bruised body standing over a dead man whose family would probably utter his name in mourning this very evening.

I laid a hand on his arm.

"He was young, Kammani. Not too much older than I am." He rubbed his jaw. "And I killed him."

"My sweet." My voice cracked. "You had no choice."

He looked at the blood staining his hands. "When the battle ends, you feel victorious. But when you see the wreckage"—he looked around, his eyes bleak, face drawn—"there is a feeling of hollowness in my chest." He swallowed with some difficulty. "I killed him, and another guardsman, and Uruku." He looked up at me. "I killed him. *Murdered him.* And it was nearly you. I threw my dagger and it could have hit you."

The memory of the Boatman's dire warning flashed through my brain, and it stole my breath. Because without the warning, I might never have been able to react that quickly. I wouldn't have believed that death could come from Dagan's own hand.

The Boatman had *saved me.*

Suddenly overcome, I tugged Dagan away, and we trudged toward the corridor and inside the shadowy depths. Out of the sun. Out of the garish light. Away from the death and injury and blood. I had a life to live, and so did he.

"You threw that dagger to protect me."

"But it could have killed you like you said in the tent. After your—vision. You told me and I didn't believe you."

"Well, luckily, I trusted myself." I smiled into his face. His bloody, battered face that was swollen and needed tending to as soon as possible. "And you killed the others to save your life." Tears filled my eyes. "We *tried*, Arammu. Tried to end it without bloodshed. It was the best we could do. But Uruku was a man of death, and we were in his domain. I was foolish to think it would end any other way."

"No. You were right to wish it could be that way. War is destruction. For both sides."

We stood lost in thought, working through our pain, our triumph, our failure.

After a moment, I placed my hands on his big chest. "You didn't come to me right after we'd won. You carried Ummi on your shoulders instead. I thought you'd run to find me."

He smiled, his eyes guarded, scuffling his sandaled feet in the dust. He blinked thick, black lashes, and he lifted his amber eyes to mine. Took my hands in his. Both of ours were bloody, filthy, coated in the dried remnants of lives lost, but neither of us cared in that moment.

"Aren't you tired of me chasing you?"

"You never need to chase me again." I squeezed his hands with all my might. "I am here with you now, and with you forever, Dagan, if you will have me." I pulled him close and stood up on my toes. "You told me that we are in this life together, and I know that it's true. I can be the healer I want to be, and I can *also* have you. I can have it all, and *want* it all. I want to be with you for the rest of my life, more than you can ever underst—"

But before I could finish, he was crushing me to him, his warm lips pressed to mine, his hands tangled in my hair. And I pulled him to me, too. Together, we let go of the grief, of the pain, and reminded ourselves exactly how it felt to be wonderfully and completely alive.

"Kammani!"

Iltani's voice, echoing in the corridor, tugged me out of our intoxicating embrace.

"What?" I demanded.

She stood there, a hand on her hip. "Maybe you could get your tongue out of his mouth long enough to give me a hand?"

Blushing, I turned back toward Dagan, trying to lean away, but he held me fast, grinning.

"With *what?*" I answered her, but I couldn't tear my eyes away from that perfect divot above his lips.

"Good gods of the morning sky. Look at me."

I sighed. She always had a way of ruining a moment. But I'd forgive her for it. It was just her way.

And above the noise of the crowds celebrating around the Pit, I heard a scream. A *woman's* scream. Planting one last kiss on Dagan's fiery mouth, I walked out into the sands of the Pit, shielding my eyes from the sun. Another groan echoed off the blood-spattered walls. The sound was coming from the direction of the viewing box.

Gudanna. *The child.*

"She's pushing?" I asked Iltani.

"The foot of her evil spawn has emerged and the cord is all wrapped around it, and if you think I'm going anywhere near whatever else comes out of that womb—snakes, spiders, what have you—"

"Iltani, be serious." Wiping a hand down my face in exhaustion, all I could do was laugh. It figured.

Dagan joined me in the sand. "You have to go?"

I sighed. "It appears that I am needed."

He wrapped his big arm around my shoulders and kissed me on my forehead. "Then lead the way. I've been told I'm a brilliant assistant."

CHAPTER 29

WRAPPED IN ONE of Shep's old tunics, Shiptu stood in front of the door as Dagan and I trudged up the path to their home. He was limping significantly less since I'd mixed him and Nasu a pain tincture and tended to the worst of their wounds. Gudanna and the babe had been delivered into the safety of the Koru's care until Arwia decided what to do with them. Alive, the child was a threat to her, and she knew it, especially if the other five ensis who didn't support her rule decided to use the babe as a figurehead to spur their own takeover.

But for now, they were safe.

Iltani went to her old hut to find her ummum and abum. She was gifting them Gala's home. She said she'd never live there—*ever*—but her parents were welcome to it.

"My son!" Shiptu ran down to meet us, her feet still unsteady beneath her, the days spent in a dungeon sapping her strength. She'd need a sturdy bone broth with fat and water-cress to strengthen her. Maybe some chamomile for her nerves. When she reached Dagan, she threw herself into his arms.

As she cried into his chest, he rubbed her back and sank to his knees before her. "Ummum, I lied to you about Shep."

She pressed a hand to her mouth silently as tears streaked down her face. "I know. I heard from Marduk and Qishti. But you protected me with your silence. Had I known . . ." She dropped her chin, swallowing, and cupped her hands around Dagan's face. "It was better that I did not know. Now I can properly mourn my son." Her voice broke, but she tugged him up to stand. "Now, both of you need to get cleaned up. You're filthy, and you'll scare Rish and Kasha."

"They're here? And Nanaea?" I followed Dagan and Shiptu inside, and the smell of old wood, smoke, and the faintest scent of cinnamon hit me. It was *home*. It smelled a lot like home.

"Not yet, but they are on their way. They'll be here before nightfall. Assata is here, sleeping in the other room with some arnica and hemp for the pain in that arm. She asked a band of the warrior maidens to go to Laraak to get Nanaea and the boys."

She ushered us through the main living quarters, out the back door, and around a grove of tamarisk trees into a small, walled courtyard where a large washtub was filled to the brim with fresh water. Climbing flowers and thick green vines crawled overtop a lattice overhead, providing privacy and much-needed shade. A cake of Aleppo soap, linens, and clean tunics lay nearby on a set of matching chairs. A lounging pallet, covered in thick quilts, sat in the corner. She'd gone to a lot of trouble, despite her weakened state. "When Assata wakes, she'll need that arm fixed, Kammani. She says she'll be burying what's left of her family and going back to Manzazu with Ummi to join the Koru. She'll need to be whole to do it."

"Yes, of course. I'll be more than happy to help her with whatever she needs."

Her eyes were sadder than I'd seen them, but her chin remained resolute. She was a strong woman. She'd survive this pain, as she'd survived the dungeon. "All right. Then I'll leave you two to get more presentable." She smiled briefly, wrapped her arms around herself, and left the courtyard, closing the wooden gate behind her, her footsteps falling away until the door to the house slapped closed in the distance.

Dagan stood and contemplated the bath, turning bright eyes to me, the briefest flush rising to his cheeks. "You first. I'll go draw more water."

"No!" I shook my head. "You've been through a bigger trial. I'll just go after you."

"Stop it. I'm covered in gore. I won't have you washing in that. Please, take my kindness." He covered his heart with his big hand, his amber eyes bright but weary behind his thick lashes. Lashes that were impossibly dark and full.

Longing filled my belly. "All right." I met his eyes. "I won't be long."

He stood, looking at me, biting his full, cracked lip. He put his hands on his hips, crossed his arms over his chest, then left them hanging at his sides. He cleared his throat, red creeping up his neck. He jerked his thumb behind us. Toward the house. "I'll go get the buckets . . . um . . . while you bathe." His face flushed even more, and he headed toward the gate.

But that wasn't what I wanted at all. It wasn't what my heart told me to do. I'd spent the last few years pushing him away, setting him aside. Not realizing how much goodness I had when he looked at me and whispered my name.

We were *alive*. I wouldn't waste one more precious second of that gift with doubt.

So right before he reached the gate to leave, I walked to him in two quick strides and slipped my hand into his. He looked at me, a question in his warm eyes, and I pulled him close, wrapping his big arms around my waist. On my tiptoes, I wound my arms around his neck, pressing my chest, my hips, against his. I didn't care that I was bloody. I didn't care that I was covered in sweat and stink and dirt and horror. None of it mattered.

He mattered.

"No." I kissed him on his lips. Once. Twice. Then again, longer, my mouth moving against his with all the heat I had inside.

"Don't go," I murmured. My voice held a quaver, my nerves bubbling through my bravado. "Stay with me."

But more than anything else in my life in that moment, I was sure.

More than *anything*.

He blushed red all the way to his ears.

But he did.

CHAPTER 30

Six moons later

A BRIDE ALWAYS felt nervous on her wedding day.

Or so I'd once heard.

But since I wasn't technically a bride—no father giving me away, no dowry paid, no bride price offered, no tradition followed at all—I shouldn't have been nervous.

Nevertheless, my stomach flitted with butterflies.

The ceremony we had agreed to, a simple meeting of minds, a promise to be united as one without the technicality of an actual marriage, settled my nerves. Though Arwia had said she'd revoke any laws that gave husbands power over their wives, her new council—made up of the seven men who'd supported her and five women—had yet to meet to strike them down.

The remaining five council members who'd opposed her rule had been given the choice of leaving the city or facing Arwia's new guardswomen and men who'd been trained in Manzazu. A particularly dour-faced former councilman had tried to lead a small insurrection against her and had ended up at the end of a rope, staring into Arwia's eyes.

The rest fled.

Currently, Arwia's concern about unrest in Sidu, a seaport city, was more pressing of a concern, so for me, when the law benefitted the man and not the woman, I wouldn't agree to marry under it. Fortunately, Dagan hadn't cared. He wanted me at his side, hand in hand for the rest of our days, marriage tradition upheld or not.

I smiled at myself in the looking glass hanging on the wall of Dagan's old chamber and smudged a bit more of the jade on my eyelids, per Nanaea's command.

A crown of roses around her head, she stood on tiptoe and pinned a sprig of yellow chamomile to the shoulder of my tunic.

"Stand still, Sister. I swear to the gods of the skies that you're the absolute worst when it comes to being prettied."

She ran her hands down the length of my turquoise tunic with the pockets I'd insisted she sew on, though she protested that they took away from the beauty of the garment. They were practical, I'd told her. I could keep my tinctures in there. I could put the gift in there that I needed to give to someone, should Nasu succeed in his quest. She'd grumbled, but she'd done it.

"I'm fidgety, because there are more important things than being beautiful."

"Oh?" She lifted a thick eyebrow in a perfect arch, pursing her ruby-red lips as she tugged a loose string from my shoulder. "And those would be?"

"Whether Nasu was successful in his mission, for one."

"Do you think he got them to come?"

"I hope so. Plus, my healing tent is low on burdock root, and I cannot continue to treat Iltani without it."

"You'd worry about your work on a day like today?" She frowned as she reached up, adjusting the blooms around my head. "A day centered on love?"

"It's not my *work*. It's my *friend*. Iltani is as glib as ever, but giving up the drink has been difficult for her."

She pursed her lips as she fussed with my hair. "She certainly doesn't seem like she's struggling. She works day and night in the Libbu with the merchants!"

"The burdock root helps the shake in her hands, but she suffers whether she appears to or not. She was sad in Manzazu. Missed her family terribly. And now after being forced into marriage, she realizes she's not infallible. That's been difficult for her to accept."

"Well, hopefully Nasu gets some more from that new Manzazu healer, and you can wipe that worry line from between your brows." Nanaea met my eyes.

I smiled. "I promise I will relax."

Impulsively, I pulled her to me in a quick hug. She'd been my partner these last moons, helping me set up things in the healing tent, and getting Bikku, my new assistant, started while building a dancing troupe for Arwia's Palace, too.

I released her but held her at arm's length. "You know you've been my solace since we won the city back. I couldn't have done all this without you."

"I know." She winked and picked a pot off the table by Dagan's pallet, and dabbed something on my cheeks. "It's about time you realized how great of a sister I really am."

Laughing, I wiggled out from underneath her fussing hands, and adjusted my tunic around my hips. She'd sewn it too tight at the waist, and I wanted to feast and dance and laugh until the stars came out, and this gown would only restrict my movements.

"You're certain I can't wear something else? This is tight!"

She adjusted our ummum's shawl around her elbows. "It fit you fine a moon ago—"

"Well, not today. Shiptu has been feeding us well." Just this morning, she'd treated us to roasted duck and eggs cooked hot and sizzling. Fresh honeycakes and sweetwine. Finally, finally, I was beginning to feel stronger. Healthier.

The door squeaked open and Kasha and Rish tumbled in, laughing, both of them scrubbed clean in brilliant red tunics, though Rish had a smear of fig jam across his tawny cheeks. He wiped it off with his hand. *His only hand.* I sent the forlorn thought away, putting it in a box where I kept my failures and my disappointments. My ummum's death. His arm. Warad. Iltani's forced marriage. I brought them out from time to time like old cloaks to take a good look and shake out the moths, but I'd tuck them back away for another day of examination. Maybe one day, I'd open it up and set fire to the contents, and finally, *finally* forgive myself for the harm I'd caused.

Maybe one day.

"Dagan says it's time, Sister. It's dusk." Kasha took two steps into the room and swiped an apple from the platter nearby. "Besides"—he took a bite and crunched—"you have a visitor."

"You have two! Three! A whole pack of them!" Rish added, smiling brightly. "Come on!"

Nasu had done it.

They disappeared down the corridor, whooping and laughing, and from the grove of tamarisk trees out back, the sounds of the celebration floated in with the twangs of lyres and chings of bells.

"Are you ready, Kammani? This is your one and only chance to back out." Nanaea pulled a hair off her melon-colored tunic and cast it aside.

"Back out of what? I'm a willing participant. *More* than willing. It's a commitment, not a marriage."

This commitment to one another was bringing me every-thing I hadn't realized I wanted before: a home with Dagan. A life filled with work that inspired me. Safety. Rest. Love. My cheeks heated.

"Oh yes, but what of children? Will Selu bless them if they're not born in marriage?"

I colored. "Maybe Selu is more accepting than we all think,

Nanaea. Besides, I'm not *having* any children, as I've told you before."

She raised an eyebrow. "As far as I can tell, you're well on your way to a house full of them. You believe that you are quiet, but let me say—"

"Nanaea!" I shrieked, my cheeks growing even hotter.

She laughed. "I am merely telling you how it is."

"As you've been doing too much lately." I opened the chamber door and walked down the corridor, Nanaea trailing behind. The thought of children filled me with worry whenever it came up, so I knew motherhood wasn't right for me. Not now. Maybe one day. *But not anytime soon.*

"But if you have a child in the next year, she'll be friends with baby Huna!"

Arwia had been enjoying her own sort of motherhood these days, having adopted Gudanna's daughter as her own. She figured she wouldn't have to worry about the child being used as a pawn against her if she became her own heir.

"Stop pestering me!" I growled, pinching her arm lightly as she pushed open the exterior door, and we stepped out into the dusk. The sunset was a dusting of rose against a golden western sky.

A sky that Gudanna would never see again. She sat in the dungeons, living out the rest of her life under lock and key. I'd convinced Arwia to let her live instead of putting her head on the wall as she'd wanted to do. She had no real power or claim to the throne, and she was already ill, deteriorating in bits and pieces as the days went by. Arwia allowed Gudanna to see the babe from time to time, though the sullen woman refused the treatments I offered her. "Why heal only to live like a rat?" she'd said. Nevertheless, I tried. I told Arwia she wouldn't last until spring, and even *I* realized that was for the best.

Torches lined the perimeter of the courtyard, and a crowd stood around, laughing, chatting as musicians played in the corner. Shiptu, Iltani, and Nanaea had hung red linen tapestries tied with big bouquets of yellow chamomile. The low tables were laden with fruit and rounds of bread and sikaru.

"So where are these visitors?" I asked Nanaea.

Marduk and Qishti were threading ducks onto poles for roasting. Sarratum Arwia, surrounded by new guards, was chatting with Enzi Puzu and Ensi Adda. A group of Dagan's new farming friends were tipping flagons to their mouths near Iltani, who was playing twenty squares with Nasu and some other guardsmen. From time to time, she took a sip of water sweetened with honey and mint, her new favorite drink.

Nanaea tugged our ummum's shawl around her shoulders as the breeze picked up. "Who knows? But I would have liked to have seen Ummum's face today, wouldn't you? And Abum's? They would have loved to have seen you settled with Dagan, even if you're defying tradition." She smiled at me wistfully.

"And I would like to see you with me as well." Dagan's voice was a low whisper in my ear, and it heated me from my toes to my cheek.

I turned around, joy dancing in my chest. "How long have you been standing behind me?"

He grinned, and I could barely contain myself. Nanaea murmured something and drifted away to join the other dancers she'd put together to perform this evening, but I didn't quite catch what she'd said. For right then, all I could see was him. He wore a dark blue tunic with gold stitching that made his amber eyes shine like torchlight. His beard was oiled, and his thick, black hair was pulled back from his face.

"You're so handsome," I murmured, and I was filled with so much happiness, I felt as though I might burst.

"Young love," a woman said from behind us. "May Linaza grant you lots of children in your future."

Startled, I looked over Dagan's shoulder and found a group of women standing there as if I'd conjured their spirits: Sarratum Tabni with a regiment of Koru surrounding her, including Ummi and Higal. My dear friend Simti stood behind them. My throat tightened as my eyes filled. "Nasu got you to come. He did it."

Sarratum Tabni inclined her head. "Yes, he asked, but I came because Sarratum Arwia requested my help with the unrest by the sea. It appears she wants to work out some sort of an arrangement involving my warriors. But she requested that I come talk to you first. You had something to tell me?"

"First"—I bowed my head—"I am honored you would grace our humble home with your presence. And second, I never thanked you for your favor. Many of your warriors

357

died—" My voice hitched, and Dagan wrapped a strong arm around my waist. "I never even got to thank Humusi and Taram for their sacrifice." I reached into my pocket and pulled out the gift I'd saved for her. The scorpion amulet.

"You gave this to me to grant me a favor; now I give it back to you with the same intent. I owe you. Should you ever need to collect, I am yours. Your warriors saved us." I nodded to Ummi and Higal behind her. They both solemnly opened their arms in the Linaza salute.

Dagan placed his hand over his heart. "It's the truth. I am also in your debt, Sarratum. And I will repay it when you need me to.

"And, uh . . ." He scratched his neck. "If I may be so bold, I also have a field full of barley I could sell you if you'd like?" He raised his eyebrows hopefully.

Sarratum Tabni took the amulet and fastened it around her graceful neck. She smiled shrewdly at him, then met my eyes. "The Koru who have died know that you've thanked them. Linaza tells me in my dreams. But you can be sure when I need your help, I will call on you. You can be sure."

She nodded graciously at Dagan. "And send along a selection of your finest crop for me to taste. I'd be happy to have our farmers consider it."

"I will, Sarratum. I will. Thank you."

As she wandered off toward the fire, the Koru warriors flanking her on all sides, Dagan grinned at me excitedly. "Did you hear that? An expansion of the crop!"

"Yes, Arammu. I did." I laughed. "And I'm proud of you."

"Kammani!" Simti, nearly exploding in her impatience, flung herself awkwardly into my arms.

"You're well, Simti?" She was practically glowing, so the answer to my question was obvious.

She laughed and pulled my hands up and kissed them. "Yes, my friend. So well. Ilu is the best husband. He's here somewhere." She waved her hand and beamed. "And," she whispered, "I am with child!"

"Truly?" Chills of happiness for her flooded my body. "You're sure?"

"Yes!" she squeaked. "I've missed two cycles of the moon!"

"I am glad for you, my friend. So glad!" After I danced her around and found out about what we'd missed in Manzazu, she released me with promises to talk all things married life later, and went to find Arwia.

Then it was just Dagan and me and our futures spinning out in front of us like threads from Nanaea's spools. Long, and golden.

"Arammu." He wrapped his arm around me once more, and we walked toward the crowd under the tamarisk trees. The red climber flowers along the courtyard wall lent a sweet fragrance as the cicadas buzzed somewhere in the dark. "They're waiting for us."

He inclined his head toward the group of our family and friends who'd quieted the closer we'd drawn to Dagan's ummum, who stood in the center of the courtyard, a woven crown of flowers on her head.

"Let's not keep them waiting a moment more."

With a grin so wide and bright it lit up the dusk, he dropped his arm from my waist and I took his hand, and together, we walked down the path that led to our expansive future. As the crowds grew tight around us, Kasha near Dagan's brothers, Nanaea, Iltani, and Simti cheek to cheek, both sarratums with their warriors behind us all, Dagan's ummum draped long beads around our necks and asked us to promise one another our love. To swear to hold each other dear. We each laid our hands over our hearts and vowed to speak kindly to one another for the rest of our days, and prayed to Selu to protect us all our lives.

And as the sky darkened and the torches burned brightly, moths flickering around the flames, I looked up into Dagan's bright eyes, and knew, with all I had in me, that this life with him would be full of joy and likely heartache, too, because life was both. But no matter what was thrown at us—new life, death, war, or disease—we could handle it all because together, we were a force, united.

❉❉❉

I'm standing on the river.

Beneath me, the water bubbles and churns, frothing blue and white. Fish, their scales rainbows underneath the water, flit by in schools.

I'm not alone.

A man stands on the bank, and he's pulling a rickety boat

to the shore by a golden rope. I've seen him before in my dreams, while I lie asleep nestled in Dagan's arms in our little house, built on the south side of the farm for him and me, Nanaea, and Kasha.

The man raises a sharp, angular face to mine. He's dressed like a warrior with a leather chestplate and greaves on his thick legs, but his face is at peace, no longer tortured as it once was. He smiles at me, and his relief is as thick as honey. It flows over me with sweet warmth.

It's the Boatman, and I recognize the man for who he really is.

A woman with a scorpion tail appears from the reeds behind him, expands mighty, gold wings and lifts into the air, then descends into the boat. As she settles on a bench, her wings flutter once before she tucks them back in.

Linaza!

I gasp, shaking. The goddess of love and war, called such because those two passions often flow from the same source, is present before me.

Another man stands on the shore, and he's glowing white. I can't see his figure as great gusts of wind swirl around him, consuming him, but I hide my face, knowing I'm looking at Selu. The same honeyed warmth spreads throughout my chest as I look at his whirlwind, and slowly, so slowly, he points down the shore at a pair of figures walking toward the Boatman.

Confused, the Boatman squints into the distance, but

after a moment, his face crumples. He drops his head into his hands, and sobs rack his strong shoulders. He looks up again as if in disbelief, and the figures run toward him at full speed.

It's a little boy. And a woman. They're wearing tunics from an age long ago, light bursting from their skin. They race toward the Boatman, the creature of whom I was once so afraid, and they throw themselves into his arms. He captures them both and lifts them from the ground, his face breaking apart in joy. After a few moments of him crying and squeezing them to his chest, he looks over their shoulders at me, standing on the water, gazing into a reunion that appears to have been long overdue.

Mudi's words about the Boatman's intent come flooding back to me, and I tremble, remembering: *He was once a warrior, cursed to his post for murdering innocents in war. He is trying to gain his freedom by helping prevent the deaths of as many lives as he took.*

Selu holds his swirling arms over the trio who cling together, and they climb into the rickety boat with Linaza, and push off from the shore, toward me.

The boat slides near, and when it does, the man I once called the Boatman holds two rough hands out and cups my face.

"Thank you," he whispers in his familiar voice. He lets go and they drift away down the river, and in no time at all, the boat comes back, empty of its passengers.

As I watch it dock itself at the shore, I see a speck of red, malevolent light glowing next to Selu, who has his arm held up high, summoning the wind. The rain. The thunder and lightning. He disappears in a swirling tornado as the air turns into fire and whips into a fury, blowing my hair violently all around. The water begins to rise into rough, choppy waves as the speck of light grows and grows and grows until it is the shape of a hideous woman, seven curved horns growing from her head, bloated black tongue lashing from her mouth. *Alani.* She screams as she wrenches herself from the depths of the seven gates, lifting her claws into the sky and pulling a chained man up from the depths. He wails in torment as he is formed from fire, formed from wind, formed from the darkness itself.

And when I look at his face, I suck in my breath.

For standing in the center of that firestorm is a man who once stole life from me. Who once wrecked my little family and hurt more people than I can even recall. Than I likely even *know*.

Uruku.

At once, the flames roar and Alani shrieks as Uruku stands on the riverbank, consumed with fire. His face contorts in an agonized scream, and his flesh bubbles and melts and drips from his body until there is nothing but his rattling bones left behind. He's wrapped in chains and covered in a dark cloak, like the Boatman's. Racked with terror, I listen as a song, as if unbidden, encircles Uruku, enslaving him to his task. With black tears falling down his bony cheeks, his breast a torment of horror, he lifts his face unwillingly to the murky sky and sings the ghostly refrain:

The river is wide
The river is deep
I take their souls to earn my keep

The end of day
Is the start of night
I bathe in horror
Bask in fright

My queen is beauty
My queen is fair
I'll bring her souls
I'll do my share

For the river is wide
The river is deep
I take their souls to earn my keep.

⬚⬚⬚

I startle awake, awash in sweat, tangled in Dagan's embrace. Carefully lifting his heavy arm from around me so as not to disturb him, I grab a quilt from the chair near our pallet and walk, trembling, to the window. The night sky is scattered with stars, spots of brightness against the gloom. The moon illuminates my healing tent on the far side of our home, a lone candle burning inside. Likely Iltani, awake again, yearning for a drink.

I should check on her.

Looking back at Dagan, bathed in moonlight, his chest softly rising and falling, I tug the quilt more closely around me, breathing in the freshness of the cool, night air, and shiver.

It was only a dream.

As I tug on my cloak, I know that now is not the time to think about such evil. For out in my tent, the one I have built with my own two hands and the support of Dagan, the one I have staffed with a young mother named Bikku who was once a fishmonger but had always dreamed of being an A-zu, is my friend who battles her own kind of darkness.

And I, as her healer, must be her light.

ACKNOWLEDGMENTS

I'd love to take credit for bringing this book to life and sending this series off into the world all on my own, but I'd be a liar, and that's really more of Iltani's thing than mine.

Thank you to Kelsey M. Horton, my incredible editor, who asked all the difficult questions and pushed me, again and again, to home in on the story this was destined to be. You made me a better writer because you never gave up on getting it right. And to Beverly Horowitz, Barbara Marcus, Adrienne Waintraub, Tamar Schwartz, John Adamo, Timothy Terhune, and Dominique Cimina, thank you for giving this series its home at Delacorte Press. It means the world to be part of this community of authors.

Thank you to Kari Sutherland, my dream agent, who is the best cheerleader, advocate, and friend a writer could ask for. This series was such a challenge, and you listened to me cry, talked me through difficult plot points, and rooted for me from day one. I can't thank you enough for believing in me and for encouraging me to believe in myself, too.

Thank you to my publicist, Elena Meuse, who has been ridiculously organized and positive during my book and blog tours (spreadsheets for the win!). You're an absolute rock star, and I don't deserve you.

Thank you to copy editors Colleen Fellingham and Jen Strada, who questioned all my dangling modifiers and made me sound smarter than I am; to Sammy Yuen for the incredible cover artwork, Alison Impey for the lovely jacket design, and Andrea Lau for the perfect interior; to Janine Perez for patiently answering all of my annoying marketing questions and Nathan Kinney for heading up the production; to the entire GetUnderlined team, including Kate Keating, Elizabeth Ward, and Jenn Inzetta, for your digital shout-outs.

Thank you, a million times, to my community of fellow writers who had a hand in shaping *Warmaidens* from the ground up. To Lillian Clark, Gita Trelease, and Heather Christie, thank you for your beautiful friendship and thoughtful critiques that helped me craft this jumbled pile of emotion and words into a story I'm proud to have my name on.

To my Tampa writers' coven—Sorboni Banerjee, Dominique Richardson, and Linda Hurtado—I'm blessed to be included in your witchery. Long live handsome pirates and good wine. Huzzah!

To Lillian Clark, Erin Hahn, Keena Roberts, Brigid Kemmerer, Isabel Ibañez, Natasha Díaz, Rory Power, Shelby Mahurin, and Calvin Dillon, you don't know how often your texts and messages have saved me from writing gloom and general publishing angst. Thank you for understanding and for always being there no matter what. To RuthAnne Snow and Sarah Lyu—WOW, we friggin' made it (dies a little inside)—and I love you both to pieces. To L. D. Crichton and Shelby Mahurin, thank you for prying me out of my self-imposed technical jams just because you're kind. We need more people like you in this world.

To Kell's Skeleton Crew, you are mighty and I adore you! Thank you for launching my books with me and for being the most creative, inclusive, and accepting street team on the planet! Wooo!

To the booksellers and librarians who have stocked my stories, invited me to come hang out with you, and cheered me on from afar, your support has literally been one of the most unexpected blessings in my life.

Thank you to my bestie, Hez, who sends me feminist podcasts and videos that make me tear up; to my cousin-sister, Lacey, who sends me memes that make me die laughing when I'm under deadline; and to my entire mom squad—including my Moms Gone WOD team and my MTC Moms group—who show up for me over and over again.

To my mom and dad, thank you for being proud of me and getting both your bingo and church friends to buy my books. I love you! To Michael, thank you for faithfully listening to me talk about my stories and then reading them under duress. To Kimmy, thank you for always supporting my social media game, no matter what nonsense I've posted that day.

Thank you to my husband, Matt, who is the kindest man alive and has shown me empathy, compassion, and patience from the minute we met on the beach. (You gonna kiss me or what?) To my three boys—Brady, Kaden, and Brennan—you inspire me to be a better human. Thank you for being a light on my darkest days.

And lastly, to my readers—to YOU!—thank you so much for reading this series. You've made my dreams come true and I am forever grateful for your generosity. Here's to many more years of storytelling adventures together.

Cheers!

ABOUT THE AUTHOR

KELLY COON is the author of *Gravemaidens*, an editor for Blue Ocean Brain, a former high school English teacher, and a wicked karaoke singer in training. She adores giving female characters the chance to flex their muscles and use their brains. She lives near Tampa with her three sons, her brilliant husband, and a rescue pup who will steal your sandwich.

kellycoon.com

@kellycoon106